L.C. Lewis

Award Winning Author

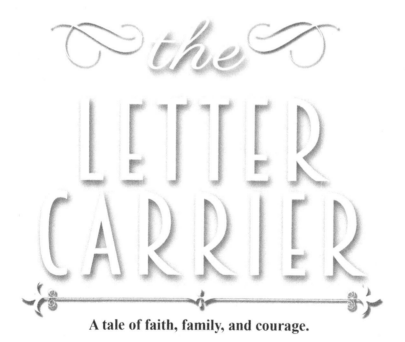

A tale of faith, family, and courage.

THE LETTER CARRIER

A tale of faith, family, and courage

An Historical Novel

L. C. LEWIS

Copyright ©2022 by Laurie Lewis

ISBN-13: 978-1-7338236-1-6

Published 2022 by Willowsport Press,

an imprint of JATA Inc.

Saratoga Springs, UT 84045

Cover design by Sheri McGathy

www.laurielclewis.com

To my cherished friend,
Michelle Naget Rogers,
upon whose courageous life
this novel is based.

PROLOGUE

May 6, 1994

My knees quivered like homemade jelly as I stood behind the curtain watching college students meander in and out of the auditorium. A few headed directly to a seat. Others chatted with their peers, as if conducting a survey about whether to stay, before many of them left. My heart broke a little . . . for me, but mostly for them.

The community college French professor arrived with four other guests—two journalists and two other people on the day's panel. We exchanged greetings as the teacher praised each of us for our courage. I noticed that, like me, the other two survivors also lowered their gaze in discomfort. Though we knew our stories must be told, we did not enjoy the attention.

The teacher turned to the press and gave idealized summaries of the events that defined the rest of our lives as if they were chapters from a fictionalized novel. We three knew better.

A journalist asked a question, and the professor replied, "We don't do these programs often enough anymore, I'm afraid, but I'm sure other classes are also marking the fiftieth anniversary of D-Day in some way."

Another panelist rubbed her hands nervously. "We can't afford to forget," she muttered under her breath.

Though she was a stranger, our similar experiences and memories bound us to each other, and I clasped her hand. The professor noted her worry and smiled.

"World War II history is part of the World History curriculum," the teacher assured us. "Aside from offering that, and programs like this, there's not much more we can do."

Her resignation sent chills through me. It took me back to France before the fall, when so many of my people hung their heads in futility, believing there was nothing they could do, and then the Nazis marched in.

"Let's teach those we can reach," the teacher added, "and do what we can do."

Her words had a familiar ring, like the echo of a saying my mother often repeated—"We do what must be done." Remembering the Naget family motto stiffened my resolve and caused prickles to rise on my arms. I rubbed at them and said, "Let's hope we can awaken some of them. Even just one."

The teacher smiled and left to welcome the audience and offer introductions about her guests. I took a deep breath and straightened my back to calm myself before facing the group. *Should I smile or face them with the worry weighing down my heart?* We would each have time to tell our personal stories, and then we'd take questions. I said a little prayer, asking to know how to reach the hearts of the young people today. I decided to amuse them long enough with my tiny size and my French accent to help them know me. Perhaps then they would care about what I came to share.

Remembering what I'd survived was awful enough, but the responsibility to awaken a new generation to the truth bore down on me. Could I make it relevant to them? Did they realize I was once as carefree and blind as they were?

The introductions met with a smattering of weak applause. I was scheduled to speak first, and my childlike size, barely four-feet ten and one hundred pounds, amused them as I had expected. I realized that I was my own visual aid, a living reminder of how the deprivations of war affect a child.

When my time came to speak, I waved and smiled, offering a cheery, "Allo!" in my native French. The students giggled at the tiny older woman before them and responded in like manner. I felt them relax and lean forward expectantly, as if they were anxious to hear more. My heart and theirs were in synch. Emotion rose in me. My lips quivered.

"My name is Michelle Naget Rogers. I came here today to tell you a story. My story. A story I tell because I don't want it to ever be your story."

And then I began.

CHAPTER ONE

I f truth is the first casualty of war, then surely childhood and innocence are the second and third. I was only eleven when the Nazis invaded France. Life had dealt our family a few early blows, but those hardships did not prepare us for what was to come.

My mother was Yvonne André, whose father's aristocratic bloodline did not spare her or her proud mother from financial difficulty. My papa, Adrien Naget, was also born to modest circumstances. He learned the value of work from his parents, the proud heads of a large farming family with fourteen hungry mouths to feed.

Papa was an architect and builder of some of the grandest buildings in France. My brothers' stories are the only memories I have of him. On July 29, 1929, mere weeks before my first birthday, Papa was killed when his motorcycle was run off the road by the driver of an automobile. Mother never spoke about what happened to Papa's share of the business or about the financial need that landed us on *Grand-père* Naget's crowded old farm with Papa's unmarried brothers, but nine months later, Papa's younger brother Joseph married Mother and adopted Armand and Jacques and me.

Joseph was only sixteen years older than Armand and more than five years younger than Mother, but he was a hard worker, a self-taught mechanical engineer who could disassemble anything and rebuild it into something better. His willingness to take on a ready-made family was not welcomed by the grieving boys, but their acceptance of Joseph grew over time as they tinkered by his side on the farm equipment. His steady manner won our trust as he brought security back to our lives. Our papa was dead, and we buried that reverential title with him, but over the course of three busy years, Joseph became Father.

A calm peace settled into our family again. When a new baby was expected, Joseph declared it was time for us to move to a home of our own. Our family landed in the small village of Braquis, a few kilometers from the Naget family farm. Father opened a mechanical repair business at the edge of the village, fixing automobiles and farm equipment, and fashioning metal tools and parts. With a growing family of five children, Mother and Father took a long lease on the largest house in the village, set right in the village square, where the community's telephone was installed.

When Mother wasn't handling civic communications, she and I could be found birthing the village's babies or tending the sick. Meanwhile, Father and the boys applied their skills to mechanical pursuits, like fashioning replacement parts for neighbors' broken tractors or helping them bring in crops before the first frost. I wondered whether the location of our house made us the hub of the community or whether our parents took that particular house to be more centrally located to the people who would need us.

Our home sat like a two-story block of butter directly across the street from the town's two most important structures—*La Mairie*, our Town Hall, and the church. Our village's school filled the Town Hall's main floor while the mayor's office and an auditorium filled the upstairs. A revered monument was erected in front of the building as a tribute to the local men killed in the Great War. It stood like a guardian, proof that evil had been defeated years ago, and while it belonged to the entire village, it faced my house watching over my family, or so I believed. And adding to that sense of protection was the comfort of having God as my neighbor.

I've always loved God.

The parish priest who served our little village was also assigned to other parishes, allowing us to have formal services only one week each month. That didn't stop our worship. The caretakers of our little church were an aged couple named the Dumonds. They made sure the church doors were always open, welcoming faithful villagers to enter and light a votive candle or offer private prayers whenever needed. I felt peace in the church's smoky scent and the glow of the candles' light, and though I didn't fully understand their connection to God and prayer, I would come to understand the power of light over darkness, soon enough.

I marveled that even I, a tiny girl, could enter that chapel and speak to God as if my little cares were as important to Him as those of adults. But it wasn't in the chapel's silence, connected to God only by whispered prayers, that I felt closest to heaven. The Dumonds gave me a special, singular way to commune with Him.

Mornings in Braquis began with the ringing of the church bell, which also pealed at midday, in the evening, and for special occasions like weddings and funerals. The seemingly ancient Dumonds climbed the steps to the bell tower at each scheduled time to pull the rope that rang the bell. Around my tenth year, I heard Father comment that the once-bold clang of the church bell had become little more than an anemic clink, owing to the Dumonds' weakened muscles and withered state. In that instant, I saw my purpose.

I hurried across the street and up the stairs to the bell tower to offer my services as their volunteer apprentice bellringer. My offer was received with less enthusiasm than I had anticipated. Monsieur Dumond looked down his long skinny nose at me and asked, "Michelle, how old are you? Seven?"

I tried to hide my frustration over yet another joke about my diminutive stature. "Nearly ten," I replied firmly, devoid of the deference the man was owed.

"Are you sure?"

Every muscle in my body tensed in embarrassment. "Yes, Monsieur."

The childless man looked at his wife, whose efforts to conceal her laughter failed miserably. He straightened as he looked back to me. "But you barely weigh more than a chicken. How will you ever pull this heavy rope?"

Without further argument, I ran full tilt and leapt at the rope, catching it as I flew past. My velocity compensated for my lack of mass, tilting the bell left and shocking it into surrendering a deep, mellow clang. As it swung back to the right, it dropped my feet to the floor. In one smooth motion, I pushed off the old wooden planks again in a leap to the other side, sending the bell into another resonant peal.

I was hired on the spot.

For the next two years, the first light of dawn and the thought of ringing that bell drew me from my warm bed before morning chores, and for a few minutes a day, I took glorious flight on the tail of that big copper bell as my muscles coaxed it into sending a loud, joyful song to God. In those moments, I felt He truly knew me, tiny curly-headed Michelle Naget, and that He heard the prayers uttered only in my heart. After twelve rings of the bell, my feet would return to the floor and I would enjoy the other gift of my apprenticeship. My view from the bell tower reached far beyond my little village in every direction, to neighboring farms and villages, past poppies growing wild between the cultivated fields of corn and wheat.

I struggled to understand the world beyond what I could see. On September 1, 1939, Germany invaded Poland. Two days later, France and Britain declared war on Germany, and nations and people far beyond my home began affecting our little village.

French soldiers arrived to dig zigzagging trenches between our house and the creek that bordered our property. The town held air-raid drills for families, and we children rehearsed our escape from the one-room school in the event of an attack. We didn't have gas masks, so our beautiful young teacher, Mademoiselle Pirot, made us each a mask out of stockings and cotton. When she rang the bell, we grabbed our masks and ran across the street, past my house, as fast as possible, and jumped into the wood-lined trenches. The bigger boys were taught to pull other sheets of wood over us to protect us from flying debris. I knew logically that the thin sheets offered as little protection as nylons stuffed with cotton, but somehow, I felt safer when I had my mask, and when the trench was covered and I couldn't see what might be happening above.

But the sky was so clear on that early morning in June 1940 that I could easily trace the approach of the tailor, Maurice Peltier, who entered Braquis from the north, furiously pedaling his bicycle. The Dumonds pointed to the young, expectant father and whispered back and forth in worried tones.

"He's in a rush," Mme. Dumond fretted. "That can't be good news."

"It must be Lydia's time," I said, giving voice to my private thoughts.

Mme. Dumond turned toward me as if I were prey. "What did you say, Michelle?" She hurried to my side. "Lydia's time? Oh . . . yes! I pray it's that and nothing more."

Her husband tried to hush her, but she pressed me harder. "Tell him, Michelle. You would know. You and your mother tend to all the expectant mothers, do you not?"

I shrank back under the intensity of her interest. I was not a licensed l'aide aux mères or mother's aide, but Mother had taught me to adhere to their rules of privacy and respect as if I were.

"I should not have spoken. These things are private matters."

"But you help your mother deliver the babies. You hear things."

"I-I-I've just been helping out as a mother's helper, cleaning for Lydia while Mother checks on her."

M. Dumond laid a hand on his wife's shoulder. "Stop, Marie. You're scaring the child and grasping at straws. We both know what news Maurice is bringing."

The old woman's hands flew to her mouth in self-reproach. "I would like to think there's a happy reason for Maurice's rush. Something joyful like new life. Let me believe it for a few more moments, Thomas."

She blanched as she looked at me, backed up against the bell tower's wall. "Of course, you're right, my love. I'm sorry, Michelle. Forgive me. Please hurry home and swing from your trapeze for me, will you? I'd like to see your tricks this morning."

Mme. Dumond had made her disapproval of my trapeze antics quite clear in the past, lecturing me on the inappropriateness of a young lady hanging upside down with her skirt flapping around her head, with only her brother's short pants between her and complete indecency. But the current request for a performance was a dual victory. I had an excuse to escape the conversation, but more importantly, she'd all but encouraged me to take a quick turn on the circus toy my brothers hung in the tree by our house.

I heard the chickens clucking for their morning corn and knew the rabbits and pigs were likewise awaiting my arrival with their feed. Knowing Armand and Jacques had likely completed their own chores of milking the cow and cutting wood for the stove, I nevertheless ran across the street and leapt to the bar with the same skill I used to pull the church bell's rope. Once my hands gripped the smooth wood, I pulled my knees in tight, slipping my feet and then my legs across the bar. I swung upside down, increasing the range of each arc while checking to see if the Dumonds were indeed watching my performance. They were not, but their ruse didn't dim my pleasure at turning a few before-school flips from my high perch.

I noticed a new audience in the backyard staring at me from

between the plants in Mother's garden. They were ragged, soiled strangers, three small children and two parents, each of whom watched me carefully as they picked precious early greens from our carefully tended rows, and dug the soft earth for last season's missed root vegetables. I jumped down from my trapeze and stared at them. Their eyes issued an apology as they continued to stuff what food they could into pockets.

I ran into the house to report the offense, crying out the news ahead of my arrival, but my oldest brother, Armand, caught me as I flew through the kitchen door. He wrapped his arms around me as he attempted to direct me from the room, but I would not be deterred.

Mother's eyes looked wary as she extended her arms my way, softly asking, "What is it Michelle?"

The masked worry in her voice and her use of my real name jarred me. For the first time since entering, I noticed that her expression looked much as it had the day she told me our newest baby goat had passed away in the night. My brother Jacques, three years older than me, stood as stiff as a broom against the kitchen wall, his narrowed eyes barely more than fiery slits. My news suddenly seemed less important than the conversation occurring in the kitchen.

Armand released me, and I made my way to Maurice. "Is Lydia all right? Are you here to call us to your home to deliver the baby?"

Maurice's eyes slipped to Mother's and then to the floor. "No . . . no, Mimie. No baby yet."

"But the Dumonds and I saw you hurrying down the road. You seemed excited."

Again, he checked with Mother before speaking. "I simply came with news from the north. It's just politics."

Politics . . . That explained so many things. Politics had interrupted our evening music programs on the radio for weeks, leaving Mother and Father hovering over the set as it blared the news. I missed our old fun, when Father and Armand played their instruments while Mother and Jacques and I grabbed the little boys to dance around the kitchen. I hated politics and its associate —war.

Though the battles were still far away, politics and war brought a variety of soldiers to our village and into our home. Officers commandeered our dining room for their headquarters and two of our bedrooms for their quarters, while their cooks used our kitchen to prepare food for the troops as they made their way to the battle-front. French troops arrived first, then the British, then more French troops.

Many of the soldiers became family friends. One French officer gave my mother a copy of a letter found in St. Sepulcher, or The Church of the Holy Sepulchre, in the Old City of Jerusalem. The church guards the site of Jesus' empty tomb, and the letter contained a prayer written centuries ago, promising believers who respected the Lord's holy day protection against violent death. Mother treasured the sobering promise, copying the letter many times for friends and neighbors, and handing a copy to each of us to tuck away.

Other gifts from soldiers came also, and we learned about the families they'd left behind, but though the soldiers were kind enough, their arrival meant further disruption. I was tired of their chatter about fighting and death and politics, and I hoped to change the topic with my own news. "A family of refugees is in our garden."

Before answering, Mother looked at Maurice, whose eyes seemed increasingly burdened. When she returned her gaze to me she said, "I know. I saw them too. They mean no harm, Mimie."

"But the vegetables aren't even ready for picking."

Mother's eyes glistened as she bent forward, speaking to me with measured deliberateness. "They take what they can find because they are hungry." She handed me a loaf of bread. "Take this to them." She straightened and turned to Armand. "Go to the cellar and bring up two empty wine bottles and fill them with milk.

Then wrap some cheese in a cloth for them. Jacques, run to the shop and bring your father home."

Refugees had been passing through for weeks, but none had engendered quite this level of assistance from Mother. I stood in my place, pondering the change. "There are more of them every day. Why?"

Jacques' anger seethed. "Because of the Nazis."

"Stop it," Armand warned as every eye in the room flew to Jacques. "At least spare Mimie while we still can."

"Spare me what?" I demanded.

Mother rose to her full five feet four inches, wiped at her eyes, and cleared her throat. "I'll take the bread to them, Mimie. You take the little boys outside and play with them for a few minutes before chores and breakfast, please. There'll be no school today. Instead, we'll bake bread. Lots of it. Okay?"

"No school? And it's Wednesday . . . laundry day. Not bread day."

"This week, Wednesday is bread day. Now go."

I gathered the boys: Ives—my Titi, nearly seven years old—and Gilbert, only three. Mother suffered several devastating miscarriages in between. A few took her so close to death that I dreaded the news of another coming child. She called me to assist when the fearful labor began, but blessedly, that reach across the veil of heaven brought Gilbert into this world. I was the first to hold and to bathe him, and from the moment his eyes met mine, he was like my own.

While the boys ran and tumbled in the grass, I studied these *refugees*. I feared the word and the people it described—dirty, needy, ragged wanderers. The hungry children were gnawing on a raw parsnip when Mother arrived with the bread. The displaced mother wept over the loaf, and the father's knees nearly buckled when Armand arrived with the gifts of milk and cheese. And then I felt it, the childishness peeling off my heart, allowing me to see past the soil and tears that marred the peoples' clothes, to witness the spark of divinity hidden behind their downcast eyes. I felt God expand my heart, then bathe me in understanding as Mother's phrase returned to me—*we do what must be done.*

Was that what they had to do? Flee? Leave all they had behind?

The impersonal war that had been but an annoyance to me suddenly had a face. Five faces. The war was no longer abstract but very real, standing in my own yard. I could no longer ignore the prospect of change because Hitler's forces were elsewhere, in someone else's land—Czechoslovakia, Norway, Poland, Belgium, Luxembourg, and the Netherlands. His army was near, very near, and coming our way.

As the family moved on, heading south along the road out of Braquis, the children looked back over their shoulders at us. Titi waved to them before running up to me, asking me to turn a flip on my trapeze, but I no longer wanted my trapeze to make the world appear chaotic and upside-down. It seemed that way all on its own, and my new wish was that it could seem righted and normal for as long as possible.

CHAPTER TWO

The refugees remained on my mind as I did my morning chores. Did they leave behind a house or an apartment? A dog or cat? And if so, where were their pets? The questions prompted me to take extra time with our own animals, giving them more than a perfunctory stroke on the head as I passed out their feed. Who would love them, feed them, if we were forced to leave? I raced through the door that separated our sheep shed from our home and shut the door to stifle the thoughts.

Mother and I baked twelve loaves of bread in Father's forge oven, since he'd decided to stay home from work that day—the first workday he'd missed in recent memory. With the baking finished, we made soft cheese, gathering the curds in a cloth and squeezing out the water before wrapping them for storage. Armand and Jacques brought dried preserves and smoked meat from the cellar, while Father oiled and tightened the screws on the wagon and bicycle, adding a complimentary rear basket to match the one attached to the bicycle's front frame. No one explained the reason behind the preparations, the change in our baking schedule, or the large quantities of bread. We even packed a change of clothes for each family member into bags made from cloth squares that were tied at the corners.

From time to time, Father pulled a chair up close to the radio and turned the volume on low. No lovely music, nor any clever dramas or comedies poured out. Only news, delivered by a somber voice that rose and fell in volume and emotion as the names of endangered cities in the north were read. When the voice reported that the government was preparing to flee from Paris, Father snapped the radio off and sent us out of the room to complete our chores, but my mind replayed the words I'd already heard.

My worst fears were confirmed when our congenial mayor, a local farmer named M. Latrobe, made grim-faced visits to the villagers' homes, sharing the news of Paris's fate. In his estimation, France's last hope was our brave French forces gathered along a defensive barrier known as the Maginot Line. Frantic excitement settled into the village as neighbors arrived asking Father to mend their broken wagons and horse tack in case our soldiers were unable to hold that strategically critical position.

History and civics lessons from our one-room schoolhouse began to feel frighteningly relevant. Our teacher, Mlle. Pirot, was young and beautiful. I tried to be a good student, primarily to please her, but pleasing her meant learning about the atrocities committed during the Great War, twenty-five years earlier, and about the fragility of our country as Hitler's war machine rolled over nation after nation. They were stories that terrified me, and it felt that they were not merely stories but our own coming truth.

Hopeful chaos broke out on Braquis' main road in the early afternoon when a man on a bicycle reported French troops in the district. Cheers went up, and the Dumonds rang the bell to herald the news, but hour by hour, more people fled from the north with sobering news of the Germans' push south. Someone pointed to planes in the sky and a rising cloud of smoke in the north. Voices chattered and then hushed at the sight. In that quiet moment, we could hear the dull boom of bombs dropping in that same direction.

The mayor went from house to house through the thickening traffic on our village's main street, begging local families not to delay their exodus any further. The scene looked like a bizarre parade—parents rushing on foot, carrying babies and leading crying children by their hands, farming families in horse-drawn wagons laden with their worldly treasures, and wealthy people in automobiles offering twice and even three times the cost of a liter of fuel to propel their vehicle on to the next town. Horses whinnied as the wagon teams' drivers attempted to navigate around the walkers, and horns honked as impatient automobile owners grumbled about wasting fuel while unsuccessfully urging the slower-moving evacuees to clear the way from before them.

While the chaotic sights and sounds continued outside, Mother and I set out a hasty breakfast—milk, sliced meat, preserves, and soft cheese over crusty bread—as our family quickly ate and attended to the day's hefty list of chores. Though Father didn't go to work again that day, we barely saw him or Jacques and Armand as they attended to tasks around our home and others'. The rest of us helped Mother pack necessary supplies in the event we too needed to evacuate. When midday arrived and the chores were completed, I noticed a change in Mother's mood. Her frantic hands, which had been consumed by preparations for our potential evacuation, slowed their pace, returning to the tasks of a normal day as she and I scrubbed the house and prepared the afternoon meal.

Traditionally le déjeuner, the afternoon meal, was the largest of the day, but Mother had us prepare an unusually hearty feast, allowing me to bring up any meats, fruits, cheeses, and spreads I chose from the cellar. She asked me to place the lace tablecloth on the large table in the dining room and set the dishes out there, and for a short while, I wondered if we were perhaps staying after all.

We heard Father's boots in the entryway before we saw him. "We're ready," he said as he entered the kitchen and froze, gazing upon sumptuous food being carried across the hall to the dining room table. He turned to Mother, confusion apparent on his face. "Yvonne? What's this?"

Mother offered him a trembling smile. "I thought we could enjoy a good meal together. All right, Joseph?"

Father held her in his gaze for several long seconds before nodding. "Quickly, eh?"

"Understood."

"Very well. I'll call Jacques and Armand inside."

Mother turned me until I faced the table. "Remember this day, and this meal, Mimie. You worked very hard to help prepare it. You're not even twelve, yet you can almost run this house yourself."

"I like helping you."

Mother wrapped her arms around me. "We are a good team, eh? I'm very proud of you." She pulled back and framed my face in her hands as she gazed into my eyes. "I know I can count on you. That this entire family can count on you."

All fears of war and Germans fled from me in the sound of my mother's praise.

"Call the little boys in to eat, and afterward, please help them dress in clean clothes."

"All right." And then I turned to find Mother's impish little boys. In that moment, she and I were more than mother and daughter, we were partners. She wanted me to know that she depended on me. And then I realized why.

I pressed my concerns down deep, turned back, and asked, "We're leaving soon, aren't we?"

Her voice was steady and stalwart. "Yes. After dinner."

We were about to be refugees. I remained silent to hide my distaste for our new status as Mother added, "Now hurry and call the boys." Before the sting in my eyes turned to tears, Mother drilled the old sentiment in me again. "Go, Mimie. We do what we must."

I stood proudly by the table, awaiting the wide-eyed expressions of delight over the dinner preparations, but Armand arrived in a dour state, and Jacques wore his increasingly frequent glare. Gilbert and Titi rescued my mood with their elation over pudding and unlimited jam. Father led us in grace, his resonant voice extending our thanks far beyond the blessing of the meal. He gave thanks for the gift of so much time in our home and for the blessing of always having had what we needed and more. He thanked God for our family and for His love. His voice broke as he pled for God's protection over us and all who found themselves in need. We could barely utter amen past the lumps in our throats as he closed.

Mother and I cleaned the kitchen in silence after our meal, and then I took the little boys upstairs to dress them in clean clothes. They obeyed my every request to hurry their entrance into what they called "the military parade" taking place in the streets. When we arrived downstairs, we found the rest of the family in organized commotion. Armand and Jacques were arranging wine bottles filled with water in the bicycle's baskets while Father tied bundles of food and clothes to the handlebars. Mother loaded blankets and other bulk necessities in the hand-pulled wagon, filling additional baskets with food and medical supplies.

She turned to me and nodded when she saw the little boys dressed and ready. "Mimie, help the boys gather the last of the eggs." She bit her lip as she straightened to her full tiny height. "Then open the pens and free all the animals."

I wanted to argue, but my questions were silenced by the painfully sympathetic expression in Mother's eyes, delivered alongside her typical logic. "They must be free to get food while we are away. Now please, see to it."

My tiny team followed me down the hall to the door that separated the house from the animals' pens. A new appreciation filled me over the wisdom of that shared wall that had kept our family and the animals warm in the winter. With newfound sorrow, I closed my eyes and listened to the animals' lowing. I'd taken the peace and normalcy of their voices for granted, and I longed to remember their songs in case we never returned to our Braquis home and to the animals we loved.

Titi and Gilbert hugged each of the chickens before sending them scrambling from their boxes. As the boys moved on to release the rabbits, I wept into the necks of our cow Marie and each of our four goats as I hugged them and set them free to happily skitter into the yard and straight to Mother's garden. I finally understood why she had been so willing to share the garden's contents with the refugees, knowing it would soon be animal feed.

The lazy pigs were less willing to leave their comfy beds. I understood that sentiment more than they realized. I didn't want to leave either. I nudged and cajoled them, finally having to resort to poking and kicking at them to get any compliance from my porcine friends.

Betina, the sow, looked at me as if I had betrayed her. I fell upon her neck and begged her forgiveness. "I will leave the outside door ajar. You leave whenever you're ready, all right?"

The entire family was standing in the front yard with our gathered belongings when I arrived. I saw no toys, no musical instruments, nor Mother's wedding clock. None of our treasures were visible.

"I have to get Gisette," I said as I bolted for the front door.

"No, Mimie. Just necessities. There's no room for your doll."

I shot a sympathetic look at the outcasts filling the street, some of whom were already scrambling to catch one of our chickens or snare one of our recently emancipated rabbits. Our situation no longer separated us from them. We were, in every way, refugees too.

Mother laid an arm across my shoulder. "Hold Gilbert's and Titi's hands. No matter what, don't let go of them, Mimie."

Father led out with a bundle resting on his shoulders and a suitcase in his hand. Armand carried a basket in each hand, and Jacques walked beside the bicycle, as Mother took the wagon handle and bravely pulled it into the street.

As we exited our village, most of the residences appeared empty. Many were the homes of people who had been at our house the previous evening, asking for Father's help in getting their wagons tightened or bemoaning their lack of ready stores to Mother, who handed out eggs and loaves of our fresh bread. Those neighbors and friends were already gone, and we were just setting out among throngs of strangers.

Within minutes, we bid adieu to Braquis and continued under a cloudless sky that carried the sweet scent of lilies and roses on the air. The pastoral beauty of fields tinged red by wild poppies lifted my spirits and evidently those of fellow travelers, some of whom began to sing as we walked. Older people, carried in the backs of wagons, added their voices to the music, as our exodus became a mingled adventure.

After four hours, we stopped at the edge of a forest to eat and sleep. I had never camped outside before, and the little boys and I found the prospect of sleeping under the stars a delight. Dinner was simple, food pulled from what we had packed, but the thrill of eating it outdoors added a special savor that made plain bread and cheese seem extraordinary.

We huddled close under blankets, aware of travelers passing by throughout the night. Some looked as if they might drop with one more step, but still, they pressed on. French soldiers marched past in the early morning hours, drawing particular attention from the refugee men.

"Why are you retreating and not returning to the battlefront?" the men shouted to them.

An officer finally called back to the hooting crowd. "We're following orders."

Father hissed at their answer. "Then don't march with civilians! You're not protecting us. You'll draw the enemy to us!"

The military didn't change its strategy. Father got us up early, had us eat and repack our things, and head out on the road before dawn. To our dismay, the route was even more crowded and jammed, in part due to abandoned vehicles that had run out of gas.

At first light, we heard the hum of engines, flying back and forth above us, in the sky. Some planes were clearly German, but to our surprise, some were Italian. Italy had also become a threat.

Father hurried us along. With his eyes in constant motion, he counted our heads, scanned the sky, and searched the terrain, again and again. The planes changed their course, their engines roaring as a few lowered their flight pattern, flying so close above our heads that we could see the pilots with their frightful gun barrels pointed our way and their national insignias emblazoned on their aircrafts' bellies. And then the game changed too suddenly for us to adapt.

On the next run, a rapid popping sound, like a hundred pots of popping corn, descended from above our heads, ripping the earth far ahead of us into a trail of dust and dirt. Snorts and cries of frantic horses filled the air around us as the animals reared and bolted, some trampling people, some falling to the ground in their harnesses. The horses' wails and commotion obscured the cries of people in the line of fire. Screams and shrieks and wails of horror echoed down the line as people dropped all around us, some in a bloody spray, some diving to safety.

Father yelled "Get down!" as Mother snatched Gilbert from my grasp. I felt a shove from behind as Titi and I dropped into the ditch by the side of the road with Armand and Jacques close behind. Mother clutched Gilbert and leapt, landing a few yards away. Groans and screams continued all around us as people fell in heaps, and the elderly, defenseless and in full view in their wagon beds, futilely hid behind raised arms as the bullets ripped through them, dropping them like ragdolls.

I covered my ears and screamed well after the first pass of death ended and the planes roared away. Survivors checked their families as wails broke lose, signaling the loss of loved ones. Some people remained frozen in place, afraid to move, while others jumped from the ditch and ran into the woods. Father called out to each of us as his panicked eyes followed the paths of the planes until they disappeared. Mother didn't respond when Father called out to her. A silent cry to Mother froze in my throat as Father made a desperate scramble to reach her. When he did, she groaned at his touch. After checking her body for blood, he gently turned her over, revealing Gilbert safely tucked beneath the shield of her body.

"Are you hit?" Father's voice, so filled with fear, chilled me as he continued to search her torso, arms, and legs.

"My back," she groaned. "When I fell."

My worry over Mother's condition became secondary as the sound of the planes' return, faint but growing louder, sent a second wave of terror through the crowd. One plane dropped low, but this time, most of our group dove into the high grass, making targeting harder. The barrage was focused on the road again, carving more carnage into the wounded still lying there and into those tending to them.

In any other circumstance, Mother and Father would have been the first ones aiding the wounded and tending to the dead, but with the threat of a possible third wave coming, everyone became focused on keeping his or her own family alive, leaving the morbid work of triage and burial to the retreating soldiers who continued to flood the road.

My parents were no different. Armand and Jacques grabbed the wagon and bicycle, and I grabbed the wailing little boys' hands. Father tucked Mother under his arm as we fled down the road as quickly as possible, past dead horses and humans riddled with holes streaming blood. The older boys called back to me and the little ones, telling us to look only at their heels without looking up. We tried not to look elsewhere, but it was impossible to avoid the scene and impossible to pull our eyes away once we saw. We ran, staying near the ditch in case we needed to take cover again, but blessedly, the planes did not return a third time.

Once we were far past the scene of death, Jacques asked Armand, "Do you think they meant to hit *us*, or were they aiming for the soldiers?" His eyes were narrowed and sad while Armand's face looked drawn and ages older than his seventeen years. Our once-happy boys had matured into men in moments.

"Perhaps," Armand answered in an emotionless tone. "I'm going to enlist when we get the family to safety."

"Me too," answered Jacques.

"You're not even fifteen yet. They won't allow it."

"Then I'll join the underground. They'll take me."

"The family will need you, Jacques. Your place should be with them."

"Please stop. No more talk about leaving," I begged as I let loose of the little boys' hands to cover my ears. Their momentary freedom from restraint sent Titi and Gilbert off at a run.

"Do you remember what Mother said your job is?" asked Armand.

My heart clutched with guilt when I saw the little boys' joy turn to fear as they became lost in the pack. I ran to them and grabbed their hands, calling back to the older boys. "All right. I'll remember my job. You remember yours. No more talk of leaving us. Promise?"

By afternoon, we reached the road that led to Doncourt-aux-Templiers and our uncle's farm. *Grand-père* and *Grand-mère* Naget and several of Father's other relatives had already gathered in the farmhouse. They welcomed us with a warmth that provided a momentary reprieve from the terror of the morning. For those few hours, we were no longer refugees but welcome family as our relatives opened their doors to us and filled our bellies and hearts. We helped our weeping cousins repeat the sad chores we faced two days earlier, loading wagons and attending to last-minute necessities like freeing the livestock they had spent decades breeding, so the animals could feed.

The hour grew late, and the men decided that we would stay the night and depart before dawn. I slept with *Grand-mère*. The sky was still dark when we ate our hasty breakfast and set off.

My grandparents rode in the wagon bed on the mattresses my uncle had packed. *Grand-mère* invited the little boys and me to join her, but having seen the fate of those perched high and most visible to the Nazi gunners, I declined the invitation and opted to walk.

The roads were already clogged with evacuees. Cars honked, and their drivers groused at the wagons and walkers slowing their progress to foot pace. One by one, their tanks emptied and their wheels stopped, creating blockages of their own. I found strange humor in watching them join the rest of us on foot.

Like streams flowing into a river, people poured into our group of evacuees each time we passed a new lane. Our cousin Dominic called out to a friend named Légère, who looked to be about Jacques' age. He was tall, with dark hair and eyes, another boy as interested in joining the fight as Jacques and Armand.

"German planes flew over our farm this morning," Légère said as he caught up to our group. "We heard that those cowards fired on a line of refugees."

Dominic grabbed Jacques. "This is my cousin, Jacques, from Braquis. His family was among the refugees the pilots attacked."

Légère's eyes widened in new respect. "And you survived?"

To my complete horror, Jacques began sharing the vivid details of previous day's trauma. I shot these thoughtless boys my darkest scowl for dredging up things I prayed to forget. Unwilling to admit that I couldn't bear to hear a replay of the horror, I nudged Jacques with my elbow and said, "Stop! You're frightening Titi and Gilbert."

Jacques abruptly ended the conversation, but Légère's eyes widened as embarrassment blushed his cheeks. He looked down at me while asking Jacques, "Is this little girl your sister?"

"Yes. Her name is Michelle." Jacques laid a hand on my shoulder. "I'm sorry, Mimie. I shouldn't have talked about the attack in front of the little ones. I wasn't thinking. Forgive me?"

Tears burned my eyes, partly because of the disturbing memories Jacques and Légère's conversation dredged up and partly out of anger for once again being minimized as a *little girl*. Mother saw me as her responsible and hardworking partner before the previous day's massacre, but the attack affected me in new ways I could not yet measure. I wasn't taller or older, but just as the carnage and the mercilessness of our attackers had changed my brothers from boys to men, whatever I now was, I was certainly no longer a child.

"I just don't want to think about it anymore, Jacques."

"I know, Mimie. I know. I'm sorry."

"It's my fault, Michelle," Légère said in a honey-sweet apology. "I shouldn't have asked about such a terrible thing in front of you and the little boys. I'm to blame, not Jacques or Dominic."

In that moment, I thought I had perhaps misjudged Légère. Maybe he wasn't a completely thoughtless boy after all. He appeared to be a mannerly, kind, and caring young gentleman. With beautiful dark eyes.

"Thank you," I said, quickly forgiving him.

He smiled my way before Jacques took his arm and led him forward, presumably to honor his apology while also continuing the gory conversation beyond my earshot. I resumed my previous opinion of him and all boorish boys, focusing on the scenery instead.

Walking through the French countryside, I was again struck by the beauty of my nation. Farmers and homeowners took great pride in keeping their fields straight and their yards tidy. Green acres of young grain stretched as far as my eyes could see, ending at roadsides aflame in poppies, bluets, and white marguerites. Stubborn trees stood like ancient sentinels amid the maturing grain. Their majestic height attested to the decades they had withstood man's efforts to dislodge them, while the submissive soil around them had been turned, harrowed, planted, and harvested over and over for generations.

Where possible, we crossed beautiful thick forests, enjoying the protective cover they provided from passing planes. By evening, we reached Doncourt-aux-Templier, the village where Father was born. Others marched on into the night, but we stopped, knocking on doors familiar to the Naget family, however, the entire village was deserted.

The doors were unlocked and open, as if welcoming all who needed rest or who could make use of the abandoned goods within. Most of the foodstuffs were gone, but Mother and my aunts were able to make soup from a straggler chicken and bottled vegetables found in the cellar. I caught sight of myself in an exquisite floor-to-ceiling mirror encased in an intricately carved frame.

The mirror was beautiful, one of the most beautiful things I had ever seen, making it all the more obscene that the reflection filling its glass was so ugly—me, and yet not me. An unfamiliar version of me, with straggly, dirty hair and a mud-streaked face and dress. Mother would never have allowed me to come into the parlor of our home looking that way. I suddenly felt unworthy to be in the house, and then I caught sight of another irresistible item —a porcelain doll with silky hair and a gentle painted face. I yearned to pick it up, to hold it close in my arm, where Gisette should have been. I looked at the doll, then down at the soiled nails of my hastily washed hands and the dirt and grass stains on my dress, then back to the doll. Mother caught me scowling at my reflection.

"A little scrubbing and all will be right again."

I looked at her in the mirror. "Are people in our house, the same way we are in these people's house?"

Mother placed her hands on my shoulders and drilled her gaze into me. "Probably." Her glassy eyes closed and tears slipped from the corners. "It's all right, Mimie. Take the doll."

Joy and horror mixed in my heart in equal portions. "But that would be stealing."

A trembling smile pulled at the corners of Mother's mouth. "You are a good girl, Mimie. I'm so proud of you. It's not stealing. The doll is abandoned. I think the family would be happy to know a good, hard-working French girl is loving her."

I wanted so desperately to believe that, but the words drew a new thought. "Do you think some other girl has my Gisette?"

A lingering tear shone in Mother's eye as she ran her fingers through my tangled hair. "I wish I had let you bring Gisette. I said we only had space for necessities, but these past few days have taught me that joy is also a necessity. Forgive me. I expect that Gisette is making some other girl very happy, and now I hope this doll can do the same for you."

I ran back to the kitchen and washed my hands once more before daring to touch the precious doll. I scooped her up, promising her that no matter what, she would not be abandoned again. To honor that promise, I found a small square of linen and tied its corners together to form a backpack with two armholes. I placed the beautiful doll, who I named Beatrice, in the sack where I could carry her and still hold Titi's and Gilbert's hands.

We started early again the next morning. The long days of walking and hiding from the planes were taking their toll on families. Some who'd passed us were worn out and were camped along the roadside to rest and tend to blistered feet or exhausted horses. People with wagons offered to carry the elderly and small children of walkers, but that meant families began to be separated. A father stopped to rest for a moment, sending his wife and the remainder of their children on to stay near the wagon carrying their youngest. He fell farther behind than he expected, and we watched him hobble frantically, checking every lumbering wagon, describing his wife and children to every group he passed as he begged for information on the nondescript rig his family was traveling beside. Another mother, traveling alone with several small children, stood in the center of the road, screaming out the name of a missing son who had scampered away to pee and never returned.

I looked down at each of the boys. "See why I hold your hands so tight? You do not want to get lost like that, do you?"

Their blue eyes widened as they shook their heads and tightened their hold on me.

An hour or so later, we reached a hill and a cemetery on the way to the village Woël, where we heard a familiar voice from the side of the road, calling for a doctor. Maurice, our friend from Braquis, had set up a bed of sorts by the roadside for Lydia. His poor wife was writhing in pain.

Father sent his extended family ahead while we stayed behind to help our Braquis friends. Mother diverted responsibility for the little boys to Jacques and Armand and called for Father and me to come with her. She grimaced in pain as she lowered herself to her knees beside Lydia there on the roadside. Before examining Lydia, Mother directed Father and Maurice to hold up a blanket to provide the poor woman some measure of privacy. She quickly confirmed that the first-time mother was indeed in the late stages of labor.

Father fetched water while Maurice dug through their supplies for the linens Lydia had packed for this very eventuality. Again, I felt Mother's trust in me and my ability, instructing me to prepare a clean area for the birthing and to ready towels and clothes for the arriving infant.

Planes began flying sorties over our heads, causing chaos on the road as travelers scattered in our direction, seeking cover in the woods. We hoped that terrorizing the evacuees was their only objective, but on the third pass, a few planes came in lower, as they had the first day, before unleashing their rain of bullets and death.

Father ordered everyone to move into the tree line, but Lydia was too deep into her labor to be moved. Maurice's normally happy eyes were fearfilled, but he encouraged Mother and Father to head to safety with the children while he stayed with his wife and the arriving child. Father bent low and reached for Mother's hand to lift her and carry her to safety, but Mother had other plans.

"No. I cannot. You go. Take Mimie. I'm needed here, but the children—they need you, Joseph, to get them to safety."

My parents' stalwart attention to duty and the practicality of Mother's argument overruled the emotion evident in my father's twisting features. I had occasionally wondered about my mother and Joseph, our father. Did she love him as much as she had loved our papa? And would he have married her if he had not felt a sense of obligation to rescue his brother's widow and children from poverty? I didn't know what type of love they shared. It certainly wasn't the eye-batting, giggly flirtation girls showed Armand, but in that moment, as I watched Mother tearfully withdraw her hand and my father's mouth drop open as he nodded his silent under-standing, I knew that this marriage, born of duty and loss and need, was filled with real love.

Father took my hand and pulled me away from my mother, fighting against my struggle to free myself and run back to her. In the tree line, I could hear Jacques' and Armand's questions, and the terror-filled pleadings from Titi and Gilbert. Father seemed old in that moment, his face haggard and filled with defeat as he looked back over his rounded shoulders at Mother. His attentions were torn between her and the rest of the family off in the trees. Halfway down the hill, I broke free. He didn't fight me further as he bent low to scoop up and contain the frantic little boys, who had escaped Armand's and Jacques' hold. The popping sound of bullets mingled with screams as the planes fired on the people scattered along the road. I reached Mother, and she grabbed my hand, yanking me to the ground with a groan. She wrapped an arm across me, drawing me as close as a second skin as we waited out the barrage.

I began reciting the little rhyming prayer Mother taught me. I repeated it over and over with a need and urgency I had never before known, asking God to remember every candle I had ever lit and every little prayer I had uttered in the empty chapel. I asked Him to remember the joyful conversations we'd shared as I flew on the tail of the church bell's rope, and I begged God to hear me, to save us, or to take us to heaven.

A family abandoned their wagon as it pulled up near the birthing site. It proved to be our salvation as bullets ripped into the bed, splattering wood chips on our huddled little party while shielding us from the gunner's sight.

Lydia was nearly mad with pain and fear. As soon as the planes passed, she sat forward and gave out a loud wail, bearing down as if this one chance was all she had to bring her baby into the world. Gerard Peltier arrived with full voice and a head of curly dark hair. Born under a canopy of smoke from Nazi planes, his arrival was heralded by the cheers of strangers celebrating the hope his birth symbolized.

The planes flew on, evidently having sated their lust for terror with whatever dead they left in their wake. Father and the boys raced to us, nearly knocking Mother and me over. The owners of the wagon returned, carrying a dead old woman who they loaded into the wagon bed and covered with a sheet because they were too afraid to linger and bury her. Others assessed their dead and injured, and, again, Father pressed us to move on quickly.

The wagon owners offered Lydia and the baby a seat in the wagon bed. We bid adieu to Maurice and to Lydia, who was propped up with Gerard in her arms as they sat beside the dead old woman. Life and death. Both so real, so close, and becoming all too normal.

We found our Naget clan early that evening, safely camped outside a small village where a family in a large house welcomed us to take shelter. The place was already filled with people staking out footage on the floor for sleeping. Everyone brought their food together to form a poor man's buffet. We ate what was provided, and then we all lay down to rest before beginning anew the next day.

We heard the roar of more planes and the boom of bombs dropping nearby. The explosions caused the old house to rumble so badly that mortar began to crack and fall. Father and Mother woke us and told us to gather our things. We grumbled at being moved yet again, but Father insisted we were safer outside than inside where the house could collapse and crush us. We bedded down in the yard while Father sought out better cover. After an hour, he returned, and we were moved again to a castle situated in the center of the town. One by one, all the people in the old house filed along after us to the block-and-stone castle.

The owners of the ancient bastion had refused to evacuate, believing the old stronghold that had withstood previous invasions could also withstand the threat of Nazi bombs. They opened their doors and welcomed us all into the cellar.

The bombardment soon ended for the night, but the chance to rest gave families the first real opportunity to assess their members' health. Almost every family group had someone who was sick or wounded or struggling emotionally. Mother's efforts as a midwife also identified her as a nurse, and soon a line of people came, begging her to attend to their wife or husband or child.

Gilbert refused to let her out of his sight, and though standing was a struggle because of her strained back, she set the toddler on her hip and went about attending to the calls for help. As she was coming down the stone steps from the first floor of the castle to the cave or basement, her foot somehow slipped. She tumbled down the stairs, clutching Gilbert to her bosom while her back scraped along the carved stairs, leaving her in a heap on the cold stone floor.

Father arrived in a rush. Mother's pain was so severe that he feared she had broken a vertebra, but he was helpless to relieve her suffering or to find someone to attend to her. God was our only available healer . . . and so, we prayed. A priest among our ranks led our supplication. Together and individually, we begged God for yet another miracle.

New families arrived and others moved on, heading south to lands we hoped were beyond the Germans' reach, but our Naget clan remained together in the castle for several days while Mother healed. She lay prone for two days as rumors of advancing Nazi troops and retreating French divisions reached the castle walls. When the risk of staying seemed too great, she hastened her recovery, asking Father to help her sit up, and then to stand. Eventually, she was able to take some steps.

On the second day, a company of French soldiers knocked on the castle door, asking to take shelter for the night. They were welcomed in and peppered with requests for a true assessment of the battlefront. The news was worse than we feared.

While Mother was recuperating, our beautiful Paris had indeed been overrun, and so had our nearest city, Verdun. The Germans controlled both. Our only hope was to race east to the Swiss border or south to Spain before the German line reached us.

The captain of the little French band looked at Armand and my uncle's son, Pierre. "How old are these boys? Sixteen? Seventeen?"

"Seventeen," answered Father.

"We're headed south to join forces and mount a defense. Your boys will be safer joining us than they will be if they are found with you. The Germans are taking all military-age boys, soldiers or civilians, as prisoners. These boys'll at least have the chance to stand and fight if they're with us."

It all happened so fast. One minute, my handsome, dark-haired, oldest brother, Armand, was just a sweet, gentle boy who loved the violin. The next, he was a willing but dumbstruck soldier being ripped from our family. Both he and Pierre gave a nervous nod to the captain. Jacques stepped up, willing to enlist, but Mother's gasp led Father to take his arm. "Not you, Jacques. Please, no. Not yet."

"Very well. We leave in the morning, men," said the captain. "Spend this last night with your families."

I snuggled close to Armand that night, crying into his sleeve. "You will come home to us, won't you?"

"Of course, I will, Mimie."

I could feel him shudder as he breathed. Armand was afraid too.

In the morning, the captain unrolled a map and pointed to our location. Then he offered the rest of us advice and a warning. "Get off the main road as quickly as possible. German lines with tanks and trucks will control it shortly." His finger traced a narrow, dirt farm road surrounded by woods on either side. "I'd head this way. This route winds, and it'll take you longer to reach the border, but I think you'll be able to travel safely on to Switzerland this way."

Father and his brothers were familiar with that route, and they thanked the captain for his help. The officer turned to Armand and Pierre. "We're pulling out in ten minutes, with or without you."

Pierre's family swarmed him, as we gathered Armand into our arms. Father offered poor Armand a few words of wisdom, expressing his confidence in this stepson and nephew he had raised as his own. Mother offered a final tearful hug before Armand wiped the back of his hand across his eyes and pushed away. With a handshake to Jacques, and a pat on my head, Armand and Pierre turned for the door and were gone from us.

We bravely collected our things, determined to make our way down the alternate route the captain suggested. Our host's wife shared small bundles of food with our group to sustain us that day, but as we thanked them for their generosity and said goodbye, a firm knock sounded on the massive wooden door. The owner of the castle hushed us, directing us to move into a side room, out of easy view. We quickly hid around the corner and held our breath keeping the room's door ajar as we listened for the scrape of the heavy front entrance and the conversation about to ensue in the foyer.

The first voice we heard was not the cheery greeting of our host, but the commanding snarls of two young Germans. We felt completely undone. None of us spoke German, but we soon understood what they wanted as they pushed past the host and began searching the rooms across the foyer from where we were hiding. Our host attempted to deflect them to the recently emptied basement, but when it became apparent that these soldiers were intent on searching every inch of the castle, Father opened the door wide and stepped into the foyer, urging us to follow. The little boys cowered behind Mother, and I held Father's hand while a more subdued Jacques, stood beside me. One by one, everyone in our company stepped out as another German officer arrived delivering his message in broken French.

"My friends we'd heard this house was providing safe haven to refugees. I see that this is true."

The wife of our host stuttered until her husband replied. "There's been a misunderstanding." His voice lacked its former boldness and defiance, instead taking on conciliatory, formal tones. "These are our friends."

"Are they? And these friends . . . ?" the German officer asked as each step of his boots echoed on the polished stone. "Does a man of wealth such as you, keep company with pig farmers and old women? Yes . . . you see, we stopped more of your *friends* at the edge of your property."

Our host froze and then swallowed. When he spoke again, his voice regained its defiant, brave essence. "Is it now illegal for a Christian man and woman to provide shelter to unarmed families who have been shot at by German war planes?"

The castle owner's last syllable echoed off the stone walls as a deafening silence filled the foyer. The German officer's steps slowed and softly echoed on the stone, resembling the more thoughtful tone of his voice. "An unfortunate set of events. We heard French troops were marching on that road."

"Can your pilots and gunners not differentiate between a farm wagon and a tank?"

Another silence ensued as the officer burned his gaze into the man. When he spoke, his words were clipped and stern, signaling that his patience had been exhausted. "Invite your remaining guests to come forward now, or my men will rout them out as they continue their search. I mean no harm, but I assure you that voluntary compliance will be much more pleasant."

He turned to the castle owner. "Good sir and Madame, we are requisitioning your beautiful home as our headquarters. You may remain here as our guests, with the understanding that we will call upon you to assist in the operation of the property and food preparation for my men so long as you choose to remain here."

Shock showed on the faces of our hosts who had, in a minute, gone from a life of wealth and privilege to one of servitude. The officer turned to our group.

"You're all to return home. France has surrendered, and an armistice is being drawn up. You will hear the terms soon. For now, consider us ambassadors of a sort, inviting you to go home and live your lives. Farmers should farm. Builders should build. Families should care for their children and maintain their normal pace of life . . . with a few adjustments, which you shall learn. Some of your homes will be requisitioned to house military leaders who will assist your local governments. They will restore order and see that the normal production of food and goods occurs. You need not fear us if you obey, but you must all be gone by morning."

And that was that.

The priest led us back to the basement, allowing us time to take in the new reality we faced, and then he led us in prayer.

We left the next morning, different parties heading east, some west, most north. There was little conversation in our northbound ranks as we headed back the way we had come. We were grateful to not be bombed or fired upon as we made the three-day journey home.

Our armed guards kept us moving at a brisk pace, allowing little time to eat or gawk at the bullet-riddled towns with their sacked and pillaged homes—homes that were pristine and welcoming mere days earlier. I was glad I stole Beatrice. So glad she wasn't left to the looters who shot at her home or who might have left her in the street with the other goods they dragged outside and abandoned. No human bodies remained on the road, but their blood still stained ground littered with dead animals and debris. German soldiers and vehicles were everywhere.

My questions about Armand went unanswered, but Mother's

shining eyes told me she was worried about him. Father's pleas to allow us to forage in the woods for mushrooms and berries were denied, but some rolls were found, and we devoured them as if they were cake.

We spent one night back at our uncle's farm, saying bitter good-byes to our family as we parted the next morning. The destruction of the once pristine land shocked us as we drew closer to Braquis, wondering if we might find there what we saw here, bomb-pocked fields with their crops destroyed and waste and debris left instead.

A moment of joy filled us as we approached the once sleepy village now teeming with German soldiers and vehicles. Our cat, Mirette, wandered up to us. She was the only bit of normalcy left in our little world. Every home and the few businesses in the town had been ransacked. Abandoned goods littered the yards. Ours was no different. We knew without checking the cellar that all our food was gone. Empty baskets and bags that were once filled with root crops and dried fruit were now empty and strewn across the yard. Bottled vegetables, meats, and jams, we had canned, were scattered on the lawn, evidence of hungry, desperate people eating whatever they could wherever they found it. Easily carried food items like dried fruit were likely taken as the people moved on. We couldn't complain. We had eaten other people's storage as we journeyed, but the abandoned, half-filled jars testified to the panicked rush these last evacuees had been in to flee France. And for what, as they were almost assuredly headed back the way they came, along with many of our possessions.

What caused a deeper ache in our hearts was the waste spread across the village. We were, primarily, a farming community, so we had but a few businesses in town. A young couple ran a small general store out of the front half of their home. We were not surprised that the groceries were gone, but hardware items of no use to evacuating people had been pulled from the shelves, adding to the melee in the streets. A woman in the village ran a small bakery to supplement her husband's wages as a farmhand. Her pans were bent and her bowls were broken. I wondered if either of these families would do business again, and if they didn't, how would they survive?

Father had his shop where he repaired almost anything from appliances to cars and tractors. His welding tools and fabrication machines were still there, but his materials had been ransacked and his meticulously kept work area was in total disarray as if a mob had searched under every hammer and nail. Father muttered something about the mess more likely being the result of a Nazi search than from hungry, fleeing citizens.

Abandoned clothes, shoes, and personal items lay scattered across the yards and streets like the refuse from a tornado. None of it looked familiar, and we could only assume that some people exchanged their things for items that were clean, or that some people's goods were simply abandoned in their race to flee south.

I gritted my teeth and stared at the garbage dump my village had become. Mother cradled me against herself and said, "They didn't do this to us, Michelle. They thought everything left behind was abandoned. They didn't think we'd ever return."

Neither did we think we'd return to the German version of France. But we had, and to the additional horror of trucks and tanks, and armed uniformed men who barked orders at the stunned and terrified people of Braquis. They ordered us to clean the debris littering the streets and yards. They wanted a clean and orderly occupied Braquis, as if their role in the ruination of our village and country eluded them.

I could forgive the missing food. Even the missing clothes and toys and dishes. What I couldn't understand was the sight of precious personal items, not taken or used, but maliciously broken, like Armand's beautiful violin. The other losses angered me but seeing my brother's beautiful instrument smashed into the dirt unleashed my pent-up sorrow. Hot tears burned behind my lids as I fell to my knees. Armand was gone. And also lost was his violin. It felt like a dark omen.

A pair of highly polished boots approached me. Before I looked up, I saw slate-colored trousers tucked into the boots, and I knew the man wearing them was a German officer. He gently picked up the neck of the instrument. Its strings and pieces of battered wood dangled below in a sad little dance. He said something in German and shook his head as he gazed upon the once beautiful instrument. *"Je suis désolé."*

Though his French pronunciation was poor, his voice did seem truly sorry about the treatment of the violin. I hoped his regrets were for more than the loss of an instrument, extending to compassion for the people who loved it and its owner. With a final wiggle of the fractured mess, he allowed it to slip from his fingers to the ground. Afterward, he extended his arm, and a soldier rushed over, extending a handkerchief to wipe any dirt from the officer's soiled hands.

He moved to where Mother and Father stood, surrounded by the boys, and introduced himself. The soldier beside him served as his interpreter. "I am Colonel Lange. Is this spacious house your home?"

"Yes," Father answered.

"It's being requisitioned for my headquarters. You and your family will be permitted to remain in certain areas. In return, I would ask that your family assist us by cooking and cleaning for me and my immediate staff. Any questions?"

And so it began.

CHAPTER THREE

S oldiers had already taken possession of our home. We stood and watched as they moved more of their things into the house—duffle bags, file cabinets, office equipment, and trunks. Not knowing our place or what to do, we set the bike and wagon in the shed, laid our bundled belongings on the front stoop, and set about clearing the debris field of discarded clothing, empty bottles and jars, and broken treasures from our yard.

One delight awaited us. We heard, "Maaa," a cry like that of a child calling for its mother. We followed the welcome sound to the thicket that ran in the deepest part of our yard, between the creek near our property line and the zigzagged air-raid tunnel our French soldiers dug for the village before they left to confront the Germans. There, feeding off the sweet grass along the creek, were three of our goats, who either evaded being captured by hungry refugees or who returned from a weeklong holiday in the woods. We hugged them and clung to them, apologizing for leaving them for a week. Mother wondered aloud if some of our other stock might likewise have remained near. Jacques brought grain and poured some into a tin feeder. The familiar sound of corn hitting the metal pan brought a few chickens scurrying and clucking as if scolding us for going away. Father found two of our six rabbits huddled under a bush. This man, who generally warned us against emotional attachments to animals that might end up on our plates one day, pressed his face into the rabbits' fur as he held them.

The German officer who commented on the loss of Armand's violin, seemed to be in charge. The thirtyish man had eyes that held the prospect of friendliness. As he had earlier, he allowed the slightest hint of caring to cross his face as he watched our reunion with the animals, then, with an abrupt shift in mood, he straightened and cleared his throat.

"Family Naget!" he called out in a loud, commanding voice.

He had our attention.

He then relayed his message to a younger soldier who informed us in broken French that Captain Bruhner was inviting us into the house so he could explain the living arrangements, going forward. It neither felt nor sounded like an invitation.

The meeting was abrupt and definitive. He was the kommandant, the law, over Braquis and the surrounding area. There was no discussion, and no apologies were made as the interior of our home space was carved up like France herself, into friendly and enemy territory. Our house had become theirs, less a home than the *Kommandantur*: the Nazi Command Post for the area. The downstairs was divided into sectors—spaces in which we were welcome to move freely and those into which we could enter only when directed, either to clean or to serve our oppressors. The hall that ran from the front door to the back of the house served as the border. Nagets to the left, where the spacious kitchen sat. Nazis to the right, where the parlor and dining room spread. At the back of the hall stood the staircase and bathroom, and a door that led outside to the backyard. Halfway down the hall a door sat to the right. It led to the sheep shed where the animals lived. The structure was attached to the house and situated in the space behind the dining room and the parlor, the rooms designated as the

Kommandantur. My room had always sat over the sheep shed, but no more.

Upstairs, the two bedrooms on the right of the staircase were commandeered to house German officers and dignitaries when they were in town, which was not every day and night, but often enough that the sleeping quarters and office spaces were considered theirs at all times. Our family of six was squeezed into the two remaining bedrooms situated to the left, over the kitchen area. Relegated to one of the rooms across the hall, I sorely missed the soothing lowing of the animals beneath me.

Braquis was likewise divvied up to accommodate the German soldiers' encampment, which was an emerging tent city housing many more soldiers than the total population of Braquis. Their camp was set in the wooded area on the road that led out of town to Étain, but soldiers roamed the village freely, and were always within sight.

Cities and regions of France fell like dried stalks in a windstorm during the following weeks. After our defeat came the reorganization, as our land was carved up like a victory cake. The Germans offered a small piece of our country to their ally Italy while the rest of our land was divided up to meet their battle needs, with little regard for the people whose homeland it was.

Braquis sat in the northern part of France, just within the lines of the Occupied Region, where French cities and villages maintained their local leaders while operating under the watchful eye of German troops. To our west sat Vichy, renamed The French State, though Father declared it to be but a puppet regime led by a World War I hero named General Philippe Petain, who seemed all too willing to dance for his German handlers. Access to our coasts and border cities was by permit only or completely denied as Germany set up defensive perimeters several kilometers in from the shores, to prevent Allied attempts to liberate us.

A pervading fear hung over the land like a lingering cold that fatigues its victims and makes drawing a full breath challenging.

Even before we knew the extent of change coming, we all felt the suffocating restriction of our freedom, but we carried on in wary obedience as we worked or attended school and awaited what was coming.

Our school, our happy, safe place, where Mlle. Pirot challenged us to learn from the past and set our sights on a bright future, was not so anymore. Our education was transferred to the tutelage of a German instructor, Herr Schmidt, when Mlle. Pirot did not return after the evacuation. Some people said she died in the air raid. Some said she escaped to Spain. I refused to accept any speculation about her death. Rather than seeing her beautiful red hair spread across a blood-soaked road, I preferred to imagine it gleaming with light as she sunned herself on a seaside veranda while making lesson plans for the day she would again return to us.

Work, in one form or another, filled the hours after school. Mother and Father saw to that, keeping us close when the Germans were near. In addition to caring for our family's needs, Mother and I served as the maids, laundresses, and cooks to whichever German officers and staff were currently occupying our home. As I increasingly became Mother's partner, I felt important and perhaps a bit superior to the little boys. Titi noted the unpleasant shift in my attitude with stinging clarity.

I had delegated several menial tasks to the little boys and was ordering them about in what I felt was a polite but suitably responsible way when Titi snapped his heels together and raised his hand in a forward salute while saying, "*Sieg heil, mein Führer!*"

My laughter caught in my throat, but Mother gasped and shot forward, capturing Titi and drawing him close to stifle further comment. Mother's nature was quiet, tender, steady, but at that moment, she was a whirlwind of fear.

"Where did you hear that?" The quietly uttered question tore from her throat with the intensity of a scream. "Where did you hear that, Titi?" she repeated.

The egregiousness of his error seemed to register as Titi

cowered and cried. "Jacques' friend Raymond did it at Father's shop. He pretended to be a German. All the boys laughed."

Mother pulled Titi close again as her eyes fixed on me and little Gilbert. "Never say that again. Do you children understand? Never. Promise me."

Something new, something uneasy settled deep into Mother that day. I saw it in the way her eyes constantly darted to the windows and doors, as they did when she heard rumors of a wolf attacking livestock in the area. With jittery hands, she gathered us to her side at the first squeak of the door or stomp of a boot. We didn't understand the meaning of Titi's phrase at that time, but we knew without question that Mother sensed a threat in her home as insidious and perilous as a wolf.

Our family withdrew as much as possible from interaction with our boarders. Some of the officers sensed the change and tried to be particularly courteous to our family. Most paid us little regard, seeing us merely as a means to an end—a pressed shirt, a full belly, a clean bed. The worst of them took pleasure in intimidating us, staring us down or flailing their hands at us as if they were going to strike and then laughing when we cried or flinched. Mother avoided their eyes, and Father rarely smiled or sang or played his accordion.

Our oppressors moved in and out of our home like waves of the sea, sweeping away one group, carrying a new squad in. Hopefully, they'd be better. At times, they were worse. The tides that moved them were battles marked on maps they kept pinned to our parlor walls or spread across Mother's dining room table in the half of the house to which they had laid claim.

Leaving school each day had always been a delight for me and my brothers. Our house sat across the street like a happy face, greeting us, calling us home. It had been built like a square box some forty meters from the road. The home's front door sat in the center of the wall like a mouth poised in surprise. The kitchen window and dining room windows flanked the door left and right, like two happy eyes, and above them sat two bedroom windows, the eyebrows of the home's happy face.

But our happy house was no more.

Titi noticed it first. My friend Lorraine and I were talking, and we nearly ran him over as he stopped suddenly at the edge of the road, his small shoulders stooped, his head tilted to the side, staring at our home. I linked my arm in his and said, "No time for daydreaming, Titi. Our chores are waiting."

He took a step and halted. "Our house is sad, Mimie. Look."

When I finally did look up, a chill coursed over me, through me, leaching away the warm feelings the view always provided. Posters and bulletins, announcing policies and warnings, scarred the home's face, and like a blackened eye, a Nazi banner hung from the kommandant's right upstairs window to identify the house as the local German headquarters.

"It doesn't feel like home anymore," Titi lamented.

I forced a smile and hugged Titi, even as I shivered in anger over the change in another aspect of our world. "I suppose there are some advantages to having the Germans take over half our house. We're now sharing a room with Jacques. He'll be near if we have a nightmare."

Titi didn't smile or even show any relief.

After a few moments of quiet grief, I tried a different approach. I studied the house, hemming and hawing, angling my head this way and that as a smile crept across my mouth.

"What's so funny?" asked Titi.

"Look at the house again. Do you see what I see?"

Titi leaned forward, anxious to join in whatever revelry could lessen the somberness. "What do you see?"

"Imagine that flag is an eye patch. Who wears a patch over his eye?"

"A pirate! A German pirate whose eye was knocked out!"

"Aye," I said in my best pirate voice. "And how did that pirate lose his eye?"

"It was slapped out of his head by the tail of a giant whale!"

My eyes widened appreciatively over Titi's creativity. "You're right! It was exactly as you say."

"And the posters aren't pieces of paper," he added.

"They aren't? What might they be?"

"Purple-colored, whisker-covered moles."

"Ooohhh! Eeeeh!" We groaned in disgust and then squealed in delight as we linked our arms.

"Be ye ready to meet that pirate face-to-face?" I asked as I took the first step into the street. To my complete relief and joy, Titi matched me, step for step, as we bravely made our way home.

We headed into the kitchen and found Mother staring at the table where the ingredients for the evening's meal were spread. The more pleasant items—three loaves of Mother's bread and a round of creamy cheese—were joined by some rather disconcerting foods, supplies sent to our German guests—a hindquarter of a pig and long links of pinkish sausage. Our looks of wide-eyed disapproval were answered with a long sigh from Mother.

"We have no vegetables. No fruit. Anything edible was stripped from the trees and garden, and the pantry is nearly bare. I hope I can find a few potatoes in the rows."

Our property was narrow and deep, running from Braquis' main road past our side yard, where chickens roamed and goats fed, through a sizeable backyard, beyond the air-raid trenches and thickets, to a creek and woods. Foraging in those woods and that stream changed from joyful to needful once war broke out. Our family ration amounts, set up when Britain and France declared war on Germany, supplemented the foods we grew and those we acquired through bartering. The German military's troop rations were unreliable, and we had more mouths to feed.

I remembered what enticed the goats to remain near the house while we were away. "Berries were growing in the thicket. I could see if there are any left."

"Good girl." Mother turned to Titi. "Go with Mimie and look for leeks, wild onions, and mushrooms."

"Can Jacques come?" I asked. "We need him. Jacques or Armand always took us foraging. They're much better at finding the good plants."

Mother's lower lip and chin trembled as she answered. "You know that Jacques is needed in Father's shop now that Armand is gone to war, don't you?"

Yes, we knew, but we didn't like it. Was it not enough that we had lost Armand? For all intents and purposes, Jacques was also gone from us. He'd become too busy to build forts under Mother's large kitchen table and too tired to tell stories at night as he did before the Germans arrived.

The Germans . . .

Even the timing of Jacques' employment seemed influenced by our unwanted guests. With tools and parts in scarce supply, old and broken things needed to be mended, and new things needed to be fabricated. Unfortunately, money was also in short supply, so most jobs paid little to nothing, and yet Father was busier than ever, and Jacques' help seemed justified. But it didn't go unnoticed that his apprenticeship was announced the day after Titi's disclosure about Jacques and his friends' mocking the Germans while playing in Father's shop. The arrangement provided Father with much-needed help, but it also provided supervision for his impulsive, impassioned stepson. What was harder to understand was Jacques' pleasure at assuming the new responsibility. He chattered on about work around the dinner table and in the evenings, asking Father how to use this tool or that as if metalwork was the most exciting thing in the world. He had outgrown us, and I sorely missed his company.

Mother placed her gentle hands on our shoulders. "You two will be excellent foragers. Father and I taught Armand and Jacques what to look for, and they have taught you. It is your turn to carry on the tradition."

She lifted her chin and eyed us. A hint of worry tinged her smile.

"But listen carefully to me. Stay together. Never go past the air-raid ditch alone, understand? And never enter the woods if the German soldiers are near. Never. Promise me."

"We promise," we said. No further explanation was needed.

Stay away from the wolves.

CHAPTER FOUR

C ertain moments stand out in time, in the same way a bent corner holds the place of a favorite page in an oft-read book or the way a scar on one's knee forever reminds you of the day you learned to ride your bicycle. I remember such a day.

It came after weeks of muted wariness. We moved quietly from our beds to the kitchen, to the yard for chores, and then to school and work. We said little to one another or to anyone else, for that matter, because the Germans were near. The hours inside the house passed slowly, like time spent by a graveside—quiet, eerie, and mournful over the loss of the life we had known. Things were a bit freer outside the house when we foraged for food.

We worked from sunrise to well past dark, gathering food from the garden, the meadow, and the stream, canning and drying whatever we could, and eating what couldn't be preserved. When the berries were all picked and the jams made and stored, we turned to drying and pureeing the fruit from our trees. Canning jars became a precious commodity, so we saved them for preserving larger fruits and vegetables, employing wine bottles for beans and peas, which we could stuff down the bottles' narrow necks. After the bottles left the boiling hot water bath, we sealed their narrow openings with corks or melted wax.

In the period between the garden's busy summer harvest and the ripening of the root crops, we turned to the stream to harvest its bounty. Father took a few rare days off to fish, which meant Jacques was also available to us to capture frogs and crayfish and to pluck watercress from the water.

In late August, Mother made a poor man's bouillabaisse using fish Father caught, and the frogs, crayfish, and leeks we children gathered. After serving the Germans until they were filled, she spread a blanket in the backyard and served our dinner picnic-style. As we finished our stew and bread, she disappeared, returning with a delicious loaf under an embroidered napkin. She lifted the cloth, revealing an apple cake I assumed was for the Germans.

"Happy birthday, Michelle," she said with a smile that took me back to happier days.

I had all but forgotten my birthday. At the very least, I expected little in the way of celebration, but as Mother cut and served the cake, Father leaned back and pulled his handkerchief from his pocket. Wrapped inside was a fancy hair clip he'd made in his shop. Father's love was practical—food, a roof, an example of faith, a guiding hand, and discipline. He was not a man who cared about fashion, nor one prone to displays of emotion. His gift showed a new sensitivity to both. The shiny metal band was beautiful and elegant, edged in intricate scrollwork, with my initials cut into the center.

The words, "Thank you, Father," eked past the lump in my throat.

"He made and rejected a dozen clips before he got that one just right," said Jacques.

My fingers traced the elaborate design. The value of the gift doubled upon hearing the effort it required. "It's very beautiful."

"You're welcome." Father blinked rapidly and coughed to clear his throat. "Twelve . . ." he sighed. "I can hardly believe it. You're a good girl, Mimie. I probably don't take the opportunity to tell you that often enough. You deserve something special. More than a hair clip."

I longed to wrap my arms around his neck and feel the comfort of his around me, but years of stiff courtesy held me back. Jacques broke the awkward pause when he opened his hand to reveal a flower-shaped pin he'd created using Father's tools. Though not as detailed as Father's piece, it too was intricate and beautiful.

"You made this, Jacques?"

His head dipped shyly. "Father has been teaching me to use his tools.

"I can't believe you made this . . . and for me. Thank you."

We ate and laughed and told old stories, and for an hour, life was as it should have been. We held on to the peace and promise of that moment through the next few weeks, sharing more smiles, being patient on hard days because we knew that no matter how we tiptoed or whispered around the Germans, inside, we were still The Family Naget.

And then one day, things shattered.

Father left early that morning, as he did most days. Mother's hands were buried in a mound of sticky bread dough when the phone in our kitchen rang soon after first light. Since we had the only phone in Braquis, an early call generally signaled important news for a neighbor or for the entire village. The potential import of the call, made so early in the day, caused Mother to freeze as it rang. She looked at her dough-bound hands and then to the open doorway that gave her a view of the closed dining room door. Our Nazi houseguests were assembling in the room beyond. She pulled her hands out and stared at the mess as the phone rang again.

I dropped my cheese-spread piece of bread onto my plate and pushed my chair back from the table. "I'll get it so the soldiers aren't annoyed."

Mother's eyes widened as her mouth formed the word no.

"I will be careful," I replied as the contraption rang again. I headed for the device to answer the call, but Mother's eyes darted to the closed door that separated us from the German officers.

"Wait!" Her whispered warning came out as a groan, causing my knees to shake. She struggled to scrape the dough from between her fingers, but we both knew a fourth ring would bring an annoyed Nazi soldier through that door.

"I know what not to say," I assured her, as I reached the earpiece and pulled it to my ear. "Hello?"

I was able to recognize the nervous whisper of Mme. Berger, a telephone operator in the larger, neighboring town of Étain. "Yvonne?"

"No, Madame. It's Michelle. Mother is kneading bread dough. Can I help you?"

"I've called to prepare your mother. But first, child, where are your guests?" Once again, her words rushed out in anxious, hushed tones.

To prepare my mother? The hairs on my arms rose on prickled flesh. I considered the caller's question about the location of our unwanted guests. Mother and Father had drilled the warning into us—never speak openly to or about the Nazis—so I used a weather phrase the locals had designated to indicate that our guests were in the house and possibly listening. "Yes, there is a good chance of rain."

She sucked in her breath. "I understand. I must speak to your mother. Ask her to call me when she is alone."

I stood with the receiver pressed to my ear for several seconds after Mme. Berger hung up. There was something about her voice —concerned and bordering on frantic—that sent chills down my back.

Mother remained silent, but her widened eyes and hanging mouth spoke volumes about her own fears. *What?* she mouthed.

Before I had a chance to answer, I heard the scrape of the dining room door as it opened, and I saw Mother quickly close her mouth and return to working her dough.

Two of our resident Nazis crossed the hall to the kitchen. They swept the room with their eyes, stopping at me. I leaned back against the wall, nearly melting into the mounted phone.

"Is everything all right?" asked the junior officer who possessed at least a modest command of French. "We heard the phone ring several times."

Mother forced a tepid smile as she glanced at her dough-covered hands. "Just a friend in Étain. I told her I will return the call when my hands are clean."

The more senior of the two officers burned his stare into Mother, who somehow managed to summon a calm dignity that returned his gaze with equal scrutiny. He eventually nodded and stepped toward me instead.

The junior officer again spoke. "Please ring the bell at three for a town meeting."

Mme. Berger's phone message and her voice's nervous timber filled me, and though I tried to mimic Mother's strength and poise, all I could do was shiver and nod.

This younger officer stepped forward, between Mother and his superior. In that moment, beyond the view and scrutiny of his commander, he lowered his eyes and offered Mother a soft smile as he laid a list of the chores the officers required on the table beside Mother's bread bowl.

"If you please, Madame Naget," he said, "by two p.m."

He smiled once more, a gesture of kindness and gratitude, and then his superior grunted, and the young officer stood erect as his body and expression stiffened.

Mother remained at a stoic sort of attention until the two men snapped their heels, nodded, and returned to the dining room. She continued to remain that way for seconds after the dining room door clicked shut, seeming not to draw a breath until she was sure they wouldn't poke their heads out to catch her in some ruse. When she at last breathed, her shoulders rounded and remained that way long after the dough was in its pans and until I was heading out the door for school. That morning provided my first recognition of the onerous toll our guests' presence was taking on our angel mother.

My mind was not on my work that day. At two-fifty, Herr Schmidt tapped my school desk with the yardstick he used to point to the new unrecognizable map of German-controlled Europe. I closed my books, set my pencil down, and left the room, glad to be excused from more of the man's propaganda but unhappy about my errand.

I still rang the bell morning and afternoon, but I had been called upon to ring it for the occupiers' two previous town meetings, and each had brought further unpleasantness and change to our world. I was only the summoner, not even the messenger, and yet I somehow felt like their tool. Their co-conspirator in bringing further sorrow to my people.

The first meeting, soon after their occupation began, had been called to introduce multiple prohibitions. The mayor stood on the rise in front of the beige stucco school/town hall, flanked by the German officers. His hands trembled as he read the notices being handed to him, one after another. The first notice was a warning about the penalty for possessing a weapon. All firearms had already been confiscated, but our Nazi occupiers sent us a stern reminder that any and all weapons were banned, and that being found in possession of a weapon, including items fashioned into weapons, would be met with the most severe punishment.

The next notice announced changes to daily life. A ten p.m. to five a.m. curfew was installed, and lights-out hours were established where curtains were to be closed and lights dimmed to complicate the Allied pilots' efforts to target ground sites. *Der Ausweise,* or photo identification cards, were to be issued to every person twelve and over. Being found on the streets after ten p.m. without one's card could lead to arrest.

And lastly, as if our occupiers hadn't achieved a sufficient level of control over us, their next notice indicated their plans to control our very movement. Local festivals and balls were prohibited.

Nationalism was prohibited. Instead, the Germans offered activities of their choosing to keep us engaged after work or school. In larger towns, youth sports teams and clubs were established, and the youth were strongly encouraged to participate, if not on the field of competition, then in a musical group or a service club. In smaller villages where work and the growing of food left little free time, no additional diversions were offered, but the messages were clear:

EMBRACE their vision of a German France.

It was much easier to monitor a herd than a stray.

And busy, tired people had little time for insurrection and rebellion.

THE NOTICES WERE NAILED to building fronts where all could be reminded of the new laws.

During the second meeting, held days after the first, the mayor, who was again flanked by his German handlers, read another notice, which explained the new rationing rules. We were familiar with rationing. At the start of the war, France introduced her own system to fairly distribute items in short supply, but in September of 1940, the Germans instituted a new, broad rationing system, with new coupons. Nearly everything was on the ration list. Tobacco, cloth, coal, and alcohol were doled out with coupons that controlled all food products as well. We were assured that the food amounts assigned to each person were based on an individual's "caloric needs" as determined by their age, gender, and occupation, but even the adult allotment of 1200 to 1300 calories provided barely enough food to avoid prolonged starvation.

As days went by, it became clear that city dwellers were the most affected—those without land to grow gardens or to raise animals, and without access to farms where they could barter for more food. But even the farms themselves fell under German control, as the bulk of our harvests were loaded into wagons and trains and spirited away. Some said our food was taken to feed troops. Some said it was sent north, to feed Germany's people, whose economy was failing as her workers went to war.

Farmers began hiding a portion of their harvest for sale on the emerging black market or for bartering with their neighbors, but the city dwellers with coupons found it hard to get their meager share. The suffering increased amid reports of uprisings over food. These riots were quickly crushed by the Germans.

But what news would be delivered in today's meeting?

Mme. Berger's tremulous earlier whisper haunted me this day with each stair I climbed on my way to the bell tower. *What message had she tried to deliver that morning Was it the very news I was calling the residents of Braquis to hear?* Dread, not joy, filled me as I pulled on the rope, not hard enough to make it sing, but with just enough force to usher forth a dull, hollow peal.

I stood in the tower and watched as the good people of Braquis slowly laid down their tools and brooms and rakes to leave their shops and gardens and homes. Farmers unhitched plows and attached wagons to carry their wives and little ones into town. Children poured from the school and into the arms of worried parents who held them close, bracing for the coming news. I left my bell-tower perch and found Mother, standing in the street. Her arms were spread wide as she counted her little chickens making their way to her from school and Father's shop.

Everyone gathered in the town center, spilling into the main road through Braquis, the Rue St. Georges, which filled with anxious arrivers on bicycles, on horseback, and in horse-drawn wagons. Once again, the mayor took his place before the town hall, whose front elevation was nearly covered with earlier notices and warnings. Through the church window next door, I could peer into the chapel and see the statue of the crucified Christ. I wondered if He wept as He watched hammers nail each edict and warning into the town hall's cement flesh, another public crucifixion, not of a God, but of His children's God-given freedom.

Anger had reddened the mayor's face as he delivered the previously forced announcements, but not that day. Instead, a pall fell over him, leaving a sickly countenance that frightened me. His eyes scanned the crowd, stopping upon certain faces with obvious sympathy, but for what? And then he looked at his German handlers as if begging for a reprieve, but none came, and the reading began.

"The following enlisted men of Braquis and the surrounding area have been captured and are being held as prisoners of war in Germany. Before the list is read, know that those guarding them will look favorably upon them if their neighbors obey and adhere to the law. The reverse is also true. Communities that resist and disobey will bring harsh treatment upon their incarcerated soldiers. I will now read the list."

"Armand . . ." My brother's name broke from Mother's lips in a guttural moan as she spun to face Father, clutching his fisted hands. Seconds later, her worst fears were confirmed as Armand's name and that of our cousin Pierre were read from the list. Angry tears streamed down Jacques' stoic face as moans and cries split the somber stillness of the crowd.

I felt numb, fragile, and papery. Armand was in prison. My handsome, gentle, violin-playing hero was a prisoner of war in a German camp. I did not fully understand the import of the decree, but I was well aware of its impact on our village. Families huddled in sobbing heaps or moved from group to group comforting one another.

Father's tightly held jaw looked as if it might crack. Mother buried her face in Father's chest and gathered her remaining children close. Ironically, those packed streets, among a noisy throng, allowed our family the greatest privacy to speak freely.

Jacques doubled over with a groan. When he stood, he said, "I swear I'll kill these Germans if they hurt Armand."

Father pressed Jacques' face into his shoulder to quiet his rant. "Shhh . . . That kind of talk will get us all killed. People are rioting over the pitiful rations. The Germans are using threats to our imprisoned family members to quell the Resistance. They think if they shock us, we will submit."

"I won't submit," Jacques argued. "I'll never submit. I'll fight."

"For now, we will submit, for Armand's sake, and for the family's. But we will also wait, and we'll plan and prepare, and then, when the time is right, then we will fight."

After the initial jolt wore off, angry eyes turned on the Nazi officers. The kommandant seemed unmoved by the display. He leaned close and spoke to his French-speaking junior officer, who paled and pulled a small notebook from his pocket as he attempted to calm the crowd.

"Please. Quiet please. Understand that your loved ones are safe so long as you help us maintain the peace. Return to your homes now. If you don't, if you riot or demonstrate rebellion"—he held up the notebook and his pencil—"I'll be forced to record your names, and your loved ones will suffer." He struck his sad smile again, as he had in our kitchen. I understood then that his earlier kindness was offered as a credit in advance of the news they were about to deliver. I almost hated him more for showing that kindness. For allowing me to think for a moment that he was different. That he might be a friend.

I couldn't imagine how we would continue to live under the same roof with these oppressors, but drained and exhausted, we all heeded the Nazis' counsel and returned to our homes. Most of the Germans huddled in the dining room, appearing as uncomfortable in our presence as we were in theirs. But the kommandant entered the kitchen and tapped his watch. "Supper at six?" he asked in broken French.

Numb. Expressionless. Mother looked at him as if she were looking through him. "Yes." She was a study in brittle dignity, her broken heart on full display while she stood in silent grief. The officer could not meet her gaze for long. His eyes dipped, and he backed two steps away. "My apologies for your son," he said in a mix of German and French. His left arm swept to the dining room. "Serve us there. Be with your family tonight."

I was not prone to hate, but I knew if I had ever hated anyone, I hated this man, feared him, and yet pitied him as well. I wondered whether he had a family, a son, perhaps. Whether he had any idea what pain he'd caused us and what weapons he'd unleashed. Father was not merely his opponent, but his newest enemy. Jacques too. And Mother, and me. As little as I was, I would wield my only power against him. I would light a candle and ask God to protect Armand by rendering these Nazis powerless to hurt him, and then I would pray for God to touch their hearts. To let them feel what we were feeling. The full agony of the unknown.

I was feeding the chickens and planning my conversation with God when two boys on bicycles rode into our yard—our cousin Dominic and Légère. They jumped from their bicycles before their rides stopped, tossing the bikes aside as they rushed over to me.

"We heard the news," said Dominic. "The Germans got Armand and Pierre."

The mention of Armand cut through my shield of anger, reopening the pain. With my throat too tight to speak, I nodded and wiped at my eyes.

"You shouldn't be here, speaking of this." I looked at the dining room window. "The Nazis will hear you."

Légère turned in the direction from which he'd come, twisted his face in anger, and spit.

"They're up the road checking papers," said Dominic. "They checked us before allowing us to come. We told them we were here to read the notice."

"They're afraid of a riot," added Légère. "It's good to see them afraid for a change."

Dominic chuckled, "Where's Jacques? Out planning a revolution?"

"Stop!" I grabbed Dominic's sleeve. "Please! Don't say such

things, and don't stir Jacques up. I've already lost one brother. Please don't do anything to make me lose another."

Dominic picked up his bike and tried to explain his comment away as a joke. Légère, on the other hand, stared at the ground as if hoping to find some words of comfort there.

"Jacques is smart . . . and he loves his family. He won't do anything foolish."

I wiped my eyes again and hoped what he said was true, but I had overheard Father's conversation with Jacques, and I wasn't sure anymore.

"All this has frightened you, hasn't it?"

The tears began again.

"Michelle, I don't have a sister. In fact, I'm the youngest in my family, so I have no one to watch over. I know I'm no replacement for Armand, but what if I help Jacques watch over you and the little boys? I could be your secret brother. You could write me letters and tell me about your fears. Perhaps they won't seem so frightening if you write them down. What do you say?"

"But . . . I hardly know you."

He extended his hand to me and smiled. "Hello. My name is Légère Dubois. Very nice to meet you."

I tried to maintain some semblance of dignity, but my resolve melted into a giggle. I took his hand, and he shook it up and down as if he were pumping water. "I'll take that as a yes." He looked at our house and saw the numbers over the door. "I'll write to you first. Then you'll have my address, and you can write me back."

I heard myself laugh once more. A few minutes earlier it had been a sound I doubted I'd ever hear again, but this dark-eyed boy with the gentle smile took me in as a friend, easing my fear and coaxing hope back into my broken heart.

CHAPTER FIVE

The number of French soldiers taken prisoner was staggering. Some placed the total at two million men. Mother begged the Germans for information on Armand's situation and whereabouts. All they would tell her was that he was in Germany, most likely in a work camp on a farm or in a factory. Farm work was a better assignment, we were told, with better rations and more freedom to move, so we prayed each night that Armand was a farmer.

Légère kept his word and sent me a brief note peppered with humorous details about his lazy dog. The last line was written to give me hope about Armand. Légère explained that a friend's uncle was sent home from a German prison camp because he was too ill and weak to work. His words were intended to give me hope, but I began to wonder whether I should pray that Armand was a healthy farmer or a sickly one who might come home.

Jacques' life was also about to change. A few days after the prisoner announcement, the kommandant and his French-speaking comrade entered the kitchen earlier than usual, in time to catch Father and Jacques still at home. I didn't make eye contact with any of them, keeping my eyes fixed on Father to weigh his response to the enemies he despised.

"We are being transferred to Paris soon," the younger officer began.

Chills coursed over my body at the news. I didn't like these men, but we tolerated one another without much interference. Could the next group be even worse? I studied the faces of my nemeses and wished they were staying after all.

"The kommandant has a few last details to tie up before the next command takes charge. He would like your son to be the new PTT officer for Braquis."

Father's head cocked back in surprise. "M. Zavich has been the Post, Telephone, and Telegraph officer for years."

"But he is an older gentleman, more suited to riding a tractor than a bicycle laden with goods. On the other hand, your son is a strong young man with time on his hands."

"He goes to school and helps me after class."

"The kommandant understands your concerns, but we are adding an additional responsibility to the job that makes it more suited to a younger person with strength and speed. The PTT officer will now also handle the delivery of rations from Étain to Braquis. This plan is more efficient, eliminating the need for most citizens' trips outside the village. Better to use one bike than many cars or trucks. It will conserve the already dwindling supply of petrol."

"His education comes first, and his help at the shop is necessary to keep up with all the equipment repairs and the manufacture of new parts."

The younger officer translated the response and came back with the kommandant's reply. "The population of your village is small, so the run should be short. Jacques can help in the shop after he finishes his deliveries of the mail and rations."

And with that, Jacques became the area's PTT officer.

He was given a new bicycle and a small monthly stipend for his work. Each day, villagers called in their orders for rationed items, small goods, and medicine. They also called to alert Jacques if they had mail going out or a package ready for pickup. During the break at midday, before Jacques sat to eat, he tallied the orders to decide if he could carry all the ordered goods and make all the requested stops that day. He also organized his route to hit every home with a need in the most efficient and timely way.

As soon as the school bell rang, he dashed home to grab his list and slide on his armband with the letters PTT emblazoned on it. The length of his route varied day by day, so he jumped on his bike and hurried to the first home or farm to pick up their ration coupons or outbound mail. On and on he rode, from door to door. The heavily wooded road took him past the German encampment as he made his way to Étain, some nine kilometers away, even without stops and long farm lanes.

He generally returned home with his belly full from all the food grateful neighbors offered him as he made his stops. Along with the snacks, the neighbors also filled his pockets with extra rolls, potatoes, eggs, and other offerings which greatly blessed the family pantry. The most wonderful gift of his work were the stories and gossip he picked up along his route. Each family he visited seemed as hungry as the next for a good tale or bit of news to brighten the dark evening hours, and Jacques developed a comedic wit from repeating the tales at each stop. We waited up in joyful expectation of his return and the telling of the day's news. We felt certain he saved his best performance for us, to ease Mother's sorrow.

Upon arriving home, he'd attend to his studies. More often than not, Father was back at the shop, so once Jacques' school-work was complete, he rode his bike down the street to join Father, and then both men came home just in time for bed. Those late nights in the shop worried me and wore on Mother. Questions about the work that required such long hours were met with diversion and dismissal. Adding to our worry was the conversation Jacques and Father shared the day the prisoner list was read.

The long days also wore on Jacques physically. Sundays proved to be his salvation, both figuratively and literally. He was in our pew on the Sundays the priest held services, then back in bed soon after. Likewise, he rested on every Sunday the priest was serving elsewhere.

The young German officer knocked on the kitchen door one evening soon after Jacques and Father returned home. He held a pair of soiled uniform trousers in his hand. Mother reached a hand out to take them.

"When do you need these?" she asked.

The soldier looked back over his shoulder in the direction of the dining room where his comrades were meeting and asked in a loud voice, "Can you remove this spot now? We are leaving tomorrow."

The question was simple enough, but as he passed the soiled trousers to Mother, his expression implied that there was more to his message. He turned to Jacques and Father, his gaze moving back and forth between the two as his voice dropped to a whisper. "Despite your long day running the PTT route, you almost always find time to work in your father's shop." His attention became riveted on Father. "The kommandant has noticed the sudden increase in your workday hours, yet the number of clients has decreased this month. He is leaving a note for his replacement to check on this inconsistency."

Mother's hands shook as she returned his pants, which had a large wet mark on the seat.

"*Danke,*" he said with a slight bow. "I'm glad your work is so consistent, M. Naget. Men with a shop and the tools at your disposal might foolishly get a notion to fabricate items other than farm equipment. That would be a perilous thing, don't you agree? For the shopkeeper, and for his family?"

The color drained from Father's face, and Jacques slipped into a chair.

"Such a man would indeed be a fool," replied Mother as her arm slipped around Jacques' shoulders to quell their shaking. "We wish you well on your assignment in Paris."

The soldier nodded again. "*Ich danke dir*. The nightlife will be most enjoyable."

"We never knew your name."

He paused, appearing to freeze at attention while debating Mother's comment. "Sergeant Meier."

"Godspeed, Sergeant Meier." Mother stepped closer and smiled before pressing her hand to her mouth. Questions tumbled from her trembling lips. "Do you know anything about the men replacing you? Will my family be all right? What can we do?"

His face tightened, and his brow became pinched as her panicked questions rattled out. He backed up a step, preparing to leave without answering, and then his tight face slackened, and he said, "Occupation is unpleasant. Our orders are to maintain a happy population, but the rioters and rebels require stiffer laws and penalties. Be as happy as you can. Obey." His gaze settled upon Father once more as the dining room door opened and a fellow officer called for his return. With a final nod, he said "Good night," closing the door behind himself and leaving us alone with his warning.

Mother didn't say a word for several long moments. She stood before Father, her eyes burning into his, pleading with him, as tears welled in her eyes.

His shoulders straightened and then slumped in resignation. "We will be home for supper tomorrow."

"And after that?"

"I cannot say."

"What are you doing in your shop if the clients are few and the work is slow?" She gasped and covered her mouth with her hand, drawing her own conclusions, unabashedly challenging Father.

"I can easily justify long days. I am always making parts,

building my inventory of bolts and clamps, things people often need, so I'll have them on hand."

"Joseph . . . talk to me."

"All right, Yvonne. I didn't know the kommandant was monitoring my shop so closely. Now that I do, I'll pace my hours to the volume of work so I don't draw their attention. All will be well. Don't fret."

WE HELD OUR BREATH AS THE NEW NAZI COMPANY ARRIVED. Six officers moved into our home, replacing those transferring to Paris. The rest of the armed soldiers walked the streets, establishing an imposing presence that seemed to shout their power without saying a word.

The new kommandant was a Captain Hoffman, a large, muscled man with deep lines etched into his brow as if his eyes were perpetually pinched. He spoke some French, mostly expressed as demands at a decibel range more suited to calling out across a field. He stomped as if announcing his presence with every step, and his junior officers seemed as nervous in his presence as we were.

For the next few months, we were a perfectly obedient family. Everyone worked or went to school, came home at noon for the midday meal, and gathered again for supper. That is, all except Jacques, whose PTT route seemed to bring him home later than ever before.

The new kommandant ordered inspections of all homes and businesses in town, including the small grocery with nearly bare shelves, the plumber's home, the family baking extra bread or taking in sewing. All the local farms were inspected, including their barns and sheds that held blades and sharpeners that could double as weapons. The inspections were not so specific that the soldiers noticed if a single tool or medicine or measure of metal appeared or disappeared, but they were detailed enough to make it clear that the owners were being watched.

Our obedience brought Mother additional freedom to care for the village's sick during the winter, when colds and flu set in and when unreliable rations left people undernourished and weak. The Germans' rations also continued to fluctuate. A lamb or hog might arrive one week and then nothing but potatoes and flour the next. The Nazis had inspected every inch of our house, including the cellar. They knew how many jars and bottles remained on our shelves, the number of chickens in the hen house, and which rabbits remained in the hutch. Regardless of the military rations that arrived, our guests expected a hearty meal. On more than one occasion, a vehicle stuffed like a September hog's belly conveniently arrived at mealtime with officers from other districts. It appeared as if news of Mother's cooking, rather than military business, drew them to Braquis. Mother wrestled to feed all the mouths that arrived at her table. She also struggled to hold back a pot of soup or a stew to nourish the sick and the hungry.

France had many suffering people.

One of Légère's monthly notes was an overt attempt to lift my spirits. It included a drawing of a little stick-figure girl with a frown that reached the ground. Beside the drawing was a list of books he recommended I read and a brief mention of a truckload of sickly prisoners returned to France from German prisons. His final lines, intended to bring me comfort, only added to my fear.

IT APPEARS *that prisoners are either well enough to work or returned home when sick. I trust no news means Armand is well.*

HIS MENTION of that truckload of sickly prisoners reminded me of a whispered conversation shared between my parents regarding the return of a truckload of sickly French prisoners. Instead of being welcomed home to their communities, some residents mocked them and called them cowards for surrendering instead of fighting to the death. The thought of my sweet Armand being maligned by our own countrymen left me confused and angry.

One of the German soldiers noticed my distress and confiscated my note, saying he needed to read it to check it for subversive content. I wanted to argue, but I saw no wisdom is escalating the already tense situation in our home, so I stood by and watched the soldier laugh about the prisoners' pitiful situation.

I wanted to believe the people of Braquis would never turn one of their own away, but things were changing, even in our village, as a growing unrest bubbled within people. The restrictions took their toll, as did hunger and the cold winter. Local men cut down trees, but there was too little petrol to run tractors and splitters to split and haul the logs efficiently, and too few men to do the jobs manually and effectively. Time seemed to revert back fifty years as horses and wagons and brawn replaced machines that sat idle for lack of fuel.

Mother's fancy wood-fed cookstove kept our kitchen toasty while heating its large reservoir so that hot water was always at the ready. When the cold temperatures caused the dining room windows to ice, the Germans demanded that all the downstairs doors remain open to allow the woodstove's heat to circulate throughout the lower floor. Doing so destroyed what little privacy we had, so Father fashioned a small woodstove and chimney for the corner of the dining room to keep our unwelcome guests comfortable and content.

The same could not be said for Braquis' hungry, cold citizens. The mayor proposed a Christmas Eve church service to give the people hope and to calm their worries. To our surprise, the kommandant agreed, and Mother planned the program. The service became quite a topic before and after school. We chatted about former town parties and celebrations, and the more we spoke of the coming program, the more we dreamed of taking that simple musical service and turning it into a pageant followed by a community supper.

For the first time in many months, conversations buzzed with pleasant hopes of a community Christmas. We children chatted about it at school, and neighbors shared the hope as they passed on the streets or entered the church to pray. We knew the planned meal wouldn't be grand, but the women spoke of setting aside small portions of their sugar and flour rations to create their favorite breads and desserts for that day.

Father pulled out his long-silent accordion that had somehow survived the looters, and practiced a few hymns to prepare for the sacred night. As music filled our home once more, the Germans filtered into our large kitchen, spilling through the doorway and into the hall, seemingly as hungry for some holiday peace as we were. I felt a momentary kinship with them, as fellow Christians, anxious to remember a gentler time.

"And what is the cause of this revelry?" asked the kommandant.

Mother set a hand on Father's knee, bringing his song to a halt. "Joseph is practicing hymns for the Christmas Eve service at the church."

"Ah, yes." The kommandant's response dragged out like taffy. "The Christmas Eve service. I planned to speak to the mayor about that. I approved but a brief church service."

Titi was unaware that our fragile dreams of enjoying more than just a religious service, of having a festive community party, were still just dreams and hopes. In his innocence, he piped up and said, "We also want to have a party and supper, with cake and cookies!"

The kommandant's face hardened like concrete. "I had heard such rumors. It's why I planned to speak to the mayor. The event may need to be canceled."

Mother leapt to her feet. "Please. Please don't! It's just the innocent chatter of excited children. It doesn't mean anything. Please let us have our service."

The kommandant remained immovable. "I generously approved a small religious service for a few dozen village dwellers, but news of a party has spread outside the village. My men and I will not be able to control the crowds."

Father remained silent, but I watched how his knuckles whitened as they gripped his accordion. Mother took a deep breath and tried again to reason with Herr Hoffman. "You wanted to improve goodwill in the village. This is a good thing you're doing. Canceling the service will undo your generous goodwill. Surely you can see that?"

The kommandant's shoulders hunched up near his ears. "The cancellation will disappoint your people for a single night. But if so much as one person were to use that gathering to create mayhem or to launch a rebel attack, my men and I would spend the rest of the war in a Russian prison, and the SS would arrive and level your quiet village. Do you understand that?"

His emphasis on the last phrase caused Mother to pale and slump into her chair. Father turned and kept his eyes dipped and his voice cool and even. "I give you my promise that the people will abide by your rules and go home peacefully afterward if you allow us to gather in the church on Christmas Eve."

Captain Hoffman's face took moments to register any reaction. We held our collective breaths and waited as his eyes moved from face to face. He finally nodded. "I will speak to the mayor tomorrow and enlist his assurance on this matter." The square of his shoulders softened and a forced smile tugged at the corners of his mouth. "You will find that we are not unreasonable. Obedience brings rewards. If things go as you say and there is no trouble, perhaps we can schedule a dance to welcome a happy New Year. You would like that, yes? But I warn you, we will bring the full weight of the military upon this town at the first sign of any trouble. Do you understand that?"

Father nodded. "Yes, Herr Kommandant."

"Good. It is very good that we understand one another. Now return to your meal, Family Naget."

Once the door was closed, Father's reaction was visceral. He brought his accordion to life with a loud wail that voiced in melody what he could not . . . dared not say. Anguish poured from the instrument's bellows, a heartache equaled by the sorrowful absence of Armand's companion violin. I saw the haunt of hopelessness and grief in Mother's eyes and the bulge over Father's jaw as he bit down his anger and squeezed the instrument through his pain.

The Nazis, including those gathered in our kitchen, were the cause. They were the invaders of sovereign neighbors like our beloved France. Their planes caused us to evacuate through the streets, only to be cut down, and it was the threat of their brutality that tore our gentle Armand from us and made him a prisoner of war. Permission to hold a church service, along with the dangled possibility of a dance, could not erase all that.

Nevertheless, the neighbors poured into the little chapel on Christmas Eve. The hymns and carols were those we had always sung, but on that night, they weren't as bright and joyful as they had been in previous years, because never before had our sacred assembly been held under armed guard.

At the conclusion, the kommandant walked up the aisle, stopping in front of the altar. He seemed to enjoy holding our rapt attention. After a considerable pause, he said, "I commend you on your obedience, and to prove to you that cooperation and obedience bring rewards, I make you this promise. If you do not linger, if you return home peaceably and quickly, and if this order and peace continues through the next week, I will permit you to hold a community dance in Herr Naget's shop." He looked at my father and smiled. "Does that meet with your approval, Herr Naget?"

Father smiled a forced smile and offered a tense bow to the kommandant.

"Very good. I'll leave it to Frau Naget to organize the event. Now make haste to your homes and remember that your comfort and peace is in your own hands, through your cooperation and compliance."

People offered one another quick, terse hugs and Christmas

wishes as they emptied their pews. When I filed out of my row, I saw Légère standing at the end of a pew.

"What are you doing here?" I asked as he slid in behind me. "Didn't they allow you to gather for a service in Doncourt-aux-Templiers?"

"My grandmother isn't well, so Father sent us here to spend the night with her. He'll join us in the morning after the milking is completed."

I felt him reach for my hand and press a tiny object into it. He leaned over my shoulder and whispered, "It's a piece of my grand-mother's fudge. She's saved nearly all her sugar rations for weeks to make it."

The thought of that fudge on my tongue made my mouth water. "Thank you, Légère."

"It's not much, but your surrogate brother should give you something for Christmas."

I giggled and he hushed me. I could feel him back away and straighten as we neared the doorway where the Germans were hurrying people's exit.

When my feet touched the grass, I turned around and walked with Légère, who took hold of his grandmother's arm. "Will you be at the New Year's dance?" I asked before he walked away.

"I wouldn't set my hopes on that dance, little sister."

"But he said—"

He jerked his head to the right, tossing a dark wavy strand of hair from his eyes. The corner of his lip rose in a sneer. "What good is a Nazi promise?"

His mother took the grandmother's other arm, and the family turned right, away from the village square.

I tucked the fudge deep into my pocket until I was home and in my bed. The temporary hope of a community dance and party had been dimmed by Légère's words. Burrowing into my covers, I drew the quilt over my head, leaving a flap open to catch a sliver of moon-light as I turned the chocolate over and over in my hand, unable to stop thinking about Légère. His normally kind, gentle face seemed so filled with contempt and mistrust. I licked my fingers, sticky from where the candy softened and seeped around its wrapping.

We all knew that the Germans could promise anything, like a dance, and withdraw even that tiny morsel of happiness from us . . . and do worse. Poor Légère no longer allowed for better possibilities. For hope. As I tasted that fudge, I thought of his aged grandmother, who sacrificed and scraped together enough sugar to make this delicious treat. The Nazis could take and take and take from us, but we were resilient, and we held to the hope that we would always find a way to keep the sweetness of life alive.

CHAPTER SIX

Contrary to Légère's prediction, we were allowed to hold our dance. Mother and I spent an hour sweeping Father's shop floor while he busied himself locking tools and materials in the drawers of large wooden chests where inquisitive fingers couldn't reach. Mother offered to help him, but he scooted her away saying, "You do not like me nosing about in your kitchen. Well . . . this is my—"

"Kitchen?" she finished with a laugh.

Father turned back and leaned against the workbench where he was standing. "I've missed that."

"What?" Mother chided as she smiled back at him.

"Your laugh." He held her in his gaze for several long moments before tossing a rag onto the workbench with the frustration that had so long bubbled within each of us. "But then, we haven't had much reason to laugh lately, have we?"

Mother moved to him and laid a hand on his arm. "Tonight, eh? You'll play, and we'll laugh and dance. It will be good."

The moment ended in a brief kiss that restored normalcy to our world, if only for a short while.

Légère attended the dance, though he never took a single turn on the floor. Instead, he and Dominic skulked off into a corner with Jacques. Their lack of interest in the few girls who attended sent the young ladies off into their own corner. They seemed to draw more pleasure from fussing about the rude boys than they could ever have had dancing.

Father played his accordion beside a few other local musicians who formed our village's little band. Mother moved through the guests, offering a smile and some kind words here, placing a hand of comfort there. Few of the adults chatted as they once did, or as the boys still did. There weren't many safe topics to chat about anymore, and a prolonged tête-à-tête of any kind eventually touched upon our abhorrent oppressed circumstances, which were dangerous topics when soldiers were listening, and weighing every word.

Mother and Father suffered the additional burden of having every word scrutinized by the locals, who believed our housing position gave our family unique insight and information about our oppressors and the future. In any case, it left my parents in a rather sad state of isolation, even when they were among friends.

I twirled the little boys around. Gilbert was in his heaven, and it saddened me to think how little fun and joy he had known in his brief life. I tried to make up for that lack by kicking up my heels and making funny faces as we skipped and stomped through some traditional *bourrées*. Titi, who was turning eight in a few weeks, found himself in the awkward position of not wanting to be lumped in with the giddy little children, while still longing to play and have fun. I cajoled him onto the dance floor for a few dances and found him to be quite a good partner. As we moved through a line dance, I watched the people in attendance. They appeared to fall into one of two categories—those who were overly joyful and eager to show the Germans their gratitude for allowing the gathering to occur and those sober-faced attendees who remained immune to the moment's pleasure, visibly mourning the days when we could gather and dance and sing at will rather than when permitted. In each person's own way, we were all twirling every day, each of us caught up in a dance of bowing and genuflecting.

Life moved on in waves as our German occupiers arrived and left over the next year, establishing new prefectorial rules and guidelines. They led, and we followed in our dance of compliance. Our family lived under the same roof as before, but the family living under it had changed. We measured every word and hid our frustration, becoming nearly mute within our own home. The situation was worse for Gilbert. The long winter left the four-year-old restless and bored at a time when we were adjusting to a new kommandant, one who found the little boy's exuberance intolerable. He ordered Mother to quiet him, and Mother read an implied threat that the officer would gladly do the honors if she were unsuccessful.

Her body shook with a rage I feared might burst from her eyes like a torch, but she held her tongue and apologized for her son. I watched her heart break from sorrow as she hushed and scolded our sweet little Gilbert for merely being a child. The retraining was effective. After a few weeks, the tamed boy barely resembled our joyful imp, as if he had been poured into a mold and squeezed until he was someone else entirely. The quieter Gilbert became, the angrier Father and Jacques grew until Mother gladly released them to the solitude of the workshop and their previous pattern of long days at work.

I hardly recognized France when spring arrived. We became so accustomed to the roar of planes above us that we rarely ran to the air-raid shelter anymore. We could hear the drumbeat of the Allies' bombing runs pounding Paris and cities near the German border in their efforts to free us from Germany's grip. Paris was being decimated, and despite Allied efforts to avoid civilian casualties, many innocents died, and still we remained prisoners, trapped within the Nazi fist.

Our land was also left ravaged, not by bombs, but by neglect.

With most of our men already gone to prison or labor camps in Germany, our work force was depleted, leaving few men to work the farms. Many fields were left unplanted. The pungent smell of freshly plowed and dunged earth had always signaled renewal and life, but weeds and ruts festered in the dormant, fertile fields, as if the land was also grieving.

As Easter approached, we applied for permission to hold our annual Passion Play. The Germans were reluctant in their permission, but plans moved forward. The men in the village pulled the crosses from Father's shop. Two were set up in the yard behind the church. The third remained in the shop, where the play would commence.

Mother readied Father, who played the part of the Christ. Eyes were especially moist in our house as Mother helped Father dress in the robes of the Lord that year. Suffering was a concept we understood more deeply since the occupation, and Easter took on a new, more personal meaning.

We walked to the end of town near Father's shop, where he lifted the cross on his back. As he walked down the main street of Braquis, we followed along, singing hymns and reciting prayers, until we reached our little Calvary, where Father's cross was set between the other two and he was bound to the wood, like the Christ.

I felt a curious new intimacy with God, and with my neighbors that day. Even the voices of the children were stilled as the spirit and meaning of the play sank deep into our hearts. I wondered how it felt for the Germans who watched from a distance with their guns slung over their shoulders. Some of them mouthed the hymns and the readings, showing that they had been Catholics at some point in their lives. It seemed impossible to me, but then, so many things seemed impossible.

Three letters began to be whispered in our home like a curse over the next few months—STO—and though they were never explained to me, I knew Jacques understood their meaning. I could only imagine that he and Father talked openly in the freedom of the workshop about things that could not be discussed at home. And as the village's PTT representative, he entered homes not housing Nazis under their very roofs. Homes where people were still able to speak freely to each other and to him. I envied him and his freedom, and I watched for opportunities to pull him aside and speak to him away from our house.

On a rare afternoon, he was still at home, kneeling in the front yard, fiddling with the chain on his bike, instead of racing off with the day's list of pickups and deliveries. When he saw me crossing the road from school, he looked up and called, "Michelle!"

Not Mimie. And I had a fairly good idea why.

"I saw you by my bike this morning, and now the chain is off. Do you want to tell me how that happened?"

I opened my eyes as wide as possible and shook my head convincingly, or so I thought.

"Mimie . . ."

His disappointment stung me. "All right. You're always racing off here or there. I miss you." I glanced at our house where a swastika hung. "I just wanted a minute alone with you . . . to talk."

He stood and rolled the bike back and forth to make certain the chain was in place. When he had his answer, he tipped his head toward the rear of the bike and said, "Get on the back. I'll take you for a short ride to test the chain."

I got on the bike and wrapped my arms around Jacques' waist. He had grown strong and tall, more man than boy, but still impetuous and playful and, hopefully, willing to speak to me about things Mother and Father would not. That shared moment made me realize how badly I had missed my brother. Both of my brothers . . .

As we moved away from Braquis' tiny town center, filled with listening ears and narrowed eyes, Jacques pedaled harder and faster, until the fragrant summer wind warmed my cheeks and tangled my hair. I spread my arms wide, allowing the breeze to ripple through my fingers while a familiar happiness returned momentarily to my heart. I felt freer and more alive than I had in months, and I dreamed that we could go on and on, faster and faster, beyond the village and ragged fields to another place and even back in time to those gentler, more peaceful days of my early childhood. But it was not to be.

Jacques pedaled a little past Father's shop and stopped. "Get off. I think the chain needs tightening." I slipped to the ground and watched Jacques kneel beside the bike as he tugged and checked the chain's links. "What were you so desperate to talk about? It had better be worth making me late for my run." His sharp words were delivered in playful tones.

"Mother and Father won't talk to me about anything that has to do with the Germans or politics. What does STO mean?"

"*Service du travail obligatoire.* The Germans are forcing French citizens into compulsory labor. Hundreds of thousands of Frenchmen have been sent to Germany to man their factories and farms, and some of the women are being sent into camps to serve as domestics for the German army."

Diverse horrors passed through my mind, of Father and Jacques, being bussed away or of Mother dragged off to a work camp. "That's why they whisper about it. They're afraid our family will be divided."

Jacques nodded at a soldier who was studying us from afar. He exaggerated his efforts to check the chain. "Mother and Father think we will be spared. Mother is practically their slave already, and Father's work is necessary to keep the equipment running on the few farms that are still producing."

"But what about you?"

He gave a slight shrug, brushing my concerns away, but I could see worry and anger flash in his eyes.

"The kommandant knows you are strong enough to work."

"And headstrong enough to be a problem." He chuckled sadly. "I hope my work as the village's PTT officer will exempt me." He stood and tugged on my hair. "And now I'm delayed from doing that very work because of you."

"But what if it doesn't exempt you?"

"Get on the bike, Mimie. I'm late for my route."

"No. Tell me, Jacques. What if they come for you?"

"It won't happen."

"How can you be so certain?" His brow furrowed and his eyes narrowed. I knew that look of defiance. "What do you know, Jacques?"

He glanced down the road at the German soldier, whose attention was fixed on us. Jacques moved the bike back and forth, and as if still checking the chain's safety, he jiggled the links, but he spoke to me.

"Families are already hungry, and now they're being torn apart. Parents and children are mourning loved ones they might never see again. That won't happen to me."

The hairs rose on my neck and arms as a chill coursed over and through me. "You're not thinking of joining the Maquis are you? You've heard Herr Schmidt warn us about what happens to anyone who sympathizes with them or any other Resistance group."

"Watch your tongue, Mimie," he spat back in a whispered growl. "Do not even speak of the Maquis. Never. Promise me."

"You're frightening me, Jacques."

When he turned my way, his expression appeared pinched in pain. "I'm sorry, little one, but . . . I can't . . . I only say"—he shook his head—"a quiet defiance is growing in France, and the Free French Forces are gathering to General DeGaulle in London. He is my hope. That is my plan. Now get back on the bike. I'll give you a ride home, and then I must be off on my route."

I didn't believe what he said about General DeGaulle's being his hope and plan, but I wanted it to be the truth. With all my heart, I prayed for it to be true, but I saw changes in my brother. He'd taken on a belligerent posture around Herr Schmidt, and he and two of his friends, Paul Brunet and André Moyes, lingered together behind the school after class, whispering as if they were in league together.

I also worried about Légère, who I'd not heard from in months. He was also in danger of this STO and its ability to yank him from his family.

There were too many things to worry about, and still a new concern presented itself. Herr Schmidt, our teacher, had taken a sudden dislike to me as the school year ended. He called on me to answer questions and then picked my answers apart, or he found fault in my written work and used my unsatisfactory performance as a reason to assign me extra work or punitive tasks in the class-room. On several days, I left class nearly in tears and ready to quit school altogether and not return in the fall. But life was quickly put back into perspective.

Légère's father parked his rig in front of Father's shop one after-noon. I made my way there, hoping to get some word about Légère, but the nearer I drew the more certain I became that the stop was not a friendly visit.

Father's shop doors were open wide to welcome what breeze he could catch. When he saw the wagon pull up, he exited the shop, soaked with sweat, with a piece of white linen tied loosely around his neck. "Have you something to be mended?" Father asked as he untied the fabric and wiped his reddened face.

M. Dubois glanced down the street to where two soldiers sat, engaged in a game of cards. "My plow," he answered in a voice far louder than was needed for Father to hear, as if his desire was to inform the soldiers as well. He jumped from his wagon seat, and as Father drew near, M. Dubois's voice lowered to a whisper, and he led Father to the bed of the wagon. "I found a family near dead, camping in the woods by my farm. My first thought was to bring them here, so Yvonne could help them, but I know nothing about them besides that they fled from Paris. What if they're part of the Resistance? I was afraid to drive up to your house for fear of how the Germans might react."

Father jumped into the wagon bed and then stood and said, "Save both our backs, Charles, and drive your rig into the shop so we don't have to carry that plow." I noted that Father was also speaking louder than usual.

From his wagon-bed perch, he saw me and waved me near. When I arrived, he jumped down and led me inside, to the back of the shop, where a second door stood. "Mimie, I want you to wait five minutes, then hurry through the backyards to our house and fetch your mother. Tell her to bring her medical supplies and some of the broth she has bottled. If the Germans ask questions, tell them I became dizzy from the heat while mending Monsieir Dubois's plow, and I fell against the forge and burned my hand. Explain that I need her to tend to me. Can you do that?"

I looked at his two previously scarred but otherwise perfectly good hands. "Yes, but—"

He tipped my chin up and said, "Good girl. Now wait outside the door for a few minutes, and then go."

I did as I was told, and when the time had passed, I hurried to the house and found Mother in the kitchen, preparing the midday meal. She remained calm as she listened to me deliver my message in wary obedience.

"Is Father *actually* hurt?" she asked, as if she already knew the answer to my tale. The telling of tales had become a necessary weapon of defense, and I could see by Mother's reaction to the message that she had been summoned similarly before.

As she gathered her satchel of herbs, salves, and bandages, I ran to the cellar to bring up two bottles of her broth. I called to the little boys in the backyard, but when I returned with them, one of the new arrivals, a nosy, German noncommissioned officer, was standing in the kitchen, questioning Mother.

"Where are you going, Frau Naget? Is someone ill?"

"Yes, Sergeant. My husband was hurt at work. I need to tend him, but I won't be gone long."

He looked at his watch and then scanned the kitchen, where preparations for dinner were under way. "And what of dinner?"

"It will not be delayed." Mother smiled brightly. "And I'll make sure I have something special for dessert."

His eyes moved to me. "How old are you, little daughter?" he asked, scanning me from head to toe. One menacing eyebrow rose. His grin incited a new fear within me, a fear I had never felt before.

Mother's arm slid around me, drawing me near and behind her. "This tiny girl is my helper. We won't be gone long." Without being dismissed, Mother took my hand and headed for the door, but the officer stepped in front, blocking our exit.

"If she is old enough to help you tend wounds, then she is also old enough to tend to dinner. I've seen her work in the kitchen myself. Leave her." His gaze moved from my face to my toes and back. "Then everyone's *needs* can be met without any disturbance."

I grabbed handfuls of Mother's skirt fabric, anchoring myself to her. My fear seemed to transform her, making my mother appear taller, stronger, and more fearsome than I had ever before seen. Her words, *We do what must be done*, ran through my mind, and I knew in that moment that Mother would fight this officer, to her own peril if need be, to protect me and the boys.

Her courage surged through me as well, and I let go of her skirt and fisted my hands, ready to defend my mother against this menace, this beast of a man, but salvation arrived from an unlikely source as the kommandant walked into the house.

"What is going on here?" he asked.

Mother remained stiff and still with her arms spread slightly in front of her huddled children. "My children and I are going to tend to my husband who is injured . . . as soon as your officer gets out of my way."

The kommandant growled a few German words that rounded the sergeant's shoulders and sent him back several steps. "Sergeant Gass was making a joke, but clearly his humor was mistaken for something more. My apologies." He and the sergeant bowed slightly. "He will cause you no further trouble, Frau Naget. I've told him how unwise it would be to rile the woman who seasons our soup." He smiled and bowed again, waving us on.

Mother glared at the sergeant when she walked past, adding a grateful nod to the kommandant as she ushered us out of the house. She remained poised and collected until we were beyond the view from our windows, and then she began to shake and quiver like a feather in the wind. Behind us, we could hear the kommandant's angry voice drilling into the sergeant. Gilbert giggled and cheered that someone else was getting in trouble besides him. Titi ruffled his hair and laughed as well, but Mother and I held hands and clung to one another.

Father met us at the door of the shop. "Yvonne, are you all right? You look shaken."

Mother forced a smile and said, "It will keep. Who is hurt?"

"First, Mimie, please take the boys to the backyard to play."

"No!" Mother's reply was forceful and final. "She stays with me."

For the first time, Father's face began to register the cause of Mother's distress. The color drained from his face and then returned in a flash of crimson. He cradled my shoulders in his hands and asked me, "Did they—"

"No," Mother snapped, pulling me close while her eyes sent a message ending the conversation. "We don't have much time. Who do you have inside? Refugees?"

Father's reply was delayed and more a question than an answer, as if he was still processing the earlier revelation. "Yes. A family of four. From Paris. They're very sick. Charles Dubois found them on his farm."

"Were they hit in a bombing raid?"

"No. Just sick. But very sick, Yvonne."

Mother moved past him, pulling me along like an unwieldy appendage. Four people lay on canvas tarps on the shop floor. Two were children, about Gilbert's and Titi's ages. They appeared lifeless, with sickly yellow skin and gaping mouths. Only their breaths, coming in gasps and moans, gave any indication of life. I huddled against Mother, who moved to the man, presumed to be the father, and the person most alert. She asked him when they became ill and what they had eaten.

He explained that they'd made their way on foot from Paris, believing they'd fare better in the country near farms, where they hoped to find food. He explained that in the city, even bread was scarce and the only meat was from organs, which the children wouldn't eat. They had picked wild rhubarb wherever they could find it. The plants' leaves had become the staple of their meager diet for weeks. They ate it raw or boiled it into a soup with whatever else they could acquire while they searched for work. The illness had come upon them slowly, finally overwhelming them and forcing them to stop and camp.

Mother moved to the two children. When M. Dubois returned with a jar of water, he offered sips to the listless children without success.

Mother looked at Father. "I've read of many similar cases as hungry people try to supplement their rations with wild rhubarb greens. People don't realize that the leaves are poisonous in large quantities. They might have just had stomach cramps if they had eaten them sparingly, but prolonged use?" She shook her head. "The father is a large man. He's better able to tolerate it, but these children need to be taken to a hospital."

"It will take hours to get them to the hospital in Verdun by wagon. What can we do here?"

"The best antidote is milk if we can even get them to drink. They're also dehydrated from vomiting. They need fluids."

M. Dubois jumped to his feet. "I'll run to the nearest farm and get some milk."

As he left, Mother pulled a syringe from her bag, filled it with water and tried squirting some of the fluid into the children's mouths. Most pooled back out.

"Mimie, I need to gather the boys and get back home to prepare dinner or the Germans will ask questions. I don't want these people's welfare to depend on Nazi mercy. I need you to nurse them. Can you do this?"

I nodded yes, believing in her confidence in me.

"It will be tedious, but it must be done. The man should be able to drink on his own but stay with Father and try to get a syringe-full of water into the mother and the children until the milk arrives, then give them each a few syringes of milk. All right?"

Mother left, and Father and I took over. He lifted their heads, and I squeezed water into their inflamed mouths and past their swollen tongues. M. Dubois returned with the milk but it took an hour to get a few meager syringes of milk into each person.

I heard the school bell ring. "Herr Schmidt will punish me if I'm late for class."

Father was so focused on the family that he missed the fear in my voice. "I'll write him a note. Besides, you only have one week of school left before summer vacation."

I bit my lip and looked over my shoulder in the direction of the school, glad it was Friday and hoping against hope that Herr Schmidt would forget my absence by Monday morning. The thought of only five days left of school had cheered me earlier in the morning, but summer meant long days at home under the gaze of our Nazi houseguests, and they frightened me even more than Herr Schmidt.

CHAPTER SEVEN

To our great relief, Sergeant Gass received a **hasty** reassignment. The kommandant gave no explanation for the beast's departure, other than a nod to Mother as the sergeant carried his things to the waiting vehicle for transfer. Gass's replacement was a quiet man who followed the kommandant around like a puppy, and for a season, we had relative peace under our roof.

But peace was a rare thing in France.

I learned so many hard truths about mankind during the occupation, the hardest perhaps being how oppression and fear can numb anyone—even the most God-fearing among us—to the suffering of others. We knew some Jews were being "relocated" as early as the summer of 1940, when we were fighting to save ourselves. We had no voice with which to question the move, and as we were unable to free ourselves, we were likewise utterly powerless to help them. And so we prayed and hoped and feared for them. And then life built a defensive scab over us, perhaps to protect us from the death of self that occurs when we witness injustice we cannot stop.

But the scab was ripped from us when the Menchers, the

Parisian refugees, were strong enough and trusted us sufficiently to share their story. They explained that they were Polish Jews who moved to France three years earlier when M. Mencher took a job in Paris as a civil engineer. People in their religious community worried when the Nazis began creating barracks in the high-rise housing complex they confiscated in Drancy, a northeastern suburb of Paris. The Germans first used it as a police barracks, but large open areas were being fenced with wire, reminiscent of the stories Jewish elders told about World War One.

Fearing a massive roundup of Jews, the father quickly sold as many of their belongings as possible to bribe a friend, a Vichy government official, to smuggle him and his family out of Paris. But the roundup of foreign men began sooner than the official expected, on May 14th, when the detained men were sent to a commune-turned-internment camp called Beaune-la-Rolande, in the Loire Department. Instead of smuggling the family on to Switzerland as promised, the sympathetic official placed them on the only truck he could. Unfortunately, the truck was headed for a place of equal danger—the Occupied Zone of France.

The truck stopped in Doncourt aux Templiers, leaving them in a small enclave where newcomers were overtly conspicuous. By bringing the family to father's shop, M. Dubois had made them equally obvious. There were no other Jewish families in Braquis or any of the neighboring communities where the population was primarily comprised of interrelated families with deep generational roots. The Menchers would surely draw the curiosity of the Nazi occupiers.

M. Dubois returned to Father's shop five days after delivering his "broken plow" to carry his mended equipment home. The weak Mencher family crawled into the front of the wagon bed and under the canvas tarp draped over the plow. Their satchels were filled with cheese and loaves of Mother's bread. M. Dubois promised to drop them off on a back road with a map to Spain. We never heard from them again.

The plight of the Menchers was just the beginning of the swarm of new refugees fleeing Paris for the countryside in search of food. A crime wave of counterfeit ration coupons sprang up, and theft of the coupons from municipal buildings was also on the rise. Both activities only further crippled an already broken system of food distribution. Malnutrition was such a threat to the city's children that vitamins and vitamin-enriched biscuits had been issued to them by schools to avert disease and death. Good bread remained a luxury. Some dark, heavy loaf was provided as an alternative. Families sliced it thinly to make it last, but there was little to pair it with as there were few butchers providing safe meat for the average family.

As sorry as I was for those suffering, I was grateful I lived in Braquis, and I knew I would never again take for granted the mouth-watering smell of freshly baked bread or the tang of cheese on my tongue or the sweet joy of an apple or berry. Such things were no longer rights, but gifts, and we counted ourselves blessed that we still had access, though limited, to such delicacies.

But the threat of hunger was always near, so in the spring of 1941, we readied more beds and planted a sprawling garden. From sunup to sundown, there was no time for summer boredom. We planted, weeded, harvested, and prepared or stored everything we could. Rabbits, chickens, and whatever we could scavenge from the creek kept us and our guests well fed during the summer, but we braced for another long winter, when we could rely only on what we had stored.

The shortages spurred creativity. Coffee was sparse, so a hot drink made from chicory became popular. While some found it satisfying as it went down, its laxative effect left them distressed in the evening.

The lack of rubber for soles led to a new fashion—platforms shoes that added inches to one's height. Because I was still short by everyone's standards, I found these quite a fine substitute. Hand-me-down clothes were nothing new, but shortages in textiles led to the repurposing of all available fabric—blankets, linens, curtains, and even flour sacks—into clothes, tea towels, and diapers. Mother and I spent many an hour embroidering designs or crocheting borders to make these repurposed items as lovely as possible.

She and I spent nearly every free hour together, partly because I had become, as she said, her third arm, able to assist her and, in some cases, even relieve her at sickbeds and in the kitchen. I scrubbed laundry on a board, entertained the little boys, and sewed clothes. Mother had taught me to hand sew from the time I was small, but she began to teach me the finer points of tailoring. I learned to make patterns and to sew clothes on the peddle machine, remaking children's clothes from Armand's and Jacques' hand-me-downs. In the evenings, we worked together to mend socks and torn clothes, and to crochet and knit sweaters, scarves, and socks. I loved every minute spent with Mother, and as helpful as I was to her, I came to realize there was another reason she made me her shadow —to protect me. Mother was wary of leaving me home alone with any of the soldiers.

The changes began in my twelfth year—the rounding of my hips, the development of a bosom, and the thinning of my face until a little chin, once hidden by my round cheeks, appeared. My thirteenth birthday was celebrated quietly, as if the occasion was a secret, because, in truth, we hoped to keep it so, to avoid drawing attention to the fact that, even though I was shorter than Titi, I had become a teenager, in every way a young woman, who could no longer count on even the limited protections of childhood.

I wore my clothes baggy and avoided eye contact as much as possible. We already knew that some German soldiers and the Schutzstaffel, or SS, believed they could have or take whatever or whomever they chose. And so, I remained Mother's third arm that summer.

Though we loved being together, we huddled like silent ghosts, afraid to laugh or speak or do anything that would draw the Nazis' attention to us. She whispered her instructions to me as we knitted or crocheted, and I communicated back like a mime, in nods and smiles and looks of understanding or confusion. I mastered a new stitch that had troubled me for days, and when she smiled her approval, I forgot where I was and gave a little cheer of joy. In an instant, panic lit Mother's eyes. We both turned toward the door, fearful the Nazis would find us in good humor and misread a welcome in our momentary fun. Despite it all, I cherished that period of closeness and relative safety with Mother. I would draw upon her strength and the security I felt in her presence to meet the changes that lay ahead.

The busy summer of food production and storage left us little time to grieve Jacques' and Father's complete preoccupation at work. Our hands were always busy, and the little boys worked in the garden or fished or tended the animals until dark most days, so they were occupied until bedtime. Father and Jacques were discontented at home, like two caged animals penned in the kitchen or bedroom. The risk of flaring tempers was high in the circumstances at home, with no privacy and with the constant reminder that Father and Jacques were powerless captives instead of free men. The shop became their pressure-release valve, a place where they could speak freely, feel useful, and in control.

I asked Mother what they were doing to fill all that time. Her answer was vague and wistful—"What men do." I no longer felt jealous of Jacques' inclusion in Father's adult world. Mother and I were likewise a team, and I began to appreciate the subtle differences between the needs of men and women. Both needed purpose. Both needed freedom. Men needed space. Women needed each other.

Needlework and mending were more enjoyable when we were permitted to listen to the radio. Some of the kommandants allowed controlled use of the radio. Others forbade it altogether, believing the Allies used the programs to broadcast coded messages to the Resistance, with information about troop movements and military campaigns that might stir up rebellion among the restless populace.

Regardless, news still managed to trickle down from one traveler to another and through carefully worded phone conversations. In August we heard about another roundup of Jews—over four thousand, some foreign, some French—who were sent to the internment camp in Drancy. Most of us took the easy route, assigning full blame to the Germans, but to our great shame, we discovered that the French leaders of the Vichy government were so anxious to appear loyal to their Nazi puppet masters, that they ordered the roundup and ran Drancy prison. I began to wonder about France. What would be left of her, even if the Allies were able to free her from Germany's grasp?

After months of silence, a note arrived from Légère, apologizing for his failure to meet his promised goal of a letter a month. It detailed his excitement about beginning school after a busy summer of hard farm work. There would still be long hours of harvesting each night after class, but his love of learning was evident, and his gentle nudge convinced me to also return to class with the assurance that Herr Schmidt's disapproving glare would be less onerous than staying home with the soldiers.

This letter touched me differently than his previous posts. Perhaps because Jacques took so much pleasure in teasing me about it or because, at thirteen, I enjoyed the attention the letter raised. In truth, as I read it, I sensed that the summer had changed Légère, that he'd grown and matured, much as Jacques had. And perhaps I was changing too.

Most of the two-page note detailed his summer's work and shared news of the books he had read from his grandfather's shelf. And these lines, filled with insight into the man he was becoming, touched me beyond mere brotherly kindness:

I LAY on a hay bale and studied the night sky, thinking how those same stars that shone over our free France still shone over us now and would shine over a liberated France one day. I considered how people all over the world look at that same sky . . . free people in America and Britain. It made the world seem smaller and closer. It made freedom feel close. I want to see those places someday, when we are free. And we will be free again, Michelle.

I TORE those words from the letter and folded them into a tiny, obscure square which I tucked into my pocket, carrying it wherever I went, to keep those words near—*we will be free again*—and to keep the writer of those words near as well.

CHAPTER EIGHT

Freedom appeared an elusive dream as fall arrived and we returned to school. Many of the older students did not return to class. Some of the boys were needed to carry on the harvest, and many of the older girls were maintaining hearth and home as mothers picked up the load of missing fathers who'd been imprisoned or sent to work camps.

Herr Schmidt's dislike of me seemed to have been stoked by the summer break. As one of the oldest girls in class, I was assigned daily duties from tutoring the younger children and washing the blackboards to cleaning the classroom—all the while being expected to maintain my own studies. Jacques said the added attention was because I was Herr Schmidt's favorite. It didn't feel that way to me.

When the first plant-and-vine-chilling frost hit the ground, hearts chilled as well. Most everything had been picked bare or dug up already, but the wilted vegetation was a stark reminder of another long, hard season ahead. Bottles and jars had been filled, the root cellar packed, and animals fattened. We prayed the Germans' provisions would add to our food supplies, and that our rations would be filled. And if those prayers failed, we prayed that what we stored would somehow be enough.

We prayed over everything. Mother often stole away to the church to pray. To their credit, our German oppressors respected the sanctity of the church. It became Mother's solace and refuge—the one place where she could get away from her houseguests and pour her heart out without watchful eyes upon her.

Her anguish over Armand increased with every report about the conditions of the work camps and their prisoners. Even if Armand had been sent to a farming assignment, the passing of the growing season likely meant he'd be moved somewhere else for a factory assignment, where the conditions were reported to be much worse.

And so we prayed. And I wrote to Légère.

He became more than a faithful brother to me. I could write to him of things I longed to discuss with Jacques, who was so busy that we rarely saw him except at dinner. None of us had much time for friends, and with his schedule, he had less than most. He found a few moments to chat with Paul Brunet and André Moyes. What little free time he and I were able to share was too precious to add to his worries, and so I shared my concerns with Légère.

I told him of Herr Schmidt's cruel eyes upon me and how he singled me out in class. I wrote about the newest German contingent, and the arriving kommandant's new rules and threats, intended to remove complacency and instill obedience from the first day. I described all the new soldiers, from the older dumpy sergeant, who flirted with Mother to get extra helpings of food, to the youngest of the officers, a skinny goose-stepping follower with a pointy nose that made him look like a half-starved mouse. He stared at me and smiled as if he knew a secret about me. I was most afraid of this wily little man.

Légère wrote back quickly, encouraging me to have Mother and Father arrange a fall dance. My parents posed the idea to the kommandant, telling him that past gatherings had been very successful in calming nervous villagers. To our delight, he approved our plans and a November date was chosen. Soldiers used the time to visit each small community, where they extended the invitations along with warnings about the penalties for any acts of insurrection or disobedience. Once again, weeks were spent with musicians loosening fingers stiff from summer work. Women prepared special treats from their meager rations, and we readied Father's shop.

The dance presented new excitement and frustration—how to enjoy my first dance *as* a teenager without revealing that I *was* a teenager. The careful protections Mother and Father built around me felt like a cage, keeping me safe but preventing me from enjoying the privileges that, by right, were mine. I longed to alter one of my boxy-cut dresses to fit as it should, but Mother forbade it. In frustration, I lashed out at her. It was the first time I could remember doing such a thing since I was a child. I expected her reprisal, but none came. Sorrow equal to my own spread over her, and I realized that the loss of this time in my life was her loss as well, that Mother longed to enjoy this season of firsts with me. Her arms spread to me, and we cried together, as she offered me two concessions—a cute bob cut to my curly red hair and the loan of one of her hair combs. I also stepped into my homemade platform shoes that Father had crafted. All in all, I was pleased with the changes. I still looked like a ten-year-old, but at least I looked like a ten-year-old who was ready for a dance.

The dance afforded me the first opportunity I'd had to gather with the girls who had not returned to school. While Jacques and the older boys huddled in a corner, we girls chose to chat in our own corner and study them. We eventually lured one of them our way, resulting in a dance invitation to one of the girls. Mother spent most of her time herding Titi and the other boys his age away from the dessert table while dragging Gilbert along from the dance floor to food-protection duty. I relieved her for a time and danced with Gilbert while I watched the door for Légère's arrival.

Gilbert and I were spinning around when Légère entered. I

stopped my dancing and turned his way, noting how handsome he looked. His clothes were worn but clean, and the great care he'd paid to styling his freshly cut dark hair was apparent. His brow furrowed as he stared at me, pretending not to know perfectly well who I was, and then his head cocked to the side, and he mouthed my name, questioning my identity. I rolled my eyes at his game, missing the intended compliment, that despite the boxy-cut of my dress, Légère saw me in a new light.

I straightened and stood taller, foolishly ready to toss aside my cage of protection and assume my rightful age. Légère was handsome, and hard work had chiseled away what remained of his boyishness, leaving behind a young man with a lean face and strong arms. In that moment, I loved him and feared for him at the same time. If I saw the change, then surely the Germans did too, and they would see threats in his strength and confidence.

Though he towered nearly a foot above me, I sensed a note of awkwardness in the confident sixteen-year-old's bearing. His eyes drifted away from me and then back. Even his smile had a certain shyness to it. He wiped at his grin with the back of his hand, as if he were stalling at the blackboard while trying to formulate a correct answer.

"You look very nice, Michelle."

"As do you," I replied, doing my best to steady my voice and speak as Mother would.

"You've grown since I last saw you."

"Not really. I'm still four feet eight inches."

He laughed and tapped my head. "Yes, little sister. You are still a tiny little bird."

No matter how I felt about Légère, he still saw me as his little sister. I blushed hot with embarrassment and nodded in the direction of the older girls. "Don't blame me for monopolizing your time. There are plenty of girls to dance with who aren't your little sister."

The awkwardness left, and his confidence returned with laughter that filled the space between songs, catching the attention of those standing nearby. "Ahhh, still as feisty as ever, I see. I was wrong to call you a little bird. You are a bandy rooster."

My hands flew to my hips. "And you are no gentleman," I teased back, but the merriment left his eyes as they scanned the room, falling upon the mousy German soldier who was staring our way . . . the very soldier I had described in my letters.

Légère leaned down as if he were addressing Gilbert. "Michelle, take Gilbert and stand near your mother for a while. Let's not draw further attention right now, eh?"

The worry in his voice froze me, and I did as he suggested, moving near Mother, who appeared ashen and shaky. She kept me busy for half an hour, arranging and rearranging the same few pastries and cookies a dozen times. During our efforts, the mousy soldier came to the table to peruse the offerings, as if I were one of them.

"You look like a big girl tonight, Michelle. How old are you?"

My eyes shot to Mother, who hugged me close. "Only a day older than yesterday. She wanted to look special tonight, so we cut her hair."

"Ah, yes. That's it. The hair. Very pretty."

He extended his hand to me, but I remained frozen by Mother's side.

The smile that instilled so much fear in me spread across his face. "You wouldn't offend me by denying me a dance, would you? I saw you speaking to that older boy."

"He is as a brother to me."

"Then think of me as your brother as well." His hand extended closer, but Mother stepped forward with a nervous chuckle. "We've been so busy since the occupation. I'm afraid I've neglected to teach Michelle how to dance. Please allow me to be a substitute who would be less likely to step on your toes."

His eyes remained fixed on me. "I have good boots, Madame. I doubt this little bird can do me harm."

Mother gave me a nervous nod, and I shuffled my feet as the

corporal led me to the center of the floor. He released my hand and placed his own hand breast-high on my right side. My entire body began to shake. After a momentary pause and with a smile that clearly indicated how much he relished my discomfort, he slid his hand slowly down my side to my waist. Father stopped playing, and the music ground into a silence that, like a spotlight, drew everyone's attention to us. From the corner of my eye, I saw Jacques stand and take a step forward. Thankfully, Légère held him back. Tears burned in my eyes, but I knew if I showed fear, my family would do something that could ignite the tension in the room. Fearing that outcome more than the German, I shook my head at Jacques, willing him to remain in his place. Then I straightened my back and offered the soldier my left hand.

"Play on, Herr Naget." The soldier's words were a demand rather than a request, and all eyes shifted to my father.

The other German soldiers, most of whom were relaxing on bales of hay, rose and leaned in while the villagers froze in their places. Father's jaw bulged and flexed, and his eyes slipped to mine. "What would Michelle like?"

I studied the intent of his words, finding more than an invitation for me to name a song, but permission for him to throw caution to the wind and defend his little girl.

The soldier said, "Request a polka."

I swallowed and eked out, "A polka, please, Papa."

The use of the word Papa, reserved only for discussions about my birth father, Father's brother, undid the stalwart man. His mouth quivered as he nodded to the other musicians and the music began.

The soldier was not as tall as Légère or Jacques, and as the dance began, he pulled me closer than the dance required. When I stumbled, he righted me on my feet and danced about, more carrying me than leading me.

As we spun, Jacques took another step forward, and Légère again pulled him back. A moment later, I heard a playful argument break out from the boys in the corner. Between laughter and bravado, I heard the words American, German, and fútbol being bandied about, and soon the German soldiers joined in the good-natured discussion until it, rather than our awkward dance, commanded the room's attention.

Légère raised his voice. "Let's see what this man has to say on the matter," he shouted as he moved to the corporal and me. Making no eye contact with me, he addressed the soldier.

"Who would win in a sporting contest if nine Germans played nine Americans in a game of American football? My friends and I are divided. We say German soccer players are better athletes, but American football players may be able to take them. What do you say?"

The corporal released my hands and became animated over the question. In a moment, he was in the corner, a glass of beer in his hand, arguing the cause of the Germans point by point. I returned to Mother's side with Father watching my every step. He struck up the music, and Mother used the diversion to sneak me and the little boys away to the safety of our house. I grabbed a quick look back at my protectors—Father, Jacques, and Légère, who each met my eyes before I slipped beyond the door. And then there was my brave Mother, my greatest hero, who had willingly stepped forward in my place.

I had never felt more loved and less safe as I wondered if the Germans would ever again see me as a child. But that was another day's worry. And no one could predict what the next day would bring.

CHAPTER NINE

C hange was constant, so I held fast to the few things that remained somewhat stable. But even though my anchors were there, they seemed different to me, because I was changing.

Oppression brought new, albeit forced experiences, and experience gave way to new understanding. Some understanding came slow and steady as we, like dough under a roller, succumbed to the daily pressure of occupation. Some of that understanding came bit by bit, as one difficult life experience blended into another, like a final crystal, dropped into a saturated solution that instantly crystallizes the whole, transforming it into something new altogether. And some enlightenment arrived instantly, with the nailing of a notice and its new rules to the door of the town hall. Sometimes, that last change affected everything I knew previously, as it did on the morning of Sunday, December 7, 1941.

I rang the bell early, but I no longer swung from the bell rope when I pulled it as I once did. I hadn't heard God's voice speaking to me joyously in the wild abandon I had previously felt as the bell rope lifted me physically closer to Him. Instead, I heard His voice as a calm cadence resonating in the solemn echo of the bell's ring, as if He were reminding me, "I'm here. I'm here. I'm here."

The church services I had attended all my life nourished my famished soul during difficult days. Instead of relishing the lazy priestless Sundays of private worship, I wished the priest could come every week instead of once in four. And though I knew God heard and answered my simple prayers, I felt a special security and peace as I listened to the priest pray and as his resonant voice led our hymns.

And communion . . . How I loved feeling one with God.

I looked into the face of Christ that day. His crucified image, portrayed in stone, hung behind the altar. I studied his complex expression, a mixture of love and grief. I considered the mockery of his crown of thorns and the brutality evidenced by the marks in His hands and feet and side. I knew Him more deeply that day. Perhaps because I too had become acquainted with sorrow and grief, with mockery and pain. The experience of occupation helped me under-stand His sacrifice in a new way, and as that revelation struck me, I felt the promise of His love extend not only *to* me, but *into* me. In that moment, I knew in a personal way I had not known before, that we were not alone. None of us. That even in our current circumstances, He was still with us.

And then I thought about the Jews. His people. And what was happening to them. I tried to push the thoughts and images away, thoughts the boys had planted in my head before school as they repeated tales of things too horrific to be true—of concentration camps and death squads. I had walked away from their conversa-tion, but the thoughts still came, along with questions. Why did He not stop it? He created worlds. He was surely mightier than the Germans. Why did He not stop it?

I felt my lip curl in doubt and anger. In my heart, I screamed, "Why do you allow such things?" But even as my wretched heart broke, I knew the answer. It was displayed in those marks on His hands and feet. In the trail of blood seeping from His crown of thorns. In the look of love worn during His own hours of greatest suffering.

Man must be free to choose.

To rise or to fall.

While His arms were ready to catch those who reached out to Him for succor and salvation.

His healing was complete and sufficient, but justice and mercy were His.

Recalling these truths did not erase all the pain and worry but remembering them strengthened me. I allowed Him to write His love on my heart, like a letter which I carried in me:

Man is free to choose.

Justice and mercy are God's.

I ADDED them to Légère's words, which were also written there:

We will be free again.

———

FATHER WAS LIKE A CAGED CAT THAT COLD SUNDAY afternoon, circling the kitchen, his tiny lair, looking for a diversion. I noticed that he was home more often since the night at the dance. I didn't know what power he could wield if the corporal again requested my attention, but having him there made me feel safer and brought a more ready smile to Mother's face as well.

He grabbed a sharp knife and a sack from the cupboard. "Let's harvest what remains in the garden."

"What's left?" asked Titi.

"The *crucifères*," Father answered. "Like broccoli and cauliflower."

The term was old and antiquated. I knew what plants it referred to, but not why. The little boys wrinkled their noses at the mention of the chore, but we children were just as delighted as Father to have an excuse to leave the tight confines of our allotted space and head outside, so we quickly complied, donning jackets, scarves, and mittens.

"What does *crucifères* even mean, Father?" I asked as we stood at the edge of the scraggly bed.

He knelt down and cut a broccoli plant near the root. "This is a healthy plant that used its energy to create this tasty vegetable we eat. If the ground gets too warm or too dry, instead of making green heads, it will use its energy to bolt, which means to make seeds prematurely to assure the plant's survival. But before the seeds form, the plant first makes bundles of little flowers shaped like tiny crosses."

"Ahh . . . Like Jesus's cross."

"Yes." He smiled and nodded as understanding came to me. "Crucify . . . cruciferous. The cross."

"Reminders of Him are everywhere."

Father's eyes shone, and his lips trembled as he testified, "They are, Mimie. Even in these hard days. Sometimes I forget." He hung his head. "Thank you for reminding me that God is here. With us still, and everywhere."

"And He will answer our prayers and set us free."

"Yes. In His time. He will make us free once more."

The image of a loving God spread before me again. Twice in one day.

We cut the last of the broccoli, cauliflower, Brussels sprouts, and cabbage before the deep freeze arrived and ruined the plants. The counter was stacked high with our harvest, and the kitchen smelled sulfurous and dank. We had plenty of work to keep our hands and minds busy as we cleaned and trimmed the vegetables. Some were set aside for the day's meal, but most were packed into mesh bags and carried down to the root cellar.

The bumbling sergeant poked his head into the kitchen once, slowly breathed in the cabbage-rich scent and smiled. "*Das ist gut.*"

Of all our oppressors, he was actually someone we didn't mind.

Mother smiled back and held up one finger to indicate that it would be one hour until supper. He backed out of the kitchen nodding.

Bowls of steaming cabbage and broccoli were set on the table next to plates of thinly sliced pork and cheese. We called the Germans in to eat first, as was the custom, and they took their time, enjoying their food. Mother, Father, and I stayed nearby to serve and clear as was needed. When their meal was finished, the kommandant and his aides returned to their maps and radios and teletype machine, to do what they did behind those closed doors.

Mother and I quickly washed the dishes and reset the table for our family's meal. What food remained was spooned into the bowls and platters. We finally sat down to eat around eight when our meal was disturbed by a flurry of excitement that could be heard from behind the Germans' door. The mousy corporal ran out of the room and through the front door of the house. His excitement had been hard to read. Fear? Celebration? Moments later, the chubby sergeant and two of his comrades returned with equal urgency as the entire group holed up behind the closed door.

We ate quietly, drawing no attention to ourselves as we strained to hear any snippet of news pouring through the radio or from the tangled threads of the Germans' frantic conversations. Something had happened. Something big and disruptive, but to whom? To us or to them?

We were given no word that night, though we cleaned the kitchen slowly, hoping to catch a word, a phrase, a look that might give us some hint. The responses to the news seemed as varied as the faces that passed by our door. Father's eyes widened, and his head tilted to the side as a look of wonder brightened his face.

"What? What?" asked Mother.

"I can't be sure, but I think they're talking about the Americans."

Mother's eyes flashed with bright optimism that quickly faded. "I don't want to get my hopes up."

But my hopes soared at the thought that the neutral Americans might finally be entering the war.

Details trickled out over the course of days and weeks about the Japanese attack on the American fleet based at Pearl Harbor in the American territory of Hawaii. The death tolls were staggering—over two thousand dead and many more injured. The American president had declared war on Japan, but Japan was part of the Axis powers, the league of nations supporting Germany's seizure of Europe. Did that mean the Americans had declared war on Germany as well?

Hope bubbled within me at the thought, and then I remembered the reason they were entering the fight—the unprovoked Japanese attack on their base. Thousands dead. Countless injured. Their fleet and planes destroyed.

With what would they fight?

America was France's friend. She would find a way.

When Mlle. Pirot taught a unit on America, she proudly explained France's courageous participation in America's Revolution. I loved imagining the brave Frenchman, the Marquis de Lafayette, who crossed the Atlantic to fight for America against British oppression, eventually petitioning the French military to stand with the young country. Though Lafayette was buried in Paris, Lafayette, the leader hailed as "The Hero of the Two Worlds," slept in both French and American soil because his son George, named after Lafayette's friend and comrade, President George Washington, brought soil back from Bunker Hill and scattered it over his father's grave. America would not forget that. Our ties were deep.

In The Great War, America helped the Allies push back against German aggression. America's Revolutionary oppressor, Great Britain, had become a trusted friend. France and Great Britain had also warred with one another, and they too became friends and allies. Enemies to allies . . .

Politics was a curious thing. For a fleeting moment, I wondered if there would come a day when Germany would also become a friend and ally to France? I could scarcely imagine that such pain and loss could ever be forgiven. At least not until we were free. We held our breath and prayed that the mighty nation we supported long ago during their struggle for freedom might return to Europe a second time and help secure ours again.

Our wary hope remained that and no more in the coming weeks and months as the Germans reacted to America's entrance into the war. A new smugness swept over our captors, who verbally assailed the Americans, believing that Japan and its mighty navy had done Germany a great favor. By tying America up in the Pacific, Japan was keeping America too busy to bother with Europe, giving Hitler and his followers a free pass to reshape the world map.

I refused to listen to their blather. The Americans were coming. We just had to hold on and wait.

CHAPTER TEN

As we turned the page to the new year, we had no more power over our circumstances than we had before, but the events of December 1941 caused us to reassess our capabilities and become more strategic in our response to our oppression.

America's entrance into the war, however distant from our situation, left Jacques emboldened and me naïvely optimistic. The hunger for news almost exceeded our physical hunger through the early spring of 1942. The German soldier's advances toward me at the dance left Mother wary and Father enveloped in a simmering anger, so Father and Jacques lengthened their days at the shop to put distance between themselves and the Germans to avoid confrontation, while Mother sought ways to keep me occupied and beyond the soldiers' reach.

By February, many pantries in Braquis were nearly empty. The rations were too unreliable to be counted upon, so what remained on shelves and in cupboards was primarily cooked into a soup or stew and served with bread to fill hungry bellies.

That is, as long as the miller had flour for bread. Flour was no longer a commodity we could count on.

We noticed that Jacques returned home from his PTT route despondent most days. He used more force than was necessary to lower the bike's kickstand when he arrived home. His roughness caught Mother's notice.

"What happened today to leave you so upset?"

"Not just today," he snapped. "Nearly every day." He dropped into a chair and rested his head in his hands. In a moment, he looked up, no less anguished, but more apologetic. "I'm sorry. It's not your fault. I'm just frustrated and angry and . . . and sad. I take families' ration coupons, but some days I can get nothing for them, and I have to tell the people waiting for bread or cheese or meat that there is none today."

"I'm sorry. You're too young to have such a difficult responsibility. How widespread are the needs this month?"

"Everywhere. Mothers cry because they have nothing to feed their children. Everyone's clothes are too big or too small, or so tattered that they offer no warmth at all. And most people's shoes are falling apart." His eyes turned red, and he jumped from his chair to face a wall where he could hide his tears. Mother moved to him. She stood inches shorter than he did and wrapped her arms gingerly around him.

When he was again composed, Mother asked, "How old are the children who need shoes? We have extras. They're old but they still have wear. Would any of those fit the children you mentioned?"

Jacques' face brightened. "Yes, but even shoes that are too large would be a help."

The next day, Mother loaded Jacques' basket with shoes, sweaters, and a few extra loaves of bread, which he delivered on his route. In return, the recipients offered Jacques some of what they had in abundance—milk or butter or dried beans. In a few days, neighbors noticed the swapping and wanted to join in, and Mother made a plan.

There were some positives to having the food supplies dwindle to ingredients for a meager pot of soup or stew. Such meals required less work and time. Mother made her bread dough early, and once she'd set a pot of broth to boil with what soup bone or vegetables she had on hand, she was out of the kitchen early and able to tackle other needs.

She sent us to school and used those hours to attend to the laundry, mending, and cleaning. After school, she took the little boys and me with her on "rounds" to check on the health of community members. As we traveled from house to house, Mother found shortages of food, fabric, sundries, and seeds for spring planting. As Jacques reported, no household had everything it needed, but she saw that almost every household had something to share, and Mother devised a system to help everyone make the most of what we all had.

Articles of clothing were generally patched and remade many times until the fabric was threadbare, leaving only swatches of good cloth which were saved to mend other garments or cut into squares for quilting. The squares were like trading cards between the women—blue squares from denim swapped for green plaid from an old work shirt, or yellow, or red, to add color to quilts or to create a patched adornment that would cover a hole and extend the life of a garment. Wool, strands of yarn, and thread were similarly saved and swapped so socks and clothes could be made or mended.

Buttons, zippers, hook-and-eye closures, trims, and notions were removed and stored like precious commodities. Shoes and boots were traded and resoled to fit growing feet in many homes. Flour and sugar sacks' seams were opened and the linen fabric used for clothing, dish towels, diapers, and bandages. Seeds harvested from the previous years' gardens were portioned and traded so each house had a variety to begin planting in pots before spring.

Jacques jotted down the needs and brought them to Mother, who knew who had what. The little boys and I were her able helpers, and as such, we were kept busy moving items from house to house and assisting Mother in her nursing duties, both of which kept us out of the house and away from the Germans as much as possible.

They noticed the change. We came home from our rounds one afternoon in early March to find one of the German soldiers standing watch by our front door. As soon as he saw us, he hurried into the house, returning with the kommandant, who wore a look of stern expectation on his face as he waited for us to reach his position.

"*Frau* Naget, your services were needed today, and you were nowhere to be found. What enterprise suddenly keeps you so occupied?"

Mother tensed and stepped forward, scooting us behind her skirt. "I'm sorry, Herr Kommandant. What did you need?"

"My laundry."

"Washed and folded early this morning, sir, and placed in your room."

He visibly harrumphed. "And tonight's meal?"

"The bread is baked, and the soup is begun." She smiled guardedly as she extended her hands to reveal a linen-wrapped parcel. "But tonight, we have a fat ham hock to add to the pot."

One of the kommandant's eyebrows raised. "Is that the errand you were on today?"

"One of many, sir."

"And these *errands* require *so* many hands?"

"There is much want in the village, Herr Kommandant. Not every household is as fortunate as ours to enjoy the added blessing of your rations to draw upon, so we do our best to address whatever needs we see and to relieve what strain we can. As we have been taught by your predecessors, happy people are more cooperative people."

I watched my shy Mother's shoulders hunch up near her ears and saw the quivering smile play across her virtuous lips, signaling her discomfort at placating the Germans with a lie. We all knew the Germans' "bounteous" rations were insufficient to cover the number of mouths they added to our home. She feigned calm when I knew she was a quaking mass of nerves, but she was in rare form.

"Well said, *Frau* Naget, but how does your service to others make a ham hock magically appear?"

Mother's shoulders slipped down into a rounded hump as she drew a deep breath. When she began again, her speech was earnest and true. "Every home has unique resources. I'm just organizing those resources to help us fill one another's needs. For example, Madame Brouchard is ill and can't make bread, so I made extra for her family, but she has butter stored, so she asked me to take a pound to a family who needed it, and that household repaid me with a ham hock."

The German's eyes widened in awe. "*Ist gut* . . . but what else have you carried home today?"

Mother signaled to Titi, who pulled a parcel from his pocket. He unwrapped it, revealing several folded papers containing various seeds.

"We'll start planting these inside very soon to ready seedlings for the garden when the frost is past."

The kommandant nodded with veiled skepticism. "All of you . . . empty your pockets and baskets."

We flinched and then obeyed, pulling everything from our empty pockets, down to the lint. When the kommandant was satisfied that he had seen all that could be seen, his eyebrows narrowed, and he leaned forward toward Mother.

"Know that we are watching, *Frau*. Tell that to your husband and son as well. There is a reason when creatures change their habits. Today you are innocent. Be sure to keep it that way. There is talk of sympathizers aiding the Resistance and Allies. Do not make the mistake of joining their cause." He glanced at each of us in turn. "Allow me to tell you a story, Family Naget. Before the war, a feisty little dog wandered onto my property. I occasionally threw him table scraps, and in return, he barked and warned me of intruders. Like that dog, a vagrant also made his way to my property. The dog barked, and I chased the vagrant away. But over time, the wily intruder began bringing my dog scraps of food until the dog saw him not as a vagrant, but as a friend. He stopped warning me when the man entered my property, and when this intruder robbed me, do you know what I did?"

My lower jaw began to tremble at the cold tone in his voice, but it was Mother's face, devoid of color despite the air's chill, that cemented the warning in the kommandant's words.

"I shot the vagrant *and* the dog. The vagrant for defying me, and the dog for betraying my trust."

THE KOMMANDANT'S WARNING PIERCED MY BALLOONING courage, but Mother maintained her rounds, helping where she could, and enlisting us in the work. Her head seemed to dip lower in prayer after the officer's ominous warning, as if her very thoughts carried the weight of his threat, and yet her expression took on a steeled air of inevitability.

I held her hand as we left the empty church together the next Sunday. "Are you all right, Mama?" I asked.

She smiled too brightly and swung our hands too playfully, as if to distract me from my question.

"Are you afraid of what the kommandant said?"

She stopped us at the bottom of the stairs and tapped my chin. "The only thing we should fear in this life is disappointing our Lord. And in that, I think we are fine."

"I think so too, Mama."

Her courage and faith had a profound impact on me that day, and like her, I decided that I too would face the kommandant's warning head on, deciding that no matter what happened to us, we would serve others and do what must be done because we cared more about being right with God than with the Germans.

We walked across the street that day, swinging arms, and

smiling at the Germans who watched us through the window, seemingly marveling over our joy. I felt another shift in Mother's attitude toward me. I was still her daughter, her little girl, someone she wanted desperately to protect, but I also sensed that in addition to knowing I was capable and responsible, she had also come to know that I was brave and as clearly in the Germans' crosshairs as she was.

That evening, Father and she exchanged glances across the dinner table, and then their eyes rested on me. "Michelle, after we get Titi and Gilbert tucked in for the night, you may come back down for an hour."

My bedtime was always the same as the little boys', but no more. I'd been invited to join the adults. I'd crossed a threshold from child to young adult.

"We want Michelle to come up with us. She's fun. And who will tell us stories?" cried Titi.

Mother laid an arm across his shoulder. "Michelle is growing up, and so are you. It's your turn to do for Gilbert what Michelle has always done for you."

Titi recognized his own rite of passage. He squared his shoulders and motioned to Gilbert to follow him upstairs.

"Would you like me to help you, Titi?" I asked.

With a flip of his hand, he waved me off. "No, thank you. I can do it."

Another threshold had been crossed.

I was anxious to be initiated into the grown-up fun that occurred after the children were in bed, but the rewards of my maturing age were not at all what I imagined. No secret desserts were shared. No parties were held. No guests arrived. Mother picked up her needlework, Father and Jacques read, and I just sat in utter disappointment.

Mother smiled and tittered behind her embroidery hoop. "You look bored, Mimie."

"Being an adult is not what I expected."

Jacques gently pulled on my hair. "Sometimes being an adult means I get to put in an extra hour or two of work at the shop. Doesn't that sound like fun?"

Father scolded Jacques with a click of his tongue. "It's a quiet time, Michelle. A time to reflect and think and talk together. You'll grow to love it."

"Perhaps," I conceded. "But if it's all right with you, I'll just go to bed tonight and tell the boys a story."

Mother smiled and winked at me. "As you wish. Good night, Mimie."

It took a week before the evening ritual of quiet hour enticed me away from an extra hour's sleep and time with the little boys. I came to look forward to my parents' whispered recounting of the day's news as much as to the fairytales I told Titi and Gilbert. Like those bedtime stories, there were villains and heroes, but few happy-ever-after endings, at least so far. But the local gossip did provide a certain context to the vaporous changes occurring around us, and knowledge provided greater peace than ignorance had thus far.

The news in our village came to us, one ragged piece at a time, like the quilts Mother and the other village women assembled. By gathering an overheard word from here and a snippet of gossip from there, the adults struggled to make some coherent sense of the limited information they received.

The miller's reach was broadest and generally most reliable because his customers came from the widest range of communities. Merchants picked up news from suppliers and clientele, and Doctor Joliet from the neighboring city of Étain moved within communities and therefore had occasion to overhear reports. In the quiet evening hour, my parents and Jacques processed all they had heard during the day.

"Maurice Brouchard had me weld a broken wagon tongue today," whispered Father without looking up from his book. "He said unless he receives a shipment of new wheat, he'll soon have to mix other grains in to grind enough flour to meet demand."

Mother dropped her hands and her knitting into her lap. "The bread will be dense."

"But at least there'll be bread."

Father glanced at the closed door, the only guarantor of privacy between us and the Germans. His voice lowered to an almost imperceptible volume. "Brouchard also said the Allies conducted a successful attack a week or two ago."

Mother's eyes widened as she glanced my way. "Where? In France?"

"Yes," Father replied.

Mother picked up her knitting and began again. "That must be the cause of the kommandant's warning to us about collaborating with the rebels."

"Was it the Americans?" I asked.

"No," Father replied with a shake of his head. "The British."

Over the course of the next few days, tiny bits of information were added to the story—

The attack was on the port city of St. Nazaire, part of the Atlantic Wall of defenses being built by Germany to ward off Allied attacks by sea. This specific port served as the repair station for German warships patrolling the Atlantic. The port had been all but destroyed when a British ship, loaded with explosives, rammed the primary dock, however, the victory came at an agonizing cost. British casualties and the number of men captured had been painfully high.

The victory meant little to me until Father put it into context. "Without the St. Nazaire dry dock, damaged German warships will have to limp farther away to another dry dock for repairs. That will extend the amount of time they'll be out of service. But more importantly, their longer voyage means they'll be forced to sail past British waters . . ."

"And British warships and planes," added Jacques.

I found it hard to cheer the victory. I had experienced the kommandant's brutal intimidation days after the attack. The Allied victory had not brought bread or medicine or meat to Braquis. It merely incited the Germans to further violence and coercion. I tried to focus on Mother's counsel, to find courage in doing God's work. What more could we do? And then one day, Mother put the final scraps of information together—the human side of the victory.

One April day, the kommandant called Mother into the Germans' office—our former dining room—to clean up a spill. While wiping the soup from the table, she discreetly read a scribbled note. The numbers 5 through 8 were written beside the names of six French communities along the River Loire on the western coast of France. One was St. Nazaire.

That evening, during our quiet hour, Mother mentioned what she read. Neither Jacques nor I responded, but the way Jacques' eyes darted from the tabletop to each of my parents told me he had news he was dying to share.

"I've heard that a few of the British soldiers who participated in the raid on St. Nazaire escaped German capture," he whispered. "French civilians in those towns you mentioned along the Loire helped get them south to Spain and back to England."

Mother's head cocked back. "French civilians?" she asked, as if another question lay embedded within the first.

Father closed his book and leaned close to her, placing a hand on her arm. "I suppose someone eventually connected them with the French Resistance."

But Mother's attention was riveted on Jacques. "Who told you so many details like city names and the route down the Loire? No mere civilian would know such things."

Father hushed Mother and set his eyes on the door. Jacques sat back and slumped into his seat as Mother pushed closer until her face was barely inches from his.

"But I know who would know those details. Are you friends with someone in the Maquis?"

The last whispered word came out like a curse. Jacques pushed his chair back with enough force to cause a squeal as the wood scraped the floor. I was instantly reminded of Jacques' own panic the day I simply mentioned the Resistance group by name.

We froze as sounds could be heard outside the door, then there was a creak as it opened a centimeter at a time. The kommandant's face peered through the slowly widening crack.

"Herr Kommandant. Can we help you?" Father said with an obvious annoyance in his tone.

"Forgive me. I heard raised voices. I was worried. Is anything amiss?"

Father leaned back into his chair and picked his book up off the kitchen table. He opened it with a forced nonchalance as he offered the kommandant a hint of a smile. "Merely a small family disagreement. Please forgive us if we disturbed you."

The kommandant's eyes scanned every member at our table. His sneered grin prefaced a one-word, exaggerated reply. "Indeed."

As the door squeaked closed, Mother burst into tears, muffling her cries into her knitting. I was caught between pain and fury over the agony of her situation. She was a parent who feared to discipline her child, knowing that a single word could alert the enemy and endanger the very child she was trying to protect.

No one spoke until we heard the heavy stomp of the kommandant's boots as he ascended the stairs with his men close behind. Jacques offered no apology or explanation as he left the room, also headed upstairs, with me following behind.

He glared my way and pressed a finger to his lips in warning. I kept silent until the door was closed behind us and we settled into the farthest corner of our shared room. I didn't know what to say. My hurt and fear communicated my concerns, and Jacques seemed to read them clearly. He took me by the shoulders, gently but firmly, as his eyes flashed alternately between anger and love. His voice, softer than a whisper, roared with the emotion twisting his face.

"I want to protect you, Mimie, and the little boys, but I can't. And neither can Mother or Father. We are powerless. Do you hear? Powerless. Our only hope is the Resistance."

"But the Ameri—"

His hands flew from my shoulders to his head as he spun away in frustration. When he returned, a cold calm steeled his expression and voice. "The Americans are going to fight Japan in the Pacific. They're not coming here anytime soon."

I wanted to disagree, but his lack of faith had exhausted my own as I reviewed the grim future he painted. No hope was coming. Our destiny was in our own hands. If we resisted, we would probably die. If we didn't resist, we might still die or, worse, be forced to surrender our will and dignity. I felt utterly powerless.

Jacques must have seen the dimming of my hope and regretted his successful pitch for resistance. He took my arms, pulling me close, but I didn't have the will or the strength to step into his offered embrace.

"I'm sorry, Mimie. Forgive me," he begged as he stepped to me. "I was an idiot. And angry. I didn't mean what I said."

I wanted to believe his new position. With everything in me, I wanted to believe.

He pressed his lips to my hair and whispered, "Please don't give up hope. Keep praying for the Americans to come. Pray that all the Allies come. I hope they do."

I responded to the emotion in his voice and the change in our situations. He suddenly needed *me* to comfort *him*. "You do?"

"I would love for them to come, so keep praying, all right? You have the most amazing faith, Mimie. I hope God answers your prayers. For all our sakes, I hope He does."

I wasn't convinced that Jacques believed the Americans were coming, but I knew he needed me to believe they were, and so I prayed. And hoped. And waited.

CHAPTER ELEVEN

Between school, his work at Father's shop, and his PTT route, Jacques certainly seemed too busy to be part of the Resistance, but there was no denying that he knew people who were, people who fed him information. Everyone he spoke to became a suspect.

I scowled at Paul Brunet and André Moyes who waited for Jacques after school. The two boys were older than Jacques and from neighboring villages, but André attended our school. I wondered if they were secretly working for the Maquis and trying to recruit my brother. And then I thought about Légère. He had expressed his outrage over the Germans after the tension at the dance. Letters arrived weekly for several months after that, letters addressed to Jacques with only a short note to me tucked inside. But his correspondence had grown more sparse since February. I wondered what nefarious activities had previously required such regular correspondence with Jacques and why he was currently unable to write. He too made my list of suspects.

The kommandant was promoted and reassigned. The new colonel wasted no time in telling us he was watching our family.

More changes were coming, he warned. Unpleasant changes, I assumed, but at least the hunger that remained after our rations were eaten might soon abate. Spring warmth would make the chickens lay, and the stream would teem with life again. I focused on the pleasant constants that anchored my life.

The last smell of winter snow in the air gave way to the musty scent of freshly turned and dunged earth, prepared and ready to receive the tiny seedlings we had nurtured for weeks. With the coming warmth came the fragrance and beauty of spring blossoms and on to summer's scent of freshly cut alfalfa and timothy from the few fields that were planted.

Summer also brought horrid rumors that more Jews had been rounded up and sent to the camp at Drancy, outside Paris. These persecuted Jews were packed into rail cars and transferred to camps where horrors were reported. We felt powerless to stop any part of the travesty, so we tried to block the images out and pretend they weren't true. Poor Father could not. He knew what was happening, and his helplessness increased his frustration, sorrow, and anger.

Jacques had been right. The Americans were not coming to our aid anytime soon. They were embroiled in battles in the Pacific, halfway around the world, and Japan's ability to keep them occupied pleased our German captors, who believed America would never enter our conflict. It seemed as if everything was working out as Hitler had hoped.

I turned fourteen with little fanfare. Mother greeted me with a kiss and gave me the one gift I would most adore—a few extra hours of sleep—as August signaled the rush to can, dry, bottle, salt, jelly, pickle, and otherwise store everything we could before the growing season ended.

Lard was already a household staple, but aside from its value in making soap and in baking, its popularity and demand increased during the lean years until it eventually became one of the most sought-after food items on the black market. The calories fueled us beyond what bread and thin soup could. The Germans loved the rendered fat as a spread on bread, akin to butter, and they considered fried pork rinds a delight.

Mother heard reports of people in the cities who were so hungry that they had turned to eating plant matter humans normally couldn't digest. They discovered that when leaves and stems were sautéed in lard, the fibers broke down enough to be digestible by humans, and the lard flavored the greens to make them tolerably palatable as well. And so we baked extra bread and traded it for pig fat which we rendered into lard for winter storage.

I was elbow deep in pig fat on the day Légère passed through Braquis in a wagon filled with young men. Titi and Gilbert raced into the house with their fingers pressed to their lips, shushing me, as they checked for the Nazis who, fortunately, were out for the afternoon. I barely had time to wipe the grease from my hands before they secreted me out the back door to the rabbit hutches, where Légère was waiting.

My breath caught, and I felt my cheeks flame at the sight of how much he had grown in the past nine months. He was tall and muscled and sweaty, with his dark wavy hair tousled about his face in complete disarray. A canteen hung around his neck by a canvas strap.

He was more handsome than I imagined in my daydreams. Even though he had never professed to be anything to me but a good friend, I had been cross and angry with him for not writing for so long. I missed his sage advice, his recommendations of books, and his promises of freedom. His silence wounded me more personally than the mere absence of our discussions could. I assumed that the delay in his correspondence was a sign that I'd been replaced by some farmer's daughter in his community of Doncourt-aux-Templiers. To my shock and delight, he seemed equally disarmed by the sight of me, and we stood there gawking as if seeing one another for the first time.

"You . . . look . . . well," I said, refusing to offer him anything too complimentary until I knew the reason for his visit.

"You look . . . so tiny."

I prepared to issue a prideful harrumph, but I saw true concern etched into his face.

"You're wasting away." His hands balled into fists. "This war . . . these Germans . . ."

"I'm well enough, Légère. Don't fret. And to what do we owe this visit? If you're looking for Jacques, he's out running his route."

Légère stepped back and smiled at me. "I didn't come to see Jacques."

The words, "You didn't?" squeaked out of my mouth with the volume of a mouse. I was grateful our conversation bored Titi and Gilbert, who ran off to play in the stream.

"No, Michelle. I came to see you."

I shivered at the thought. "Your little sister?"

"If that is what you want."

None of Mother's sewing magazines nor her back issues of France's most popular women's magazine, *Mon Ouvrage,* nor even Father's worn copy of *Les Misérables,* which I had read at least twice, provided me with a single suitable response. I stood like a lump, a hand-wringing little girl lump, before his handsome, nearly grownup presence.

"Didn't you get my notes?"

"The little notes tucked into the letters you sent to Jacques?"

His eyes crinkled at the corners as he leaned down to my height and smiled. "Did you read the letters I mailed to Jacques?"

"Of course not!"

"Well . . . you couldn't have even if you'd wanted to, because they were blank pages wrapped around your note. I didn't want to draw attention to you and have the Germans think you were old enough to have a suitor."

My tongue grew too thick to speak.

"I'm sorry I haven't written more. I've had to keep myself

productively engaged so the Germans would think me too essential here to ship me away to a work camp."

Thoughts of romance flew from my mind as I immediately worried about Jacques. "Are they still sending young men away to Germany?"

"Some, but over a million French men have been conscripted to work on the German defense barrier along the Atlantic coast. They call it the Atlantic Wall."

"Like St. Nazaire."

"Good girl, Michelle! I didn't know you were interested in politics."

My pride reared its ugly head again. "I hear things."

"I know you do. You face your fears head on. I admire that in you. I wish we could sit and discuss important things as we once did, but there is neither a safe place nor the time for such discussions."

"A wise plan." I smiled at his humorous explanation, but the seriousness of the plan was not lost on me. It all made sense, and I blushed at my selfish childishness over his failure to write me more notes. "What brings you here now?"

"The men in my town organized a crew to help the farmers get their harvests in. We're going from farm to farm."

His goodness and wisdom made him seem even older than his seventeen years. "You're a fine young man, Légère. I'm proud of you."

"And I of you, Michelle. Jacques told me about the work you have done here in Braquis—delivering babies, organizing food drives, tending the sick. You inspire me."

I felt the skin on my arms prickle at his words. "I just help Mother."

"I think you would do it anyway. It's who you are."

His kindness overwhelmed me. I had to pull my eyes away to hide the moisture welling within them. My parents loved me, but work was an expectation, not something worth much praise.

Légère's praise felt like water on the parched soil of my heart, and I realized such gentility was yet another casualty of war.

He reached for my hand and placed something in it. When I opened my fingers, a delicately carved wooden crucifix on a black silken cord lay in my palm.

"It's beautiful," I whispered.

"I carved it for you, so you will always feel Him watching over you. And know that I'm watching over you too."

Completely disarmed, I ran the cord through my fingers. Voices could be heard in the front yard. The German soldiers had returned and were questioning the other members of the work party, asking them why they'd stopped. Our moment was over.

"Will you come by again?" I asked.

"I'll try. Now go inside the house so they don't see us talking. My friends will say I'm filling a canteen with water from the stream, but they won't be able to delay my return for long."

I did as he asked, catching a final glimpse of him as he ran back toward the stream. I stood by the front window, watching for his return to the wagon, hoping the Germans didn't harangue him. I knew I was powerless to stop the abuse if they did, but I felt a need to watch over him, as he had watched over me.

Before the wagon lurched away, Légère looked back at the house and found me watching from the window. With one hand raised to wave goodbye, he touched the other to his smiling lips and blew a kiss my way. He'd never claimed to care for me as anything but a sister, but my fourteen-year-old heart hoped his feelings had grown into something deeper. And though we were still children by age, we understood what some adults might have missed in times past—that the one freedom neither governments nor armies could control was the power to love. In that moment, with Légère's blown kiss warming my heart, I knew I would love him forever.

CHAPTER TWELVE

In addition to all our household demands, Mother's work as a midwife and nurse kept us both increasingly busy. While Mother attended to the laboring woman and new child, I watched and cared for any other children in the house and over the house itself, by cooking and cleaning so the new mother would have a meal ready and her chores done when we left. Mother and I returned several more times, if additional help was needed, and when the birth was difficult and dangerous, I was called in to assist in the delivery.

I was no stranger to the sights and sounds of labor, having helped Mother deliver Gilbert before I was ten, with but a little aid from Father. I pushed slippery emerging infants back while Mother unwrapped cords, and I caught new babies in a warm towel when Mother attended to birthing women who were struggling themselves. I relished the joy of washing a newborn babe while Mother sewed up the mama. Birth was a moment of ecstasy and pain for the strongest and healthiest of women, and so it was with more fear than joy that I learned that Mother was expecting again.

She hid her own pregnancy from everyone but Father until her bulge became obvious, and she replied to my questions with the news that we were being joined by a new baby in the fall of 1942.

We were all lean from our poor diet, but Mother seemed but a skeleton, with a bump that further strained her already weak back, causing her to resort to bed most days. The tiny child arrived too early and lived only a few hours before its sweet life ebbed away, taking a bit of Mother with him. She openly mourned the loss of another son.

Those words hit me hard. We prayed endlessly for Armand, but I felt Mother's hope flee that day, as if she had already accepted that Armand would never come home to us, and I wondered if she was already also mourning Jacques, whose interactions with the Maquis seemed impossible to ignore.

We buried Ètienne in the church cemetery down the street. I worried that Mother would throw herself into the grave with the little child as the shovels of dirt fell upon the lovely box Father built to hold his remains. The loss of the baby was more than the loss of one precious irreplaceable child to Mother, whose gaze slowly moved to each one of us. Her hollow eyes reflected love burdened by sorrow and grief, as if she feared she'd eventually lose each of us as well.

Father wrapped himself around her, steadying her as he carried her home and put her to bed. His raccoon-like eyes were ringed from the strain of the past few weeks, and he dropped into a chair before me with a thud as if his rail-thin frame carried a thousand pounds upon its shoulders. His eyes glistened with denied tears and he coughed to clear the emotions from his throat as he reached for my hands.

I braced for the worst—news that Mother was dying. I tried to imagine a world without her, but I could not. If that was the world we were to face, then I too would have preferred to leap into Ètienne's tiny grave.

"Mother is very weak, Mimie. I don't know what we're going to do. The Germans will still expect to be fed, to have their laundry washed and pressed, and their quarters cleaned. I don't know how they will respond when I tell them Mother needs to rest for a time."

To rest for a time?

Relief flooded over me. This was a problem we could manage. A problem for which I was trained. I felt like Esther in the Bible, prepared for such a time as this.

"I'll do it, Father. I'll do it all. I know how."

His lips trembled. "I'm relieved and embarrassed to tell you that I hoped you'd say this very thing, Mimie." He took my hands and pressed them to his damp face. I'd never seen this proud man brought so low. His fear of German retribution was evident in the gratitude and renewed determination that flickered in his eyes when he looked back at me. "We'll all help. All of us. You tell us what to do and we'll follow. Yes?"

"Yes, Father. It will be all right."

In truth, the primary care of the household had fallen to me on the day Mother went into labor. I knew her routine, and I soon had a plan of my own in place, using the rest of our very willing family. The work was hard and never ending, but I was grateful to be of service, and because I was so sorely needed, the Germans left me to my duties without placing any additional impositions on my time or workload.

The food was simple—café au lait and bread with soft cheese or jam, or eggs for *le petit déjeuner*, or breakfast. I occasionally made a pot of oatmeal with dried fruit. *Le déjeuner*, or our main meal served at midday, had become a more modest meal, resembling *le dîner*—bread with soup or stews made from our stored goods or from what I could gather through trades. I went to school when I could, but I preferred to stay at home rather than submit myself to more of Herr Schmidt's ridicule and abuse.

By the end of November, word trickled down that America and Great Britain were challenging the Germans in North Africa. That battlefront did not impact us directly, but we could feel a change, a further tightening of control over us by our Nazi captors, and we could only imagine that their aggression toward us would increase as the Americans neared.

On the first Sunday of the Christmas Season—*l'Avent*—Mother was able to join us at church. Her attendance was a Christmas miracle, and by Christmas Day she was nearly back to full health.

The new kommandant didn't authorize any gatherings aside from a church service, so families huddled together to worship and pray, and then we hurried home. Légère's grandmother passed me a Christmas note from Légère which he'd sent in her own Christmas letter from him. It was the only gift I received and the only gift I needed that year.

Father brought out his accordion to play the old familiar carols. Our thoughts were on our lost brother, baby Ètienne as we sang *"Il est né, le Divin Enfant."* "He Is Born, the Divine Infant," the tender song testified about the beautiful baby Jesus's birth. But the final chorus, with its lyrics about Jesus as our all-powerful King and Ruler, left us hushed and prayerful. In those days, in our oppressed circumstances, the words had new meaning and power. We wondered if God in Heaven and His Holy Son knew how desperately we prayed for Him to deliver us. If He knew that our hopes and faith hung on these words:

Oh Jesus! *Oh All-Powerful King*
Such a little child that you are,
Oh Jesus! Oh All-Powerful King,
Rule over us entirely!

One of the younger German officers knocked on the kitchen door to ask Father if he knew how to play *"Stille Nacht"* or "Silent Night." Father nodded, but our lyrics were different from the original German, so Father pointed to the man, indicating that he should sing.

Without hesitation, he broke into a gentle rendition of the carol. His tenor voice was trained and mellow, and though I didn't know the words he sang, I felt his testimony of their meaning. Once again, I was confused by the brutal juxtaposition these gentle moments created, showing us a glimpse into the men our captors were before they were soldiers. We wondered if they or we would ever be able to recapture the gentle natures that were ours before the war.

CHAPTER THIRTEEN

The turning of the calendar page to a new year did not bring celebration. Rather, it brought a reminder that we were facing the leanest months of the year when stored food ran scarce, ration cards seemed worthless, and the unforgiving winter delayed the hope of spring far too long.

Herr Schmidt enjoyed using his position as teacher to remind us how fortunate we were that our generous German leadership allowed such a bounteous flow of goods to come into Braquis. When anyone questioned his assessment, he would tell us horror stories about Leningrad and the siege Germany was inflicting upon the foolish citizens who refused to capitulate. Hundreds of thousands starved, and those still alive were reported to be boiling their belts and shoes. They'd drink the leather broth and chew on the softened hide for want of anything else to fill their bellies. Others were pulling the wallpaper off their walls and boiling that because the paste contained flour. The starchy broth tricked bellies into feeling full while the bodies slowly died of malnutrition. When that story didn't inflict enough shock and awe in the class, Herr

Schmidt told stories of Russian mothers who fed their starving children on the flesh of dead siblings.

I made the mistake of flinching at his stories and drawing his attention. He called me to the front of the room and asked me to explain the meaning of capitulation. After stuttering in fear, I gave a reasonable definition, which he accepted with a grimace.

"Yes . . . but I want you to help the class understand the meaning of the word and have them feel the consequences upon a people who are either too proud or too stupid to know when they are defeated. Let us demonstrate its meaning. Get on your knees, Madmoiselle Naget."

I shot a glance in Jacques' direction and saw his jaw tense and his hands curl into fists. Herr Schmidt made a point of walking to the row where Jacques' desk sat while his yardstick flicked back and forth in his hands. "Did you hear me, Mademoiselle?" His voice rose in volume while lowering to a menacing timbre. "Get on your knees," he ordered again.

Jacques' rebel friend, André Moyes stood in protest. Herr Schmidt turned and raised his yardstick, as if he were preparing to strike him for his insolence.

"I could beat you, Herr Moyes, and the kommandant would applaud me for squelching your disobedience, but that would only encourage you further, so instead, I will inflict your punishment on Mademoiselle."

My blood turned to ice as I imagined what a man who took pleasure in stories of human depravity might do to me in order to prove his authority. I saw hate transform Jacques' handsome face, and my sweet little Titi began to cry. Both responses delighted Herr Schmidt.

"Michelle Naget, you will not only kneel before me, but you will lie prone on the floor in complete capitulation. Do you hear me?"

Hot tears burned in my eyes. I wanted to cry, but I knew he would relish my fear, and a part of me refused to give him what he wanted. I looked at the window and saw my house, where my mother would be. I thought about running out the door to her, but there would be no safety in that for me or for her. Herr Schmidt had the support of the Nazis, the oppressors who saw his abuse as successful behavior modification.

I stiffened and slowly lowered my quaking knees to the floor, hoping against hope that this offering would be enough to satisfy his need for control. But no. He slapped his yardstick on Jacques' desk, repeating his demand that I lie prone on the floor. With all the dignity I could muster, I placed my hands on the floor and slowly lowered my torso to the wood. I wanted to vomit, but I pushed back my disgust by imagining that I was simply doing a push up. Nothing more. Just in position to do a pushup.

I pressed my forehead to the floor, hiding my shame, not wanting to see my enemy's pleasure over his victory or the sympathy and anger on my brothers' faces. I wondered how long he would make me lie there before claiming his victory. Instead, I heard his footsteps move my way until he stood at my feet. I feared how my humiliation would play out. Would he beat me next or step on me and proclaim himself victorious as if I were a prized kill on the African savanna? Or would he dishonor me in some further way, before my brothers? Before the entire class?

Instead, I heard the classroom door open, and the combined gasps and then silence of the class. I turned my head enough to see black boots enter the room. They belonged to the German tenor who sang "Stille Nacht" in our kitchen Christmas Eve just a few months earlier.

He spoke sharply in German. His words were unclear to me, but their impact was immediate. The teacher shuffled his feet like a skittish mouse while mumbling something unintelligible in response. When Jacques stood to testify against the instructor's heinous game, the officer turned ferociously toward him, instantly quelling any notion Jacques might have had that the young officer was interested in his testimony.

Instead, the officer pointed to the window, where Titi stood. Through the open door I could see villagers gathering and gawking, and I assumed they were responding to Titi's pleas through the glass. The officer then looked at me and mentioned my name in another angry German question. Herr Schmidt nodded and quickly signaled for me to stand. I rose on legs that shook like saplings. When I was again erect, I faced the man who had humiliated me and saw his bloodless complexion, as if he too were about to faint. I next turned to face my savior, to reward his kindness, but all I found was the same disregard he'd shown Jacques.

His only concern was for the loss of order in the room. When he was certain all was restored, he motioned for me to return to my seat, offered Herr Schmidt a final sentence of stern counsel, and exited the building.

My lips quivered the rest of the afternoon but not as badly as the instructor's hands or body. Herr Schmidt spent the rest of the day in his seat as we read from our textbooks. I sent a trembling smile of thanks to Titi, my hero, but I worried about what the day's events had done to Jacques, whose chiseled jaw was set like stone. I knew that whatever interest he had in the Resistance before had been cemented within him.

Father came home early and waited for me outside our house, staring at the school. I hoped Herr Schmidt saw him there. As he guided the three of us into the house, his mouth was clamped shut and his hands shook. Mother looked as she did when standing by Ètienne's grave. She pulled me close and then stepped back, studying me through tigerlike eyes. She said nothing, but her trembling body spoke to me with a power beyond words.

I saw the same conflict in Father's twisted face, the desire for retribution tempered by the knowledge of the cost—from the Nazis and from God. As Jacques had said some days before, we were physically powerless against the Nazis. But God balanced our helplessness with an outpouring of blessings, beginning with His incomparable power to make beauty from ashes. To make something good from something that was devoid of good. And so it was with Herr Schmidt's abusive actions toward me.

The tale of my abuse traveled throughout the surrounding area, though the Germans made every effort to downplay the event as a teacher's misguided lesson plan. And while the villagers didn't riot or rebel in outward ways, the Germans felt our solidarity with one another and our utter contempt for them.

That solidarity brought an extra measure of community good-will to our family in quiet ways. First, the Nazis were careful around us for a time, lessening their demands on Mother and especially on me. Self-preservation more than empathy seemed the cause, as if they knew that they had pushed us to a breaking point where heaven seemed sweeter than mortality, a point where people are capable of acts beyond what they might do in a calmer state of mind. Since we cooked and served the Germans' food, they not only needed us but had cause to fear us some days, a fact proven when they asked us to sample the food before we served it.

We enjoyed their fear. What they didn't know was that our silent and somber strength was not rooted in our hatred and need for justice but in our faith. That honoring God mattered more to us than obeying evil men.

We also felt a new level of compassion from our neighbors. We knew we were loved and respected in our community, but news flowed from Paris about French loyalists who became sympathizers and even German collaborators in return for additional rations to feed their families. Though no such accusations reached our ears, we felt some in the community believed we benefited from housing the officers. Herr Schmidt's treatment of me settled any such concerns, and the added indifference of the officer to my abuse solidified the truth—that we suffered as much as, and perhaps more than, our neighbors.

The Nazis were always watching and listening to us, and the community had seen how anxious our oppressors were for any opportunity to make an example of the Family Naget. As a result, our neighbors rallied to us, and the Germans knew we did not stand alone.

The third blessing arrived suddenly and unexpectedly one Saturday afternoon in April when the memory of that humiliating day again brought me palpable pain. Father and a neighboring farmer left early for the mill to pick up the town's flour rations. When he came home, he entered the kitchen and handed me a small, slightly wilted nosegay of purplish-blue forget-me-nots. The sentiment caught me off guard on a day when such a small token easily overwhelmed me.

"For me?" I questioned with a shake in my voice.

"For you. From a new worker at the mill."

"What? A new mill worker sent these to me?"

"Yes . . ." Father drew the answer out as he tapped his lips in thought. "I believe I've seen him before. Now . . . what was his name?" As if surrendering to the effort required to remember, he shook his head and turned for the door to pick up another sack of flour.

I followed him every step of the way. "Have you seen him before?"

"I believe so. What was his name? Hmmm . . . Louis? Leon? Lionel . . . ?"

"Légère!" I didn't bother to conceal my enthusiasm. "When did he start working at the mill?"

"He put his name on the list some time ago. The miller just called him up today. Imagine that. The day of your father's turn to pick up the flour. What are the chances?"

I saw it not as chance, but as a gift. A tender gift from God.

My head dipped. "He heard about Herr Schmidt, didn't he?" I wondered what Légère thought of a girl singled out for such derision.

Father tipped my chin up. "The shame was Herr Schmidt's. Not yours. Légère knows it too, and he thinks you are very brave. So do I."

The affirmation caused my eyes to burn. I ran the wilted blossoms upstairs and pressed the petals within the pages of the white leather Bible I received at my confirmation when I was ten, acknowledging this gift as coming from both Légère and from a loving, listening God.

CHAPTER FOURTEEN

J ust as farmers forecast coming weather by the color of the sky, we assessed Allied successes or failures by the behavior of the Nazis. Their bearing eased and their conversations were tinged with boasting and bravado after the Japanese attack on Pearl Harbor. We also noticed that they were more regular about taking their meals in the kitchen, where they loved to discuss how the Pacific theater was keeping America too occupied to threaten Germany's conquest of Europe. Even the Allied arrival in Africa didn't seem to worry them, as if the Nazis were not yet threatened by the Americans' entrance into the war.

But things began to change in May 1943. The officers spent more time holed up in the dining room with their radios and maps, their lists and charts. The regular soldiers no longer patrolled to simply deter unruliness or to enforce curfews. They began to see imminent threats in the quiet villagers of Braquis, and small infractions were met with brutal force until people feared to congregate or talk as neighbors.

Any questions we children posed to Father about the changes were met with strict warnings to focus on our work at school and then come home without delay. But Mother and Father shared knowing glances when the Germans entered or left the house, and they slipped into a corner with greater frequency for private whispered conversations. When I asked Mother if she'd heard any news, she repeated Father's advice, and Father refused to discuss anything but the most mundane family topics during our evening quiet hour.

But one night in May, long after Titi and Gilbert were asleep, and after Mother and Father had gone to bed, I whispered my question to Jacques. I saw the struggle within him. He was dying to share the latest news he'd heard, but he was also cautious enough to know the cost if our conversation were overheard. He whispered only that the French underground had built an extensive communication network, and the current rumor was that the Allies were having success in Africa.

I held my breath and prayed their march would carry them north to France. It appeared that Mother had the same thoughts and hopes, because the next day, she brazenly pinned a map of France and our surrounding neighbor countries to the kitchen wall. It immediately caught the Germans' eyes as they entered the kitchen for their midday meal.

The kommandant stood at the table for several long seconds, staring at the map. "I see we have a new addition to the décor this evening, Madame Naget."

Mother offered the map a quick glance before we set about serving a particularly bounteous meal that day. "The map? Herr Schmidt has taught the children that it is ever changing. It is good for us to know the boundaries, is it not, Herr Kommandant?"

The two stared at one another. A serene strength filled Mother's face, but the kommandant's face was unreadable, a shifting palette of wariness, showing both respect and mistrust.

He called his minion, Sergeant Weiss, to come forward. "Madame, let us make your map more accurate." With a nod, the sergeant left and returned with a marker which he used to draw lines on our map, distinguishing the Vichy area from occupied France. Other lines identified portions of our country that were prohibited to French citizens, and the area given to Italy. The sergeant looked back at the kommandant as if waiting for his approval. With an almost imperceptible nod, the kommandant dismissed the sergeant and turned to Mother.

"Now your map is accurate. This is the new France."

We couldn't know it at the time, but Mother's little act of patriotic pride proved to be inspired, and even more, it saved our flagging hope, and eventually, it saved our lives.

THE GROWING, GATHERING, PREPARATION, AND STORAGE OF food once again consumed our days. The work was mundane and tedious, but it kept me busy, and the tedium allowed my mind the freedom to wander as it so frequently did. My thoughts were about the future, my future in particular, and whether the inconstant, oft uncommunicative Légère Dubois was worthy of any of my thoughts at all.

While snapping peas and bottling beans, I heard muffled bits of conversation through the Nazis' door. I understood very few words in German, but the names of places and nations were easier to decode—*Allies . . . Americans . . . British . . . Mediterranean . . . Sicily . . .*

The Allies were in Sicily! And the menacing mood of our houseguests assured me the Americans and British were prevailing! My heart secretly pounded within my chest, but mistrust grew across France as the Nazis' iron fist came down upon us in increasingly horrid ways.

Reports trickled in from friends in outlying communities of missing relatives, people who had been called in for interviews with the Nazis and never returned. There was no recourse to investigate a missing person. No sympathetic body to which a family member could plead their case. The Nazis claimed the missing people were arrested because they were part of the Maquis or some other resistance group, but little proof was needed to make one a suspect, so people stayed locked in their homes, unwilling to speak for fear that something they said might be misconstrued. Summer was long and lonely, but one day, Mother took a sewing pin with a blue head and pinned it to the island of Sicily. The gesture was hardly noticeable to anyone but our family, and yet we cherished that little pin and the hope it represented.

The tension in our home reached a new level by September. The officers were again holed up in the dining room, demanding that their food be brought to them in there. I answered each request without a word. In truth, I had barely uttered ten total words to any of them since the day of Herr Schmidt's abuse. They mistakenly assumed the event had shattered me, rendering me less than a shadow, a girl they believed was without will, a ghost devoid of fight, and evidently a person they thought was also without ears.

While clearing their dishes and dodging stares and teasing, groping hands, I heard the radio mention the Americans . . . and two new clues—*Italy* and *Mussolini*. The Nazis leapt from their chairs. One all but shoved me, knocking the gathered dishes to the ground, in his rush to draw nearer to the set to hear more. As I cleaned the mess, I observed the grim expressions in the room, assuring me that the Allies, including the Americans, had reached the mainland of Italy!

Without revealing my understanding, I left the space quickly, closing the door behind as I raced to press a blue pin into the map where Italy was drawn. I wanted to believe that deliverance was nigh, but within a week, during a static-filled radio transmission, a cheer went up from behind the Germans' door, and I feared the worst—that the Allied efforts had been defeated in their push through the Italian nation.

We barely stopped to eat or drink that morning as our sobering assumptions underscored the absolute need for us to prepare for yet another long, hungry winter of occupation. The boys were carrying in bag after bag of freshly picked beans and setting them in the sink to be washed. The table was spread with jars and bottles I was hurriedly filling with cleaned and snapped beans. Mother lifted racks of boiling food-filled vessels from the large canning pots on the woodstove and set them on the counters. The jars with lids were left to cool while the bottles were sealed with hot wax. Amid all this orderly chaos, the kommandant requested that he and his officers be served their midday meal in the kitchen that afternoon.

Mother spread her arms wide over the canning chaos, in case the officer had missed the obvious—but despite acknowledging the chaotic industry underway, he simply replied—"At one o'clock."

With our spirits sagging, we broke down our production line and turned our efforts to readying a sumptuous formal meal. The Germans entered, precisely at one o'clock, to a fully set table laden with the rewards of a fall harvest—breads and cheese, fish and fruit. The kommandant eyed the spread and nodded as he moved to his chair at the head of the table. He pulled the seat out with great deliberateness. Pausing, he touched his finger to his mouth as if processing a new thought. With equal care, he pushed the chair partially in, and marched to the wall where the map was hung. He pointed to Mother's box of pins sitting on the counter nearby, and asked, "May I?"

She returned a cautious nod as he opened the box and pulled out a red pin which he held up for all to see. His pivot to the map was done with the military grace befitting an honor ceremony, then he pulled out the blue pin of Italy, replacing it with the red one.

The message was clear. Our fears were real. The Nazis still held Italy. More terrifying, would they question how we got the information in the first place?

To our great relief, relishing the moment of dashed hopes seemed enough as the officers cheered the kommandant's theatrics. Mother reacted with subdued grace, nodding her defeat as she pointed to the head chair, inviting the kommandant to sit. We children followed her lead, silently serving the meal. When the Germans finished and left the room, we ate what remained, and returned to preserving what food we could for a future that once again seemed grim.

I CONTINUED MY GAME OF EAVESDROPPING ON THE GERMANS, pretending to be a shadow with nothing on my mind but cooking and cleaning and serving them. In truth, I was in turmoil. Jacques had finished school. Though he was smart and deserved his certificate, everyone concerned was grateful to put distance between Herr Schmidt and him. He would no longer be subject to the whims and demands of that Nazi puppet. Neither would he be Father's assistant.

He had been assigned to work at the agricultural cooperative in Étain, the destination of his PTT route. Since his day was long and busy, he took the ration orders with him early in the morning. During the day, he worked his shift at the co-op fixing delivery trucks or sorting what produce and/or grain arrived that day for shipment elsewhere. Little was left in the community that grew it. After work, he picked up the mail and exchanged what ration coupons could be used that day to fill waiting families' orders. Then he rode the route home, delivering the mail and goods along the way. He arrived home exhausted and much later than we expected. After eating, he generally headed to bed and slept in order to repeat the grueling schedule the next day.

I knew Jacques' day was hard, but I still envied him and his release from Herr Schmidt. I did not want to return to school, and I desperately longed for one person's advice on this matter—Légère's. He encouraged me to broaden my mind with study and literature. He would be disappointed in me. He'd perhaps think I was a coward, but I'd remind him that I had turned fifteen, and that I'd served as a tutor to the majority of the class during the last year.

Most of the older girls were so badly needed at home that they'd left class as well. And besides, I could teach myself what I yet lacked to get my certificate, or perhaps I would get a job as *une aide aux mères*. I was young, but I was more than qualified and could easily pass the licensing exam. Or maybe I would tell Légère that I was considering turning my life over to God as a nun so I could serve His neediest children. Perhaps my altruism was partly because, except for the flowers, I hadn't heard from Légère in months.

He was eighteen, no longer a boy, and most assuredly under the scrutiny of the Germans. My last note had not been answered, meaning only one of a few things. Either he was excruciatingly busy at his farm or mill work, or he'd been shipped off to a work camp, perhaps as one of France's conscripted workers reinforcing the Atlantic Wall. The third possibility was personally devastating —perhaps he had grown tired of playing older brother to me.

In any case, I had options. Returning to Herr Schmidt's class-room was not one of them. Waiting for Légère was becoming another option that might be closing.

My parents readily approved my exit from school. As my public education ended, Gilbert's began. I ached for Mother as she watched little Gilbert take Titi's hand and walk across the street for his first day of class. Her baby was growing up, and she would have been utterly alone in the house with the hostile German officers. Instead, we joined forces to fill the cellar with what food we could for the winter, and we helped wherever we were able.

The Germans' summer jubilance over their hold in Italy turned to suspicion in mid-September. Their frustration meant the Allies were gaining ground, but we suffered along with our captors as another fall turned to the winter of 1943. When everything we loved, believed in, and trusted, was about to change.

CHAPTER FIFTEEN

Our Nazi oppressors became increasingly belligerent and frustrated from fall to winter. The Allies' early victory in Italy was reversed when Germany rescued Mussolini, but the Allies held on, and their foothold in Italy remained an irritation to victors who had enjoyed complete submission in France. They appeared to sense that their control was threatened.

More changes came. More rules. More men torn from their families to work in camps or to provide support for the German military until the only men left in villages and towns were older and those vital to the support of the local economy and the farms.

More soldiers passed through our little village because of its fated location, positioned in the crossroads of the more strategic cities of Étain and Verdun where the area Kommandanturs were located. The kommandant sat at the big map-strewn table in their area, barking at his junior officers, who scrambled to find requested documents or maps. They in turn barked at us and the foot soldiers who stayed as busy as ants, knocking on doors and issuing warnings about gathering on the streets, threats that were unnecessary since the fear of gathering had been instilled in us months earlier. The soldiers' uniforms sagged, and their haggard faces attested to their meager rations. Morale was low, and tempers flared easily.

Such stress and commotion generally signaled an inspection by the kommandant's superior or a change in local leadership. We braced for what was coming and did our best to stay out of the Nazis' way, knowing it would already be a hard winter for all.

We didn't know how hard.

Despite Jacques' busy schedule, leaving as early as he left every morning should have made it possible for him to be home hours before he was most days. Tension at home was high, and we could hear the all too familiar warning in our heads, like the whistle of the valve on Mother's pressure cooker, telling us that if Jacques didn't have an outlet, some space to vent his ever-increasing frustrations, the explosion would come . . . at home . . . with the Nazis. And so we asked few questions, and we looked the other way.

As painful as it was to admit, we knew things we pretended not to know. Perhaps we denied truths we were powerless to change. In any case, fuzzy truths eventually came together with unwanted clarity at the end of 1943.

The morning of December 5, 1943, was particularly rushed. The day before, the kommandant informed us that an inspection of the area was scheduled, and he requested that a sumptuous meal be served at midday. Mother and I rose especially early to prepare breakfast so we could begin work on le déjeuner, which was to be ready by one.

Jacques and Father ate quickly and hurried to leave in order to avoid the Nazi officers. As Jacques headed into the December chill, Mother noticed that he had forgotten the day's ration requests. When she called him back in for them, he scoffed sarcastically, "What good are they?"

A flash of fear lit her eyes as they shot to the hall where Germans would soon be. We held our breath and waited for a bellowed rebuke or a heavy-handed arm grab in acknowledgment of Jacques' perceived insolence. None came from the Germans, but

Mother held the list out to her son until he returned and took the paper from her hand.

And then he was gone.

The expected general and his guards arrived around ten and were escorted into the kommandant's office, where we served coffee, bread, and cheese. The door closed behind us, and we hurried to the chicken coop to gather eggs and to the cold storage to retrieve the bird she'd killed the day before for the afternoon's stew. We fed the little boys during their break from class and sent them upstairs to rest for thirty minutes while we served the Nazi entourage. By two thirty, the boys were long back in school, the officers were packing to leave on their inspection, and Mother and I stared at a kitchen filled with dirty dishes.

The commotion that preceded an inspection gave way to a quiet afternoon as the kommandant left the house to lead his superior on a tour of the encampment in the woods, of the village, and of the surrounding farms—the pride of his leadership—where food production and exports to Germany had exceeded his district's quota.

During those precious quiet hours, as we cleaned the kitchen, Mother's eyes repeatedly darted to the door. When I questioned her about it, she confessed the ache she felt over the way she and Jacques had parted in the morning, and she invited me to enjoy a delicious reward—the opportunity to head upstairs to read for an hour. Not long into my quiet time, I heard a ruckus below and the sound of Mother's cries. I raced down the steps and gasped over the scene at the back doorway. Jacques' limp, blood-soaked form half walked, half hung between two young men.

"Has he been shot?" I cried.

Mother's ashen face reflected her dual worries. She was grief stricken over her son's wounds and absolutely terrified about what this event could mean to our entire family. She muffled her anguished cries by biting on her palm as she turned and ran to the kitchen, ordering the boys to bring Jacques along. I followed, more tripping than running, as Mother swept the table clear. André Moyes and Paul Brunet, Jacques' older friend from Ville-en-Woëvre, a village two kilometers away, laid my groaning brother down. Jacques' coat fell open, revealing the bright red patch spreading across his shirt. I knew this was bad . . . very bad, but I had seen a far worse view from behind.

"His back! Check his back," I moaned. The patch of blood on his chest spread, but the bullet's exit through Jacques' back left a gaping hole in his jacket, as if the bullet had exploded as it left. Tissue-strewn blood flowed freely from the wound.

I raced upstairs to gather bandages and towels. When I returned, Mother was trying desperately to keep Jacques awake while the boys removed his coat and shirt and the black-and-white PTT armband.

Mother turned to me and said, "Go through the woods and get your Father! Don't let the Nazis see you!" Then without waiting for my reply, she alternately hugged her boy and attended to his care.

I ran down the hall and out the rear door to the woods, barely able to see past my tears as I raced to get Father. No words were needed. As soon as he saw my face he ran to me, and I pulled him along to the house the back way, unable to answer any questions with more than the words, "Jacques' been shot!"

Mother was pressing a blood-soaked towel to Jacques' chest when Father appeared in the doorway, aging twenty years in a second.

Jacques' breathing was ragged and hollow, as if each could be his last. Time seemed to stop as the catastrophic shift occurred in our world. A surreal and nauseating swirl of odors filled the room—chicken stew, fresh bread, fear-induced sweat, pine tar from the forest, and the dank warmth of Jacques' blood. Paul's and André's sniffs blended with Mother's anxious breaths and the rustle of her apron as she pressed a fresh towel to Jacques' wound, shushing his cries.

The shuffling of Father's feet sounded like sandpaper on wood as he nervously paced, fearful for Jacques and fully aware of the perilous circumstances we were all in. He offered to relieve Mother, but she shook her head and bent over my brother, pressing her forehead to his.

"André called for the doctor to come with his car. Where is he?" She broke into quiet sobs.

Father joined the sacred parental huddle over Jacques while I leaned against the wall and watched what felt like the death of my family. I knew the consequences of breaking the ban on weapons. We all knew. Arrest if you were lucky. Execution if the Nazis were having a bad day, and this day, a day when the kommandant's superior was in town, was the worst possible time for such an infraction.

As if hearing my thoughts, Father spun on the boys, grabbing Paul by the boy's arms. "Where did you get a gun? And how did Jacques get shot?"

A smeared palette of blood and tears covered Paul's face as he cried out, "It was an accident!"

"Do you know what you've done? What the penalty is for such an offense?"

The boys hung their heads without reply.

"Why? Why?" Father snarled.

"For the Resistance." Paul's hands jutted forward in defense, and his words came out in rushed heaves. "Jacques has been tooling gun parts in your shop late at night. He brings the parts to André on his PTT route. I pick them up and carry them to my farm for assembly. We were testing this gun today. I thought the safety was on."

And the reality we had all feared came true. The next concern was more chilling—whether or not Jacques survived being shot, his association with the Resistance could still get him killed, and us as well.

The rest of the story came out in pieces. Paul had joined the Resistance months before. Jacques and André wanted to join as well, and once the local Resistance leaders heard that Jacques was the son of a machinist, they welcomed him in and gave him a gun to use as a template to tool new parts.

The news devastated Father. He pressed his hand to his face as he muttered something to God and paced in a circle.

Mother stood, revealing Jacques' pale face. "He's barely breathing. Where is the doctor?"

Father moved to Jacques and bent over him, begging him to be strong. The room remained silent for several long seconds, and then Father stood, revealing a new expression of even greater distress. He turned on Paul with an urgency that frightened me. "Where is the gun now?"

"I-I-I dropped it when it went off. It's still in the forest."

Father's hands crumpled Paul's shirt as he drew the boy near. "Did anyone else see you or hear the gun fire? Anyone at all?"

The twenty-year-old shivered and hunched his shoulders around his ears. André Moyes stepped forward. "No one saw us. We were in a thick stand of trees. But I don't know if anyone heard the shot."

A car pulled up in front of the house, and Father rushed Mother's friend and mentor, Dr. Ouvrard, into the house. The physician drew back a step as he came upon the gruesome scene in the kitchen. Pulling himself together, he moved Mother aside and checked Jacques' wound. His expression was grim, as he turned to Father and asked, "Who shot him? The Nazis?"

I could feel Father's wrestle over what to say as he studied Mother's twisted face and then Jacques' ashen one. The reply would seal everyone's fate. If the doctor reported the shooting, he would also have to report the gun and its owners, and there would be grievous consequences. If the physician hid the truth, he would be a conspirator. Men had been executed for less.

With a gravity that belied hope, Dr. Ouvrard went into action without waiting for Father's reply. He moved to the phone and made a call to St. Catherine's Hospital at Verdun, leaving a message for a surgeon named Dr. Durant. I heard the word surgery and the doctor's instructions as he hung up.

"I'll pull the car around back. Carry Jacques out that way. It's best to delay our interaction with the Nazis until you have a story that will hold up."

Mother slumped and nearly cried anew in her relief as she took the man's hand. "Thank you, Dr. Ouvrard. Thank you."

"The obvious questions will be raised over this shooting. I will say that there was no opportunity to take a report. It will give you time to prepare one, but I must hurry and take him now."

Mother rushed to the hook on the wall and grabbed her coat and purse. "I'm coming with you."

The doctor stopped in his tracks and raised an eyebrow at Father. "Monsieur..."

Father took hold of Mother's arm. "You cannot, Yvonne. I will go."

She slipped free and moved to the door without further argument.

"Madame Naget," the doctor pled. "Are you prepared to deal with the trouble this shooting will surely arouse? Do you understand what you may face when we arrive? Interrogation? Perhaps even arrest?"

Mother exhibited the same steeled determination she showed as she remained at Lydia's side to deliver her baby amid the shelling from German planes, and the day the kommandant checked our pockets and threatened our family. I knew she would do what she felt was right in the eyes of God, regardless of the consequences.

"All I know, Dr. Ouvrard, is that I most assuredly am not prepared to send my son to Verdun alone."

Father stepped toward her, but as she touched her trembling lips with one hand and raised the other to hold him in place, Father stepped back, accepting that no earthly force would prevent her from going.

He nodded and gave her a stoic smile, and then she gazed at me with eyes that seemed to transmit a sacred promise between us. Momentary panic again flared in her eyes as she looked around the blood-stained room. "The Nazis will be back. They will see . . . They will know what happened."

Father's shaky voice testified to the struggle he was having. "Go," he said. "Michelle and I will take care of it. Go be with Jacques."

"No matter what has happened here, they will still expect dinner."

"Shhh . . . Go. We will handle all of it. Just go be with our boy."

With a final look back at Father, Mother headed down the hall to the doctor's car. I wondered if I'd ever see my brother again and perhaps whether Mother would ever again return to our home.

Father managed to calm his nerves enough to set the plan in motion. He turned his attentions to Paul and André. "You two will help me scrub this room until there is no evidence, understood?" It was not a question. "And then we will call your families and prepare a defense." There was no hesitation in the frightened boys as they set to work gathering buckets and mops and bleach.

Father next turned to me with tears shining in his eyes. The trembling of his lips frightened me more than Jacques' blood. He was afraid. More than that, he seemed lost, and unsure how to proceed from that moment. He sat in a chair and took my hand. "Gilbert and Titi will be home soon. What will we say? What will we do?"

I wanted to fall into his arms and cry. I wanted our old life back, the one where the kitchen smelled like flowers instead of German cigarette smoke. When we laughed and sang and ate until we were content. When Mother smiled and Father played his accordion at night. The life when Jacques and Armand built me a trapeze and I spoke to God as I swung from a bell. Those days were gone. We didn't know how long it would be before we knew our fate and whether we'd have a life at all.

The feeling of being anesthetized returned. The same dead

feeling I experienced after the Christmas dance and after Herr Schmidt humiliated me, leaving me too numb to cry, too numb to fear. Everything felt temporary and fragile. Heaven seemed nearer and sweeter than life. I accepted that we might have only days, or hours, before the Germans arrested us and asked us what we knew. Father and Mother would protect Jacques to their death, and I could never protect myself at Jacques' expense. How could I live with that on my conscience? And what assurance did we have that any of us would be safe from the Nazi judgment no matter what we said?

I thought of my sweet younger brothers who knew nothing of how much the world had changed since midday. They would be home soon. I'd protect them as well as I could for as long as I could.

"I'll meet Titi and Gilbert at the door and send them upstairs to read. They'll be happy to stay out of sight while the kommandant's superior is visiting. Then I'll make the evening meal."

The gray pallor of Father's face brightened a little, and he squeezed my hand. "Good girl. Our situation is very dangerous, Michelle. Not only for Jacques, but for all of us. No one can ever know that he and his friends made a gun. We must never speak of this . . . understand?"

I nodded.

"There is very little time and much I need to attend to before the Germans return." His eyes drilled into mine. "There are . . . things I need to do in my shop. The Germans will surely search there. And I must speak to Paul's and André's parents. I may not be back before the Nazis return."

The implications were terrifying . . . that I might have to face the Nazis alone. And what pressing matter in Father's shop could possibly be equal to our current emergency?

I began cooking while Father and the older boys cleaned to make all appear normal. After the floors were mopped, the table sanitized, the walls wiped of bloody smears, and the blood-soaked towels burned, Father, Paul, and André left the house as if the afternoon's tragedy had never occurred.

Except Mother was gone.

And Jacques might be dying.

And Father was trying to save all our lives.

I checked the clock—three thirty-two.

We do what must be done . . .

Gratefully, Mother had baked enough bread in the morning for the evening meal as well, and knowing that this was not the time to worry about rations or future hunger, I gathered the ingredients for three quiches, and I baked a cake as well. Anything to keep busy. To push back the thoughts of Mother and Jacques.

I had run the house many times when Mother was sick or when she was called away, but that day was different. I couldn't run upstairs for advice or send the boys with a note to ask her a question. My throat grew tight with fear that I might never get to speak to her again, and as panic swelled over me, my sweet Titi and Gilbert arrived, arguing over some moment at school and jabbering with gladness because the Germans were away. They inquired about Mother's whereabouts, quickly accepting my reply that she was out. For a few minutes, all felt calm again, and I marveled at how thin the line between normalcy and insanity had become.

They happily accepted the offer to play upstairs while I finished the meal preparations. When all was ready for baking, I fed the fire in the cookstove to have it hot at the first sight of the Germans' return. Like a mouse on a wheel, I kept busy, doing all I'd promised Father. All I *physically* could do to help.

I realized I had not prayed.

I'd uttered exclamations to heaven and desperate cries for help, but I'd voiced no faith-filled acknowledgment of His constant love or expressions of confidence in His will. Only fear. Only panic.

I ran upstairs and pulled my rosary from my drawer. I hadn't recited the prayers in a while, but that day, in my hour of need, the prayers passed through my mind at the first touch of the beads and, with them, strength, comfort, perspective.

It matters more that we are right with God . . .

I set a chair near the window to watch for the Germans' return and prayed.

CHAPTER SIXTEEN

D usk settled in at five. The Germans had yet to return. Father wasn't back and Mother hadn't called, so I fed the little boys and sent them back upstairs with a caution to remain in their rooms and be quiet until bedtime.

A lone figure approached from City Hall, carrying a lamp. I jumped from my chair and backed against the wall to hide before gathering the courage to face the pending knock on the door.

"Michelle . . . It's M. Latrobe," a voice whispered through the wood. "Let me in."

The hushed greeting from the village's mayor calmed my nerves like warm milk on a cold night—comforting, reassuring. I opened the door, and as the middle-aged man slipped his round torso through the entryway, his eyes scanned the rooms to be sure we were alone.

"Your father came to me and explained about Jacques' *accident.*"

He closed his eyes and crossed himself quickly, and though his manner seemed caring and helpful, I wondered how much Father had told him, and whether Father or the Germans had sent him to our door.

"Your brother didn't complete the PTT route yesterday, and people are asking why. Little things create such a stir in the village these days. Everyone feels so unsettled." His eyebrows rose as he finished his thought. "And we don't want to draw attention to Jacques' absence."

The mayor had been Mother and Father's friend for years, but the Nazis had forced him to also be their mouthpiece, using his history with the community to soften the delivery of their edicts. Being unsure whose cause he served that day, I stood blank faced and silent as he continued.

"We must have a PTT officer, Michelle, and the transfer must appear logical and seamless to avoid upsetting the German leadership. You are the obvious choice."

An hour earlier, I was certain we were going to be arrested or lined up and shot. Instead, we began discussing tomorrow . . . a future. No assignment, no matter how terrible the job of PTT officer could be, was more frightening than the outcome I had previously expected.

"I'll do it," I said.

"Very good." He sighed long and low. "Thank you."

Headlights appeared at the edge of town, headed for our house. I whimpered at the sight, and the mayor's arm slid around my shoulder. "I will stay until your father gets home. You were preparing le dîner? Continue, and I'll handle the Germans."

I slid the quiches into the oven and finished setting the table when the kommandant, his guests, and officers entered.

"How long until dinner?" he asked with his characteristic brusqueness.

His arrogant tone and the normalcy of his question calmed my nerves a bit. "Twenty minutes, Herr Kommandant," I replied with my head dipped in submission.

He squinted at the mayor and asked, "M. Latrobe? Why are you here? And where is Madame Naget?"

I watched the mayor's fretful face assume a look of calm concern as he danced around the question with the nimbleness of a ballerina. "Good evening, Herr Kommandant. Before you take up your business with Madame Naget, I had hoped to have a word with you, but I see you still have your guests."

The officer's head drew back, and he barked. "What business do you have with me today?"

"Nothing of importance. I take it the tour of the area went well . . . that your superiors can see what a fine job you've done here in Braquis?"

The kommandant's face softened a little. He turned to his junior officer. "Show the major and his party to the facilities and allow them to refresh before dinner." The officer did as he was instructed, leading the major and his entourage upstairs to shed their coats before relieving themselves.

When the leaders were out of earshot, the mayor dipped his head slightly and said, "My apologies, Herr Kommandant. I should have chosen a better time. My item is barely worth your consideration, but I always like to run everything past you before I implement any changes, and I've heard rumors among the soldiers that if all went well, you could be promoted to a new post. I thought I should tie up loose ends with you before your departure."

The kommandant puffed at the mention of his promotion. "It's true. I'm being sent south to replicate the success I've had in keeping the Resistance out of Braquis."

The mayor glanced out the window as a smile spread across his lips. "Well deserved, Herr Kommandant. And when must you leave?"

"Tomorrow."

"So soon? . . . Well . . . thank you for the leadership you've shown here in Braquis. I will not monopolize your time with my petty concerns when you have esteemed guests. I'll leave you to attend to them. Perhaps we can speak in the morning?"

The kommandant's ruffled impatience returned. "This village's petty concerns are your own now." He flicked his hand to dismiss the mayor and his issues. Then, with a satisfied grunt, he turned and headed up the stairs.

"Don't leave," I begged the mayor.

"It's all right, Michelle. Look outside. Your father's coming."

I ran to the curtain and saw Father approaching across the street, pushing Jacques' bike along.

"See? Have faith, child. All will be well. Come see me in the morning, and we'll discuss your new employment."

My new employment . . .

The mayor slipped through the doorway, nodding to Father as they passed one another in the street.

I waited what seemed like hours in the few moments Father took to park the bike and reach the door. As soon as he crossed the threshold, I rushed against him, giving him no choice but to carry my stress-exhausted body into the kitchen as I hung from his arms. He raised a finger to his lips and gently closed the door before lowering the two of us into a chair. Love effused from him into me as his hand stroked my hair and he whispered, "My brave girl. My brave girl."

My hammering heart slowed while I was wrapped in the strength and comfort of his arms. "Jacques?" I asked. I held my breath as I awaited the answer.

"Alive. Barely."

I bit my bottom lip and posed the next terrifying question. "And Mother?"

"Dr. Ouvrard drove her home. I left a bundle of clean clothes for her in the church. She's changing out of her bloodstained dress, and then she'll be here. The Germans won't have cause to question her tonight."

"They're already here."

He nodded. "I know. I've been watching from the church window. You serve *le dîner*. I'll handle them."

There was something in Father's demeanor, a tranquility that underscored his immediate concerns. I knew that, like me, he was prepared to die because of the day's events. Having faced that, we could withstand the Germans' threats and power.

We heard the clomp of boots on the stairs, and I quickly laid the three quiches down the center of the table with bread, cheese, and fruit compote. We were expending three days' worth of food to maintain the ruse of calm.

The kommandant bragged about the abundance his district enjoyed, and the men set about to eat without noticing Mother's absence.

I heard footsteps in the back hall and then gentle feet coming forward. My beleaguered mother arrived with tired eyes and a too-cheery smile. She and Father exchanged a knowing glance that moved to include me as she rushed to fill the Germans' glasses.

"Madame Naget, where have you been?" asked the kommandant.

"Attending to the sick, Herr Kommandant," Father interjected. "We knew you and your guests were in good hands." He waved my way, and the kommandant nodded.

We proceeded to keep ourselves so engaged that no further conversation was needed on our part, but the Germans spoke openly in our presence, as if news of the war was of no consequence to us and as if we posed no threat.

When the meal concluded, the kommandant walked the major and his party to their vehicles and watched as they drove away. While we waited for the kommandant to return to the house, we wondered whether he'd received a radioed report from Verdun about Jacques' shooting. Was he merely hiding the report from his superiors to protect his promotion? We held our collective breaths to see what would happen next, but to our relief, he and his officers requested a bottle of wine to toast their good day.

After delivering the wine, we excused ourselves and returned to the kitchen, closing the door and pulling every curtain tight. When we were huddled alone, Mother finally leaned into a corner and cried out, "I watched my son receive the last rites. The surgeon took one look at Jacques' wound and sent the nurse to"—she stifled a sob—"to bring the priest."

Her voice broke, and she crumpled over the counter. Father pulled her close, wrapping his arms around her as she wept into his shirt. Moments later, after a few privately whispered words, Mother wiped her tears, looked into Father's eyes, and nodded before they turned their attention to the kitchen. I still felt fragile, jellylike, but my parents appeared solid once more, as if they had tucked their grief and fears away into some sacred place where the Germans held no authority or power. Despite all that our oppressors had done to us, they had not broken our family.

But what about Jacques? "He's alive, isn't he?" I asked Mother.

She extended an arm and drew me close. "Yes. He's alive, thanks to Dr. Ouvrard."

"Then when will he come home?"

"Not for a long time, I'm afraid, Mimie. But we can visit him when the doctor says he's ready."

"His heart . . . is it damaged?" asked Father.

"Dr. Durand thought so. After seeing the location of the bullet hole, he said there was no hope for Jacques at all, but Dr. Ouvrard prevailed upon him to at least make an attempt at repairing it, and the surgeon reluctantly agreed. I barely had time to say goodbye before they whisked Jacques away, and then Dr. Durand appeared again just a few hours later. My heart caught in my throat because I assumed the worst had happened, that Jacques had died in surgery."

Mother's voice caught. When she pulled back from Father and looked at us, her face was lit with wonder.

"The surgeon came down the hall toward me, and Dr. Ouvrard took my hand as we braced for the worst. I watched Dr. Durand pull down his face mask, expecting to hear the news that my son was gone. Instead, he said, 'Madam Naget, what I found when I opened your son's chest is nothing short of a miracle.' He said the bullet passed directly through the space where the bottom of Jacques' heart sits, but there was no injury to the heart itself."

"How is that possible?" asked Father.

"The heart contracts as it beats, drawing upward. The bullet must have passed under the heart in the fraction of a second during a beat."

"A miracle," I repeated.

"Yes, Mimie. A miracle. God was with Jacques, and He is still watching over us."

"But the blood," said Father as he stepped back and stared at the table and floor that had been covered in red mere hours earlier.

"The bullet missed his heart, but it punctured a lung and his stomach. That's why there was so much blood. Another surgeon was called in to assist in the repairs." She looked at the clock. "He'll be in surgery for a few more hours, and his recovery will be long and difficult, but I have faith that God spared his heart because he intends for Jacques to survive."

Father closed his eyes in silent prayer. "I'm surprised you agreed to leave the hospital and come home."

"I didn't want to leave him. It was the hardest thing I've ever done, but Dr. Durand and Dr. Ouvrard insisted that going home was best for everyone's sake. They are required to report the shooting to the police, who will notify the Germans so they can conduct their own investigation. Dr. Durand delayed the report so I could get away. He said he will tell the police that Jacques was nearly dead and unable to answer any questions about the shooting when he arrived home. The doctor will not allow anyone to interrogate him for a few days."

"But people in the hospital saw you. They know you and Dr. Ouvrard brought him in."

"Yes, Joseph, but as far as the staff is concerned, all I knew was that my son collapsed after he arrived home, and Dr. Ouvrard rushed us to Verdun to St. Catherine's."

Father paced some more.

"They will be here soon . . . tonight or tomorrow . . . but they will come," said Mother.

"And we'll be ready," replied Father. "I've spoken with the boys' parents, and we are agreed on a plan. I'm afraid there will be consequences . . . at least for some of the boys, but I think we can survive this."

"And the kommandant? Is he suspicious?" asked Mother.

"I don't think so."

I remembered the news I'd overheard that night. "The kommandant is being promoted and transferred tomorrow, Father. I heard him tell the mayor."

"Another miracle!" Father lifted his face to heaven and smiled. "Thank you, God."

"See? God is with us," said Mother. "Even in the darkest of times, He is watching over us."

"Yes. And we will need more of His mercy before we're through. We are like Abram and Sarai from the Bible, traveling through a political Canaan, surrounded by people who would kill us over the truth. I don't think God wants that, nor do I think the kommandant will want to risk his promotion by discovering that the Resistance has been operating under his nose the entire time he was here. We will obscure the truth and lead him to a more, shall we say, *acceptable* conclusion for all of us."

"And what do *you* know of this Resistance, Joseph?"

Father's jaw bulged, and his teeth ground as his eyes remained fixed on Mother's face. "I knew nothing of Jacques' involvement. I swear it."

The determined look in his eyes said all that would be said on the matter, but I had a very good idea what errands Father had needed to attend to in his shop all afternoon.

I BARELY SLEPT THAT NIGHT, IF I SLEPT AT ALL. I STARED AT Jacques' cold, empty bed, wondering if I would ever see his face again or hear another magical story rise from his lips. His choices had altered so many lives. I feared the kommandant's response when Mother and Father told him about the shooting. If we weren't shot on the spot or jailed, I would run the PTT route. Our new reality was unfathomable, and I wet my pillow with fear-filled tears.

The next morning was Saturday, and it began as normally as possible. Mother fed the boys and sent them out to tend the animals while we served a hasty breakfast to the Germans, who'd been scurrying about since dawn, packing the kommandant's personal items and tidying up the office for the newly arriving officer.

Before the kommandant rose from his meal, Father asked for a private word with him and shared selected details of Jacques' shooting:

THE BOYS FOUND *a gun in a satchel in the woods.*
Jacques had been shot.
The boys helped get him home where he collapsed.
Dr. Ouvrard rushed him to St. Catherine's in Verdun.
Jacques was unable to provide any details.
He was in a coma.
We weren't sure he would live.

THE OFFICER STOOD ABRUPTLY, kicking his chair back with a crash to the floor. His fists hit the tabletop like synchronized hammers. "Why did you not tell me this yesterday?"

Father didn't flinch. "Saving our son was our first concern, Herr Kommandant. And I thought you'd prefer to hear this news privately rather than in front of yesterday's guests."

The color alternately drained from and then reddened the kommandant's face, which contorted from a landscape of angry folds along his lips and brow to a palette of doughy fear. As Father had predicted, the man responsible for controlling the Resistance in our sector, suddenly saw that his entire career, and perhaps his personal fate, was in jeopardy.

He reigned in his emotions and answered in a voice that grew colder and more devoid of feeling with each word. "We will conduct an investigation, Herr Naget. We will tear up your shop and everything in it, as we will do to the homes of the other two boys. And if we find so much as a single bullet or a gun part or a piece of evidence that any of you have had part in the Resistance, you will regret this day."

And he kept his word. More bayonet-wielding troops than could possibly be needed were called in to rifle through Father's business and the home of André Moyes. We rightly assumed the same was being done at the residence of Paul Brunet in Ville-en-Woëvre.

The village houses remained shuttered, and the streets remained empty while the sound of crashing and shouting echoed from Father's shop. Bales of straw were run through as were mattresses in their search to find and kill rebels. Our kitchen table felt like executioner's row as we awaited the results of the search, knowing our fate rested on how well Father had performed his errands the previous day. Would the boys' stories hold up? Would anything incriminating be found in their homes? Had Jacques left evidence in Father's shop? Had Father? And would it be found during the search?

When the kommandant was satisfied that no evidence was found, he returned and approached Mother and Father.

"I see that your son's bike is here. There's no blood on it. If Jacques was bleeding as badly as you say, we would see blood on his bike. Jacques did not ride it home. How did it get here?"

Father remained calm. "I brought it home. Once Yvonne and the doctor left to take Jacques to Verdun, I went searching for it, to see where this tragedy occurred."

A glimmer of hope fell across the kommandant's face. "And where was this bike?"

"Near the woods . . . by the road to Ville-en-Woëvre."

The officer's eyes twitched as he pondered this piece of evidence. "My men have taken Paul Brunet to those woods to retrieve the gun. Ville-en-Woëvre . . ." He slapped his gloves against his thigh. The kommandant raised an eyebrow. He glared at us, pinning us in place like the map we pinned to the wall.

"Oh, Naget family." The corner of his lip curled into a sinister little smile. "We got on so well," he gushed before dropping his pitch like a musical leap into an abyss. "And then this happened." He took obvious pleasure at our extended discomfort. "You and your son have marred our rather cordial relationship, and now I will leave the determination of how to proceed with this matter to my successor, an officer who knows nothing of you and who has no reason to care about you. For my own part, I will say that after living in your home and carefully observing your activities and after having conducted an exhaustive search of each boy's home and your shop, Herr Naget, I have found no evidence of conspiracy."

My shoulders, which had been hunched up near my ears, dropped as we all took a collective breath.

"But," continued the kommandant, "as my findings are inconclusive, I will advise my replacement that further investigation is warranted. Pray that he is as merciful as I have been, Herr Naget."

Father didn't thank the kommandant. He merely nodded his understanding as the officer turned and stormed away. Before he closed the door, he spun back around and offered a final warning.

"And I would advise you to have the contents of your shop cleaned and put in order before the new kommandant arrives."

Judging from the pleasure the soldiers took in the thoroughness of their "inspection," which had left tools and materials spread into the street, salvaging much from Father's shop, let alone restoring it to its previous order, seemed an impossible task if given an entire week, let alone a day.

"I'll see to it," Father replied.

With a grunt for an acknowledgment, the kommandant left us to attend to his final packing. When he was behind his closed door, Father moved to Mother. "You know what to say to Jacques if he is awake?"

She nodded.

"All the boys must tell the same story. That they found the gun in a satchel in the woods and that Paul pulled it out and it went off. Nothing more. I've proposed this to the other boys' families, but Jacques must say the same. Rehearse it with him until it becomes his truth."

"I understand, Joseph."

Father took Mother's trembling hands. "He can do this. He is a strong young man. He's going to be all right."

Mother didn't debate Father's assessment. She nodded again and took her coat from the peg on the kitchen wall.

"I will send Paul Brunet's brother Robert to visit Jacques as soon as he is well enough to receive guests. They must not appear guilty. It must all look innocent, like an accident, with friends coming to comfort—"

"Please." Mother raised a hand as the color drained from her face.

"I'm sorry. I've said enough."

Father said his goodbye and headed down the street to see what remained of his livelihood. Moments later, Dr. Ouvrard arrived to drive Mother to St. Catherine's to check on Jacques.

We hadn't received a call about Jacques' health. We assumed no news was a good sign that he was at least stable. *Stable* . . . We had already adjusted to that new routine:

The family divided between Verdun and Braquis.

A life hanging in the balance as if that too were normal.

I was tasked with feeding the exiting German officers and

preparing the house for the arriving kommandant and his staff. A cold rain began falling as the old guard packed their vehicles. They grumbled about the cold and the mud and the rain as they departed, slamming the door shut as if underscoring their misery.

For a few sweet moments Gilbert, Titi, and I had the entire house to ourselves. No Germans. No cigarette smoke. No commands. We looked at one another and counted as the sound of the German vehicles sputtered away. When we could no longer hear them, we shouted and jumped and danced around the kitchen as if we had won the entire war, until Gilbert asked, "Where's Jacques? And where's Mother?"

And reality closed in on us once more. I sent them to Father's shop for their answers while I set about preparing food for the new regime.

Another tender mercy was granted us that day. The rain fell in torrents, and the country roads that had been churned by heavy military vehicles, quickly turned into mud pits. Mother and Dr. Ouvrard walked the last kilometer home because his vehicle became mired up to its axles. One German patrol pulled the good doctor's car from the ooze while another dropped Mother off at home before driving the physician back to Étain.

Soaked to the bone, Mother headed straight upstairs to change into dry clothes. I thought I heard her crying, but her eyes were dry when she returned downstairs. She immediately found things to do in the kitchen, skirting around me as if I were a pole standing there, awaiting some news of Jacques. She finally allowed herself to make eye contact with me.

"Jacques has not yet awakened. The damage to his left lung and stomach have been repaired as well as they could be, but he . . . he lost so much blood, Mimie. He is very weak. Healing will be slow, and so many things can still go wrong. Dr. Durand says we must pray for the best and prepare for the worst."

"Do you still believe God is watching over him?"

Mother pasted on a weak smile. "Yes. And we have more good

news. The soldiers told me that the kommandant's arrival was going to be delayed a day or two due to weather. We can have a family dinner . . . just the si—" She caught herself and blanched before repasting her smile. "Just the five of us."

I warmed at the thought of a family dinner like before the war, and yet not at all as it once was. Armand was absent, and Jacques was fighting for his life. We did our best to enjoy the blessed reprieve. We talked without hushing our voices, and we ate the best of the scanty meal instead of the scraps, never knowing if that moment might be the finest moment we would know for the rest of our lives.

Father used the hours before the kommandant arrived to solidify our stories with all the boys' families before the interrogations began. I used it to settle my nerves before my PTT duties began and I was forced to accept yet another new normal.

CHAPTER SEVENTEEN

I had hoped the road conditions would delay my first PTT run, but the temperatures dipped Sunday, causing the mud to freeze and the roads to become passable again. When I arrived downstairs, Mother was waiting to rehearse the route to me for the hundredth time.

"People will bring their outgoing mail, their orders, and their ration stamps here by noon. I will help you organize the stops— mail, pharmacy, groceries, meat, and then a stop at *la Mairie*—City Hall—to get the new ration stamps. Understood?"

I nodded that I did, in theory, understand, but terror prevented me from absorbing the details.

"You drop off the outgoing mail at the post and pick up the incoming mail. Organize it by house number. If you stay organized it will all go smoothly."

Mother's voice sounded abnormally high, as if she were as nervous as I was. "Push your bike inside every place you go or people will steal it and everything on it. You have a few requests for grocery items, two for meat, if there is any. And two orders for medicine from the pharmacy. It's a light day. That's good for your first run." Her voice pitched higher still from her normal mellow calm.

"And the last stop is always to *la Mairie*—City Hall, the grand building in the center of town, at 1 Place, Jean Baptist Rouillon. You've gone there with me to get our ration stamps, remember? Before the Germans came."

Yes, I remembered *la Mairie*. The grand stone block structure had always seemed more suited for a president than a mayor. No wonder the region's German officers had selected it as their headquarters.

"The ration office is on the first floor." Mother smiled unconvincingly. "In and out. Don't linger. Just get the stamps and get on your bike for home."

We both avoided all mention of one universally terrifying truth —to get to Étain from Braquis, I would have to take the road through the forest, where the German troops were bivouacked. I swallowed and took the list from her to end her pain. "I understand."

We spent the morning together, sweeping the same floors, wiping the same tables and straightening the same beds, waiting for the new kommandant, and watching the clock. Our breaths came in shallow wisps as if our lungs were too tense to inflate. We looked everywhere but into each other's eyes, knowing we were living on a razor's edge of lies and prayers and hopes and denial of danger, knowing full well that anything could happen.

Four vehicles pulled up—a large truck, two smaller trucks, and a reconnaissance vehicle in which the kommandant rode. Mother sent Titi to get Father as we hurriedly set food out. There were three knocks on the door, and then it flew open as if the knocking were simply a warning for the inhabitants to get out of the way. The kommandant eyed the food, removed his hat, and sat down, gesturing for his men to do the same. His second in command, a sergeant named Ohler, introduced our new leader, Captain Guntz.

It was soon apparent that no one spoke French in this group. The meal was eaten, they nodded, and then they began to unpack.

No firing squads.

No arrests.

No questions about Jacques.

Our anxiety remained as high as our relief. We wondered if they were merely toying with us, enjoying the suspense as we awaited our fate, but nothing out of the ordinary happened, and it appeared we would carry on, living on the razor's edge a little longer.

All the village's outgoing mail and ration requests had been phoned in or delivered to our home. The time had come to face my fear. Mother suggested I wear a pair of Titi's pants to keep my legs warm, and I pulled an extra sweater over my bony frame. Even with the addition of the sweater, there was still enough room in my coat for another person. I slid my hands into the warm woolen mittens Mother had knitted, and she wrapped her warmest scarf around my neck, adding a tug and a smile as she pulled a cap over my head.

"Keep your hair tucked into your collar."

I understood the cause for the advice. Small frame. Long pants. Hidden hair. She was making me look like a boy.

"And if anyone asks why you're doing the route instead of Jacques, simply reply that he is sick." Much more silent information was delivered by the look she gave me—a mother's worry for her son.

And for her daughter.

She then placed two hot baked potatoes into my coat pockets and handed me a wine bottle filled with water. Warmth for the ride to Étain, and a snack and drink for the ride home.

"Father has a surprise for you," Mother said as she opened the door.

Father stood holding a bike. It was not Jacques', but a modified boy's bike built to my size and mounted with a front and rear basket.

"For me?"

He bobbed his head modestly. "I know you've been nervous about handling Jacques' large bike. The town's new PTT officer deserves a bike her own size."

"But where did you get it?"

"Parts from here and there. Get on. Try it out."

With Father's instructions, I mounted the bike the way a boy would, stepping on the pedal near me and pushing off while swinging my other leg behind and across the seat until I was seated. After repeating the process to Father's satisfaction, I stopped the bike and Mother wrapped the black PTT armband on my right arm. She adjusted it numerous times as if shifting it a centimeter left or right would enhance the band's power to protect me. They were each doing their best to disguise the fear we all felt, but there was no avoiding the moment. The villagers were depending on us. The Germans were watching us. The time had come for me to take Jacques' place.

I pedaled into the street, headed down the block and back twice, as some confidence returned. With a final glance and a forced smile at my parents, I took off down the road, headed for Étain, before my apprehension released into a flood of tears.

I dipped my head as I pedaled past the guards at the edge of town. If anyone could help me, I knew it would be God, so I sang a hymn as I set my sights on the halfway mark, Boinville-en-Woëvre, three kilometers ahead.

My heart began to thunder within me as I saw the first tents and trucks at the edge of the German encampment. My chattering teeth interfered with my ability to form the hymn's words as my eyes met those of miserable-looking soldiers, whose ragged uniforms hung over their scarcely fed frames. We were suffering. They were suffering. I considered yelling, "Go home to your families, and let our men return to ours." The answer to war seemed so simple—"Just go home to what's yours"—and therein lay the insanity. These men probably wanted nothing more than what they had waiting at home, but Hitler and his allies wanted more.

They wanted everything.

Some German soldiers called out to me, breaking my thoughts, shooting searing terror into my heart. I pedaled faster and crouched lower. How does a boy ride? A frozen rut caught my tire and threw me. I scrambled to straighten my bike and noted my first PTT lesson—"Watch the road."

Three farm lanes broke off to the right. Two broke off to the left. I knew the families that lived at the end of each. I'd have business with three of them on the way home. As an oncoming military vehicle passed, I tried to focus on the faces of the people depending on me. I was grateful the soldiers in the vehicles ignored me, allowing me to ride past without much notice.

The guards posted at Boinville-en-Woëvre glanced at my armband and likewise let me pass without question. My legs and lungs felt the effects of two years of poor nutrition and limited activity. There had been stairs to climb and gardens to weed, and trips to the creek to forage, but more of my day was spent cooking before a stove or mending clothes while seated in a chair than in activities that strengthened my body. I sipped on my water bottle and quickly put it away as a convoy of trucks roared by, nearly pushing me into a ditch. Lesson two was learned. Better to take advanced refuge in a ditch than to be forced into one.

My nervousness upon entering Étain was matched by my shock and curiosity at changes in the town. *La Mairie* and its open, welcoming courtyard was now enclosed within an imposing iron fence with a guard gate. German military vehicles were everywhere, and a sea of armed and unarmed soldiers moved in and out of stores and gathered in clusters on the streets as if Étain were their home.

Citizens of the outlying villages relied on the PTT representatives to shop for them and deliver their mail. People without PTT armbands—locals, I assumed—stood in lines with their own ration stamps at shops where a few chickens and bread and rolls lay behind store windows. The people likewise lined up at the post office to drop off and collect their mail. It appeared that the people of Étain had adjusted to German occupation far better than the people of Braquis . . . until I noticed the smaller details, like their eyes, which were downcast and wary. Few locals gathered in groups on the street. They conducted their business and hurried on.

I got off my bike and pushed it along to the post office, past stately homes my mother and I had admired on previous trips. Trucks and officers' sedans sat where beautiful gardens once grew, and soldiers poured in and out of the loveliest homes, assuring me that, like our home, these had also been commandeered.

The line moved quickly at the post. People dropped their mail off in the outgoing mail slot, and those picking up mail had few letters to retrieve. Two pieces of mail were waiting for my route. I would make those deliveries on the way home. The lines at the bakery, *la boulangerie*, and the butcher, *la boucherie*, were long and filled with silent people who looked at the ground or their feet rather than chat or joke with a fellow shopper. I saw frustrated people shake unredeemed meat coupons and grumble under their breath as they left empty-handed. But I clearly understood Jacques' angered sorrow when I witnessed mothers weeping as they left with just a small loaf or a few rolls to feed a passel of clamoring children. For all the hardship we knew, I had to admit that life was easier in Braquis, just a few miles away, where large gardens and local farms eased the pinch of hunger.

I headed to *la pharmacie* and was able to pick up cold medicine for the two families who requested it and soaking salts for another. The next stop was *l'épicerie* or the grocery for salt and sugar for one of the families who had also needed the cold remedy. The clerk took my ration stamps and told me take my bike outside and await a worker who would bring my items to me. I dared not argue. While I stood by my bike, someone came up behind me carrying two cloth sacks. I flinched at his nearness and stepped back to find Légère's eyes peering back at me.

"Let me help you pack your basket, friend," he said a little too loudly before his lips quietly shushed me from reacting to the surprise of seeing him. "The clerk is my friend," he whispered. "I asked her to send you outside to give us a brief moment." His attention moved from me to the items he was packing and tying down while he spoke to me in a whisper. "So it's true. You are the new PTT?"

"Yes." I was torn between joy and indignation at his appearance. "Why have you ignored my last four letters?"

"To protect you from the very scrutiny Jacques' involvement has set upon you, little one."

"You? You are also in the—"

A fiery warning flew from his eyes, stifling further reply. "You are doing an adult's job, so I will speak to you as an adult," he whispered more sternly as he adjusted the packages for the second time. "The Allies have suffered heavy casualties in Italy, but they are holding their ground, and they are not backing down. They will prevail, and the Nazis will not take it lightly. In fact, I believe the Nazis will make things much worse for our people before we feel any relief from the Allies. So hear what I say to you. If you must be the PTT, keep your eyes straight ahead. Do not look left or right as you pass the German encampment or convoys. Promise me."

I shook as I stuttered out a weak, "I promise."

"No matter what you see, keep riding. You can't help anyone else, and you can't stop what's happening. The only person you might be able to save is yourself, if you mind your own business. Understand?"

The coldness in his voice frightened me more than his words. "Why are you acting this way? So cold and hard?"

"Because I'll be leaving soon, Mimie. General DeGaulle is

calling every able-bodied citizen to his army to fight when the Allies arrive."

The sting of tears burned behind my closed eyelids. "Will I ever see you again?"

His hand brushed mine as he completed his task, and for a moment, he allowed our eyes to meet once more. I saw a trace of a smile before his head dipped again. "Remember how I told you we would each fight in our own way? You would pray for God's help, and I would fight as a man must. If you see me again, it will be as a free Frenchman. Now wipe your eyes and remember what I've told you, Mimie."

Then he turned and walked away.

The echo of his one endearment—Mimie—replayed in my head as I counted the young men lost to me—Armand, Jacques, and lastly Légère.

I wiped my eyes and pushed my bike away without looking back. I knew he would be watching me, and I wanted him to feel confident that I'd heard his warnings. That I was not a child, but fully capable of the job entrusted to me, even as I shook like a reed in the wind.

I stood in yet another line as I waited my turn at *la Mairie* to pick up the town's ration coupons for the coming week. The time passed in a blink as I rewound my encounter with Légère. I pondered how he had avoided all contact with me to keep me safe in case his involvement with the Resistance was discovered. He loved me. Perhaps still as a brother, but he loved me, nonetheless. And he too, like Armand and Jacques, was gone from my life.

I picked up the next week's ration coupons and mounted my bike for the ride home. I thought of Légère's haunting words each time I passed a soldier.

Keep your eyes straight ahead.

Do not look left or right.

No matter what you see . . . keep riding.

. . . Save yourself.

I made my stops and quickly sidestepped the questions waiting for me at every home. The sun was already setting, and my nerves were raw as I pedaled home. *Home* . . . It had never looked so sweet as it did that day. Worry darkened Mother's face when she heard me enter.

"Mimie? Back so soon?"

She grabbed me and pulled me into the kitchen, scanning me for injury or worse.

"I'm all right. I finished the route."

She stepped back and looked at the clock. "You've only been gone three hours. Jacques never made it home before . . ."

We stared at each other for several long seconds as understanding passed between us . . . understanding about how much time Jacques added to his route to work for the Resistance. I understood him and his choices better. He never intended to endanger us or to upset our world. He had fought in his own way for hungry children and weeping mothers, to restore the nation and life we loved.

As Légère was about to do.

As we all had to do. Including me.

CHAPTER EIGHTEEN

I shook each time I mounted my bike and left home. After the fifth day, I became almost invisible to the Germans encamped near Braquis, a tiny boy barely worth the fun of taunting. I was not as invisible to the Étain guards, who blocked the path enough to force me to slow down or stop completely. With my hair secured under my cap, I could still pass for a boy, but it wouldn't always be December, and I wouldn't always be able to hide under a heavy winter coat.

Riding the PTT route did have some benefits.

First, riding the bike made me stronger, but it also made me as hungry as a bear cub, leading to another benefit—the kindness and sociality of the families I served.

I saw their suffering and bore the sorrow of informing my neighbors when their requests could not be filled, but when I could fill them, I was received like Saint Nicholas, with joy and cheering. My very appearance was heralded as I pedaled up families' lanes. Children raced outside to the porch to greet me as if I were a celebrity. Families shared what little they had with me to thank me for my service—a roll here, a parsnip there, a sliver of cheese or a boiled egg or a bacon strip or even just a chance to warm my frozen fingers by their stove. I ate what I needed to fuel my ride, but I almost always had a little something in my pocket to share with Titi and Gilbert when I arrived home.

I was invited to witness the arrival of a new litter of kittens or the birth of a baby goat or calf. Families welcomed me in like a member of the family for a birthday treat or to join them in song. These were small celebrations, to be sure, but they were celebrations, nonetheless, moments filled with hope, Moments when I felt God's love. Still, it was easy to see how one day's route could be finished in three hours while another day's trip, delayed by hospitality or requests for news from Étain, could easily require an extra hour. I remained mindful of the stress and worry any delay caused my parents, and I tried to keep the pleasantries to a minimum.

Mother and Father alternated riding to Verdun with Dr. Ouvrard to sit with Jacques, who finally awoke from his deep sleep in terrible pain on the fourth day. The surgeon was able to hold off the authorities' interrogation for nearly a full week as doctors addressed issue after issue resulting from the damage the bullet caused to Jacques' stomach, lung, and other organs and tissue. The haggard expressions etched into my parents' faces spoke of the agony of watching a loved one's suffering. A hopeful report one day often reversed to a warning for them to prepare for the worst on the next. The seesaw of hope and decline continued with hope looming as a brighter possibility with each day he survived.

Robert Brunet, the older brother of Paul, arrived to visit Jacques soon after he was lucid and before the expected interrogation, to be certain Paul's story would align with Jacques' and André's. Everyone feared Paul would be punished for handling the gun instead of reporting it to the Germans. The more important question was where he would be sent and for how long.

When the police and Germans finally questioned Jacques, he recited the story Father had pieced together, matching Paul's and André's with enough accuracy to satisfy the authorities in Verdun.

Our family worried and prayed the night after the interrogation as we awaited the authorities' decision regarding the boys' futures. Mother was with Jacques when he received word that the German investigator would place severe reprimands in André's and Jacques' files, but the pair would not be prosecuted. The news was not as hopeful for Paul Brunet, who was ordered to stand trial.

A canon from the church in Ville-en-Woëvre sought a meeting with the authorities to plead for mercy for Paul. While we prayed the cleric's pleas would be heard and heeded, we also prayed about our outcome as we awaited our new kommandant's reaction to the report we felt would surely reach him soon.

A young corporal who spoke decent French was assigned as the kommandant's interpreter. The two men lingered after the evening meal, two days after the investigator's decision was announced. We no longer feared execution, but we knew the infraction gave the kommandant cause to make our lives more difficult and miserable.

Captain Guntz whispered to Corporal Beutel, who stood and snapped his heels together. "The nature of your son's injuries has come to the kommandant's attention in a report from Verdun. Captain Guntz was most disturbed to hear that his wounds came from a gun he and his friends found while they were idle and hiking through the woods."

The voice was the corporal's, but we kept our eyes on the captain, whose gaze shifted from Mother to Father and back again.

"The captain wants to know about Jacques' condition."

Father bowed in deference before answering. "Thank you for asking. He's still critical, Herr Kommandant."

The kommandant nodded and whispered again to the corporal, who translated. "The kommandant has heard that you, Madame Naget, are an excellent seamstress and that you have taught your daughter well. We have need of such talents. Our men's uniforms need repair, and such work will keep idle hands busy and out of further trouble."

And there it was. No prison or removal to a remote work camp.

Home would be our work camp. We would fill our minimal free hours mending German uniforms. I heard Mother sigh in relief, and I quickly moved from irritation to gratitude that work was all the penance required of us.

A pile of soiled uniforms was promptly delivered and stored in a corner of the kitchen. The stench of sweat and tobacco rose from the pile like invisible smoke that masked every good smell our kitchen produced. Mother and I mended tears and tightened the stitches on patches while the little boys brushed the loose dirt off with whisk brooms. Washing the woolen trousers and tunics was backbreaking work. From first light until I left for my route and from my return to lights out, we were never without a chore, but we were together, and Jacques was still alive, so we counted ourselves blessed.

Christmas rolled past, and we children were granted our first visit to see Jacques. He was nearly as pale as his sheet, and his body was emaciated from the liquid diet he was on while his stomach healed. His once mighty arms and legs were barely as thick as mine, and his handsome face reminded me of the awful stories circulating about the condition of the Jews being held in concentration camps. While Mother beamed about how much better he looked, I shuddered to consider how much nearer to death he must have been. He was too weak to walk, and the doctor avoided all questions about a discharge date. For all intents and purposes, Jacques was not coming home anytime soon.

He asked for a moment to speak to me. His hand reached for mine, and he closed his eyes as he said, "So you are the new PTT officer." I felt his weak, bony fingers tighten around my own. "Did you hear that Paul was sentenced to four months on a work farm?"

"Yes. I'm sorry about your friend, but Father said his sentence would have been much worse were it not for the canon's intervention."

Jacques closed his eyes. "I was so afraid he'd be sent to Germany . . . like Armand." His eyes were glassy when they opened and gazed at me. "And what of your sentence, Mimie? I'm sorry that you too are paying the price for our choices. I never intended—"

I rushed in. "It's all right, Jacques. I'm getting along. I just want you to be well."

His brows knit together as his expression grew more earnest. "You may see some terrible things, Mimie. Don't peer into the German camp or make eye contact with anyone if you can avoid it."

When the chill zipping down my spine finally calmed and I was still again, I returned his squeeze. "I'm very careful." I forced a little smile. "I think they believe I am a boy."

He released my hand and tugged on my hair. The hint of a smile he allowed to grace his lips disappeared as sobering worry darkened his countenance. "But you're not a boy, Mimie. You're a beautiful, brave young woman." He bit his lip and looked away. "I'm very proud of you."

My throat grew tight at the compliment and his concern. I left his room that day, humbled by the way he took no thought for himself. His concern was for others, particularly for me, and I added his cautions to Légère's warning.

I believe the Germans will make things much worse . . .

Do not make eye contact.

Keep your eyes straight ahead . . .

Do not look left or right . . .

No matter what you see . . . keep riding . . .

. . . Save yourself . . .

I headed for the church when I got home and studied the image of Christ as I poured my heart out to Him with a depth I had not before known. I prayed that He would spare Jacques, and I begged Him to watch over me as I took Jacques' place as the letter carrier.

I never stopped looking for Légère in every face I passed in Étain. In time, I became familiar with the town and its mood until I was able to recognize the normal movement of its citizens as they dodged contact with the German military, and the abnormal bustle of people in fright or flight. I became adept at appearing invisible, to the extent that I could occasionally overhear people sharing whispered gossip with vendors or trusted friends as they stood in line.

I learned that the Allies were indeed continuing to gain ground in Italy and that, as a result, Hitler was sending a feared man named General Rommel to secure the Atlantic Wall. The whispers of the locals grew angry and more fearful over expectations that tens of thousands more French men were to be pulled from their homes and conscripted to labor on this western defensive barrier. I worried about Father. How long would the Germans find him more valuable as a mender of farm equipment than as the builder of walls?

I also wondered how some people knew so much about what was happening outside our tightly controlled little district. Over time, I pieced together bits and pieces of conversation until it became clear to me that the Resistance was disseminating cryptic messages to its members via radio, newspapers, and word of mouth. They knew of Nazi troop movements and offensive operations, of Allied advances and the rescue of downed Allied fighters. They whispered about Resistance fighters, German deserters, and the roundup of Jews. And though I caught but tiny snippets of rumors, it brought me comfort to know that France had not completely capitulated. As Jacques and Légère had said, the Resistance was at work.

I became a regular fixture in Étain. Vendors and locals acknowledged me with a nod or a smile, and though I attempted to remain aloof, I felt my guard lower among some of the people with whom I had regular contact. There were benefits to living in a town Étain's size, where clubs and sports teams were organized to entertain the youth. Posters described the opportunities Germany provided to the youth of larger cities like Verdun, where camps operated to teach skills like sewing and knitting and where young people with particular skills were trained to excel.

I saw a poster that featured girls forming a pyramid. It offered to train young gymnasts, and for a moment, I thought of my trapeze. How wonderful it would be to not only swing and turn somersaults, but to be trained to perform them well. I mentioned the poster to Father, who chewed on his pipe and then pulled it out, pointing it my way.

"Do you know why they hold those camps, Mimie? They do not want to merely train your body. They want to train your mind. To fill it with propaganda until you think what they want and believe what they want. That is a high price to pay for a few somersaults, eh?"

I never looked at those posters with longing again.

My trips to Étain made me aware of the social dynamic of the town. A few locals were highly respected by their neighbors. Children flocked to them as if they felt safe in their presence, and the adults nodded deferentially to these men, who were rumored to be *Maquisards*—members of the Maquis. One particular man, referred to simply as Leo, was a source of particular pride to the locals who whispered that Leo was always armed and that, at times, he brazenly carried a machine gun strapped under his pants leg, covered by his long coat.

I marveled that he could walk so freely about the town, appearing unafraid that so many knew about his association with the Resistance and with the infamous Maquis. Jacques had been so secretive about his involvement, and Légère acted as if a mention of the Resistance alone was cause for arrest.

I had mixed feelings about these fighters. The movement had nearly taken Jacques from us, and though Mother and Father were confident that he was improving daily, they still spent as many hours as possible in Verdun to assist Jacques' recovery. We hoped to have him come home in a few weeks, but he would still need months to regain his strength and mobility. Our family's daily struggle since Jacques' shooting was our personal offering to the Resistance. And it had taken Légère from me. I felt I had nothing more to offer the fight.

I wondered if Légère would agree with me.

Leo reminded me of Légère. He was an affable man with a ready smile for his adoring neighbors. I eyed him for weeks, building up my courage to approach him, to ask if he knew Légère and where he had gone. I finally appointed a day in March to introduce myself, but my ride to Étain that day was met with unusual scrutiny. My person and my nearly empty baskets were checked at each stop. As I entered Étain, I noticed that a strange pall had fallen over the town. Except for German soldiers, the streets were practically deserted. No children played ball on the fields. Few shoppers were out redeeming their ration stamps. Leo was not to be seen anywhere.

A sense of eerie alarm swept over me at my conspicuousness, an almost lone figure in a very quiet town. I pushed my bike to the post office hearing every squeak of my tires and the crunch of gravel under my feet. After mailing my village's letters, I asked if there was any incoming mail. The postmistress handed me three letters and whispered, "Conduct your business and leave Étain quickly today."

"It's very quiet. What's happening?"

"The Gestapo is sweeping every home, looking for members of the Maquis. Just hurry on with your business and go."

I spoke to no one else that day as I rushed from place to place, completing my list of chores. I noticed the gray-green uniforms worn by the Leitsellung or district staff of the Gestapo, with their spit-and-polish black boots, whose shine matched that of the black sedans guarded by a convoy of military vehicles. Members of the secret police, dressed in suits like respectable businessmen, were also in plain sight, and yet they seemed to blend into the walls and scenery. Their very presence seemed to breathe in people's will and joy, expelling fear, suspicion, and capitulation.

My cargo was checked again as I exited each checkpoint. I made four stops on the way home, and the mood at each house was unusually guarded and apprehensive. A few neighbors mentioned they'd had German military "visitors" that day, conducting searches of their homes, outbuildings, and property.

Why were the Germans suddenly so alarmed by the Maquis and the Resistance? Had Légère been right, that the Allies were making progress in Italy, drawing nearer to the French border? He also said General DeGaulle was calling the Resistance fighters to his side. What if Légère was right on both counts? The thought of the Allies' arrival excited me, but Légère's warning returned again —"I fear the Germans will make things much worse . . ."

Fear struck me as I hurried to Braquis to see if our home had again been raided, and there, in front of our house, sat two black sedans. The sight of the vehicles gave me such a start that my foot slipped from my pedal, gashing my ankle against the pedal's gripping metal teeth. I barely noticed the sting of pain and the trickle of blood soaking into my sock as my attention was fully drawn to the armed soldiers standing guard on the front stoop. I slid off the bike and walked it to the front yard while being scrutinized by the guards as I parked it. Not knowing the protocol to enter one's home when guarded, I stood before the men, dipping my head as I addressed them with a sideways glance.

Before I uttered my request, the door opened and a Gestapo officer, dressed in his signature gray-green, swept his hand, inviting me in. Mother, Father, Titi, and Gilbert were standing behind kitchen chairs. My parents' arms were wrapped around the boys. They shot me a strained smile.

"You're limping," said Mother as she took a step to better see me. "And your leg is bleeding." Her attempt to move to me was halted by the officer, who raised one hand to hold her in place while offering me his other. He led me to a chair and sat me down.

"You must be Michelle, the PTT officer. Bonjour, Michelle," he said in rather fine French. "I am Colonel Gott, and I've come to check in on your family after hearing about your brother's tragic shooting. We feel confident the gun that was used was dropped by members of the Resistance operating in this area. We wanted to assure your family that we're taking the strongest measures possible to round up all remaining members . . . and their support network."

I saw his glance shoot to Father before his attention returned to me.

"We wouldn't want to have another tragedy befall your family, now would we?"

I couldn't feel my heartbeat nor hear a single breath as the implications rained down upon us.

"But let's take a look at that wound." He motioned for a subordinate who drew near as the colonel knelt in front of my chair. He cupped my heel in his hand and set my foot on his leg. "What do the mademoiselle's papers tell us, Sergeant Beinhauer?"

The young NCO snapped to attention, seemingly delighted to be of service as he read from my *ausweis* document. "Michelle Rose Naget, born August 30, 1928—"

"Ahhh!" The colonel raised a hand to stop the reading. "That would make this little thing fifteen years old. Not a child as she appears, but a young lady."

Terror zipped through my body at his touch, his voice, his cold stare. He removed my shoe and my sock, making only a cursory glance at my cut as he slid his hand up my pant leg to my knee, moving the fabric north with his hand. He chuckled when I gasped and shrank back, shivering as tears burned in my eyes. I watched his gaze move past me to scan the pleading faces of my parents. With a final sneer, he dropped my foot and stood beside Sergeant Beinhauer. The weasel's eyebrow was arched, and his lip was curled in a half smile over the potential show.

"She is lovely, is she not, Sergeant?"

The sergeant responded in German, and the two laughed and eyed me as if I were little more than an item in a store window.

The kommandant entered with his junior officers, and though he himself deferred to the Gestapo officers, it became clear that the secret police weren't as willing to harass us in front of colleagues and witnesses.

"I leave your care to your mother, Michelle. Perhaps we will visit again sometime and continue our conversation."

I didn't like the kommandant, but I regarded him as a savior as the door clicked shut and the Gestapo officers' vehicles pulled away. Mother and Father made little mention of the incident. Mother hugged me, and we carried on as if there had been no assault on my security, and no threats of worse. But the Gestapo, and perhaps the SS, was aware of us, and I knew that these men, who saw themselves as demigods, would return again someday.

CHAPTER NINETEEN

April, the month of nature's awakening and rebirth was anything but that in 1944. The sun shone and the rain fell in earth's pas de deux of spring, but nature's few life-affirming glimpses of hope were overshadowed by the increased ferocity of the war.

Still, God blessed us with a few moments of joy that dismal spring, as a counterbalance to the sorrow swirling about us. Our first bit of good news was the return of Paul Brunet, who was sent home at the end of March after serving four months on a prison farm for Jacques' shooting. Our second joy was celebrated in mid-April. After five months of surgeries and hard-fought healing, Jacques was finally released from the hospital. The shriveled young man who hobbled through the doorway of our home was a greatly reduced version of my strong, handsome brother, but he was home, and Mother seemed ready to face any hardship or horror so long as at least one of her lost sons was safely returned.

We celebrated these happy milestones, but they were the only days worth celebrating that April as Jacques' and Légère's predictions about the worsening of the war came true. Whispers about the

Allies' advances hung in the air like smoke, emboldening the Resistance. But every tiny victory of the Resistance or advance of the Allies brought the boot of the Germans down upon the citizens. As the PTT officer, I could not be spared from hearing fragments of the horrid reports being shared on the streets of Étain.

In the early days of April, a German armored division was on a train approaching the *Gare d'Ascq*, a railway station near the village of Ascq, France, where three rails intersected. An explosion blew the rails apart, causing two train cars to derail. No effort was made to determine who actually set the charges that caused the accident, but vengeance, not justice, was the German officers' desire. They rounded up every adult male from every house on either side of the tracks, and when the final toll was taken, eighty-six men were dead.

The massacre created a tumult in France. Sixty thousand workers held a demonstration in Lille, and twenty thousand mourners flocked to the village of Ascq to attend the funeral services for the murdered men. The rest of France still sizzled with tension, but despite the size of the protests, our people were powerless to do anything more. Over two million French citizens were in Germany or under German watch in work camps and along the Atlantic Wall. Previous attacks on Germans had been answered with the execution of French and Allied prisoners, men like Armand who were as yet unaccounted for. The constant threat against our imprisoned and confiscated men suffocated the will of our nation's people, who feared for their captive loved ones. The mourners and demonstrators held their peaceful protests and returned home.

Six days later, rumors circulated about a raid on a home in the quiet village of Izieu in central France. Reportedly, the Gestapo brought trucks up to a home where forty-four Jewish children, many of them orphans, were being hidden. Observers said the Gestapo forcibly tossed the crying children into trucks, then the seven caregivers were shoved inside, and the caravan drove away. Most people presumed the ride would lead to the group's eventual deaths, given the abusive treatment of the tiny captives and their caregivers, whose efforts to provide safe haven to Jews violated Nazi orders. Adding to our national horror was the admission that information from French citizens led the Gestapo to the safe house. This was happening in my beloved France.

We knew there were Nazi sympathizers in France, people who gave comfort to the enemy and who fed them information in return for favorable treatment. We were ashamed of the entire government of Vichy, but the danger spread beyond the Vichy government and a few sympathizers. Germany had relocated many of her own citizens to the Lorraine region, creating an entire swath of Nazi sympathizers within France.

The spread of Nazi influence in our country was destabilizing, emboldening the Maquis, whose raids caused agonizing suffering to the very compatriots they were attempting to liberate. But there were stories of quiet French courage. Whispered tales told of physicians who risked imprisonment or execution for falsifying medical documents to prevent otherwise healthy young French men from being sent to work camps. We heard of Resistance fighters who disrupted Nazi communications and others who smuggled downed Allied pilots to safety in England.

Still, the knowledge that there were spies and Nazi allies among us brought a new level of fear to communities. Who could be trusted? Whose eyes were watching every move with the intent to report a neighbor? Mounting a defense was impossible when arrests could occur without evidence. And resistance was futile, bringing swift, brutal, and merciless retribution. A single accusation could make a person disappear forever.

Another merciless attack occurred six weeks after the raid in Izieu. A German armored company reported that one of their officers had been killed by a member of the Resistance while the company was enjoying refreshment near Frayssinet in central France. The retaliation for that crime was especially personal and calculated. Fifteen young men, purposely identified as an only child of their respective families, and each innocent of the crime, were rounded up and executed, leaving their parents childless.

The brutality and inhumanity of these attacks were effective at instilling terror into my people, who began to question the wisdom of the Resistance and the reality of our rescue by the Allies. No reasonable mind could predict what future horrors might be inflicted upon random people walking through town or sleeping in their own beds. The raids had achieved their intended goals. We were a fearful people, suspicious and tamed. I dreaded what was happening to my beautiful, lovely France.

CHAPTER TWENTY

Despite the great threat of reprisal for any and all infractions, the map remained on our kitchen wall. During our evening chats, we pointed out the rumored positions of the Allied and the German troops. Aside from the positions of the Germans encamped in the woods around Braquis and Étain, we knew nothing for certain, but we clung to the rumors with hope.

The occasional sprinkle of information to the citizenry had apparently turned to a more reliable trickle as the Resistance, with its curious communications network, grew broader and bolder within our communities. I found it surprising that not only was I hearing snippets of news in Étain, but Father and even Mother were privy to rumors, particularly about the Allies' progress. We were like chickens pecking bits of grain from the sand as we attempted to sort truth from rumor.

A story trickled down in mid-April of 1944 about Nazi deserters. Several German and Austrian soldiers appeared in the nearby village of Chaillon and surrendered, seeking asylum from the one hundred or so residents there. They bartered valuable information in return for their safety. Knowing they could never go home, they were even willing to fight with the Resistance.

Rumors also circulated about the Allied advances in Italy and about a large American army poised to sweep across the English Channel for a landing at Calais. And then there were rumors that no Allied Army would be able to push the Nazis back. Once again, our best indicator of the battlefront came from the changes in the Nazis' movements and in their increasingly barbaric methods. The SS and Gestapo became a regular presence, even in our rural communities, creating an aura of evil omnipotence.

I ran Légère's words through my mind as I pedaled. *Keep your eyes straight ahead. Do not look left or right.* I tried not to look, but how could I not see men struggling against the uniformed hands grappling with them as they were being dragged into the woods? And how could I not hear the pleas of people begging to have their cries of innocence heard? My eyes burned with tears as I pedaled on, afraid of what the next few rods of terrain might reveal while hating myself for ignoring the suffering behind me. I imagined that one day it would be me who was pulled from my bike for some imagined accusation. That my cries for mercy would be shouted to fear-deafened people who turned away because they were power-less to save themselves, let alone me.

I saw terror in the eyes of everyday people being marched or dragged about the German camp. I heard the sounds of single gunshots echoing from the woods and noticed deep holes being dug in the moist spring earth. Fertile soil that once welcomed seeds and returned bounty instead received the unnamed dead and returned sorrow.

Jacques was the first to recognize the toll that running the route was taking on me. I say that incorrectly. Mother and Father saw it, but being as powerless as I was, they spoke of it not in words but in soothing touches and sorrowful looks filled with helplessness. I understood their dilemma, but their silent empathy didn't relieve my fears. I wanted to scream and cry aloud about the images and sounds that were tearing my heart apart. Only Jacques spoke honestly about my anguish, of the changes he saw in my countenance and mood, the repulsive things he knew I witnessed each day, and the pervading fear of being the next victim of a Nazi interrogation. I saw that my pain was borne equally by him, the one whose place I had taken.

He still spent most of his day upstairs, away from inquiring Germans who might feel the need to question him and his story further. The confinement slowed his physical progress but being home with more family contact greatly improved his mental state, though I sensed that something continued to prey upon his peace.

Our time together was limited. We shared a few minutes after the rush of morning chores and getting the little boys off to school, and a few more during our family's scanty evening meal. Jacques was generally fast asleep minutes after lying down at night, so I relished our morning talks when Jacques opened up to me and asked me to bare my heart to him as well.

On one particular day, he finally let me see the tumult roiling inside him. His confession began when he reached for my hand as I made my way to the dresser to grab my scarf.

"I'm worried about you."

Just those small words of compassion set my eyes tearing. I remained faced away from him, fumbling with my scarf until I was composed. "I'm fine." Even I could hear how terse and cold my response sounded.

"It's my fault you're in this situation."

"It's not your fault. It's the Germans' fault. All of this . . . everything we've lost and suffered, and everyone gone from us is because of them." I heard the callousness in my voice, but in that moment, I made no attempt to camouflage my feelings.

Jacques' soft reply pierced me to the core. "Not because of all of them, Mimie."

I spun around and stared at him, awed by this change in the brother who had argued with me about my hope and faith that God would deliver us, as he spent three years spitting out pledges to fight and kill Germans.

He gave my hand a gentle tug. "I learned a few things during my months in the hospital. Not every German is a Nazi, and not every Nazi is a German. The people of other conquered countries were conscripted into the Wehrmacht, the Nazi war machine, but many feel just as victimized as we do."

I didn't know how to respond, so I stared at him and said nothing.

"Does that shock you?" he asked, his eyes pleading with me to understand.

"Yes." My reply was curt and definite.

"Try to understand what I'm telling you. I heard so many stories while lying in the hospital all those months. A few were stories from Nazi deserters who had barely escaped execution. Some were German. Some were Austrian. They initially believed they were fighting for a just cause, but time proved that they were serving a madman—"

"Hitler."

"Yes. Their families were starving, their countries were being destroyed, and they were being asked to occupy countries and kill people who had never done them harm. They said that one day they woke up and asked themselves why. The trusted few, the SS and the Gestapo, seek glory and conquest, but that is not the case for most Nazi soldiers. They fight on to avoid the shame of cowardice or a noose or a firing squad or torture, knowing that their countries' women and children and their aged suffer. The few who desert and survive are often willing to join our Resistance to fight the Nazis."

His words supported the rumors about the deserters at Chaillon, but the reversal in Jacques' thinking unnerved me. I rubbed my prickled arms and fought the swirling emotions of compassion and hate. "What are you saying? That we should surrender?"

His face pinched as he shook his head. I saw the former fire return to him. "No. We must fight, and we must prevail, but we must also accept that the German people have also suffered. And eventually, we'll need to forgive."

"You sound like Mother."

"No, Mimie. I sound like you. Like the Mimie who hears God's word in her heart. The Mimie who prayed every day, believing He would save us. You once spoke of becoming a nun. Do you still dream of turning your life over to God?"

I returned to my dresser, feigning a search within the drawers while my true intent was to hide from Jacques' question and the guilt it harrowed.

"Mimie?"

"I heard you. No, Jacques. I haven't thought of that for a long while."

"There's no guilt in changing one's mind if it's because you choose another life for yourself."

I spun around. "It's because I cannot serve God with a heart filled with . . ." I bit my lip and fought another barrage of tears.

"A heart filled with anger? Perhaps even hate?"

The tears fell in torrents, and I heard the scuffle signaling Jacques' clumsy efforts to come to me. Seconds later, I felt his thin arms wrap around my bony frame, pressing me close. Soothing whispers shushed my crying, and for a moment, I felt safe and understood and forgiven.

"Be wise, be cautious, be wary, and be angry if you must. You're entitled to all these feelings, Mimie. My fear was over what the Germans *might* do, but you're witnessing what they have done, which surpasses anything I imagined. I cannot fathom all the horror you see, but it breaks me to the core to know you're vulnerable to it because you're taking my place. I don't know how to protect you, my gentle Mimie, but don't allow what you see to taint your heart. I couldn't bear that."

I thought about that girl who dreamed of giving herself to God. At times, she seemed lost to me. At times, she seemed lost to God, not because I had stopped loving Him, but because I had stopped feeling His love as I once had. Jacques had been right, I was angry, and I did hate the war, and perhaps I hated the Germans too. Could God love me if I hated some of His children? I mulled that question over as I rode my PTT route. I tried to see the occupying soldiers as Jacques had described them—as victims caught up in Hitler's madness, but it was difficult to see anything but the harm they caused.

CHAPTER TWENTY-ONE

The calendar page turned to June, and we counted our blessings as food became more plentiful. While we all gave thanks for the chickens' eggs and peeping chicks, for new batches of rabbits filling the hutches, for the creek's wealth, and for the return of fresh vegetables and fruits, we could hardly thank God for His bounty without also thanking Him for the food's part in Jacques' improving health.

He walked to Father's shop nearly every morning, stayed a few hours, during which he tinkered with some small job Father assigned, and then they walked home together at midday for *le déjeuner*, after which Jacques generally returned to his bed to rest. With Jacques still recovering and many of my hours consumed with the route, Mother looked to the little boys for much of her help with food production and gathering. At eleven, Titi was taller than me, and seven-year-old Gilbert, whose childhood had been shaped in the vice of occupation, seemed older than his tender years. They two were a matched set who happily spent their days supplying our table with fish and frogs, crayfish and watercress. When they weren't at the stream, they were hoeing a row or picking beans from the garden. They rarely complained about any work that freed them from the oppressive mood pervading our home.

Members of the SS regularly joined the kommandant and his men to dine. At times, they evicted the kommandant and his staff and took over their rooms as well. They treated their arrival as if it were a compliment to Mother's fine cooking and accommodations, but it was also a strain on our pantry and a stress to Mother, who never knew if she was cooking for ten or twenty. Our nerves were raw from tiptoeing around men wielding the power of life and death. We felt their eyes upon us, searching our home for some offense and asking us random questions as if hoping to ensnare us with our answers. On one day, a simple swap of meat became fodder for their games.

"And how did you come upon such a fine cut of meat, Madame Naget?"

"I traded a rabbit for a ham, sir."

"And with whom did you make this fine trade?"

Mother's lips trembled before releasing the neighboring farmer's name, not knowing what repercussions might flow from that simple admission. "Monsieur Xavier."

"Is this Monsieur Xavier a rebel collaborator?"

I watched Mother's hands shake as she cleared the dishes from the table. "No, sir. Just a farmer."

On a good day, the officers would chuckle over their games. On a less fine day, they might sternly rebuke us for being insolent. On a bad day, they might take Mother's innocent answer and head to the neighbors' home to interrogate them, saying Mother provided information that required further investigation. It tore our community apart, so we stopped sharing or visiting one another.

And there were the looks the Nazis gave us, as if we lowly servants were there to serve them and their whims, no matter whether it was as the recipient of a suggestive comment or a touch or a pinch or a couched threat to the boys for completing a task too slowly. Father's powerlessness to protect his family was slowly breaking him, and the Nazis seemed as delighted in tormenting Father as they were in terrorizing us. Even the kommandant, who cared little for us but who feared the disruption of his amiable circumstances, seemed increasingly unable to distract our tormentors, and we feared a day would come when they would cross a line we could not bear, making death a more pleasant alternative to enduring further abuse.

The pop of gunfire rang through the air with such frequency since April, that we barely flinched at its occurrence, but while tanks and trucks churned our roads into dust or mud, we rarely heard heavy artillery fire in our area, or the whir of aircraft above us followed by bombing runs. The danger the secret police posed was silent, insidious, personal. Our tormenters knew us by name and enjoyed our discomfort. When we felt we could bear the scrutiny no longer, everything changed again.

A cryptic radio transmission came through one morning in early June. The kommandant gathered his junior officers into his office and had them close the door. The muffled voices carried on a brisk discussion for hours, and the number of armed soldiers on patrol was doubled.

"They're worried about something," Father whispered as he peered out the window from behind the kitchen curtain. "They're so preoccupied with their news that I wonder if we dare turn on the radio for a minute?"

"No! It's too dangerous." Mother clasped her hands together under her chin. Her voice trembled as she spoke. "What if the Resistance launched another attack? Someone will suffer for it."

"General DeGaulle has called all members of the Resistance to join him. We are a real army now," said Jacques. "The French Forces of the Interior—the FFI."

Mother was not comforted by his explanation, and Father rushed in.

"Not every family has Nazis living under its roof. Someone will know. Eventually, they'll bring the news to my shop."

"The FFI will know first," added Jacques. "The BBC has been transmitting to them in code. The news will spread once they decode the message."

"But how far away are these people who will know?" asked Mother.

Jacques studied her, as if determining whether to share the answer or not. "Some are very close. It won't be long before the news reaches our ears."

Our front door swung open and closed so many times over the next hour that we scarcely knew how many soldiers were in our home at any time. Father and Jacques prepared to head to work, but as they stepped outside, a new officer caught the closing door and stepped out, barking something in German that was clearly intended to stop them.

"We're going to work," I heard Father explain.

The soldier stood firm and shook his head. "*Nein.*"

As I peered through the open doorway, I saw one of the kommandant's regular aides appear. He waved the soldier away and addressed Father.

"No work today."

"May I ask why?"

"For your safety." His voice lacked the concern his words espoused.

"Are we in danger?"

The officer's face hardened. "In a war there is always danger."

"And tomorrow? Should I plan on going to work tomorrow?"

The officer's eyebrows pinched together, and one side of his mouth curled into a smile.

"What work is so urgent, Herr Naget, when you are out of steel?"

I saw Father swallow. "All the more need for me to repair old goods."

"I see. I'm sure your farmer neighbors know where to find you when and if they have need of your services."

The officer didn't withdraw after delivering the message. He stepped to the left, leaving the doorway clear, as if herding Father and Jacques back into the house, but Father didn't move.

"Very well. Then I'll work in the garden today."

"*Nein.* You will stay inside today."

Father's head tilted to the left. "Are we under arrest?"

The previous soldier returned with a comrade, creating a wall between Father and the garden. Father's shoulders rounded, and he nodded slightly, signaling his capitulation.

"As I have said, you and your village are under our protection. Until further notice, anyone seen on the streets will be regarded as a member of the Resistance and shot on sight. Do you understand?"

———

We believed the threat. The fear of being gunned down kept our entire community inside under house arrest for three days. Armed soldiers walked the streets as more materiel and heavy artillery passed by. Sentries stood at every intersection in and out of town, but as there was almost no civilian movement for them to check, we wondered who they were guarding against. Our conclusion was that they had word of an imminent attack. But were they preparing for an assault by the Resistance forces or the Allies? And if they feared the Allies, had Italy been taken and they were pressing on from the southeast, toward Lyon, or was the rumored invasion coming from the west, from Britain to Pas de Calais? All three possibilities brought a mixture of emotions—hope because our prayers for liberation were being heard, and fear because there would be reprisals no matter who came and regardless of the campaigns' success.

Knowing our family was still under scrutiny, we did our best to be in plain sight while also being invisible. We kept quietly busy—

mending, washing, cleaning, cooking, saying little and requiring nothing. Anything to appear indispensable and keep the gun barrels pointed away from us.

When the kommandant noticed the unkempt garden and the monotony of food on the table, we were again allowed into the garden, and Father and the boys were allowed to go to the stream, so long as the guards knew where and when they went. Our neighbors were finally given permission to emerge as well. Stealing glances at one another, we picked our way through our yards and gardens, wearing similar looks of nervous curiosity as we held our collective breaths and waited.

And then the quiet phase of the war became loud and large once more.

Days of unrelenting rain and wind turned the world into a brown ooze. We couldn't see the planes at first as the all too familiar whir of engines increased. As planes broke through the cloud cover, we stood frozen, wondering if we were the targets. And then someone panicked and rang the church bell, and we ran for the air-raid ditch that zigzagged across the back of our yard.

People poured from their houses, gathering crying children and helping the elderly along. The Nazis reacted to us while checking the sky. When the last person was in the trench, we pulled the plywood sheets over our heads and waited in the damp earth, but no bombs or bullets struck our area. Men lifted the wood from time to time and peered out as more planes soared above us from bordering Germany, less than one hundred kilometers away, disappearing into the southwestern sky.

Are they headed for Pas de Calais? The flight path didn't seem correct for an invasion from Britain, directly to the west, across the English Channel to Calais. The only thing we knew for certain was that the day's target was not us. With a prayer for those in danger's path to the west, we crawled from the dirt and returned, filthy and nervous, to our homes to await the next change.

We lived on edge, acutely aware of the heavy artillery and

troops moving past us as the Nazi army reallocated men and supplies. Whatever we were not supposed to know clearly posed a greater threat to the Nazi war machine than anything we'd seen before.

We were soon encouraged to return to our *normal* tempo of life. A more watched, more guarded, more scrutinized normal, where our freedom to move from place to place became even more limited. A curfew was established on June twelfth, requiring us to be off the streets from 10:30 p.m. through 05:30 the next morning. The curfew's hours had more impact on city dwellers than farmers and country people, who generally went to bed early and arose at dawn anyway. The return to some level of normalcy told us that the battlefront was indeed far from us and, more, that the Germans didn't believe it posed a threat to our region. That realization was both a blessing and a sorrow.

Life was a series of great oppositions, never more so than at that time. We prayed and pleaded with God to protect the Allies and bring them to us, while fearing the destruction and the ensuing repercussions their arrival would cause. And as we contemplated the moment when we could finally rise up, stand with the Allies, and fight back, we knew the Nazis were waiting for just such a moment, when they would lay down their forks, set down their crystal water glasses, pick up their guns, and, without a second's regret, kill us all.

Little by little, news began to trickle down. The Allies had landed at Normandy on June sixth at a tremendous cost to soldiers on both sides and to civilians as well. The number of dead was rumored to be tens of thousands of lost lives, and some said even hundreds of thousands were left dead. Mother's mouth hung agape as Father shared the news. It was impossible to fathom such a Biblical-level scene of death and sacrifice.

We didn't know how to feel at first. The joy of hoped-for deliverance was swallowed up in other emotions that left us aching and sad. We were grateful, of course, beyond what words could express, and laid low with humility that such a sacrifice had been made and was still being made to liberate us and the rest of occupied Europe. We thought of the men who would never go home, of the dreams that would die in bloody sand, of the lives that ended far from the comfort of loved ones. Grieving families would not know for some time that their sons and husbands died to save unknown people not their own. But perhaps that was the very point of their offering, to show Hitler that the good people of the world were all one, united against evil and oppression.

We thought of the hundreds of civilians and members of the Resistance who had also died in Normandy. Many more of us would die, and maybe our family would pay for our freedom with our own lives, but how could we bemoan even that fate when strangers willingly gave their lives for us?

As expected, reports of reprisals traveled fast. For every blow the Resistance dealt, the Nazis punched back sevenfold in places like Ugine and Tulle, where French prisoners and conscripted French workers were cut down for the perceived sins of their people. I felt certain I would not see Armand again. Mother never voiced those words, but she no longer spoke about the day when he would return home. As cruel as these tragic acts were, some of the Nazis surrendered all reason and humanity once the Allies arrived.

Whatever previous meaning man attached to the word atrocity had to be redefined after Normandy. The criminal act of taking soldiers prisoner and then executing them for sport became a regular occurrence. An even greater atrocity occurred at a small town called Oradour-Sur-Glane. It was a horror so unimaginable that Father dismissed me before discussing it with Mother. Miffed that I was still being treated as a child, I stood around the corner of the doorway and listened, but as the details of the event were unfolded, I realized that Father had tried to spare me from facing a level of depravity that would haunt my thoughts evermore.

A German Panzer division on their way to the invasion area experienced skirmishes with the Maquis. Someone said that

Oradour-sur-Glane was a Maquis stronghold, so one company diverted their course and rolled into that town with their tanks, heavy trucks, and artillery. Everyone in the town, from the youngest resident to visiting guests and tourists, were lured into the streets for a check of their ID papers. When the people were rounded up, they were separated by gender. The men were locked in garages in town, while the women and children were ushered into the church where they heard the Nazis' gunfire open on their men and boys. The women screamed in horror as the garages holding their men were set ablaze, but their screams turned to disregarded pleas for mercy as the Nazis turned their morbid attentions to their location, setting off smoke grenades that blinded them as machine gun fire bore down on the church until it too was set ablaze. Only one woman and a few men managed to survive the massacre to tell the tale. When the toll was taken, 245 women, 207 children and 196 men were lost in a few hours, an entire village, including people randomly swept up in the raid.

I shuddered as I looked at the kommandant and the SS through this new prism. Were they also capable of such barbarity? I wondered what had become of our world and what kind of world would be left to us, regardless of who won the war.

CHAPTER TWENTY-TWO

W e became ghostlike, grown children pretending that if we didn't acknowledge anyone else, they couldn't see us either. We said little, moved silently, rarely laughed or smiled or sang. We bore both the weight of our fear and of the Nazis' displeasure, knowing they measured the value of our lives daily to determine whether our service was worth keeping us around until the next morning.

Nazi-held Cherbourg and the entire Contentin Peninsula fell to the Allies on June 26th, but while the people in that region rejoiced to have the yoke of occupation lifted from them, that yoke pressed harder upon the regions Germany still held.

Planes were in the sky above us nearly every hour. My PTT run was punctuated by the percussion of gunfire and engine rumbles as planes left the airfield on the outskirts of Étain. I saw German soldiers dragging young men into those horrible woods at gunpoint. I could almost count out the remaining seconds of their lives before the pop pop pop of gunfire. The entire circumstance was surreal, that I was riding a bike to pick up mail and rations for some people while others were being assassinated mere yards away.

I questioned the sanity of it, but Mother's words returned to me: *We do what must be done.*

I was not immune to danger. My armband offered no protection from the new Nazi soldiers rolling by every day from Germany. They did not care who I was or what my purpose was. They would try to run me off the road for sport or they'd stop, exit the vehicle, and try to grab me. I felt as if God was pedaling my bike, giving me speed beyond my own strength to distance myself from their game, and when they backed up to chase me down, another vehicle always seemed to appear, requiring them to carry on with their original business.

I finally decided to become more defensive. As soon as I heard a vehicle approaching, I jumped off my bike and hid in the deep ditch by the side of the road until the way was clear. With so many stops and starts, the route took much longer, and from that hidden vantage point, I did not merely hear, but saw the end of so many lives.

On my return home from Étain one day, I stopped at a neighboring farm to drop off the family's mail. One of Jacques' friends lived there, and on that day, the sandy-haired young man was tinkering in the tool shed. He smiled and called to me as I drove up the lane, but before I could reply, he waved me away as a Gestapo car approached. I quickly dove off my bike and pulled the cycle and myself down to the ground in a patch of tall grass. From there, I watched the officers exit their vehicle and push the boy into the barn. A few loud crashes sounded within the open shed, and then I watched them walk the boy into the tree line. I saw him look back at his home and glance where I was hidden as if making sure I was safe. His pleas of innocence and cries to parents were silenced with a gun butt to his head. He dropped to the ground and was dragged deeper into the trees and then two gunshots rang out. The officers drove away from the property without so much as a word to the parents, who finally saw the vehicle exiting their lane.

They called for their boy, who never replied. I rose tearstained and trembling from the grass. In silence, I pointed to the woods, and watched them half run, half trip to the place where their darling boy lay dead.

I could barely see the road ahead as I pedaled home. I didn't dodge passing cars or jump in the ditch. I was blind to the chaos around me and deaf to the sounds of war. When I reached my house, I dropped the bike, quietly entered the house, and headed up the stairs. My anguish was too deep to lay at my parents' feet. I wanted Jacques. I needed Jacques. He would understand what I could not. How a sweet, fresh-faced young man could be alive one minute and gone the next. And what I should do with the venom raging in my heart.

He was reading a book by the window when I entered the room. My clothes and hair were still dirty and littered from the field as I dropped onto my bed saying, "I hoped you were home."

His eyes were glued to his page as he replied, "We finished early today."

My silence drew his attention, and when he looked up, the same sorrow I felt began to fill his face. In one move, he set the book down and rose from the bed. He bent low, to my height as he came to me. Worry and sympathy poured from his gaze as he took me by the shoulders and asked, "What's happened?"

"Robert Daigle is dead." My sobs released into his shoulder as I shared the details of Robert's execution. "Was he a member of the Resistance?"

"Perhaps. I don't know." He let me go and paced in a tight circle. "He was a farmer's boy. He knew how to repair things. He had some tools. Is that all the SS and the Gestapo need now to issue a death sentence?"

"Your compassion for the drafted Nazi soldiers does not also extend to these murderers?"

He stepped back in confusion, apparently stung by my sarcasm, and then he paled as he recalled our discussion about oppressed members of the Nazi army. Taking me in his arms, he said, "No.

No, it doesn't. The men who murdered Robert are cold-blooded murderers."

"I hate them, Jacques. Am I a terrible person for saying that?"

He framed my wet face in his hands. "Shhh. You are good and kind and gentle." He stared into my face, and when I could bear his gaze no more, he pulled me to his shoulder and cupped my head in his hands. "No decent person can see what you have seen and not want to cry out against the inhumanity of it. It's a sign of what a very good person you are."

"What must God think of me?"

"That you are brave. Like Jean D'Arc."

I shivered as I began to believe Jacques. Not that I was like Jean D'Arc, but that I was salvageable. Redeemable. That God would forgive my hatred. That He would get me through another day.

WE MISSED THE PEACE OF SILENCE DURING JULY AND AUGUST. The ground shook, and the whirr of engines and echoes of bombs pressed upon us day and night as the Allies advanced our way. Nazi aircraft soared over our homes, dropping their ordinance in ever closer locations. We ran into the air-raid trenches in full daylight and in pajamas and robes. The nights were the most terrifying, when we couldn't see well enough to gauge the direction or nearness of approaching ordinance except by listening for their whistles as they fell.

We felt the Nazis' fury over every inch the Allies gained. Our pin-filled map illustrated the cause of their distress. Step by step and city by city, the Allies were moving toward Germany from every direction—Normandy to the west, Provence to the south, and dozens of cities in the interior. We could see pillars of smoke along the horizon as bombs smashed cities and set the remains ablaze.

Life was frantic. Supplies were scarce. Chickens laid fewer eggs, and cows gave less milk. Soldiers ran to and fro without regard for where gardens lay, and as a result, our season of bounty was not looking bountiful at all. If the war didn't end by harvest, we would likely starve before spring. Everything people owned became precious and quite possibly irreplaceable, and Father and Jacques were kept busy making repairs.

Mlle. Portier knocked on our door holding a kettle with a broken handle. I opened the door and recognized the woman, a pretty singer who had enjoyed some small fame in Paris before fleeing the city a year earlier. She took refuge in the home of her cousin, the wife of a farmer whose property was located down the road. On that day, she came seeking Father to repair the broken kettle, but Jacques obliged and led the woman to the shop. He shared a whispered report of the encounter later that evening, as we cleaned the kitchen.

"Mademoiselle Portier told me that the Allies have reached Paris."

Mother drew in a swoonlike breath over the news, but Father was skeptical.

"Who gave her that information?"

"She didn't say," answered Jacques. "She seemed surprised that I didn't already know. In fact, she kept asking me for information about the Resistance, and where they were likely to strike next."

Mother gasped. "Why would she ask you a dangerous question like that?"

Father leaned forward in his chair and whispered, "Either she's a fool or a spy. I hope you said nothing."

Jacques smiled, pleased with himself. "She flirted with me as if she were also nineteen, and then she dangled the question before me, baiting me to answer. Something felt odd . . . forced . . . or maybe coerced is the better word. The Germans have used French women as spies many times. I don't know if Mademoiselle Portier is one of them, but I wasn't willing to take that chance. I told her I knew nothing and flipped my welding helmet down to finish the job quickly."

Mother stood and paced to the sink and back as she nervously tapped her fingers against her lips. "But what if she still says you know something. No proof is needed to have a person arrested. Only an accusation."

"I know. I've said as much to myself."

Concern darkened Father's face as well. "There is no protection against the wagging tongue of a spy once they set their sights on you."

Jacques shrugged. "I was kind and complimentary. There is nothing more I can do. I hope she is as Father said—a fool—or a lonely woman anxious to make conversation. If she is a spy, I pray she left seeing me as a friend she won't betray and that she'll move along."

CHAPTER TWENTY-THREE

We placed pins on the map marking Provence, Chartres, Avranches, Brittany, Mantes. By the end of August, rumors circulated about cities and regions that were being freed almost daily, quicker than we could verify. And then word arrived that the Allied and French forces had indeed liberated Paris as well. The news was heartening. We felt the liberation of Verdun, Étain, and Braquis was just a matter of time. Our worry was whether we'd survive to see those days.

The SS officers became regulars, far more than visitors, in our village and home. More locals vanished, leaving their loved ones with questions they couldn't answer and blame they couldn't assign. I felt confident I knew where their bodies would someday be found, in the deep mass graves in the forest by the German camps. Everyone else knew it too, though no one spoke of it publicly, and while we grieved the missing, no one dared question the Nazis over their disappearances, fearing that the same fate might become theirs.

We carried on as if life were an obscene game of "The Farmer in the Dell," where one by one, the Nazis took a farmer, and then his son, then the family's livestock, one steer or hog at a time. And then one day, they must have taken the farmer's neighbors, the entire Clerc family—an older couple, their married son and daughter-in-law—who just disappeared and never returned to their home. We assumed people would just continue to randomly disappear from the area until the blessed day came when the Allies stopped the Nazis or until there was no one left to take.

The small slivers of normalcy the Nazis allowed deepened their control. They knew that if they terrified a people and beat them down, then followed that campaign of fear with an apple or a piece of chocolate, the citizens' hope for more mercy would keep some from rising up and cause others to bow even lower. The strategy was effective.

The bit of chocolate dangled before the people of our area involved the neighboring village of Fresnes-en-Woëvre and their annual town festival, planned for late August. As early as late May, the mayor hung posters encouraging locals to prepare their entries for various competitions, and then the Allies landed, and everyone went into lockdown. When we were again allowed to open our doors, we learned that the Nazis had given permission for the festival to proceed. Desperate for some relief, the people bit at the offered "chocolate." We all recognized the obscenity of it all, that while Allied soldiers fought and bled their way across our land to liberate our country, many people of the Meuse Département of France were preparing for contests to enjoy but a momentary sliver of the freedom our liberators were attempting to bring.

The ladies sewed fabric scraps into small quilts, farmers fattened up their livestock to be judged, and young men practiced soccer skills for a match to be held at the fair. But after Paris fell, the Nazis' presence in our area increased, and their aggression became unpredictably brutal. Community leaders wondered if the event was simply a ruse to bring defenseless locals together in one place where angry Nazis could cut us down more conveniently.

With so much potential for conflict and danger, the mayor offered the oppressors some anemic excuse and canceled the festival.

The Nazis challenged the decision, but the mayor held firm. Some locals were disappointed. Others were relieved. Interestingly, most of the people enjoyed the thought that the mayor had stood up to the Nazis, ending the charade of normalcy. It took unbelievable courage, and though he didn't say those words aloud, his message was clear—that no matter what the Nazis did to him, the Allies would still come, and the Nazis knew the citizens believed it too.

Étain became more a prison camp than a community. The residents barely ventured into the streets for anything but the necessities of life. I ran the errands without speaking a word. People were again busily storing any foods they could grow or harvest from the streams and woods because the ration stamps were all but useless. Horror stories abounded about the conditions the Allies found in the poorer sections of Paris, where the deprivations were so extreme that a few parents reportedly smothered their children rather than listen to them cry from starvation pangs. We muddled on, barely surviving, because of the land and gardens, but there was almost no dairy or food to pick up in Étain, very little mail going in or out, and few medicines to answer the declining health of most everyone. I was barely more than a skeleton, expending more calories on the route than I was taking in.

On my ride into Braquis, I saw the car belonging to the German commander of the SS officers drive into town from the opposite direction. Gilbert was outside, playing with one of our rabbits. The poor boy almost never went outside alone when the Germans were at the house, and I knew the SS terrified him far more than the regular army officers. I sped up, trying to arrive at the house in time to warn him and get us both safely inside, but the car arrived before me. All I could hope was to serve as a decoy and try to deflect their attention away from Gilbert so the fragile seven-year-old could slip away.

I watched and cringed as Gilbert cowered and fell back when

the colonel's guards opened the car's door and the imposing man stepped out. The middle-aged officer was dressed in his black uniform, his gold buttons and medals gleaming, giving him the appearance of deity as he walked four steps and stood over the whimpering lump that was my little brother. Just before I reached him, I heard Gilbert cry out. I stiffened, prepared to fly off my bike and directly into the brutes causing him pain, but before I committed the executable offense, I saw the cause of Gilbert's pain and stopped. The rabbit that Gilbert innocently crushed to his chest dug and scratched at the boy's arm in its efforts to escape. Gilbert flinched, and the rabbit broke free but didn't get far. In a single sweep of his arm, the colonel snatched the creature by the hind legs, dangling it above Gilbert's head.

My brother and I froze, wondering what fate awaited our poor bunny . . . and us. The two guards laughed, enjoying our fear as we squirmed and shrank. The colonel said something to his men in German, summarily dismissing them. I assumed he wanted no cackling clowns drawing attention to his actions, or witnesses that would spread the news of his deeds around the campfires that night.

I held fast to Gilbert, pressing his eyes to my chest to spare him from seeing whatever horrid display the man planned. I considered screaming out, but I knew I would only put more people I loved at risk, so I held my tongue and faced the colonel as a sense of divine peace calmed me. I didn't know what his intentions were, whether this was just another act of intimidation or if, like so many other French citizens, we were about to become convenient targets of a Nazi's immutable privilege to destroy. I knew I was tired. Tired of cowering. Tired of starting every day more afraid than I was the day before. Tired of wondering if there would even be another day. But I also knew I was loved, not just by my family, but by God, someone who was not powerless or fearful of the Nazis, and that knowledge gave me a peace and freedom this man could not take.

I jutted my chin at the colonel, determined to make him face me squarely, and to my surprise, I saw the lines around his eyes and mouth soften, and his shoulders sag. He leaned forward, extending the rabbit toward Gilbert.

"Here you go, boy." His words were French, but they were spoken with thick German intonations. He had always spoken to us through an interpreter, never before revealing that he could either speak or understand French. My first instinct was panic as I reran conversations my family might have shared when we erroneously believed we could speak freely in our own tongue. But those feelings dissipated as I watched tender sorrow crease his brows and bend his mouth downward at the corners.

When Gilbert did not accept the proffered bunny, the colonel said, "Go ahead, boy. Take your rabbit."

I finally reached for the animal myself to end the stalemate, but my wary gaze never left the officer's.

"Your brother reminds me of my own son. He also loved animals."

Something in my expression must have revealed my curiosity over the comment, because the officer nodded thoughtfully before adding, "Is it so hard to accept that we too have families? Wives and children who love us?"

I sat as still as stone until Gilbert turned to look at the man.

A sad smile curled one corner of the colonel's mouth. "My boy isn't little anymore, like you, Gilbert. He wanted to be like me, so he joined the army. He died in an accident a few years ago, in Russia."

My emotions became confused. I felt compassion for the very man I thought might kill me moments earlier, and then I remembered that he and his kind were the cause of the war and the reason Armand wasn't with us. I locked my jaw to prevent any sympathetic words from passing my lips.

"Go," he muttered, almost as a whisper. "Go inside or put your rabbit away."

And then he walked through the front door and entered the

house without another word.

His momentary kindness was not repeated. At best, he ignored us, even when the roughness of his men increased. We soon understood the new threat they felt. The number of sorties flown over our heads had increased, and the thunder of bombs rumbled near us from the direction of Verdun. The Allies were close, and the Nazis knew it. We were living in a tinderbox, where a word or a look or a dropped spoon could be the match that would end us all.

We fled to the air-raid trenches several times, ushering crying children and helping slow-moving older people climb into the damp, muddy shelter. We almost preferred the hours spent there, huddled in shared sorrow, to life in the house, under the hair-trigger fury of the Nazis. When our duties forced us back into the house, we did what we needed to do, and then we sat, still and quiet, awaiting what came next—liberation by our victorious Allies, or execution by our angry, defeated foes.

My sixteenth birthday passed with quietly whispered greetings and tense smiles. I understood the danger my youth and gender created. The kommandants and their regulars' primary concern had been order and obedience. They were reluctant to engage in actions that could incite community chaos and rebellion, so they generally left the local women alone and satisfied their needs in the company of women brought into the camps. The SS officers posed an altogether graver threat. I was a young woman in a house filled with men who felt entitled to satisfy their lust wherever they chose, so I gladly wore Titi's pants and shirts when I drove the route, and I gave thanks that my own clothes hung on me in very unflattering ways.

I dared hope that a note or bundle of flowers might once again arrive from Légère, and then my heart clutched when I realized I had not even thought of him in a very long time. The gravity of our situation had left neither time nor will to dream of romance and love when any future at all seemed less likely each day.

The never-ending stream of vehicles pouring through the

streets included a sobering sight the next day, in the late afternoon of August 31. As I was parking my bike after the day's ride, several soldiers on motorcycles rode up to the mayor's house. One of the vehicles had a sidecar with a civilian in the seat. I didn't recognize the young man, but he looked frightened and wary. I took some comfort when the mayor stepped out to speak to the soldiers, and I entered the house, praying the mayor could settle the matter.

Another motorcycle soldier arrived shortly thereafter, and the secret police living in our home snapped their hats into place as they hurried out our door and to their vehicles. Their eagerness and the swiftness of their response made it clear they were looking forward to this errand. We relished their absence from the house, and then I thought of the young man, pitying anyone whose fate rested on the razor-thin mercy of the SS.

A few hours later, a soft knock sounded on our back door. We were startled, knowing that someone probably chose that door to avoid drawing the Nazis' notice, a signal that the matter was likely a dangerous one. Father opened the door, yet little light entered the hall as the person filling the doorway was nearly as wide as the opening. The neighboring farmer, a M. Dautremont, was bent forward, twisting his cap in his hands as he asked, "Do any of you know Jean Moyes?"

"Jean? Yes, I do," said Jacques. "I mean to say that I've met him a few times. I'm friends with his brother, André."

I thought of the young man in the sidecar and prayed he was not Jean Moyes. I wondered what new heartache had befallen the Moyes family, who so narrowly escaped having André imprisoned with Paul Brunet when Jacques was shot.

M. Dautremont made a sweeping motion with his hand as he said, "Then you must come with me now. I know the young man's father. He bought two calves from me for his farm in Hermeville," he rattled on nervously. "I haven't seen Jean in some time. Not since he was a boy—" His voice broke.

Father laid a hand on Jacques' shoulder to hold him in place as he asked the man, "Why do you need Jacques? What is this about?"

The man's reddened eyes shot to those of us huddled around our mother.

Father looked back at us and nodded, seeming to appreciate the farmer's efforts to spare the children another sorrow. The men walked outside and didn't return for over an hour. The Nazis returned before they did, but miraculously, they were so preoccupied with the events of the day that they didn't notice our men's absence. Father and Jacques slipped into the house through the side door from the sheep shed, setting up a ruse of checking the animals, creating a semblance of an alibi, in case their absence had been noted.

Once they were safely in the kitchen, their faces became a mixed palette of sorrow and anger more bitter than I had ever seen from either of them. Jacques' twisted mouth hung open and his breaths came in heaves that caused his shoulders to rise and fall. Father seemed withered, as if the day's events had sucked the life from him. I looked at Mother to gauge the moment, but the fingertips of her right hand tapped nervously against her lips while she drew Gilbert against her with the left. Whatever had happened was bad, and as much as I wanted to know what had occurred, part of me did not want to know at all. I dropped my eyes to the floor and waited for the dam of silence to burst.

"He's dead," Jacques spat out in a hateful whisper.

"Jean Moyes?" asked Mother.

"Yes. The Nazis picked him up for walking down the road. He was coming to visit his grandfather."

"Here in Braquis? Where André lives?"

"Yes. André helps on his grandfather's farm here in Braquis, and Jean helps his father on theirs in Hermeville. Or at least, he used to."

Father reached a hand to Jacques to shush his rising volume before carrying on with the story. "Monsieur Dautremont found a body lying by the side of the road near the woods between here and

Hermeville. He thought the young man looked like Jean Moyes, but he couldn't be sure. Jacques identified him."

Mother crossed herself and slumped into a chair. "Who shot him? The Nazis?"

"Of course, it was the Nazis!" Jacques spat back.

Father moved his hand to Jacques' knee, placing a warning squeeze there as his eyes shot to the door separating us from the very murderers we were discussing. "Your mother does not deserve that, Jacques."

My brother nodded in resignation and looked at Mother, who brushed his coming apology away. "You are grieving. I understand." She closed her eyes and shook her head. "His poor family."

"Poor André," said Jacques. "We took the body to his grandfather's house. André fell over Jean's corpse and wept like a child. He just kept saying, 'Not Jean! Not Jean! Jean was the peacemaker.' " Jacques wiped at his eyes. "He had no ties to the Resistance. None. Now poor André has to carry his dead brother home and give his parents the news that their oldest son has been slaughtered."

A long silence settled in as we each dealt with our thoughts. Mine flitted from the day we heard about Armand's arrest and on to the day Jacques was shot. I feared I would lose both brothers, but while Jacques miraculously returned to us, I felt sure none of us believed Armand ever would. That grief had been doled out in a slow, agonizing loss of hope, unlike the poor Moyes family's immediate anguish. They'd abruptly lost a child they'd embraced that very morning . . . perhaps laughed with over breakfast, a child they'd never see alive again. It had to be the hardest possible pain.

"I don't understand." Mother was tentative, and then she asked, "Then why did they shoot him, of all people?"

"Why not him, or any of us?" Jacques snarled as he glared at the door.

My throat grew thick. "I think I saw him today. A motorcycle patrol rode to the mayor's house with a man in a sidecar. I didn't recognize the man, but the mayor seemed to be handling things."

Father glanced at me. His brow wrinkled as he studied my face. "There was nothing you could have done, Michelle. The mayor said they picked him up along the road from Hermeville. They assumed he was a rebel because he was brazen enough to be walking alone when the battlefront is so near. The mayor tried to vouch for Jean, but one of the soldiers called the SS in, and they decided that he should be questioned by the kommandant."

"But the kommandant doesn't live here in Braquis anymore," said Mother. "His quarters are in Étain now."

"Exactly, but I don't think Jean knew that. Evidently, when the vehicle turned for Étain, Jean must have thought he was being set up, and he panicked. Dautremont said he heard shouting at the edge of his property, and when he looked up, he saw a man darting across the road, and then he heard three shots."

Mother groaned and set her elbows on the table before placing her head in her hands. "No, no, no . . . They didn't have to shoot him. All they had to do was explain."

"Why speak to a Frenchman when it's much easier to simply shoot."

We all hung our heads over Jacques' words knowing how true it all was. Jean was murdered for the crime of being afraid. His original violation was walking down the road. Just walking.

One of the SS swung the door open without knocking, his face wrinkling into an accusation as he surveyed us sitting instead of stirring or cutting or pouring something. "*Le Dîner?*"

Mother rose and held up ten fingers, following that with the words, "*Zehn minutes,*" in an automatic mix of French and German. The officer wrinkled his brow, nodded once, and withdrew.

We all sensed the morbid insanity of our situation, that we were feeding, preserving, even nurturing murderers, the men who were killing our neighbors and who posed the greatest threat to our own lives.

"I'm going with André tomorrow," said Jacques. "Some of the

boys saw us carry Jean's body to his grandfather's farm, and they're going too."

Mother's chest caved in from the force of her gasp and held breath, but she didn't ask him not to go. Neither did Father. Jacques was a man. He had secretly fought a man's war when still a boy, and he'd paid a man's price for it. He had seen that the cost of fighting and the cost of being a peacemaker were the same, and he would spend his last day, if it were to be his last day, opposing the men who made it so.

The SS officers ate heartily, undisturbed by the blood we knew was on their clean and manicured hands. We barely ate. We felt we were in a countdown.

Trucks and tanks rolled through the swamplike streets. Fog thickened the air, giving our lovely town the apocalyptic look of death.

The world was in commotion. The air shook. The roads shook. Our very house shook. And we quaked and shivered to our very toes. There was little sleeping and no true rest within that sleep. We expected death from a bomb crushing our home or a more surgical end with bayonet-armed soldiers bursting through our doors. In the morning, we sent Jacques off with a kiss. He seemed more at peace than I'd seen him in years. I envied that he knew the day would likely bring his end, and for finding honor and peace in his final errand.

We wondered if the Nazis would shoot the group before they reached the farm in Hermeville or if the young men would be crushed by a tank scrapping with them for inches on the road. Angels must have answered our prayers and been with them along the way. To our great joy, Jacques walked back through our doorway a day later, after Jean's makeshift funeral. He was somber and dirty, covered in dust and sweat from the trip, but we praised God and gave thanks that we had made it to September alive.

CHAPTER TWENTY-FOUR

As much time was spent in the trenches as above ground over the course of the next few days. We watched the flood of ragged, battle-weary Nazi soldiers and their muddy, battered vehicles retreating in the direction of Germany. We dared not show our excitement, but we believed our liberation was near.

Waves of shelling and bomb blasts continued to shake our rainy, gray world. Our Nazi houseguests received a message as they ate breakfast on September fifth. The contents of the message caused them to bolt from the table in a panic, and within minutes, they were out the door and racing off to their vehicles. Bad news for them was good news for us, so we paused a moment and drew in a peaceful breath as soon as they pulled away. All of us, except Jacques.

Jean Moyes's murder and funeral affected Jacques deeply, leaving him as somber and reclusive as he'd been after his own brush with death. Mother and Father were worried about him too.

"There's no line for the tub now," Father said in a cheery tone.

"Yes," Mother added with enthusiasm though her eyes seemed stressed and tight. "A long hot soak will do you good."

Jacques complied mechanically, heading upstairs, and Father and the little boys went to the garden to pull what remained from the muddy rows.

As I helped Mother clean up from breakfast, I dared imagine what life might be like once the Nazis were pushed back into Germany. I dreamed of filled plates, of laughter in our home again, of evenings spent with music pouring from Father's accordion and Armand's vio—

The ache returned, as it did whenever I thought of Armand. Not even the Nazis' defeat could bring Armand back if he were—

The front door opened suddenly and with such force that it slammed against the interior wall, bouncing forward again, earning a kick that nearly tore it off its hinges. Mother and I jumped and stepped back against the cupboards. We held our breaths, hoping the two Nazis would turn for the dining room to vent their apparent anger in their own space, but the assault on the door knocked a framed sketch of Paris off the wall. It became the next object of their rage.

One of the SS officers, a tall captain named Zimmerman, picked it up and spat out a string of furious words as he shook the frame in our direction. At the end of his verbal tirade, he broke the sketch over his knee, scattering broken glass and pieces of wood across the kitchen floor. Mother took my hand, drawing his attention to us. He sneered, as if enjoying our fear.

Father and the little boys entered the house through the gaping front door. Fear and rage swept across Father's face. He quickly assumed a well-taught expression of appeasement, since quelling the danger was the only tool at his disposal. His hands shot forward.

"Friends, surely whatever is upsetting you cannot be laid to our family." He glanced our way and then swept a hand toward the dining room and away from us. "Please, sit and relax. We'll bring you some wine and cheese." Without waiting for a reply, he turned to Titi. "Run to the cellar and bring a bottle of wine," but before

Titi moved, the other SS officer, a shorter blonde man named Franke, shouted *"Nein!"* and shoved Father through the open kitchen doorway, nearly toppling him to the floor.

Mother lurched forward as if to catch Father as he tripped and stumbled, but Franke shot her a warning glance, and she stayed in her place. Father grasped at a chair to stabilize himself, but the chair tipped with a crash. Titi and Gilbert began to cry, and then we heard the pounding of Jacques' feet on the stairs.

The kitchen wall separated us, so we were unable to see him, but we knew every creak of the old stairs, and we could tell that he had stopped cold before reaching the landing.

We could see the officers turn in his direction. Their gaze became fixed on what we assumed was his face before moving downward, and then the hatred burning in their eyes shifted to an evil pleasure.

They motioned for Jacques to come down, and when his footsteps hit the floor, we heard a cackle and then a thud that shook the wall.

Two officers half-dragged Jacques' partially naked body into the kitchen, where they shoved him against a wall. He was dripping wet, wearing nothing but a towel draped across one shoulder and pants that were buttoned but only partially zipped. It appeared that he had attempted to dress as he came to our rescue, but for all his good intentions, he suddenly posed the greatest threat to us. Jacques had forgotten about the scars on his chest—one from a bullet, and one from the surgery performed to repair the damage it caused.

One of the soldiers dug his forefinger into Jacques' scar, saying a word we recognized—"Maquis." Jacques winced in pain and all I could think of was his heart. Sorrow filled his every feature. His lips parted, silently forming the words, "I'm sorry," as his reddened eyes looked first to Mother and then to each of us, finally settling on Father's glistening eyes.

"Please, don't hurt him," Mother cried. "His heart! He's recovering from surgery."

Zimmerman was from Austria, and he spoke some French. "We know about his surgery. To remove a bullet he took from a Maquis gun."

"No," Father pled. "They found that gun in the woods."

Zimmerman looked at Franke and spoke in German. I understood three words—rule, penalty, and gun—meant to condemn Jacques in a court where these officers held all the power. Like Jean Moyes, Jacques was also in peril.

"Please," begged Mother. "There was an investigation. He was cleared."

Franke raised one hand to silence her while he used his other to pull his sidearm from its holster. He held it to Jacques' head and grinned at Zimmerman as two more of his comrades entered the room.

They shared another exchange in German. Any hope we had of rescue by the new pair faded quickly as their faces lit with wild humor.

Zimmerman moved in front of Mother, towering over us. He flicked a lock of Mother's hair and then cupped my chin in his hand. "We could shoot your boy without consequence. In fact, we would be justified in shooting this entire family of collaborators."

Neither Mother nor Father offered further petitions for mercy. Even I knew it would be futile to do so, and my proud, faithful parents seemed unwilling to provide the murderers the prize they wanted most—our complete and utter humiliation.

This is it, I said to myself. I felt liquid, devoid of muscle or bone. A quaking powerless mass. I looked at Mother, hoping to draw strength from her. She squeezed my hand and looked across the room at Father and her boys, giving each person a tearful smile.

Her obstinate calm infuriated Zimmerman. He pulled a chair out from under our large round table and slammed it down, telling Mother to sit. Then one by one, he sat each of us around the table, reserving one seat in between Father, Mother, me, and Jacques. Titi sat beside Father, and Gilbert sat beside Jacques. The empty seats were filled by the officers. Zimmerman sat between me and Mother. Franke holstered his gun and took the seat to my right, another officer sat to Mother's left, and the last officer sat between Father and Jacques. And then the game began.

Zimmerman placed his hand under my skirt, resting it on my leg. My body tensed, and I squeezed my knees so tightly together that my body shook. Sitting across from me was Father, who saw my reaction. His jaw looked like stone, but his eyes, his strong, sensitive eyes filled with tears as he groaned, "Stop. Please stop."

"Ah, ah ah!" scolded Zimmerman who pulled a knife from his boot. "One demerit." And with a flick of his wrist, he tossed the knife at my father.

It skimmed so close to his head that we gasped and closed our eyes, terrified that we'd witnessed our Father's murder. But the knife passed by Father's ear, landing in the cupboard directly behind him.

Zimmerman nodded to his colleague, requesting that the officer fetch his knife. When the blade was back in Zimmerman's hand again, he waved it back and forth at one family member after another as his other hand inched up my leg.

"Ah, ah, ah. You flinched. Another demerit." He flicked his wrist, and the knife flew once more, this time in Jacques' direction, just barely missing his head.

The knife was retrieved a second time, and again his hand moved farther up my leg. Silent tears slid down my face. I was going to die, but first, I was going to be dishonored before my family. I saw Franke turn and laugh at Mother, and I wondered if she too was being humiliated in the same way. That thought caused a sob to break from me. I tried to push my assailant's hand down. I begged him, "Please, please, please," but my fear only added to the jackals' pleasure.

Zimmerman shook the knife at Father again, and then, as the

other three beasts cackled and cheered, he shook it at Titi, and then Gilbert. "Don't flinch, Michelle," he sneered again. I squeezed my knees tighter, praying that I could crush his fingers and send him howling away, but instead, I felt him inch his way higher. I tried to be brave for Titi and for Gilbert, but a surge of revulsion and grief tore at me, until I leapt from my chair with a scream.

Zimmerman grabbed my arm and pointed the knife at my throat. I closed my eyes, waiting for him to end my life, when a voice growled from the doorway, "What is going on here?" It belonged to the colonel who had saved Gilbert's rabbit.

When Zimmerman and his cohorts were slow to respond, the colonel repeated the question in a more authoritative tone, adding something in German that sent the four officers to their feet and upstairs to pack their things.

Our family collapsed over the table in tears. Mother managed to rise and offer the colonel her gratitude. He took her offered hand but not her thanks.

"I am not your hero, Madame. I was motivated by the same impulse you feel—survival." He walked over to the map on the wall and touched the pin stuck in the village of Verdun. "The Allies are not here, Madame." He moved the pushpin, placing it very near to Braquis. "They are here. They should reach your village tonight."

His meaning did not hit us immediately. He seemed to understand that the previous moments' trauma had left us too numb to swing from destruction to salvation so quickly. It was then that I noticed the haunted look in his face, as if the scene he witnessed had shocked his sensibilities equally, leaving him hollowed and ashamed. With the slightest of nods to Mother and Father, he exited the room and gently closed the door.

The barrier offered no more physical protection than it had earlier, but its closing signaled something much bigger. Years of prayers about to be answered. The closing of the horror of our Nazi occupation. The knowledge that our family had survived.

Father pulled down the Nazi banner that had hung on our

home since the enemy arrived. Afterwards, he raised his eyes to heaven and gave thanks while Mother sank into a chair, set her elbows on the table, and folded her hands in prayer. We could openly speak and pray and cry once more, because of the blessed restoration of a gift I would never again take for granted—freedom.

CHAPTER TWENTY-FIVE

We huddled in the house and peeked through the curtains as the Nazi exodus proceeded out of town on the road toward Metz. The Allied fighter-bombers patrolled overhead, nudging the Nazi retreat out of our villages while also posing a threat to us when they unleashed a bomb or sent a barrage of machine gun fire to encourage the enemy along. We made a hasty return to the trenches when bombs fell in nearby fields or when the air popped with the concussion of shelling.

Eventually, the shelling slowed, and the rumble of engines and tank tracks quieted. Like nervous turtles, we pushed back the wood and slowly poked our heads out of our shelters, watching as the last trucks, those loaded with crates and metal boxes with smokestacks protruding from the top, exited Braquis. Father said these were the German field kitchens. They took longer to pack and were situated farther behind the battlefront. They rattled and shook in the rutted road, and then at long last, the final ragged soldier and cook cleared the checkpoint on the edge of the village.

The locals scurried back to their homes to wait and see if the colonel's word about the impending Allied arrival proved true.

Aside from the distant rumble of fighting to the east, all became quiet for a time. I wanted to laugh or cry or sing over the freedom of having our house to ourselves, but our joy was tentative. What would come next? Another retreating Nazi company? And if so, would anger over their defeat be unleashed upon whoever had the misfortune to lie in their path? And if the Allies were on their way, would they be any better to us?

We had heard the joyful stories of liberation to the west, but we had also heard tales of swaggering Americans whose bravado obliterated decorum, men who believed every French woman owed them a heroes' prize. Would they be any better than the Germans?

For a few hours our home was our own. Mother suggested we begin preparing *le dîner*.

For six? For just our family?

The simple notion of gathering our little family alone around the table for a meal felt miraculous, especially after the events of the morning. I made a simple stew, and Mother made bread dough, which she mixed and then kneaded with a ferocity that testified to the state of her own ragged nerves. About the time the loaves were ready to come out of the woodstove's oven, we heard more rumbling, and we braced as Father opened the door and stood on the stoop, staring down the road as trucks and tanks emblazoned with white stars appeared.

"*C'est les Allies*," he whispered back to us.

We braced with hopeful anticipation as a long convoy of tanks and armored vehicles crawled through town on the road toward Étain. The Allies peered at each French face peeking back from behind the windows of the few homes in the town center. Some soldiers waved. Some warily scanned every bush and bend in the road. We understood that caution. That mistrust.

Curiosity lured some people onto their porches to assess the newest arrivals. Jacques could not be contained. He squeezed past Father and stood on the porch, stretching his arms high as he waved back at the soldiers. Through the kitchen window, I watched emotion tug at him, wetting his eyes and distorting his mouth, which trembled as he cheered the army's arrival. I could imagine the thoughts going through his mind. Help hadn't arrived in time to save Jean, but it did arrive in time to save us. Just barely.

We opened the window to watch and hear the goings-on. The mayor walked out to greet the convoy. One soldier after another pointed down the line to a particular section of vehicles. When that section reached the village, a middle-aged officer and another soldier, a young man, jumped out of a slowing Jeep to approach the village leader. Both men removed their helmets and tucked them under their arms. The senior officer extended his hand to the mayor, whose arms were already outstretched, ready to welcome the Allies with an embrace of friendship and gratitude.

The officers' attire—muddied boots, crumpled trousers, and olive-colored button-front shirts, or blouses, with their sleeves rolled up near the men's elbows—spoke of fatigue, but their tired eyes were filled with offers of peace and friendship, and our guard lowered.

"I think they are Americans," said Jacques.

Father looked back at us and relayed Jacques' assessment.

It soon became evident that the younger man was interpreting for his older companion. After a brief exchange, the officers replaced their helmets, and the mayor led them toward our home. Father joined Jacques on the stoop.

"Joseph Naget," said the mayor, "allow me to introduce American Lt. Colonel Mark Jeffries and 1st Lieutenant Dennis Richards. They would like to ask you to house their officers while they are in the area." The mayor's eyes widened apologetically as he leaned forward adding, "I told them Yvonne and Michelle were the best cooks for a hundred kilometers."

Father smiled and huffed proudly. "They are. I must agree," he said in French. "Welcome. You seem very young to be a lieutenant, Lt. Richards."

The young officer muttered a "Thank you, Mons—," stopping

suddenly as he glanced at his superior. The two men's eyes met and held, and then Colonel Jeffries patted Richards's back and replied with a joke of his own, which Richards interpreted as, "He said I'm a lot older in dog years."

Father appeared confused, but since Colonel Jeffries was smiling, he smiled also and called for Mother and me to join him. Mother stepped under Father's arm, and, cautious of any men in uniform, I leaned into her, practically hiding my four feet ten-inch frame behind her.

Both of the Americans again removed their helmets. Colonel Jeffries's light-colored hair was cut short and thinning at the crown, while Lt. Richards's longer brown waves maintained the shape of his helmet. He ran a hand through his flattened hair and dipped his head shyly. I could not determine his age. His face seemed young, with smooth skin and a little boyish fullness to his cheeks, but his blue eyes and brow were creased as if they had spent years pinched in worry.

I studied his mannerisms as well as his voice, to confirm the goodness he exuded and to know if we had merely exchanged one set of oppressors for another, whose evil was simply less conspicuous. He met my stare and nodded, before rapidly diverting his eyes.

"Yvonne, the American officers would like to be our houseguests," said Father. "I think the aroma of your bread and stew drew them here."

"Yes, ma'am," Lt. Richards said to Mother in response to Father's joke and chuckle, but he returned the humor with only the tiniest hint of a smile. The colonel however, smiled broadly, though he seemed more lost than amused by the conversation. He spoke to the lieutenant, who quickly translated for us using a curious French accent I had never before heard.

"The whole army is coming to Braquis?" asked Father.

"No, sir. Parts of the Third Army are spread west and south. Our forward echelon will move on to Étain. We'll locate a company here. The men and supplies will camp in the woods along the road.

The colonel would appreciate it if you could house four officers and a translator."

"Are you not the translator?" I asked. His soft and lazy dialect charmed my ears.

"I'm afraid not. I'm just on temporary loan to the Third because there aren't enough soldiers fluent in French to go around. I return to my unit in a few days."

I felt certain my disappointment showed. I was fascinated by this American who spoke my language in his charming, gentle way. He was shy, but there was a definite strength to him and a sadness that creased his eyes and stiffened his mouth, barely allowing a smile to escape. His hands were rough, with fresh cuts, and scars. I found him fascinating. "Where did you learn to speak French?" I asked.

His shoulders drooped and his cheeks reddened. "Is my dialect that bad?" he asked in more of his lilting, lazy French.

I blushed for putting him on the spot. I straightened from Mother's embrace and said, "No, no, no! It's delightful. It's just different. Unique."

"I'm from Louisiana, ma'am. Ponchatoula to be exact. Have you ever heard of New Orleans?"

"No, but it sounds wonderful. And you don't need to call me ma'am," I told him. "I'm only sixteen. My name is Michelle."

"You're sixtee—?" the lieutenant blurted in French. His eyes widened in shock as he quickly glanced at my tiny frame. Then his jaw bulged as if he were biting steel. He blushed and dipped his head. "It's a pleasure, ma'am."

Father piped in. "Will Colonel Jeffries remain here?"

The lieutenant resumed his formal posture. "He and his staff will be in and out, sir. I'm afraid most of the officers you house will rotate frequently, but whoever is here will provide their own rations and additional for your family, if Madame Naget wouldn't mind cooking them up. The field kitchens will be down the road a kilometer or two. It would be convenient if they could eat with you"

"No trouble at all," said Mother. "We would be delighted, wouldn't we, Michelle?"

Mother looped her arm around me again before I could answer. She looked up into Father's face, and I saw peace replace the fear and intimidation that had ground my parents down over the past four years. Sweeping her hand toward the house, she said, *"Bienvenue. Entrez vous."*

"The colonel doesn't speak French," said Father. "Only Lt. Richards."

Colonel Jeffries piped in with a few words of French to show that he did understand her welcome and invitation to enter the house. We giggled at his mispronunciation, which seemed to make him smile wider. They moved in that night.

The church bells rang out, calling the people off their farms and into town that evening. Noise and chaos filled our village, but the bustle was hopeful. Despite that hope, when the phone in our kitchen also rang, our eyes automatically darted for the door, fearfully expecting Nazis to listen in or interrogate us over the call. Watching them leave had not immediately dispelled our fear. It took time to relax with the Americans close by. Within a week, we felt confident that we were able to move and speak freely in our home. *Our home.* What a lovely thought.

Father carried his accordion into the street. A few of his friends brought their own instruments out, and we laughed and sang and celebrated freedom again. Father's eyes glistened. I could only imagine the relief he felt over our deliverance and at being treated with respect again. A renewed sense of dignity and purpose filled each of us, as if we had been living under the shroud of an eclipse, and the sun was once again free to shine.

A new level of normalcy returned.

The summer had not been a bountiful one for a variety of reasons. The incessant rain rotted some crops, and erratic troop movements either trampled others or interrupted harvests. The winter pantry would be more sparse than we had hoped, but the Americans brought additional supplies to add to the villagers' rations, and we again set about preserving all the food we could for another lean but more joyful winter.

Guards watched the roads in and out of the village, and planes flew overhead out of the airfield in Étain, but these were our protectors, not our occupiers, and we slept knowing that whatever happened, we were at least free again. The mayor returned his attentions to long-neglected municipal business, including changing my status from Jacques' substitute to officially naming me PTT officer, along with the commensurate salary. Jacques had outgrown the assignment. He and Father were needed in the shop to fabricate parts and to weld and make repairs to whatever equipment came their way. Even though our home was not ours alone, it felt as if we were the masters of our own space again, coming and going as we pleased and doing what we felt was best without fear of reprisal. If the Americans needed something from us, they approached us with a request rather than a demand, and Mother's confidence returned under their praise and appreciation for her cooking and aid.

My heart was light as I drove my route again for the first time in days. Every stop turned into a long visit so the families could chat about "*les Américains.*" Everyone had their own story, from exultant to cautious, about their interactions with the new arrivals. Some enjoyed repeating abhorrent gossip they'd heard.

"They brought us canned peaches," said one woman.

"A soldier gave the children chocolate from their rations," said a father.

"They are wolves," said another. "They think that because they pushed the Germans back, they can take our daughters!" She then proceeded to issue me a stern warning to avoid them at all costs.

Saddest were the reports of how appalled the American soldiers were over our ragged and malnourished condition. I thought about Lt. Richards's pained glance when I told him I was sixteen, as if in that single moment, he understood the deprivations even we supposedly well-fed country people had endured over the past four years. I chuckled as I pedaled, imagining him finding Herr Schmidt and wringing his neck for me. I believed he would do it if he knew about the humiliation my teacher had forced upon me. And then I thought of Zimmerman, the man who touched me, who we thought would kill us, and I wished Lt. Richards could find him for me too. And then I shivered and changed my mind. I never wanted to see any of those Nazis again.

As I moved on to Étain, most of the neighbors' reports about their interactions with the Americans were favorable and hopeful, but we all sensed that the Americans remained as wary of us as we were of them. I noticed their kindness on my ride—a tip of a hat or helmet as they passed, an occasional whistle and smile, but also scrutiny and vigilance.

The echo of bomb blasts to the east reminded us that the war raged on for some cities and some people. Whereas Étain's streets had become almost desolate, with nothing to offer the hungry but a high risk of danger, they bustled once more with people enjoying the influx of American rations. The military added some canned goods, flour, sugar, and meat to the shops' meager supplies, and like the fable of "Stone Soup," people opened their cellars and pantries to barter jams, cheeses, milk, and eggs.

The limited supplies the Americans provided were more about optimism than about increased inventory, and that difference was incalculable. The war was not over. Hunger hadn't ended. The German border was close, with the Nazi army still amassed on the other side of the Moselle River, easily able to strike at us when they chose. But even though life and death still hung in the balance, we had hope, and hope was stronger than fear.

Even the postmistress, who grumbled about how busy her day had been, could not withhold a smile as she handed me a week's worth of mail. I thanked her and sorted the thick stack by address to make my deliveries easier, and then I headed to the shops. Nearly a week had passed since my last run, and nearly every home needed something. I filled what I could from the day's long list of ration orders and found a surplus of a few items, thanks to the Americans' gifts. My front and rear baskets were already full with mail and food items, so I tied the sacks of flour and sugar to my handlebars. The bike and load weighed more than I did, and I struggled to keep the bike upright as I pushed it through the busy streets to the road home.

A crowd of people gathered around a section of Étain near the outskirts of the city. It had been cordoned off, and guards stood before military fences. I stretched on my tiptoes, balancing the bike, as I attempted to see the cause of the stir. My bike began to tip, and as I struggled to right it a voice called out to me from behind, butchering the French language in an attempt to say what I believed was "May I help you?"

I turned and saw a soldier with a rifle slung over his shoulder, coming my way. His mature, stubbled face and the strands of dark, gray-tinged curls peeking out from beneath his helmet reminded me of Father in the morning, but the soldier had a round belly, and he laughed freely as he moved with a side-to-side gait that seemed to reduce his forward progress by half.

I yanked my bike close. "*Non, merci.*"

He pointed to my armband as his face squished into a look of disbelief. "*Vous? PTT?*"

"*Oui,*" I said defensively as I prepared to defend my size, my age, and my employment once again.

The soldier's eyebrows arched in surprise and respect as he bowed slightly and then extended his hand. "Sergeant Olivier Sciacchitano from New York City, America, little miss. *À votre service.*"

I couldn't withhold my giggle over his mangled mix of English and what I assumed were some strategic French phrases learned in a military-grade French tutorial. My laughter caused his own smile to broaden. His massive hand gently but fully encased my bony little one. I noticed a wedding ring on his chubby finger and considered that he had left a wife and perhaps a family to come to our rescue. I wanted to hug him for saving us, but I refrained when another armed soldier joined our happy little party.

The first soldier dropped my hand, and the two men exchanged a few words, of which I was only able to decode PTT. The second man, taller and younger than the first but also wearing a wedding ring, bent low and smiled at me. "Corporal Charles Kwiakowski of Booneville, Arkansas. Pleased to make your acquaintance. *Parlez vous Anglaise?*"

I knew he was introducing himself, but I understood little else other than his question about my proficiency with English, which was very poor. I pinched my thumb and index finger until they were almost closed and winced one eye shut. "*Non . . . uhhh . . . un peu.*" I knew as much English from my school days as they knew French.

The first soldier pointed to his chest and said, "*Moi,*" and then he pointed to me adding, "*une fille.*" He raised his hand about four feet from the ground and then held up ten fingers.

I took this to mean that he had a daughter back home who was ten years old. My heart swelled, and I instantly liked this man very much. "*Comment s'appele-t-elle?*" I asked, getting only confusion for a reply. I tapped my chest. "*Je m'appelle Michelle.*" I pointed to him and then measured the distance to the ground and asked again, "*Comment s'appele-t-elle?*"

This time, he smiled with a new light in his eyes. He reached into his shirt pocket and pulled out a photo of his family—he, his wife, and a little girl. "Patricia." He wobbled his head and corrected himself. "Patsy."

"*Ahhh, Patsy.* Vous avez une jolie famille.*"

He seemed to understand my compliment about his beautiful family. He coughed a little and wiped at his eyes. His companion removed his helmet and pulled out his own photo from the lining there, a wedding photo of him in his dress uniform and a young woman in a white wedding gown.

I tapped my heart and said, "*Si belle.*"

He kissed the photo and tucked it back away. Once again, I considered the sacrifice these soldiers had made in crossing an ocean to rescue strangers.

I pointed to the first soldier. "Sergeant Sciachi . . ."

He waved off my effort. "Just call me Skitch."

I nodded. "And Sergeant Kwaikow . . ."

He waved me off as well. "Just call me Sergeant Ski."

I nodded. "Ski."

"Perfect," they replied with great pleasure. They pointed to me. "Michelle?"

"Oui. Michelle Naget de Braquis."

Their eyes bulged and they looked at one another. "Naget? Madame Naget? The cook?" They made very enthusiastic stirring motions, and I knew my mother's reputation had preceded her.

"*Oui,*" I said, adding a hearty laugh. I pointed down the road toward Braquis and motioned as if I were eating as I said, "*Venez. Vous êtes invités à venir dîner.*"

Their thumbs shot up, and they smiled, telling me that they accepted my invitation for them to dine with us.

I looked at Sergeant Ski, whose voice had a similar timber to that of Lt. Richards. I wondered if he might know the lieutenant. "*Connaissez-vous le lieutenant Richards de Louisiana?*"

"Lt. Denny Richards?"

They knew him! "*Oui!*"

They glanced at one other as their expressions changed from humor to somber surprise. I wondered what that mood change meant, and then they made a finger pinch to indicate that they merely knew *of* him. Then they pointed to the cordoned area. "He's translating in there for the big wigs."

"Big wigs?"

They smiled. "The majors and generals."

"Ahhh . . ."

"General Patton is in there."

I felt my eyebrows rise. "General Patton?" I'd heard Jacques speak of him in hushed, respectful tones. "In Étain?"

"Pour une reunion."

"Ahh . . ." I assumed it must be a very important meeting for General Patton to attend.

The sergeants looked at their watches, said a few words to one another, and then quickly straightened. "En service."

I nodded my understanding that the time had come for them to return to duty and for our sweet conversation to end.

They made an eating gesture and pointed toward Braquis with hope-filled eyes. Once again, I repeated the invitation with a giggle and a nod. "Oui. Vous êtes invités à venir diner."

I received a wave and two thumbs up from each of them. An entirely different mood filled their faces as they straightened their uniforms and centered their helmets. They pulled their guns off their shoulders and carried them as they made their way to the guard post. My comical friends became soldiers before my eyes, warriors tasked to protect the Big Wigs, the high-ranking officers. I felt privileged that I also knew them as friends with loved ones far across the sea. Friends who would come to le diner one day soon.

I was grateful I no longer had to pretend to be a boy or ride like one. I pushed my heavily laden bike to get some momentum, and then I jumped on, peddling hard to keep the load upright as I headed back to Braquis. Each house was intensely preoccupied with the gathering of soldiers and some neighbors in the woods. No one had any answers as to the cause, but everyone had ideas, and none of them were good.

One of my stops was at the Daigle farm where I'd seen the Nazis drag the owner's son into the woods before shooting him. The husband opened the door, which I found odd. He was normally in the field working at that time of day. I heard the soft cries of his wife behind him, and I dipped my eyes, not knowing what to do or say.

"I'm sorry, Michelle. We're both a little in shock. We were just told the name of the person who sent the Nazis after Robert."

"Someone *sent* them? For Robert? Why? Was it someone we know?"

"It appears it was Mademoiselle Portier."

I sucked in a gasp of air as I recalled how she had come to our house under the pretense of getting her kettle welded, and how she had pressed Jacques for information on the Maquis. "Are you certain?"

"Her cousin and the cousin's husband came here to tell us. They just left. She went missing the day the Nazis pulled out. The family wondered if she had returned to Paris now that the city has been liberated, but they found it odd that she never said goodbye and that she left all her things. They waited to pack up her belongings in case she had merely gone off on a lark, but the American soldiers found her body in the woods today. She had been dead for at least a day, of a gunshot wound to the head. When the family and the soldiers looked through her things, they found notes from a German officer asking her for photos and names. She made a list. Robert's name was on it."

My breaths came shallow and fast. I couldn't draw enough air. I worried about who else she'd named, and whether the Nazis came after us that last day because of Mlle. Portier. "I-I-I'm so . . . sorry. I can't believe it. Was Jacques' name on the list?"

"I don't know, but there were other names."

"But why did she do it? And who killed her?"

"Why does anyone spy for an enemy? For money? Or perhaps they promised her protection. Perhaps they killed her as they left because she knew too much. I doubt we'll ever know."

It made a sick sense. She was among us, but not one of us. People spoke openly around her and welcomed her into their homes because they knew her family. And she'd betrayed them all.

I shared nothing of what I knew as I completed my route, wanting only to finish the work and get home. Jacques was sitting on the front stoop when I arrived.

He stood and grabbed the bike's handlebars as I dismounted. "I can tell by your expression that you've heard the news."

"Robert Daigle was murdered because of Mademoiselle Portier!"

"Did you also hear that my name and Father's were on that list?"

My legs quivered, barely keeping me upright. "I wondered if that's why they came the other day."

Jacques blinked rapidly to stave off his tears. "It helps somehow to know that they already planned to kill us. It wasn't just because they saw my scars."

I took his hand, and we sat on the porch in silence for a time. "Why then? Why did they come that day of all days, when they were about to leave?"

Jacques cursed under his breath, calling the Nazis names that seemed deserved in that moment. "They were losing ground to the Allies. Maybe they felt we were the one enemy they could destroy."

My entire body shivered at that thought. At how close we'd come to being annihilated. "Do Mother and Father know?"

Jacques nodded. "Father nearly broke down, and then he headed to the shop. And Mother is baking the Americans a cake."

Jacques' comment reminded me about the invitation to dinner I had extended to Sergeant Ski and Sergeant Skitch. "I need to tell Mother something."

Jacques followed me inside where we found Mother beating icing. "Mother," I began. "I made friends with a few soldiers who want to come to dinner to eat Chef Naget's cooking."

"Is that so?" she teased back as she added a thick swipe of buttercream to the cake.

Jacques smiled, and it pleased me to see his sorrow dim.

"I thought it would be good to be friendly to some American

soldiers. So many of them still seem wary of us," I added as I ran my finger along the inside of the mixing bowl and licked the prize from my finger. "I suppose the news about Mademoiselle Portier's collaboration with the Nazis will make them fear us all now."

Jacques' mouth set back into a thin grim line. "They have good reason. Before my accident, I heard the Nazis were embedding their own people in villages along the French border. I told Colonel Jeffries, but he was already aware of the information. It explains why the Allies question who they can trust."

I linked my arm in Jacques'. "Then they need to know that we are their friends."

CHAPTER TWENTY-SIX

W e fed Sergeants Skitch and Ski that evening, but Colonel Jeffries and Lt. Richards didn't return for dinner that night, nor did any officers come the next evening. The two sergeants must have known the "big wigs" were occupied, so they happily returned again with a linen sack filled with tins of fruit, Spam meat, and two bottles of wine. Mother received the men and their gifts happily.

Ski proceeded to pop the cork on one bottle of wine and offer a toast. We laughed over our struggles to communicate, pantomiming our conversations as much as speaking them. We played a little game where they taught us English phrases and we helped them with their French. The results were so enjoyable and satisfying that we agreed to continue teaching one another a little each week.

Mother called us all to the table, and Sergeant Skitch popped the second bottle of wine. Sergeant Ski filled mealtime with card tricks interspersed with stories that made us laugh until tears filled our eyes.

When Sergeant Skitch announced that the second bottle of wine was gone, Father sent Jacques to the cellar for two more bottles. Father opened the next bottle and grabbed his accordion. The two Americans began to sing, and interestingly enough, Sergeant Skitch's singing grew louder with every cork popped.

Rowdy as it was, joy reigned in our home that night. Father was relaxed and merry for the first time in years, and Mother's eyes were bright again. "We have new French names for you two," said Father at the end of the night. He pointed to Sergeant Skitch and imitated tipping a wine bottle back. "I will always remember you as Tire-Bouchon, The Corkscrew." We laughed and clapped, and Sergeant Ski slapped his friend on the back. Father continued, "And you, Sergeant Ski, shall forever be remembered in this house as La Blague, The Joke, because you have cheered our hearts and reminded us how to laugh."

The pair referred to each other by these silly new names, and then they asked us to call them by their new names as well. We loved these two Americans, our friends Tire-Bouchon and La Blague, for bringing laughter back into our home again and for helping us become a happy family once more. We hated to see them go when La Blague drove his tipsy friend back to camp that night, and we dreaded falling asleep and surrendering the spell of happiness they'd brought into our lives.

COLONEL JEFFRIES AND LT. RICHARDS RETURNED THE NEXT afternoon. They confirmed news we had heard, stories of captive workers and prisoners of war returning home since the Nazi pullback. They also confirmed that some captives who'd survived their captivity had been killed before the Nazis exited. Mother and I lit candles in the church that night and prayed that Armand might yet show up. This frail new hope, and the accompanying waiting and wondering, were almost as agonizing as our acceptance that he might never return.

I found it odd that I had not given Légère much thought in

weeks. Perhaps because the Nazis had made the future seem bleak at best and, at times, altogether unlikely. But hope caused me to dream again—new dreams, filled with endless possibilities and choices, like the potential of giving my life to God and His work, but I was also filled with a hunger to laugh and sing and dance and fall in love. Légère's face returned to my dreams, but so did the countless faces of young American boys who swarmed our streets, tipping their hats to me while offering me rides in their vehicles or walks in the country. I never said yes, but I thought about it. And I thought about quiet Lt. Richards, who was leaving the next day to return to his own company.

Our table was full that night. Lt. Richards was our guest of honor, but Colonel Jeffries, Tire-Bouchon, and La Blague were also there. Mother promised to fix Lt. Richards's favorite meal, so when he asked for seafood, Mother sent Father and the boys to the stream to collect whatever the water could provide. The surprise and enthusiasm with which he greeted Mother's bouillabaisse, *rouille* sauce, and homemade bread, was exceeded when she presented a platter of pan-fried wild brown trout. The young officer laughed, and clapped, thanking Mother profusely before standing to give her an awkward hug.

Mother hugged him back and laughed in return. "Joseph caught them in the stream. I hope they're all right. I tried to prepare them the way you described, just as your mother cooks them."

Lt. Richards thank Father also and then sat to eat his first bite. Pure pleasure filled his face, then his smile and happiness noticeably dimmed, with only an occasional forced smile appearing on his face the longer he sat at the table. He emptied his bowl and a plate of fish, gently refusing seconds. Instead, he dabbed his mouth with his napkin, graciously thanked Mother for bringing him a taste of home, and then quickly excused himself from the table.

All our eyes followed him out of the room, and Mother babbled an apology, worried that her food and her poor preparation of the fish was the cause of his departure. Colonel Jeffries folded his napkin quietly and apologized for Richards's hasty exit by offering an explanation in battered French mingled with hand gestures and exaggerated expressions.

"He landed at Normandy. He saw terrible things. So much death. He lost friends. In France, he sees pain, suffering. Being here, with you, in your home, feeling your kindness, and this meal, a reminder of home, is wonderful. And terrible. He returns to the frontline tomorrow. He's preparing for that."

We all sat still and quiet for several seconds as the panorama of nineteen-year-old Lt. Richards's experience and pain swept over us. Tire-Bouchon and La Blague noticeably hung their heads while the colonel toyed with the corner of his napkin.

"Did you also land at Normandy?" Jacques asked the colonel.

His face twitched as if trying to decide which emotion to convey. His head shook to signify that he had not. We glanced at Tire-Bouchon and La Blague and they too shook their heads.

I stood and walked over to the apple tarts Mother baked. I scooped one onto a plate before turning for the door. The colonel spread his arm to block my way. "No, Michelle. You will only make it harder." He drew a heart on his chest and slashed through it with his fingers. The imagery brought tears to my eyes.

"Help him," I pled.

He paused and stood, taking the plate from me before walking out the door in my place, to be with Lt. Richards. My eyes burned from the futility of our situation as I sat next to Mother, who, like me, had no words to heal the moment.

"Poor Lt. Richards." Tire-Bouchon reached a hand across the table to me. "You were kind to him, Michelle. He saw it, but"—he closed his eyes and shook his head as if dismissing Lt. Richards —"there's nothing you can do for him."

La Blague nodded his agreement. He patted his heart, then pointed to me, and slashed his hand through that drawn heart as he said, "You have also been hurt by the war. You need happiness." His eyes suddenly brightened until they were large and expressive.

He pulled a folded piece of paper from his pocket and pressed it against the table to straighten it out. It pictured a dancing couple and the heading read, *"Danse de la Liberté, 30 septembre."*

I hadn't seen the notices in Étain, but it didn't matter. I was too sad about Lt. Richards to care about a dance, and if that wasn't enough to dissuade me, the image of the happy woman in a pretty dress was. I thanked La Blague with a tepid smile as I pushed the paper back toward him.

Jacques looked at it and shot an encouraging glance my way.

"Non, merci."

Undeterred, Tire-Bouchon shared an animated conversation with La Blague. When he returned his attention to me, it was clear they were not letting the topic drop.

"We know many young, brave, handsome, American soldiers, Michelle," began Tire-Bouchon with an enticing lilt while La Blague played the part. Our Jokester stood with his chest puffed forward. He pressed his fisted hands to his waist as he struck a debonair pose, complete with a pompous expression and wriggling eyebrows. Tire-Bouchon snorted as he suppressed a laugh and went on. "We'll make a list of the best," he continued as La Blague placed his napkin on his head, held his knife as if it were a pen. With his lips pinched tight, he resembled a stern secretary writing a list. After writing a few illegible names on her invisible list, La Blague's secretary character paused, read the list, and then swooned into a backward faint. At this point, Tire-Bouchon stood and asked "her" to dance. The pair waltzed around the kitchen, stepping on one another's toes, until I could not contain my laughter. Seeing their success at brightening everyone's mood, including mine, the pair sat and asked, "So you'll go?"

I thanked them for their performance and shook my head again as I tugged on my well-worn dress. "And there is no fabric to make a new one."

The two men looked knowingly at one another, and finally let the conversation drop. Noting the hour, our friends rose to leave. I went to the window, but I couldn't see our houseguests—Lt. Richards, or the colonel. We set about cleaning, and though an hour passed, neither officer returned. It was not until the lights went out in the kitchen and went on upstairs that the front door opened and we heard the familiar scuff of boots on the downstairs floor.

I lay in bed listening to the noises that continued below. An hour later, a vehicle drove up outside. I pulled my robe on and ran to the top of the stairs in time to catch Lt. Richards hefting his rucksack and walking out the door. With a quick look back at the colonel, he caught sight of me at the top of the stairs. I saw the young soldier pause between determination and doubt. Right or wrong, a thought occurred to me, and I called to him to wait. In a flash, I ran to my drawer and found a piece of the stationery I used to write to Légère, and I jotted my address on the front.

I ran down the stairs, past the colonel's disapproving glance, and handed the lieutenant the paper. "Write to me? I'll write back."

Peace and a smile appeared to replace his doubt as he folded the paper and tucked it into his pocket. A moment later, he was gone.

I stood and watched the truck disappear on the road to Verdun. The colonel bid me goodnight as he walked into the dining room/office and closed the door. As I locked the door and headed upstairs, I wondered if the lieutenant would ever actually write or if just knowing that someone wished for him to was enough to lighten his heart. I prayed he would survive whatever lay ahead and that whatever he faced would not further injure his already broken spirit.

CHAPTER TWENTY-SEVEN

Tire-Bouchon and La Blague were regulars at our table, showing up several times a week with one surprise or another. They occasionally brought a tin of some new food item or a new card trick or joke. Sometimes, they brought a bouquet of flowers for Mother with a blossom for me or a K-ration, which the little boys adored, but there was always a bottle of wine.

Their tutoring helped my English proficiency improve rapidly, and I was soon able to communicate simple concepts in broken phrases. I often saw our American friends in Étain, and they smiled and waved or called out to me from wherever they were until soldiers I didn't know also began calling out to me as if we were good friends.

The taller and more developed girls received whistles or requests for romantic dates as soon as the Americans arrived. I did not. Instead, my diminutive size and PTT job proved to be fine assets for making friends of soldiers who saw me as a little sister or as a reminder of their daughters back home. I didn't mind. I actually preferred my situation.

Mother had gone to great lengths to dress me like a child or a boy, to hide the fact that I had become a young woman. Despite her efforts, there had been too many unwanted advances for me to wish for more of the same. But with better and more plentiful food and with less stress wearing me down, I had begun to gain a little weight and round out in my hips and bosom. My clothes were growing tight and the time had come to make new clothes, cut for a young woman of sixteen, instead of for a child.

The security in Étain was high one day, with more armed soldiers about. Such measures almost always meant that General Patton was visiting. I didn't understand the military ranks or who was whose superior. I only knew that General Patton was, as Tire-Bouchon declared, a big wig, a leader not only of men but of the entire Third Army, and therefore the superior of even General Walker, the commander over all the troops stationed in Étain.

When Walker and his troops arrived, the Germans abandoned the French military barracks they had commandeered—the *Caserne Sidi Brahim*—in Étain. When General Walker and his men moved in they became the hope of the people. We looked to them for relief and safety.

Étain's streets were again bustling with locals, who had hoped the Americans' arrival also meant there would be fuel enough to run tractors so long-dormant fields could be harrowed and readied for plentiful spring planting. But civilian requests for help with fuel had generally been denied because the army had none to spare. Rumors began to circulate that the only reason part of Patton's army had stopped near Étain was because they didn't have enough petrol to move themselves forward. When they did, they would head for Germany. I dreaded that day and worried what it would mean for our new friends.

I pushed my bike past a store window with two pretty white blouses and a checkered dress on display. One glance down at my own attire—a pair of Titi's pants and Mother's borrowed sweater—reminded me of how dowdy I looked. I knew I could duplicate the general look of the displayed items, but fabric was still in short supply. Before I could bemoan the situation, I felt a tap on my shoulder, and when I looked up, Tire-Bouchon was standing behind me.

He pointed to the clothes on display and then to me. "For you?"

I smiled and shook my head. "Too much," I replied in English. He beamed with pride over my improved English, and then he frowned over my situation and replied in the French we had likewise shared with him.

"But your English is *trés bon!*" He then mimicked sewing and with a question in his eyes, pointed to me again.

"Yes. I can." I frowned and tugged on my blouse. "But I still have no . . ." I struggled to find the English word, and settled for the French, "*Tissu.*"

He frowned back and tugged at his own shirt as if he were offering me some khaki fabric instead. I laughed and rejected his offer with a wave of my hand.

He looked at my bike's partially filled basket and asked, "All done for today?"

"No. Just beginning. I'm on my way to the post office."

"Is any of that mail ever for you?"

I shrugged my shoulders. "Not lately."

"Ahhh . . . A beau?"

I bobbled my head, not sure how to characterize my relationship with Légère and unwilling to tell him that I had not taken his advice and that I had given my address to Lt. Richards.

"You like him?"

Again, I bobbled my head and shrugged. I liked both of them, but I knew he was speaking of Légère. "Before he joined the Resistance, he wrote many notes. I saved every one."

"They are special to you?"

"Very special."

A look of melancholy washed over his face. "I understand." He pulled a letter from his pocket. "From my wife. I read it over and over until the next one comes."

"I keep mine in my Bible."

Tire-Bouchon nodded thoughtfully. "I'm sure you will get too many letters for your Bible to hold." His hands spread apart and then made an explosive motion.

I shook my head in doubt. "I don't even know if he's safe."

He tipped my chin up and said, "Don't lose hope. Some mail was held up. Older letters are trickling in." He raised his arms and wriggled his fingers in a gesture of rain.

"Ahhh . . . I see. So much mail now."

"See? So maybe your letter will come today. And if not . . . I could make a list of young American boys who would love you to write to them."

I was able to decode enough of his garbled Frenglish to understand his meaning. I waved my hand and laughed. "No more lists."

"All right . . . all right. But you just say the word."

"Thank you."

He winked at me. "Friends look out for each other, right? Gotta go now. I'm on duty."

"Will you be at dinner tonight?"

"I'm afraid not. I have night duty. Tomorrow?"

"Very good. And La Blague?"

"Uh . . . I don't think so. He has an errand to run." He winked again and then headed off. His parting smile was like that of an uncle, caring and protective, and I loved him as such.

As Tire-Bouchon predicted, the postmistress once again had a wide stack of mail for me. I searched the post dates and found that many of them were mailed weeks earlier. As I sat on a bench and sorted the mail, I believed Tire-Bouchon had seen the future.

I came across an envelope addressed to me, with a return address of Dover in Britain, but the handwriting was unmistakably Légère's. The postmark was fairly recent, September eighth. I ripped the envelope open and began reading the short note.

. . .

Dear Michelle,

Forgive me for not writing sooner. I know you have seen and experienced terrible things. I wish I could have been a protector to you, but I dared not even risk sending you a letter and adding further to the scrutiny of your family.

I have been getting regular updates on Braquis, and though I grieved to hear of Jean's murder and the loss of so many of your neighbors, I am grateful you and your family were protected until the Allies arrived. How is life with the American army as your neighbor? No doubt, you are everyone's little pet and favorite letter carrier. I hope the Americans are as good and kind to you as you deserve.

I have joined the Navy. Our Navy is rebuilding, but the Brits have generously taken me under their wing. I find that I have a passion for the sea. I love being enlisted anywhere in the cause to fight oppression, but I do love the smell of the ocean, and I believe I will take great pleasure in seeing the world.

The war is not yet won, but I believe it is merely a matter of time now. Remember always that I kept my promise. I told you we would be free once again. God has preserved you for a purpose, Michelle. Find it, whether it is in dedicated service to God and His children or simply so that you may live as an example to those who come after us, to fight to remain free. You make the world better in your way, and I will do my best to improve it in mine.

You are brave and strong and wonderful.

I am always,
   Your dear Légère

I was so numbed by the confusing messages in the note that it nearly slipped from my fingers and onto the ground. It felt like a letter of goodbye with all the references to traveling the world, and yet he signed it "Your dear Légère." I determined that I would send a return letter that was just as vague about my feelings, and I began constructing the note as I rode my bike to *la Mairie* to pick up the new ration coupons.

Even as the food situation improved, theft of the precious coupons remained a concern because of the food they could purchase. Guards were posted at the town hall to deter thieves. One young soldier, who looked barely older than me, smiled and opened the door as I drew near. I smiled back politely and headed down the hall to the left to the ration office. When I came out, the same soldier opened the door and smiled again. As I walked away, he whistled long and low, drawing others' attention to me, as if I were *une catin*, a trollop.

An older woman scowled at the soldier and then at me as she scanned me from head to toe, showing particular disdain for the men's pants I was wearing. She muttered something rude under her breath, and I felt my cheeks flush hot.

I turned back to the soldier with angry tears in my eyes, and I saw his own face flush red. He hurried after me. "I-I-I'm sorry. I meant it as a compliment. I was just trying to say you're pretty. I-I-I'm sorry," but I turned and hurried away on my bike, speeding home.

I was troubled all the way into the house. His whistle had been a small thing, and yet in that moment, it felt like so much more. More troubling, more painful than such a small thing should ever be. The soldier embarrassed me, but was he, as he said, trying to be kind? And why had that so completely unnerved me? I knew my understanding of boys and men and relationships was very limited, but why was I not able to see this flirtation as that and nothing more? Was it the woman's judgment of me, someone she did not know at all? And why had I not celebrated the proof that Légère was alive and felt flattered that he wrote to me as soon as it was safe? Instead, I was disturbed by the letter's content.

Is it me?

Légère had always made me feel safe, hadn't he? And I felt safe around Tire-Bouchon and La Blague. *But their attentions were fatherly.* Was that the difference? Did I see threatening and hurt from those whose attention was more romantic? And then a more ugly and frightening thought hit me.

I found Jacques and I told him about the young man who'd whistled at me. When I asked what he thought about the situation, a smile appeared and disappeared just as quickly on his face, settling his mouth into a thoughtful line. "It's what men do, but I can see that it upset you."

"People looked at me. One woman called me a terrible name."

He placed his hands on my shoulders and said, "You cannot control what other people say or do. Only what you do. You are a very good girl, Mimie. Enjoy the attention, but be a lady in every way. Pay those gossipers no mind."

Father's initial response was more succinct. "*C'est la guerre.*" After a moment's thought, and during my silent standoff before him, he lowered his book and eyed me over its pages. "Just a whistle, yes?"

"Yes."

"Let them have their fun. You're a good girl, Mimie. A little flirtation helps soldiers remember what they're fighting for."

I clearly needed the opinion of a woman. I pulled Mother aside and told her about the experience with the guard.

"What bothered you so much about that whistle?" asked Mother.

She held me fast in her eyes, as if every word I said from that point on mattered deeply to her, and in the safety of her glance, despite the tightening of my chest and the trembling of my lips, I pulled the terrifying words from the deepest corner of my heart.

"I keep thinking of the Nazis. How they looked at me. How they touched me."

Her face slackened and, if possible, her gaze drilled deeper into me, beyond sight to my core, and she said, "I understand, Mimie."

We spoke bravely to each other as we had before I assumed Jacque's route, when I was still her shadow and medical partner, helping people, defying the Nazis in our own way, as equals. I knew she heard what I was saying, not just the words, but the underlying insecurities and fears, as if they were also hers.

Also hers...

I knew in that moment that they were her fears also, both for me and for herself. She led me out to the sheep shed, where we could be alone. Her understanding and empathy opened my wounds wide and allowed them to bleed out in complete safety and empathy.

"A woman called me a terrible name, Mother. As if I were dirty, and I felt dirty because of how the Nazis treated me."

Mother closed her eyes. "I still struggle with those feelings too."

Saying no more about her own experiences with the Nazis, she pulled me close and held me, and we cried to the music of the sheep and pigs. I considered how many hours she had been in the house alone with the Nazis. How many looks or touches or sugges- tive innuendoes she had endured, likely terrified that at any moment, a comment or a glance would become more, an overture she would have been powerless to defend against. *Powerless to defend against.* I pushed back against the images and thoughts sweeping over me, of my good, sweet Mother alone and vulnerable to the threat posed by such men's hands.

I knew she wept for me, for all the violations against my body, my peace, my sense of self. She cried for all her children. For lost childhoods and innocence and sense of family, and I wept for both of us, for the unimaginable things we endured because we were women. We cried until we had both wept out all our hurt and pain and losses and anger. We held each other, and I cried into her shoulder, telling her about Légère's letter and my hurt because he hadn't said he loved me, and my fear of what I'd feel if he did.

We cried a few more tears, and then we clung to each other, and when we were strong enough to stand on our own legs, I said,

"What if the Nazis' cruelty and their impositions have left me suspicious of all men? What if I can't trust a man's words or be able to enjoy a young man's attentions? I still think about becoming a nun, but I don't want to choose that life because I'm afraid of men."

Mother brushed the tears away from my face, and then she finger-combed my bangs back. "I was reluctant about even Father's kind touches, but with his patience and understanding, I have come to enjoy his kindness again. Don't push yourself. Things will sort themselves out in time. If you choose to enter a convent, I will cheer your decision, but you must feel called to the order and not enter out of fear. While you wait for your answer, keep your heart open, but I believe a young man will come at the right time, when your heart is healed, when you can happily accept his kindness. You will feel love someday, Mimie."

We remained in the sheep shed until our eyes no longer burned. I decided not to assume the worst with Légère and write him an optimistic letter, hoping that instead of an ending, his disappointing letter might actually become a new beginning.

CHAPTER TWENTY-EIGHT

On September 15th, our brief period of peace and normalcy shifted into another period of controlled frenzy when General Patton moved his Third Army's base camp from outside Chalons to a muddy stretch of bomb-blasted, decimated woods to the west of Braquis and Étain. We had become accustomed to having a few hundred or a thousand men camped around us, but the Third Army was so massive that its personnel, supplies, and vehicle pool sprawled farther than a person could see.

The dreadful camp location stirred up more rumors about the army's lack of fuel, for no one would willingly select a location with so many hazards and holes by choice. The general himself spent far more time away than in camp, but the logistical marvel of his army fascinated me and everyone else in the surrounding communities as the Americans transformed that pocked and blasted acreage into an active, working city.

Tire-Bouchon was made a supply sergeant. He spent a great deal of time in a truck checking supplies or overseeing the men tasked with moving them from section to section of the grand encampment.

He and La Blague came to dinner soon after the fifteenth of the month carrying a cardboard box with a folded length of white fabric tied around it like a ribbon. When we asked to know the contents of the surprise, they extended the box to me and said, "It is for Michelle."

"For me?" Shivers of excitement raced up and down my arms at the very idea of any gift, let alone one that fit in so large a box. Whatever was inside weighed as much as several sacks of flour, and I set it on the table with a thud.

"Open it," they urged, with my family joining in.

I carefully untied the ribbon, made from what appeared to be a long length of white silk. I ran the fabric through my fingers as notions sprang to me over what I could make from this treasured fabric.

"May I keep the ribbon?" I asked in awe as I handed the fabric to Mother.

"Of course. Then you like it?" said La Blague.

"I love it! How could I not?"

The two sergeants' eyes widened, and they looked at each other with increasing pleasure. "Hurry! Open the box!" they repeated again.

The four top flaps had been folded over to close the box. I pulled the flaps back and my heart flipped. Dubious, I looked at my benefactors. "A parachute?"

"A parachute!" Titi repeated.

"Not just *a* parachute," said La Blague. "Show them, Michelle."

I sank my hands into the folds of the decadent fabric and pulled out a handful of—

"A *red* parachute!" cheered Gilbert.

I pulled the fabric close. "It is silk? For me?"

It took several minutes to communicate the information, but in the end, Tire-Bouchon and La Blague were able to say, "You said you could sew but you needed fabric. We heard about a Belgian bride who made her wedding dress from the silk parachute that saved her wounded fiancé's life."

"But we felt you needed a red party dress," added La Blague, "so we started looking for one of the red chutes paratroopers use for night drops, but no one would make the trade."

"And then the Third Army moved here, and I was made a supply sergeant. I checked the inventory and found some red chutes, and voilà!"

"Voilà!" we all cheered.

"But how can I ever thank you?" I asked. "There is enough fabric here for many things. Look, Mother! A dress and some blouses?"

"You can make whatever you want," said Tire-Bouchon, "as long as you wear a red silk party dress to the Liberty Ball."

"I will."

"Promise?"

"I promise." And with a hug for each of my benefactors, I raced upstairs to begin sketching out the dress I would sew for the dance. My excitement bubbled over, and I wanted to share my happiness with someone. My first thought was of Légère. I had not yet replied to his letter, so I took advantage of the moment to send him a note.

DEAR LÉGÈRE,

Thank you for your letter. I feel so relieved knowing you are safe and well. And thank you for worrying about our safety. It seems all our prayers were answered.

The final days of our occupation were harrowing. We still grieve for those friends lost to us, and our gratitude for our Allied saviors cannot be measured. Several of the American soldiers are now dear friends. They come by the house for dinner like family. I am just beginning to understand what they sacrificed to come here to our aid.

Mother and I do what we can to make them feel a little sense of home while they're our guests. And as you say, we have every reason to hope for a quick end to this terrible war.

Congratulations on finding such a perfect fit in the Navy. They are lucky to have someone whose eyes and heart are fixed on but one thing—freedom. I hope you find your travels as exhilarating as you expect. There has been so little joy, and we must accept it where and when it is available to us.

I'm still the PTT officer, which is a much more pleasant assignment now that the Americans are stationed near. And I'm making a dress for my first real dance, using a red parachute two sergeants found for me. I'm sixteen now, and I feel like a debutante preparing for her coming-out party.

Mother and Father, Jacques and the little boys all send their best wishes to you. We keep you in our prayers, and though we miss your company, we celebrate your happiness.

I AM ALWAYS,
    Your dear little sister,
    Michelle

I REWROTE THE LETTER A FEW TIMES, AND PROBABLY SHOULD have edited it a final time. I sent it, hoping to know, once and for all, if Légère truly saw me merely as a little sister or if I should hope for more.

———

TIRE-BOUCHON AND LA BLAGUE JUST HAPPENED TO BE driving a truck past my house the next morning at the time I generally began my route. They offered me a ride, which I gladly accepted. We tossed my bike in back, and I sat in the front seat between them, noticing that they were in a particularly playful mood. Tire-Bouchon diverted from the main road and drove past a company camped outside of Étain. When I asked what he was doing, he replied that though I had a dress, I still needed a date, so he proceeded to drive me past his single friends while La Blague broadcast my name to the men. I joined in the fun and clearly went too far.

Tire-Bouchon's sidearm was poking out beside my arm. I looked down and pretended to fight him for the gun while La Blague feigned terror. The two sergeants soon recognized that many soldiers we passed looked on with their mouths hung open in worry. My military friends sobered and rattled off a list of protocols we were violating, and we quickly resumed more respectable postures.

When we arrived in Étain, Tire-Bouchon asked, "Do you have many errands to run today?"

"No. I must visit two stores, get the mail, and then head to *la Mairie* for the new ration coupons."

"Oh, very good. I'll meet you there to take you home."

As promised, Tire-Bouchon was standing by the front door of Étain's City Hall. "You need to go upstairs today."

"Upstairs?" I questioned. "For ration coupons? They're always on this floor."

"Not today." He pointed up the stairs where two more armed guards stood and jutted his thumb to the right. "Upstairs and then the second door on the right."

I noted the parade of people still flowing in and out of the regular space where I had always gone. "But the people . . ."

"Not today."

I pointed and gestured up the stairs and to the right to be sure, and he nodded that I was correct. With a huff, I parked my bike and climbed the stairs toward the two guards at the top. These were friends of Tire-Bouchon and La Blague, some of the soldiers who waved and called to me as I rode my route. They tried to look solemn, but I thought I saw hints of smiles as I walked past and made my way to the second door where two more guards stood. These two guards were also familiar faces that knew Tire-Bouchon.

"Ration office?" I asked.

They stepped aside and swept their hands toward the door, encouraging me to proceed. I tapped lightly and stepped back, awaiting permission to enter. No voice bellowed a hasty *Entrez vous.* Instead, the door opened slightly, revealing an elegant-looking older man in an American military uniform. But he was not a regular soldier, nor even a regular officer. Four gold stars were embroidered on the officer's epaulettes. His face was also familiar, but I didn't know why for several seconds. His identity came to me at the same moment a fellow officer, standing in the back of the room, called for the officer's return saying, "General?"

"General . . ." I repeated in awe. "General Patton . . ."

"Yes? May I help you?"

My lips were frozen and immovable, whether in fear or awe.

He shot the guards an annoyed glance and said, "What are you knuckleheads up to?" His face relaxed as he returned his gaze to me, bending slightly forward as he said, "Hello, Mademoiselle. I'm sorry, but it appears my security contingent guided you to the wrong place."

My cheeks burned, as he waved me away and slowly closed the door. I wanted to run away. Instead, I eked out an apology to the general and waited for the door to shut before falling apart. I had no ready words to express my utter humiliation, so I just glared at the first two guards, who were grinning with delight as they escorted me from the door.

"Skitch was so excited to set this up for you," said one.

"You just made his day!"

I stopped cold. "*J'été humilié!*" I argued.

"*Humilié?*" they repeated as they looked at each other, hoping one or the other of them knew what I was saying. "Wait, wait, wait . . . humiliated?" one finally said.

"Yes."

"No, no, no, no, Michelle. Skitch gave you a gift. A very special gift. One to tell your kids someday."

"Yeah," entreated the other soldier. "When Skitch heard the general was coming to meet with local civic leaders, he planned a way for his special friend to meet the general."

I understood few of their words, but their intentions were very clear. This was intended to be a surprise . . . a gift, not a joke or a tease.

As I calmed down, they leaned close and put the event into perspective. "You just met the man who may save France and end this war!"

The longer I thought about that, the more awestruck I became. I had met General Patton!

I could not deny the sincerity of the four guards' excitement, and yet, when I reached Tire-Bouchon, I wagged my finger at him.

"Uh oh . . . Are you angry with me?" he asked as his look of anticipation melted into concern.

I tipped my head to the side and eyed him for a second. "Surprised. Terrified at first. But no. It was a lovely surprise. A day I will remember always. Thank you. But today, *you* are La Blague, the jokester!"

Our fun was short-lived. We had barely exited the building when a colonel pulled up beside Tire-Bouchon's truck, calling his name in a voice that clearly meant my friend was in trouble.

The color drained from the sergeant's face as he moved faster than I had ever seen the bulky man move. The colonel jutted his face forward into Tire-Bouchon's and used his finger like a dagger, pointing at my friend, and then at the truck, and then at me as he shouted about our earlier drive through the camp.

Tire-Bouchon took the stern rebuke, offering few replies. At the end, the colonel shot me a final glance and then wagged his finger a few more times at Tire-Bouchon before stomping away.

I remained on the stoop with the soldiers standing guard at *la Mairie*. They watched the entire painful display while I was torn between confessing my part in the scene and hiding from the terrifying officer. After the colonel was gone, Tire-Bouchon took a moment and then waved for me to come.

"I'm so sorry."

"No. It was my fault. I knew better."

"And La Blague? Is he in trouble too?"

"Yes. The colonel found him first. But I'm the ranking NCO. I was being irresponsible."

"Was the colonel mad because we were being silly?"

"Because we were being reckless. By putting you in the cab without restraints, we broke about a dozen protocols."

"But I am just a girl. I'm not a collaborator."

"The Germans have soldiers younger than you, and spies too. I know you're not a spy, but the colonel doesn't, and what if you *were* a spy? I allowed you to have access to my gun and potential control of a truck in the midst of hundreds of soldiers. If you had been a collaborator, you could have killed a lot of men today."

The implications caused the hair to rise on my arms.

"I need to get you home. La Blague and I have a long night of guard duty ahead."

"Is it okay for me to ride in the truck?"

"With conditions." Tire-Bouchon walked to the truck and pulled a set of handcuffs from inside. "You have to wear these from now on."

He clamped them on my wrists and helped me climb into the truck. As we drove past the site where our infraction had occurred, I raised my hands high to show off my restraints, and the men laughed and pointed at the poor embarrassed sergeants.

We'd both suffered a terrible humiliation that day, but our little adventure made me somewhat of a mascot in the camp and forever endeared Tire-Bouchon to me.

OUR HOPE THAT THE GERMANS HAD FLED HOME IN THE FACE of the Americans' arrival soon proved false. We were again reminded that the reason the American army was so near was because the battlefront was also very close. On September nineteenth, we were again greeted by the constant reverberations of munitions exploding to the east. The soldiers we regarded as friendly guests took on a battle-ready urgency as tank units and trucks loaded with GIs pushed east through mud and rain and fog toward Metz.

Even with the majority of the Third Army camped within a seven-kilometer radius of us, fears of a Nazi reoccupation and subsequent reprisals returned. I stopped Tire-Bouchon's truck on the street and asked him if we had reason to fear that the Nazis would return. His reply stung my heart and corrected my thinking. He said we didn't need to worry. The Nazis would not return to Braquis and Étain, but he wondered how many GIs that headed out today would also not return.

Several days passed before either of our friends visited us. When Tire-Bouchon finally stopped by our home, he could not speak about the battlefront, but when I naïvely asked if many soldiers had been hurt, disappointment and then sorrow clouded his face. He patted my hand with his giant paw and looked me in the eye. "Many die every day, Michelle. Many thousands every month."

I winced in disbelief. Surely, he was wrong. Those staggering monthly numbers of lost lives totaled more than the population of a thousand Braquis villages, but I saw the confirmation of the losses shining in his eyes. I wanted to look away, to avoid my own parents' humble confirmation that they too understood the cost. I longed to change the subject, to withdraw my question and erase the entire conversation, but I could not. Tire-Bouchon drilled those numbers into my heart, educating a naïve little French girl on the fundamental math of freedom. How the incalculable number of lives sacrificed to repel evil proved the value of each life they died to protect. I realized that the ink of those fallen soldiers' blood had written my personal worth into the very soil of France. They found me and every other oppressed European worthy of their sacrifice, and I needed to decide how that new understanding would change me.

Fewer than three decades had separated one deadly world war from another. The thought that another life-ending conflict could happen yet again was too grim, too defeating. Tire-Bouchon seemed to sense that.

He released my hand and sat back as his mood slowly brightened. In an animated mix of Frenglish, he explained, "And that's why you must live a full and happy life, Michelle. Not just survive, but really live. You need to make that red dress and go to that dance. You must laugh and date and fall in love and marry. And have lots of curly-headed babies with your spirit and spunk. Someday you will tell your children about this war, and my Patsy will tell hers, and others will share their stories. And hopefully, we will remember the cost and never have to do this again."

I contemplated the families whose lives were forever altered, in France, in England, in America, in Canada, and in every other nation either oppressed or sent to save them. How could anyone forget the gaping hole left in their family when a loved one's promise was extinguished by war. No one could ever forget that. Could they? I vowed to tell my children, if I had them, and congregations if I did not, but I began by doing what I could that day. I headed to the church where I lit many candles and prayed that the Allies would halt Nazi hopes of returning and that every soldier protecting us would also be protected as well.

New changes came the next day, when the commotion was in no distinct direction. I concluded that General Patton must be a genius to keep track of so many moving elements, as I could make no sense of the chaos, with tanks and men moving east and west, north and south, through crippling fog and rain and muck.

Planes began flying with greater frequency, and we could hear the echo of bomb drops and artillery blasts in the distance. By September 26th, Étain seemed to have reverted to its former state of confusion and fear. Few civilians were on the streets, and artillery fire could be heard by the *Caserne Sidi Brahim*. I ran my errands as quickly as possible. My daring trip was rewarded with a new letter from Légère, but I was saddened that I had still not heard a word from Lt. Richards. I banded Légère's letter with the others I picked up and turned quickly for home.

Légère's new letter was terse and cool. He included a photo of himself standing on a dock before a ship. Knowing so little of men, I sensed an undertone of jealousy in his admonishment for me to "be wise around the Allies, especially the American wolves." Though I wouldn't visit the post again for several days, I wrote him quickly, thanking him for his concern while assuring him that I was "being most prudent, and Jacques screens every American who passes through our door, and so far he likes each one very much." I purposely neglected to mention that the two soldiers who came to our home were both older and married.

I had been advised not to run my route for a few days, until the fighting outside of Étain ceased. Instead, I focused on my dress. Though the dance for which it was planned had been postponed, I refused to surrender to my fear that the Allies would not prevail. Instead, I cut out the pattern I had drawn upon pieces of newsprint and pinned them to double layers of the beautiful red fabric. The design was simple to avoid ostentation and allow the elegant silk and the bold color to speak for itself. I worked slowly and deliberately to not waste an inch of the silk since I planned to make Mother and perhaps myself, a blouse from the precious goods.

We missed the company of our American friends. They both looked harried and worn when they found a moment to make a quick visit. October's arrival did not lessen the intensity of the war. There was a strangeness about sitting at dinner passing a basket of rolls to the family, knowing men were heaving explosives at one another a few dozen kilometers away.

The air already carried the hint of fire on the morning of October the 8th. By afternoon, a thick plume of black crept across the skyline, and bits of greasy soot fell from the sky like black snow. The fire and smoke came from the southeast, in the direction of Nancy, a city the Americans had taken some weeks earlier. Father figured that a rubber fire at a tire factory in a neighboring town was likely the cause of the sooty smoke.

Tire-Bouchon and La Blague stopped by on October 12th. They were unusually quiet and sullen. When pressed, they explained that the base camp was being moved to Nancy. A few companies would remain to resupply General Walker's Division in Étain, as his numbers had been reduced by casualties and reassignments to other areas.

The camp packed up and moved with remarkable stealth and speed. They literally were there at breakfast and gone by supper, with a steady stream of men and vehicles heading southeast toward Nancy and the German border there, while others headed elsewhere, as if Patton's army were being sliced up like pie. We worried for our friends and for all the soldiers to whom we owed our very lives.

The skies and ground in our area were quieter, but we knew that meant the fight was merely heading on to Germany. Jacques knew a little about what awaited the Allies as they pushed on—a monstrous series of traps, fortifications, and minefields that had been laid for such an eventuality. I thought about Lt. Richards and wondered what new ugliness tore at his fragile spirit. I longed to hear from him, to simply know he was all right.

CHAPTER TWENTY-NINE

Our friends had been left to serve under General Walker, to make sure expected supplies moved forward as needed. We celebrated the happy news with a fine supper. They reminded me that the Liberty Dance was rescheduled for mid-November, and I told them I had kept my promise and was almost finished sewing my red parachute dress, which I refused to show them, insisting that they too would have to attend the dance if they wished to see it.

I collected no fewer than twelve invitations to the dance as the days passed. Mother suggested that Jacques escort me to the ball, where I could offer one dance to each of the soldiers who had invited me. The plan made me more comfortable than the prospect of an actual first date. Still, it seemed that Father understood my nervousness about my big social debut. He brought his accordion to life nearly every night so we could all practice dancing again. His music and our laughter almost always drew some neighbors and soldiers to our home, adding the sounds of harmonicas and guitars to the mix. No matter how many people played, the music felt a bit hollow, absent one musician, Armand, and his beautiful violin.

Those were happier days, and yet, in the distance, we heard the reverberation of war, and we were reminded that the battle between life and death still raged. We held on to what Tire-Bouchon said, that we must laugh and dance and live in gratitude for the gift of life and the freedom to gather. And so, we did gather often.

Sometimes our group grew so large that we had to move down to Father's shop. The American soldiers who came were of all ages and ranks. Some came to listen to the music and take a casual turn on the dance floor, seeking a respite from the ever-present crush of war. Some soldiers, single and married, flirted shamelessly with the local women, fat or thin, old or young. Ours was a safe family setting where they could feel at home in the glow of friendship and two one-hundred-watt bulbs. But some left the room and ventured into the night—men I did not know with women whose faces were familiar. Once again, Father said, "*C'est le guerre.*"

I eventually moved from being nervous when a young soldier asked me to dance to being disappointed when one did not. I learned to flirt like the other girls and found it quite fun, most likely because I knew Father and Jacques were always near, smiling and shaking their heads at my awkward steps into this new phase of womanhood.

Jacques was my prince, my knight, waiting for me to find my footing before allowing himself to leave my side and enjoy more romantic social opportunities with the young ladies in our village. The time had come for me to set him free.

One evening, during one of our impromptu dances, I flopped down in a chair beside where Jacques stood. I was exhausted from being swung around the floor on multiple soldiers' arms when each seemed determined to hop faster and swing wilder than the last.

When Jacques laughed at my frazzled state, I shot him a look in return. "What about you? When are you going to ask someone to dance?"

He shrugged off my question, but I saw his eyes drift to

Rachelle, a twenty-year-old farmer's daughter. I curbed my sarcasm and realized we had reached a moment when I could return the sibling advice he had always offered me. I nudged him with my elbow. "You're nineteen. Old enough to ask her to dance."

He rolled his dark eyes and brushed this comment away as he likewise brushed back a wave of dark hair.

"So serious," I teased.

"So big for her britches," he quipped as his lip curled into a smile.

"I promise you that in this very room there are at least five girls who will write pages in their diaries tonight if you so much as say hello to them."

He huffed and leaned back against Father's band saw positioned behind him, but I noticed that he didn't find my comments annoying enough to leave my company, so I carried on.

"They would much rather be with a local boy than a soldier who'll leave in a few weeks." I seemed to have hit a nerve.

He turned toward me, his smile gone and replaced by a scowl. "You really don't understand, Mimie. They enjoy the company of these American heroes."

"Hmmm." His poor assessment of my wisdom simmered as I added, "That's funny. I heard them call you a hero too."

His head cocked back like a rooster. "Me? A scarred man unfit to serve in the Free French Forces?"

"That's not how they see you, Jacques. You're brave, and you were injured because you tried to fight when most of us didn't dare."

He kicked at the wood floor and shoved his hands into his pockets as he turned his head away.

"I'm not so young as you think, brother. I'm old enough to catch the hounding disappointment of girls in this room over the way I've ruined the Liberty Dance for them."

"How?"

"Because you are escorting me."

He chuckled, and I heard a hint of pleasure within it.

"You're tall and handsome. And your professional prospects look good. Father says you're almost as good a machinist as him."

He huffed again. "I doubt that whether or not I can run a machine is of consequence to these young ladies."

"Well, you have another advantage over all those Americans."

"Such as?"

"You can actually communicate with the girls."

He nodded as a smile spread across his face, bursting into an even happier laugh. "Touché!" he said, rewarding my wisdom with a pat on my head.

I saw his eyes drift to the same young woman again. "I'm fine, Jacques. I don't need you to hover over me anymore. So long as I know you're near, I'll be all right."

He pushed away from the machine and stood erect. Then he gave my chin a soft pinch and shot a wink my way. "Maybe it would be good for you to have a little independence."

"I'm sure it would." I smiled as a little stitch tore in my heart. It was time to let go, but I knew in that moment that Jacques would never be just my Jacques again.

I watched the younger girls' private chatter increase as he moved across the room. Their flustered sighs also sounded as he asked Rachelle to dance. Thirteen-year-old Titi pointed while nine-year-old Gilbert giggled at Jacques. Peace and calm filled Mother and Father. We were almost back to normal. Almost . . .

I went home and tried to recall the names of all the young soldiers with whom I danced. We had no dance cards, and I could remember only a few. Their flirtatious smiles and overt familiarity seemed to blur one face into another. Interestingly enough, I found myself thinking of only two young men: Légère the most astute flirt I knew, and Lt. Richards, the least sociable soldier I'd ever met.

I pulled some stationery out to write Légère about the evening. Not to make him jealous, merely to let him know I was not pining away for him as he explored the world's shores, but my words ran on and on. The evening's dance became but a mention along with a brief note about the upcoming ball. My petty concerns and flirtations seemed just that to me. I longed for one thing from the past four years: my former chats with Légère about the deeper things of life.

As page after page filled, so did my heart, not with romantic notions, but with spiritual ones. I felt a renewed confirmation that my faith had not gone cold as I had feared. The seeds of my faith were always there. Though dormant, they'd carried me on, helping me stand and breathe and work and love when I imagined how easy it would be to just die. And they were swelling within me again, as if they'd finally found moist ground.

As I wrote, I felt like the teacher, sharing wisdom Tire-Bouchon had taught me about the exquisite value of life, even a battered life like mine, and the indescribable humility I felt when I realized that, like Christ, modern saviors literally had, and literally were, laying down their lives that others might live.

THE TEMPERATURE DROPPED, AND MUDDY ROADS TURNED thick and rutted as October turned to November. I could barely keep both hands on the handlebars for all the waving I did in reply to the helloes and cheers from soldiers I passed. My courtesy nearly landed me in a ditch on more than one occasion.

Excitement brightened one foggy, cold day with the arrival of Marlene Dietrich, a film actress, and her touring comedy troupe who came to entertain the troops. Aside from this bright moment, a sense of urgency and tension, as thick as fog, pervaded the camp, as if the soldiers were horses in harness, prancing in anticipation and ready to bolt.

Each day's weather was more dismal and miserable than the last. I was soaked and cold by the time I reached Étain each day, and then I had the uncomfortable ride home. I commiserated with the poor soldiers who were always wet without a dry warm house waiting for them. They slogged through ankle-deep mud, remaining more vigilant than before, if that were possible, in preparation for what we assumed was a critical battle on the horizon.

Many limped in obvious pain. Mother guessed that their distress was from constantly wet feet, and when asked, Tire-Bouchon confirmed that they were smitten with trench foot. Mother encouraged families to offer what meager help they could, by setting up drying stations in their homes, where the Americans' clothes and boots could finally dry.

Rain fell every day that first November week. Thunder woke me on the morning of November eighth, but stars shone through the window, and I knew the rumble was not from thunder but from artillery fire to the east. By noon, the curious smell of artillery smoke filled the air, and a white smoky ribbon floated above the land in the direction of Metz.

The sky filled with planes on November ninth. Nearly as many as the sands of the sea. The air pulsed with the hum of engines and then the concussive whoosh of countless bombs began, as if Metz was being pounded into the center of the earth.

In contrast, the air was almost still on the eleventh, and though the rain persisted, we saw very few planes and little smoke. That pattern of intense bombing and then quiet continued. Bombers flew and dropped their ordinance one day, and then they stopped while the ground troops began their push forward. Proof of our theory came as we saw a marked increase in trucks ferrying badly wounded men to hospitals whenever the number and severity of the wounds overwhelmed or exceeded the medical services available near the front.

I made my last delivery for the day and headed for Braquis in a drizzle on the eleventh, hungry for home, dry clothes, and a spot near the woodstove. I rode into the yard and jumped off to push my bike into the sheep shed, where I kept it. As I opened the shed door, the inner door, which led to the house, also opened, and there in the doorway stood a man I both barely recognized and could never forget. His hair was still wet as if he'd come fresh from a bath. He wore my oldest brother's clothes, but though four years had passed, he appeared to have shrunk instead of grown. The clothes hung on him as if they'd been sewn for someone else entirely. I could see the points of his shoulders through his shirt. His face was lean, with sunken cheeks and creases that formed at the edges of his eyes and mouth, but despite all that, I knew this was the brother I feared I'd never see again in this life.

"Armand?" My throat grew thick.

His trembling smile and moist eyes pulled me out of my daze. I tossed the bike aside and ran into his thin arms. He held me softly against his bony breast, saying, "Mimie. My little Mimie. Still so little and yet, no longer a child."

The chorus of the little boys' excited chatter accompanied our tears as Armand and I held one another and cried. When I lifted my head and looked behind Armand to the hall where my family stood, I saw both the pain that underlined my parents' love and the sorrow-tinged relief on Jacques' face. Their joy was soft and reverent and holy, in recognition of the miracle standing before us. An answer to thousands of prayers, old and new, given in quiet and watered with tears. Armand was home! We'd made it! We had all survived.

I reached a hand up and touched his cheek. "When did you get home? Where have you been?"

"There's time for all that. Right now, I just want to look at you." He took my hands and pulled back to gaze at me. "I missed it."

"What?"

"Your transformation from a trapeze artist to a young woman. You're so beautiful, Mimie. I heard how we almost lost Jacques. And the little boys! Titi is nearly as tall as Jacques was when I was captured, and I needed Mother to convince me that this lean seven-year-old was once our chubby little Gilbert. I've missed you all so much. And I've heard how brave you've been."

"Not brave. Just determined."

"Determined is a close cousin to brave."

His use of the word cousin brought to mind our cousin Pierre who was also swept up when the Germans captured the French army company the boys joined.

Jacques piped up first. "What of Pierre? Is he home as well?"

Armand looked over his shoulder and gave Jacques a thoughtful nod before closing his eyes. His expression was one of deep pleasure, as if he had breathed in the aroma of hot bread. "*Home* . . . I'll never take that word for granted again. But yes, we traveled together as far as Ville-en-Woëvre. He should have made it home to Doncourt-aux-Templiers about the same time I arrived here."

I rushed to hug him again. "I've missed you so. We prayed for you every day, but we had begun to fear you were—"

I felt him place a kiss on my head. "I know. I feared the same about all of you. We've been blessed, so come, sit. We both have much to tell one another."

He slid his arm around my waist and led me into the house as the family shuffled into the kitchen, where the table was spread with food. The door to the dining room was open, but the room where visiting American officers bunked was empty.

Mother noticed my glance. "They've left for a few days, so we could have the house to ourselves."

I was grateful for the privacy to feel and respond without curious eyes upon us. I noticed a bundle of torn and dirty clothes balled in the corner. I assumed these rags were the clothes Armand arrived in. My eyes burned as I imagined what he'd survived.

"Tell me everything," I said, barely letting go of his hand long enough to close the door to the shed.

He pulled a chair out for me and sat in the one beside it.

"Shall I bore the rest of the family with the same story?"

Their reply was an obvious yes as they each pulled out their own chairs and sat around the big circular table. Armand avoided giving many details about his capture and treatment, focusing instead on bullet points about the past four years.

"They marched us to a camp and loaded us onto a truck headed for Germany. We arrived at an island processing center, where they asked us questions about our skills and education. When they asked who had farming experience, Pierre and I raised our hands. We were soon moved to a farm where we lived and worked until the harvest was over, then we were transferred to a city where we spent the winter in a factory."

"Day and night?" I asked.

"They had a barracks. The guards rotated us in and out for shifts."

"Like a prison?" Gilbert asked.

Armand glanced at our parents' expectant and sullen faces, offering only, "Something like that."

Gilbert slipped from his chair and stood next to Armand, wrapping his little arm around his big brother and laying his head on his shoulder.

"Oh, Armand. I'm so sorry," I said.

"It followed a pattern. In spring, we were sent to a farm somewhere for planting and back to a factory after harvest. We didn't mind the farm work. We had sunshine and the food was plentiful, but people were starving in the cities, and our factory work assignments left us sick by spring, when we were grateful to return to a farm."

Titi slid to the front of his chair and said, "Tell her how you escaped!"

Armand smiled at him. "You tell her."

"He hid in cabbages!"

"In cabbages?" I asked.

"Not exactly *in* them. We were always under guard wherever we were assigned, but we believed our best chance of escape would be during a farm assignment because we were always moving. We also noticed another pattern. The age of the guards started changing last year, as if the Germans were running out of men. Military-aged guards were sent to the front, leaving young boys and old men to guard us. Last October we knew our best chance had come."

"Because you wanted to get home," said Gilbert.

He rubbed his forehead against Gilbert's. "Very badly."

"After loading produce for shipping, we planned our escape. We loaded and stacked crates of cabbage onto a truck, leaving enough space for Pierre and me to hide between them. When the truck drove past a wooded area, we grabbed two heads of cabbage each and jumped out. Eventually, we came to a village with a little church. By then we were out of food, and the weather was bitter cold. We needed shelter soon or our escape would have been for nothing, so we knocked on the pastor's door late one night and threw ourselves on his mercy. We got lucky. He was a good man, opposed to the Nazis, and dedicated to helping the people who suffered at their hands. He moved us on through a network of other sympathetic Germans who were hiding Jews from the SS. When we heard that much of France was liberated, we traveled at night and pushed on to the border. We moved slowly, opting for safety instead of speed, but"—he swallowed past the lump in his throat and scanned every face at the table—"everything I dreamed of those four years, and on my long walk back, is right here, sitting at this table. I'm so grateful to be home."

We smothered him in love as we ate and swapped happy memories around the big circular table. I had come to hate that table and the memories it held, of serving the very people who abused and oppressed us, and of sitting around it on the day when the Nazis terrorized us. But I couldn't see the faces of my Nazi tormenters anymore. I would never forget what happened, the hardships and the fear, but those faces were gone. Instead, I saw only expressions of love as we reclaimed our lives through the sharing of old memories, like those we made that night.

CHAPTER THIRTY

O ne amusing by-product of our freedom was the return of the local gossip mill, which seemed especially energized by the escape of Armand and Pierre. It took a week to track down the path of the story, but it seemed to have occurred like this.

News of the young men's return spread through Braquis and our cousin's hometown of Doncourt-aux-Templiers where Légère's family, the Duboises, also lived. When the Duboises heard the happy news, they sent a letter about the joyous information to their son, Légère, who sent me a letter congratulating our family before I even thought to write him of the news. I had just come home from my route and sat down to read his letter when the phone rang and Mother announced that the call was for me.

As soon as I heard his voice, my brain and lips went numb, rendering them completely incapable of delivering a coherent word. My only salvation was that once I managed a squeaky, "Hello?" Légère filled in the scratchy silence with ease.

"Hello, Michelle. It's Légère. I'm calling you from England. My parents told me about Armand's return. I'm so happy for you."

"Thank you . . ." As I struggled to come up with a mature second thought, Armand completely sidetracked me, making my anxiety worse by shooting me silent, silly looks to make me laugh, antics only an older brother could relish.

"It's so nice of you to think of us, Légère. Yes, Armand's return is a miracle. Then you must know that Pierre is home also."

"So I heard. How is Armand?"

"Armand? Oh . . . he is doing very well, thank you," I replied as I squeezed into the wall, trying to ignore my older brother, who threatened to tickle me. "He's thin and weak . . ." Armand stopped one form of pestering to hobble about the kitchen, exaggerating my point until I laughed. "And he's very rude."

Légère laughed as well. "He's right there, listening, isn't he?"

"Yes," I said, surrendering all hope of sounding mature.

"I wish I could be there too. I miss the sound of your laughter. I think I've only truly heard it once, but hearing it now takes me back to that moment. I miss our talks, Michelle."

I felt a shift in the mood from vigilant protector to something else. "So do I."

Armand also seemed to sense the shift. He offered me a wink and a smile before heading upstairs, as if finally seeing me as I was instead of as he wished to remember me.

"I bet Armand hardly recognized you since you've grown."

"He was surprised, but then . . . the war and time have changed us all."

"Some for the better. Like you. And I'm not the only one who notices. Mother's letters confirm that you are quite the American soldiers' favorite."

"Hardly, but please thank her. You look very handsome in your uniform."

"So, you already received my last letter?"

"Yes, and the photos."

An operator cut in, requesting that Légère add additional coins to the pay phone he was using. While he obliged and the phone clinked, I studied the photos. Unlike the toll of time on Armand, the years had been good to Légère. He was lean and muscled, with squared shoulders that filled every centimeter of his uniform. There was no trace of boyishness left in his face, owing in part to the military cut of his dark hair and the serious set of his mouth. American soldiers struck similar poses for their photos. But those penetrating eyes were unmistakably Légère's, and I was pleased to see that they reflected strength and hope.

One photo pictured him with a few fellow sailors standing in a crowded festival of happy people, many of whom were young women. In the other, he was sitting alone on a rock, thoughtful and pensive, as he looked out at the sea. It was clear that this was where his heart lay.

"England appears to have been kind to you. Besides a ship, it seems you also found some pretty girls there."

His laugh began with a choke or a cough. "A few, perhaps . . . but none prettier than the girls in France."

My heart warmed at his thoughtfulness, but I looked at the pictured young women's styled hair and clothes and then at my reflection, and I knew he was being kind. Britain had been severely bombed in the early years, but she and her people were further in their recovery than France and her citizens, whose every day was lived beneath the boot of Nazi occupation. Even then, I could hear the echo of artillery just a few kilometers away. Survival was still our primary concern.

Even Paris, the city of style and art, had been reduced to a place of poverty, where most French women would choose a baguette of warm bread over a new dress. The war had made us . . . pragmatic. Even we young women. And while, to some, pragmatism might conjure pitiable images of boring, old, unadventurous people, I knew better. I loved my moments of fun and excitement, but I clung to the timeless principles of faith, hard work, and steadfastness. What I still craved was peace.

"I'm anxious to get back to France and be assigned to a French ship. Have you given any thought to your future, Michelle? Whether you'll become a nun?"

"I'm not in a rush to decide. And what of you? Will you leave the Navy when the fighting ends, or will you make it your vocation?"

He paused before answering. I thought I heard him swallow, as if he needed a drink of spirits before releasing the words, "I believe I will stay in." His voice had an apologetic tone, as if we both knew the greater meaning of his decision. His choice to live and fight on the seas would continue to separate our once-aligned paths.

Other voices called out to Légère in the background, some male, some female, asking him to hurry back to their group.

"I'm proud of you, Légère. The Navy is lucky to have you. So is France. Your courage and optimism kept my hope alive when it was growing dim, and I'll always be grateful to you for that."

Seconds passed before he answered, and when he did, his voice was as soft as suede. "I wish I could have done more."

"You did what you could. You did what I needed. And in case you ever doubt that, I want you to know that I carried one of your letters in my pocket every day for years—the one where you promised that we would be free again. By the time I began running the PTT route, I had committed it to memory, and I carried it in my heart so no one could search me and take that promise from me. When times were the worst and I thought I really might die, I clung to that promise, Légère."

"I'm glad. Very glad. Thank you for telling me that." He cleared his throat. "And what now? The Allies will win this war, your big brother is home, and I am without a purpose. You have no need for a surrogate second brother anymore."

"No, I don't, but I'll always need my friend."

I heard the clink of glasses as voices called out to him again. He'd found a new place and a new purpose in this world. His life was large and exciting. It suited him well.

"I'll always be here for you, Michelle."

"And I for you."

We hit a moment of silence, as if we knew we'd each said all we knew to say, and yet we dreaded ending the call.

The operator clicked back and said, "You have thirty seconds, or please deposit another coin."

"We're out of time. I should be heading back to my ship soon anyway."

"Of course. Thank you for calling. It was wonderful to speak to you again."

"Like old times."

"Yes. Just like when we met."

Stilted pauses followed each line, as if finding the next word became harder for each of us.

"I'll call you next leave."

"I'll look forward to it."

"I'll always love you, my little Michelle. No matter where I go, know that you'll be tucked into my heart."

"And you in mine, Légère."

"Goodbye then."

"Yes. Goodbye."

Like the last bit of air rushing from a balloon, the call and the special bond we shared simply ran out. Out of time . . . out of shared need . . . out of common ground.

Our final expressions of love echoed in my head for a time. They weren't romantic. I accepted that perhaps, they never had been. That they were just a young girl's dreams upheld by an older boy's need to be someone's hero.

Perhaps he would call again, or we'd meet on a street someday when we were older and settled into separate lives. If that day came, I'd still love Légère, knowing he'd walked me through a dark time to a safer, brighter fork in the road.

I'd spent four years wishing away fearful days while longing for a return to past happiness. I didn't want to lose another day looking back. Pleasant or not, those circumstances made me who I'd become. It was time to inventory my gains and move forward. Time for me to claim my future.

CHAPTER THIRTY-ONE

P lanes flew continually back and forth toward Germany. We could no longer hear bombs or artillery fire as the battle moved away from us and nearer the border. The flow of supplies felt like a living organism, inhaling vehicles, food, fuel, and reinforcements from the west, and exhaling those critical men and goods east to the front. Our only measure of the ferocity of the fight was the number of Army trucks and ambulances racing the injured to local hospitals and clinics.

Tire-Bouchon and La Blague honked and occasionally stopped as their vehicles passed, but their visits were few as the push for Germany sped on. New officers arrived in our home and moved on so quickly that we barely got to know them before they were gone. The entire area felt as if it were in commotion. Cold temperatures, rain, snow, and ice made the thought of a long winter fight unimaginable.

November eighteenth, the date of the Liberty Dance, arrived, but we wondered how many soldiers would be available or of a mindset to attend. Some said it would lift morale, but it seemed almost obscene to enjoy such frivolous entertainment with war raging a few dozen kilometers away. And then Tire-Bouchon pulled out his military Bible and read this passage to me:

To EVERY THING *there is a season, and a time to every purpose under the heaven: A time to be born, and a time to die; a time to plant, and a time to pluck up that which is planted; A time to kill, and a time to heal; a time to break down, and a time to build up; A time to weep, and a time to laugh; a time to mourn, and a time to dance.* (Ecclesiastes 3:1)

A time to dance . . .

With that comfort, we moved ahead with our plans.

Jacques was taking Rachelle, and since Armand and I were each in need of some moral support, we planned to go together.

Mother relished this first chance to celebrate my teen years. She spent over an hour the night before the dance, rolling my shoulder-length hair into sections using strips of cloth which she tied near my scalp. Sleeping was hard to impossible, both because of the knotted fabric covering my head, and the butterflies in my nervous stomach.

My parachute dress had exceeded my expectations. I gave it a scooped neckline that was demure rather than daring, set off by an inch-wide collar. The bodice was form-fitted to me and unadorned, aside from the back zipper. There was enough fabric to gather it into a full skirt that floated over a crinoline. It swished and swayed around my calves when I walked, and it flared when I twirled, as if it would return to its former purpose and once again take flight. As much as I loved the feel of the unforgiving silk, I tried not to touch it and dared not eat while wearing it out of fear that it would stain before my debut.

Mother lent me her pearl necklace and earrings. Father made me a new pair of wooden-soled platform shoes for the event. I felt like a princess as I twirled in my room, but my brothers' awed silence as I descended the stairs meant more to me than their many spoken compliments. I had sewn a red silk tie for each of them from scraps, and Mother made them new linen shirts for the occasion. Their suit coats were too short for either young man, so Mother cut them down into handsome vests.

Mother, Father, and the little boys went ahead to the dance in a local farmer's wagon so Father could warm up with the band. As soon as they were gone, Jacques and Armand engaged in a fun little rivalry over who would get my sweater, who would place it on my shoulders, and who would sit with me when a neighbor's truck came to pick us up. Their assurances that I looked nice were confirmed by the stir in the room when I arrived, looking little like the tomboyishly dressed PTT officer who rode a bike through the communities each day.

The ball was held at *la Mairie*. Flags adorned the outside and were the predominant decorations inside as well. Local families made up half the attendees. They dressed in what I knew was their finest attire. For most local people, that meant mended and washed Sunday clothes because few pieces of finery survived without having been ravaged to provide a treasured satin headband for a child or some meager ornamentation for a flour-sack dress. A few women had managed to hold on to an old party dress, but already shy as I was, I felt conspicuous in a new dress made of red silk, of all things.

The evening began with a welcome and a few speeches made by Étain's mayor and an American officer. Both countries' national anthems were sung, and then the band began to play. Soldiers continually trickled in, dressed in washed Army green. Some stood near the walls before joining in. Meanwhile, others took only seconds to find an unescorted woman before setting off to the dance floor. Armand took my first dance, and Jacques, my second, giving my brothers time to be sure I would not languish alone near a wall if they pursued more romantic options during the evening. Their concerns were completely unfounded as the number of men greatly outnumbered the available women. I barely finished one dance when a new partner appeared behind the gentleman currently leading me along. While I was more than happy to see some dances end, some partners were so engaging that I dreaded to hear the music stop.

The band primarily played traditional French tunes, but as the evening drew on, and the wine flowed, some American soldiers requested songs the band didn't know. The band took on a revolving door composition to resolve that issue as soldiers with varying levels of musical talent left their partners and borrowed the band members' instruments to play more contemporary American tunes.

We laughed and cringed and sometimes were awed by the sounds the constantly changing band produced. Likewise, the dance floor opened to allow demonstrations of new dance steps. We picked some up quickly and stumbled through others, laughing as we stepped on toes and made new friends.

Jacques danced my way with Rachelle in his arms and tapped me on my shoulder.

"Mimie. Look!"

I glanced in the direction he was pointing, and saw Armand make his way to the bandstand. Father's friend, a local musician who still held his own violin, extended his instrument to Armand. My brother nodded gratefully and accepted the proffered loan. There was a pause in the room as the band waited for Armand, who visibly savored the feel and reverently drew in the scent of the beautiful instrument's polished wood.

Some soldiers, ignorant to the moment's poignancy, grumbled about the delay, but a hush fell over the room as our French neighbors whispered explanations about Armand's return from captivity and his own precious violin, destroyed during the first days of the occupation.

Armand fingered the bow and plucked at the strings, making

minor tuning adjustments, and then he positioned the violin on his shoulders, lifted the bow and closed his eyes as he brought the instrument to life.

Complex runs bled into a mournful rendition of "La Marseillaise," which bit into our hearts with earnest supplication. We didn't move or speak as verse after verse played almost as visibly upon Armand's face as it did through the violin. Those who knew of Armand's incarceration understood the pain that drove his bow and fingers, but we who lived a similar hell, and those who fought to end it, understood that his playing was more than a musical performance. It was a musical cry of grief.

Tears were shed as we counted those no longer with us and the parts of ourselves that were also lost. Then, as if the time for grief was over, Armand's brow lined and his jaw clenched, and the instrument burst into a triumphal chorus, a shout that called us to action, to which we responded in voice:

Aux armes, CITOYENS!
Formez vos bataillons!
Marchons! Marchons!
Qu'un sang impur
Abreuve nos sillons!

THE MOOD CHANGED AGAIN as Armand brought the tempo and volume down. He pulled the bow back and forth across the strings in a cadence that felt like a march. His gift returned to him as he translated music he'd heard into the violin's strings. Strains of America's national anthem played, and proud emotional soldiers sang.

When Armand finished playing, we all felt spent, needing a moment to collect ourselves. Our parents rushed in upon him, and he welcomed their embrace. The moment had been transformational for Armand, as if the hungry, weak, timid man captivity shrank had found himself in those moments. When Armand returned the violin to its owner, he stood erect and confident. Our old Armand, the inner man untouched by the Nazis' mistreatment and denial, was before us again, renewed, reborn, and returned.

He and Jacques and I rode home in the back of a truck with other partygoers as we snuggled under a thick layer of blankets. It had been a perfect evening, a glimmer of a future we could hardly imagine but for which we happily prayed.

CHAPTER THIRTY-TWO

R eality returned the next morning as more trucks and ambulances sped by, a reminder that while the dance had shielded us from the war for a few hours, the battle continued and, in fact, had intensified.

Tire-Bouchon dropped a few frozen turkeys off at our house and asked Mother if she would roast them. When she said she would and asked what occasion required so many turkeys, he replied that Thursday the twenty-third was the American Thanksgiving or day of thanks.

"May I bring a few friends to share the meal with your family?"

After Mother assured him that they'd be welcome, he wrote down instructions on how to prepare the birds in true American fashion as he babbled on about Pilgrims and Indians and pumpkins and such. Even I, the person in the family who was the most proficient at English, could not follow everything he said, but his excitement was undeniable, and we felt his longing for home.

He drew feathers and a funny hat on paper sacks. We painted the pictures and cut them out for decorations, growing as excited for Thanksgiving as Tire-Bouchon. On November twenty-second, a truck roared into town honking its horn. Men in the bed shouted the news that General Leclerc's French forces had taken Alsace and were pressing on to Strasbourg, fulfilling his oath to fight until "our flag flies over the Cathedral of Strasbourg."

We jumped for joy and cheered and hugged one another. We noticed Tire-Bouchon's reserved smile.

"This is wonderful news, isn't it?" I asked.

"Sure, it is," he said with forced assurance. "It's great news. A proud moment for your country."

He left soon after Father ran inside to turn on the radio. The news confirmed that Alsace was again in French hands. That grand news was dimmed by the reports of large numbers of German deserters and agonizing casualties on all sides as the Allies pressed on. The Allies had paid a high price to get the French soldiers through to Alsace. That sacrifice had barely been considered in our moment of national pride. It was likely the cause of Tire-Bouchon's reluctant smile.

The radio played in the background on Thanksgiving Day while our American guests shared stories of Pilgrims and home. Gratitude swelled in each of us, making throats tight and hearts full. By late afternoon, the radio signaled an important upcoming announcement. We gathered around the set and listened for the report:

UNITS *of the French 2nd Armored Division entered Strasbourg and raised the Free French tricolore over Strasbourg Cathedral at 2:30 pm.*

I WAS STILL unsure of the significance of this particular victory. "Is this the end of the war?" I asked.

"No, Mimie," said Father. "But it means that France is almost free."

We made certain not to forget all the Allies who paved the way for that glorious day. They considered the taking of Strasbourg a major Allied victory as well. I ran to the church so the bells could ring out the news, as the soldiers' joy and ours spilled into the streets. The end had to at least be close, or so I naïvely assumed, but as one day merged into another, and more truckloads of soldiers moved east toward the front, I saw how wrong I was.

MANY YEARS EARLIER, FATHER BOUGHT MOTHER A SWISS clock. Each hour, a little man exited through two swinging doors and rang a bell once for each hour of the day before withdrawing back into his little house for fifty-nine more minutes. I calculated that he spent twenty-three hours and forty-nine minutes a day waiting to ring a bell seventy-eight times. So much sacrifice for so little reward. The same could be said of the Allied troops that bitter winter of 1944/45.

The Allies and the Nazis dug in. Each tried any and all options to gain a bit of ground. We saw bombers fly sorties to the east and north on a regular basis, and we heard stories of creative Nazi strategies. One involved tying a lantern to a cow's back and having a soldier, dressed as a farmer, walk it into an Allied camp as if he were a friend. Then tank companies followed the lantern's light into the heart of our troops.

War was terrible. We heard accounts of women snipers positioned to attack Allied troops. So many Nazi sympathizers were embedded in the region that no one could be trusted.

We saw the toll on the tired faces of the soldiers left in camp—those recovering from trench foot or simply too sick in body or mind to fight, and those assigned to care for them or ferry what few supplies or fresh troops arrived. Tire-Bouchon and La Blague had been called to the front, along with other men not considered riflemen, all because too few replacements were coming. Freedom became fragile again. Time stood still. For everyone, except those on guard at the front.

Life dragged on. The PTT route that had become a pleasantry was little more than an assignment for me. Tire-Bouchon and La

Blague were gone, and there were no letters from Légère. I had long stopped hoping to find a letter from Lt. Richards, though I still wished he would write. Étain had an airbase, which required pilots and support staff, but by mid-December, they were so busy, both on the ground preparing for or recovering from a run, or in the air attacking German positions, that we rarely saw any servicemen at our home.

I drove by the airfield weekly. I knew some of the pilots and which planes they preferred to fly. When I saw my friends' planes on the ground, I cheered, and when I didn't see them, I prayed. When days passed without a plane's return, I cried, knowing that another friend was lost.

Our family huddled by our radio at night. The incessant rain left half the neighbors sick, so Mother was busy nursing people during the day, with my help when I was home. I looked forward to surrendering the PTT route to someone else so I could be *l'aide aux mères* fulltime, helping expectant mothers and caring for babies, experiencing the hope of life again.

I spent more time praying about my future, asking God to show me what life he had spared me for—as a nun or as a wife and mother. Both were lives of service. I could think of nothing nobler than the life my mother had lived, but no clear answers came to me, and time dragged on.

People arrived long before the start of our Christmas Eve service to pray in quiet and to light candles. We all had cause for gratitude and cause to mourn. Mostly, I think we gathered to pray for the success of the soldiers in whose hands our fate still remained. There was a certain selfishness to our pleas, and it did not go unnoticed that on this holiest of nights as we celebrated the birth of the babe sent to save the world, we were praying for other saviors, far from their home—some who'd died and some who would die—all who came to save the free world.

Their sacrifices had yielded no great victories lately. In fact, the news had been sobering at best. The threat of a German return loomed, and so we lit our candles and sang and prayed together, hoping the sacred smoke and our voices mingled and rose to God's ear, asking Him to give victory and safety to the men who formed the last line between the destroyers and us.

The world nearly stopped on January fifth when reports were made of a German push to reclaim the hotly contested Alsace region. We knew such a return would likely mean death for every French person living in that area, and we were not so very far away. We held our breath and prayed. Days passed before we knew the outcome of the German offensive and the answer to those prayers. Tears of joy were shed by some when the radio reported that the Germans had been pushed back, but they now had a new offensive —the Bulge.

The news reported multiple offensives through January—the Bulge, the Ardennes, Bastogne, and the Siegfried Line. Reports finally trickled on about Allied successes over the coming weeks and months. As the Allies pressed farther into Germany it became clear that the Germans were not only fighting to gain ground but to conceal the barbarism that would shock and horrify the world.

I could barely listen to the radio anymore as the eyes of the world shifted from battle lines to Soviet descriptions of a concentration camp called Auschwitz. The Soviets had found proof of a similar camp the previous summer and reported the atrocities found there, but perhaps ignorance, coupled with willful blindness, allowed us to discount how widespread and depraved such horrors were. Six thousand nearly dead humans survived death marches and starvation to testify of the depravity. The witness of hundreds of thousands more would be told only through their remains.

As the Allies pressed in from the east and south, the Soviets' press west uncovered more of these camps through the spring. While we were turning the earth for crops, soldiers were digging up mass graves. The obscenity of it all was unfathomable, and perhaps even more incomprehensible was that even knowing all this, life went on. It had to, of course, or what was the point of surviving at all? I told myself that we continued to live our lives, in part, in homage to those who died with a prayer of freedom on their lips.

A curious postcard, addressed to me, turned up in the mail in late March. I sat outside the post office and read the simple message:

Michelle,

I finally decided to take you up on your offer to write. I am well. I hope you are also. I have no doubt that we will end this war soon. I hope to hear from you.

1st Lt. Denny Richards

SMUDGES of erasure marks marred the card. Even knowing as little of the shy officer as I did, I could easily imagine how many times he wrote, erased, and rewrote his simple message before finally sending it off. That he sent anything was a marvel to me.

I returned to the post office window and dashed off a quick note in return.

Dear 1st Lt. Richards,

I was so delighted and relieved to hear that you are well. I have prayed for your safety and wondered where you are. The news has been so terrible. We have worried over you and our other friends. I trust your word and will take heart in this hopeful news! I hope you will pass our way before you go home.

You remain in my prayers.

Michelle Naget

THE LIST OF DEATH CAMPS, scattered in every quadrant of Germany, increased until the numbers staggered us—hellish places called Buchenwald, Dora-Mittelbau, Flossenbürg, Dachau, Mauthausen, Neuengamme, Bergen-Belsen, and others. Most were filled with ghostlike survivors and surrounded by mass graves. I struggled to understand how any human could do what Hitler and his followers had reportedly done, but I had witnessed the acts of depravity committed by some Nazis, and remembering that cruelty made me accept that the SS could sanction even greater suffering.

How would we heal? How would the survivors of such horror

move on? I thought of our friends, Lt. Richards, Tire-Bouchon, and La Blague, and the countless other soldiers whose smiles had passed through our doors. How could they ever forget what they had seen?

Bombers flew directly north into Germany. Reports of hits on Berlin left us wondering what of that city would remain at the end of the war. The news of Hitler's death was received with sobering gratitude on the last day of April. Heaven help us, but we were glad he was dead.

The end of the war was just a matter of time, but the return to normal? We weren't sure if that could ever truly be. The formal signing on May 8th was a beginning, but we were a nation divided and a people who had both heroes and traitors to deal with. I was glad the work of sorting all that out was left to others.

As for us, we'd done what we could, resisted where we were able, and helped those we could reach. We could testify to more than a few miracles. In the times of greatest trial, faith and love had kept us plodding on another day.

There was a knock on the door in early June. When I answered it, I found Lt. Richards standing on our doorstep. He was handsomely dressed in a new uniform. His brown wavy hair was freshly cut, and except for a scar on his chin, he seemed well and whole and unharmed. That was his condition on the outside. His darting eyes, which shifted with every movement in his range of sight, and the nervous way he fingered his hat, attested that he was still feeling the effects of the war on the inside.

"Lt. Richards! Come in! Come in!"

He dipped his head as my family rushed to welcome him. His hand rose in a tentative wave to all, and then, with a second encouraging invitation, he came inside.

His glance shifted repeatedly as if overwhelmed by our effusive welcome. He took a seat, and Mother and I set food out as he explained the assignment that brought him to Étain, allowing time for a quick visit to us. The boys fired off questions about the Nazis' defeat. He touched on some topics and was conspicuously deflective on others. We ate and laughed and listened to whatever stories he chose to tell. Most were jokes about military cuisine or tales of his enlisted friends.

When the conversation grew thin, Father looked across the table and said, "It's getting warm in here. Michelle, why don't you take the lieutenant outside for a walk while we help your mother clean up?"

Relief showed on the officer's face as I led him outside and to the backyard.

"I remember that you like crayfish. We have some. In our stream."

"Lead on," he said in his Louisiana drawl as he pointed forward with the hat in his hand.

"I wondered if you'd ever write. I'm glad you did."

He gave a tight smile and walked on without further remark.

"Why did you wait so long?"

He stuttered and stumbled for a few seconds before saying, "My mind . . . what I'd seen . . . so many hard things. I had a girl-friend back home when I enlisted, but I couldn't figure out what to write to her after Normandy, so I wrote nothing, and she stopped writing too. After a while, I figured I had nothing worth saying inside me. I just did my job and carried on. A chaplain told me to talk to someone, but I couldn't think of anyone I felt comfortable with, anyone who could understand what I was feeling. And then, you handed me your address. With all you and your family had been through, I knew you would understand."

"I would like to hear your story, Lieutenant, but why did you wait six months to write?"

He gave me a wry smile. "First, will you call me Denny?"

"Yes." I chuckled.

"Why did I delay? I knew where I was headed. I figured there was no sense in starting a correspondence when the next letter could be my last, so I waited until I felt confident I would make it out okay."

As sobering as it sounded, I understood his reasoning.

We sat in soft grass by the stream's edge and talked until the sun began to set. He opened up and told me more about where he'd been and how he'd been injured and sent to a field hospital for a time. I saw his eyes redden and fill with tears.

"Have you heard of Buchenwald?" he asked.

"No, but it must have been awful."

He nodded and drew the back of his hand across his eyes. "Human skeletons . . . piles of bodies . . . and the stories the survivors told . . ." He leaned back and shook his head as if to knock the images from his mind. He finally offered a sigh that faltered into a gasp. "It was worse than Normandy. I thought nothing could be worse than that. My senior officer called me a hero when he gave me my bronze star and purple heart. I wondered how I could be a hero when I was shaking like a rabbit inside."

He was shaking just from telling of the experience. I touched his arm and looked into his eyes. "Maybe that makes you an even bigger hero."

"You really understand, don't you?"

"Yes."

"Because you've also had to be brave when you thought you couldn't."

"Like you, many times."

"Except your battlefield was in your home." His mouth pinched and his eyes became soft and narrow. "Did they ever . . . hurt you?"

I stalled, brushing my hand over the blades of grass, watching them ripple like wheat in a field, as I considered how much to share. This time, I was the one who was shaking. "I feared they might, every day, but when I felt I was truly in danger, God intervened."

He placed his hand over mine and gave it a little squeeze.

"People say the war makes foxhole Christians. All I know is that I've never prayed so hard in my life as I have these past two years."

We laughed and cried and weren't embarrassed by the honest tears our shared pain released. I thought how the lieutenant was like Légère in some ways—brave, strong, willing to sacrifice himself for others. But the two men were very different in other ways. Whereas Légère seemed complete, Denny needed something to fill an emptiness inside, like the hollow space Légère filled in me. Légère was hungry for adventure, but Denny had seen more than his share. He longed for peace, for a quiet home, and for someone to whom he could belong. The war had left him worse for wear. I understood that very well. It had broken each of us a little, left cracks and crevices we'd need time to fill.

I regretted the end of our time together as we walked back to the house. I felt safe in his company. More importantly, I felt capable beside him, as if he saw me as an equal.

"I'm staying in theater," he said.

"Here in France?"

"For the time being. I'd like to keep writing to you, if that's all right."

"I'd like that very much. And you will visit?"

"I'd like *that* very much."

We laughed nervously, equally discomfited over what to do or say next. It was all right. We were an odd pair, a tiny French letter carrier and a decorated American hero, two human palettes etched by the war. We were comfortable in our mutual silence, knowing the other person fully understood what we were unable to put into words. We had experienced events we might never be able to speak of, events only witnesses to the war could fully understand. Others, like the Jews, suffered far worse than we did. Denny had at least saved some from those camps, but I had no such victory to erase the impotence that left France aching and ashamed.

We exchanged a few last words, and then he was gone, leaving us as two friends who would exchange letters and see where things went. Neither of us was ready for more than that. Just like France itself, we each had much personal rebuilding to do.

I retired my PTT route that summer to become licensed as *l'aide aux mères.* My aunt offered to have me come live with her in the city, where I could pursue more opportunities. I thought I might do that someday, when I was ready to leave the comfort of Braquis and my family and home, but that day was not yet.

The war had already enrolled me and my countrymen in a unique university filled with captive students for whom there was no deferment. Its catalogue of experiences touched on every discipline—the math of troop figures and death, the science of bombs and artillery, the economics of supply and demand and want. War intertwined itself into history, disintegrating borders and terms like freedom, changing the course of nations and lives, rewriting pasts, and obliterating futures. We underwent an excruciating study of the humanities and the inhumanities of a modern world. And while vague topics like hate and hunger became poignantly clear, topics that were once crisp and firm, like home and truth and childhood, had become muddled and vague.

I didn't like the path I'd been forced to travel, but I liked the person forged by the journey—from a timid girl to a young woman who was braver than she knew, part of a proud French family that was strong and courageous and good.

And when hard times came again, as I knew they surely would, I drew upon the lessons learned during the Nazi occupation of our home, strengthening others with the wisdom taught by my mother, that "we do what must be done."

– THE END –

EPILOGUE

Michelle's daughter, Beatrice, and her son, Lionel, wanted to let readers know about Michelle's family's life after the war. Thank you, both. Much love to you and your family.

— Laurie

WHATEVER HAPPENED to the courageous young woman and her family?

MICHELLE AND HER FAMILY, HAVING SURVIVED WWII, resumed and rebuilt their lives in their village of Braquis. Armand was reunited with the family. Yvonne continued to serve her neighbors with a door that was always inviting people in with their various concerns. Joseph continued in his trade so he could care for and support his family. The children grew up, married and had their own families.

Armand eventually bought another violin after he was married. Music and the arts played a big role in his family. He became a legal professional.

Jacques married, designed and built his own home himself in Braquis, where he lived and raised his children. He was a frustrated inventor in search of a perpetual motion machine. He enjoyed playing the accordion.

The two younger brothers, Titi and Gilbert, eventually went into business together. They invested and made machines to manufacture parts for use in heavy equipment and trains. They eventually sold the business to retire. They both married and raised their families in the northeast of France not too far from Braquis.

All were forever marked by the events they lived through. All have passed away.

Michelle worked for the Aide aux Mères and in the chocolate department of a department store in Reims. She considered joining a convent, but that wasn't what God had planned for her.

She married an American soldier she met while she lived in Braquis. Together they had two children, a girl and a boy. They lived together for about eighteen years in various parts of the US and Germany, where they were stationed with the Army. Michelle talked to the German people and discovered that they were as adversely affected by the war as the French. She became good friends with many of her German neighbors. This was a healing experience for Michelle.

She faced additional hardship when her husband divorced her. Life was always difficult for Michelle, but she never quit. She was ever faithful and always had a firm conviction that God would take care of her and the family. She managed to keep a roof over our heads by caring for other people's children. She did so well in managing on a meager income that IRS auditors were amazed. You see, she had always made her own clothes, cut and curled her hair, did her nails, and cooked from scratch (sometimes it was just beans and rice). No splurging on health clubs, beauty shops, or on nonessential items for herself.

While visits to France were few and far between, the family was very important to Michelle. She radiated His sunshine for several years from the confines of a long-term care facility. She was loved by her family. Cared for and loved by God.

Michelle went home to be with her Heavenly Father in January 2022. She is sorely missed by all.

— Beatrice Rogers Kiss

MICHELLE, MY MOTHER, WAS ALWAYS A VERY STRONG PERSON. When I was young, I knew nothing of her struggles during the war. Being a curious child, it wasn't long before I got her to tell me about some of the things she had experienced. My father on the other hand, would not talk about the things he had seen during the war. He was a decorated American Army soldier who didn't want to think about all that had happened. He has since been laid to rest at Arlington Cemetery.

My mother was a wonderful wife and mother. Fundamentally cheerful by nature, she would sing all the time. In fact, she had such a beautiful voice she was asked to sing in Baltimore along with the original accordionist that played for Edith Piaf (AKA 'The Little Sparrow'). His name was Norbert Slama. He even commented to my mother that her voice was the closest he'd ever heard to Edith's own.

My mother also had a big heart. She became friends with a great many people and some of her close friends included people of German descent. She was never able to forget what Hitler did to her, the family, her friends, and the world in general, but she never held it against anyone other than the Nazis.

Please enjoy the book and share in mother's memories.

—Lionel Rogers

ACKNOWLEDGMENTS

There would be no book titled *The Letter Carrier* without Michelle Naget and her family, whose experiences inspired this book. I likewise owe a debt of thanks to Beatrice Kiss, Michelle's daughter, and her generous brother and cousins. Beatrice translated documents, cheered on the project, and contacted her extended family members to get their approval for the book. I'm so grateful to her and to this generation of Nagets for allowing me to use their brave ancestors' stories. I thank them all deeply.

I was unable to find a suitable home for this book with traditional publishers. I knew it needed to be told, but self-publishing it was a daunting hurdle. My heartfelt thanks go to my dear friend, Elizabeth Petty Bentley—gifted author/editor/publisher—who not only held my hand and urged me to self-publish the book, but she also delivered a beautiful, inspired edit that made it a better story. Thanks tons, Beth.

Deepest thanks are also owed to friend and cover artist Sheri McGathy for the gorgeous cover. I also owe a million thanks to Ray Hoy and his talented army at Misty Mountain Productions for their patience and tireless efforts in beautifully formatting this book, so it was ready for prime time. I am blessed to have great, talented people in my circle.

That circle includes my team of tireless beta readers—Cathy Morgan, Mara Harvey, Jacklyn Good, Terry Deighton, Cyndi Packer, LeAnn Arave, Donna McNew, Cheri Frazier, Janet Graham, Sharon Marks, Cyndi Wanamaker, Dianne Boadle, Gail

Ostheller, Jane Waldoch, Pam Dove, and Bruce Morse. A million thank yous to this eagle eye team. Many read it several times. It's been a long road. Thanks for helping get this story out there.

No one is more responsible for this book than Michelle Naget Rogers herself, who wanted her story told. She made a few attempts at writing it down, but she was unable to complete the task. I met Michelle while visiting my mother. I had just published *The Dragons of Alsace Farm*, which featured a beloved character named Agnes, who was a French survivor of the occupation of France. Michelle's accent drew me in, and as we talked about her life, I realized she was a real-life Agnes.

A great friendship developed between us during my three years of interviews with Michelle, and that extended to her wonderful daughter, Beatrice, whose help was invaluable in translating some of Michelle's memories into English and as we searched French documents.

The bulk of the book's personal story was drawn from true accounts of Michelle's life and the lives of her family members. The Naget family lived under the Nazi occupation of their home for over four years. The accounts of the treatment they received are primarily based on Michelle's memories. I used information gleaned from researching life during France's occupation years to fill in gaps where Michelle's memory was thin. I'm incredibly grateful to Mme. Isabelle Estade, Director of Collège Louis Pergaud, in Fresnes en Woëvre, France, for permitting me to refer-ence their college's published study on the war—"Liberation des Cotes de Meuse et des environs" Volume 2, 1st edition, 1998.

Details about the military engagements came primarily from General George Patton's personal diary. Many thanks to the Patton family and the Library of Congress, Manuscript Division, George S. Patton Papers, for making this material available to the public.

All other characters in this novel are the invention of the author. Their actions are also the inventions of this author, based on accounts found in historical documents and reports.

Michelle's encounter with Patton did occur, as did the truck ride that created so much havoc, and yes, she really was handcuffed after that and given a red parachute, which she used to make a dress for a dance. Those scenes were particularly fun to write as they demonstrated hope, even in the most distressing times. Michelle believes the parachute was made of silk. Parachute fabric switched to nylon near the end of the war, and without being able to verify the material's content, we went with the silk. In any case, it was precious fabric to her, and every scrap was used.

After the manuscript was completed, Beatrice sent advanced reader copies to the children of Armand, Jacques, Gilbert, and TiTi, Michelle's siblings. The children wrote back that their fathers had been very quiet about the war and their experiences during it. Now they understood why. I'm heartened to tell you that the manuscript has brought the Naget family members of a new generation closer than they've ever been before.

Michelle's story needed to be preserved, to remind us that freedom is fragile, and great is the sacrifice required to reclaim it once it is lost.

Thank you for sharing Michelle's story.

— Laurie L.C. Lewis

ABOUT THE AUTHOR

Laurie (L.C.) Lewis is a weather-whining lover of Tom, her four kids, their spouses, and twelve amazing grandkids. She's also crazy about crabs, nesting boxes, twinkle lights, sappy movies, and the sea. It's documented that she's craft-challenged and particularly lethal with a glue gun, so she set her creative juices on writing, which was less likely to burn her fingers.

Born in Baltimore, Laurie will always be a Marylander at heart, but a recent move to a house overlooking Utah Lake makes Utah her new love. Her Maryland years, spent within the exciting and history-rich corridor between Philadelphia, Baltimore, and D.C., made her a politics and history junkie. During a seven-year stint as a science-education facilitator, Laurie honed her research skills, eventually turning to writing full time.

The Letter Carrier is Laurie's fourteenth published novel. She writes in multiple genres, penning her women's fiction and romance novels as Laurie Lewis, and her historical fiction novels as L.C. Lewis.

She's a RONE Award Winner (*The Dragons of Alsace Farm*) and was twice named a New Apple Literary Award winner in 2017 (*The Dragons of Alsace Farm*) and in 2018, winning Best New Fiction (*Love on a Limb*). She is also a BRAGG Medallion honoree, and she was twice named a Whitney Awards and USA Best Books Awards finalist.

Laurie's next book, *"Revenge Never Rests,"* is a romantic suspense novel set to be released in October 2022 by Covenant Communications.

Laurie loves to hear from readers, and she invites you to join her VIP Readers' Club or contact her at any of these locations.

VIP Readers' Club
https://www.laurielclewis.com/newsletter
Website
www.laurielclewis.com
Twitter
https://twitter.com/laurielclewis
Goodreads
https://www.goodreads.com/author/show/
1743696.Laurie_L_C_Lewis
Facebook
https://www.facebook.com/LaurieLCLewis/
Instagram
https://www.instagram.com/laurielclewis/
BookBub
https://www.bookbub.com/profile/laurie-lewis